DESTROYED

BRIDGET E. BAKER

For Jesse

Sometimes we lose the best people in our lives.
But we never forget them.

❦ I ❦

EDAM

My mouth moves along with the numbers. Thirty-two for the small freckle near her thumb, thirty-three for the blotch that looks like a sheep near her wrist. It seems like there are more spots on the back of Mom's hand every day.

"Are you counting my age spots again?" She lifts one eyebrow.

I gulp and shake my head.

She laughs. "Of course you are."

"I like them," I say.

Her strong, wrinkly hand strokes my hair, smoothing it down even though I'm sure it's not messy. "You have been a tremendous blessing in my life, Edam. You know that, right?"

How could I not? She tells me every day. I nod. "Yes, Mom, I know."

"It was a shock to me and to your father when I found out I was expecting you. Not many evians have children, once they begin to show signs of age."

I could tell her this story myself. I wonder whether

repeating stories is also a sign of age. "Analessa shouldn't have killed him."

"It was time," Mom says, but her hand trembles, and I know she's as upset as I am that my sister ordered the execution of my father. "She could have killed me too, and she didn't." Mom closes her eyes. "She was merciful and simply relocated me here, to be with you."

Us. She relocated *us* here, to a dirty little shed on the perimeter of the palace. "I hate her."

Mom sits up in bed, her arm snaking around me and pulling me against her chest. Her hands both cover my mouth, as if someone might hear me out here. "Hush, child. Never say that. She's your sister, and she's the empress. It's a hard job, and there aren't many right answers. With as fast as my body began to weaken, she had no choice but to take dramatic action. If your foolish father hadn't challenged her, she wouldn't have had him executed either. We'd all have been removed to live out the rest of our days in peace."

"You should eat something," I say. "You're getting more and more skinny."

Her smile lights up the entire room, even if the windows are so dirty that the sunlight doesn't shine very much through them. "Alright. Go and bring my dinner then, sweetheart."

I skip across the room to the kitchen where the servants left the dinner tray they brought, but when I reach it, I stop short. My hands shake. A rat nibbles on Mom's sandwich.

Senah Malessa was empress of the second family of Eve for more than nine hundred years, a number so big I can't even count to it unless I want to spend all day doing it, and now she's sleeping in a tool shed and sharing her lunch with dirty, grody rats. Anger pulses through me, and I grab the paring knife off the table and plunge it into the rat's back with a terribly loud scream.

"What's wrong?" Mom's legs swing out of bed and she walks toward me. She isn't supposed to be getting upset. That's what Phineas said. He said to keep her calm, and let her save her energy. And now she's walking over here because of me.

Before I can even say sorry, the room tilts and shifts. My body stiffens and my eyesight changes. *What's happening?* Everything in our little shed turns red—bright, dark red. Like when I color too long in the same place with the brightest red crayon in the box.

When the front door opens, I snatch the knife from the rat's back and turn toward whoever is coming inside, my lip curled, my arms held wide. Let them try and hurt me or my mother. I snarl like a wild dog, warning them to back away.

They don't listen.

The palace guards from the east garden unsheathe their swords. "Put that blade down, boy."

Something inside me snaps. "I'm not a boy! I'm prince Edam Malessa, son of your *empress!*" I leap toward the biggest one, my carving knife slashing and jabbing. Muscles bunch underneath the dark skin covering his arms as he grips his sword and shifts his feet. His eyes flash. Some part of me knows that he'll kill me. I'm a child, and he's a full grown warrior, and I can't defeat him.

Only, he's so slow.

So painfully, unbearably slow.

Slashing him is so easy, and dodging his moves is even easier. Like we're playing a game and he's letting me win.

The female guard with the white-blonde hair and the copper skin standing next to him is even slower. In baffled confusion, I slice with the same knife that killed the rat across the man's hamstrings, and then I keep jogging past him and shove it upward, right in between the woman's ribs. It slides through easily, and I yank it back out.

Neither of them has even moved—not since I started to attack. And I've never had this much fun in my life. Everything is already red, but blood bubbles out where I slash, and it sprays when I slash harder.

Someone's screaming behind me, but I don't care. I can't focus on anything but the blood, the rage, and all the unfair things that keep happening to my mom. To me. And then, without realizing what I've done, both guards are completely still. Blood pools around their bodies at an alarming rate. I back away, horrified, and yet also desperate to attack something else, someone else, anything at all.

I'm angry. So angry. My hands shake with it. My teeth grind against one another. My hands clench on the knife, and I lean toward the sword the big man dropped. I could do a lot more cutting and carving with it than with my knife. So much more.

"Edam?" a voice behind me calls softly.

It's a voice I know, but the rage turns me, not the voice. I leap toward her then, the woman calling me, eager to answer. I wave my knife in warning, knowing it won't matter that she's larger than me. She's even slower than the other two.

"I love you darling, my sweet, sweet son. Your mother loves you, no matter what you do next."

She loves me.

The world shifts again, the red fading away from the center of my vision.

"You are my light, the best gift I've ever received, the joy I never earned and wasn't worthy of receiving." Her voice, a voice I know, a voice I love, it keeps talking, keeps naming me. "Ah, Edam. You're a light in my life. Yesterday, today, tomorrow. No matter what."

The red disappears entirely, and I sink to my knees.

Tears well in my eyes. "Oh, no. What have I done?" I can't look at her, at my kind, smart mom. She must hate me. I just killed two people—people who did nothing to me. Good people. And that means. . .

I'm evil.

She shuffles over to where I'm kneeling and lifts my chin gently. "Oh, darling, you feel awful I'm sure, and I understand why, but I've known this might be your lot in life for a long, long, time."

What? "I don't understand."

She covers my mouth, takes the knife from my hand and drops it into the sink, and then she ushers me into the bathroom. "Shh, now. I'll explain everything in just a moment." She points at the tub. "Strip and get in. I'll take care of the rest."

I do as she orders, numb, confused, and guilty. Why doesn't she hate me? I hate me. How could I do that? What happened to me?

I hear her on the phone. "Yes, right away, please."

Then there's a long pause.

"Enora."

I can barely see Mom's face through the crack from the door. I climb into the tub even though the drain hasn't been plugged yet, and I watch the bloody water as it circles round and round and then disappears down the drain.

"I won't keep you for long. I'm sure by now you've heard that I'm dying." A short pause. "Yes, it's not good. Phineas says weeks, more than likely. But that's not why I'm calling." Another brief pause. "No, I have a favor to ask. There's no one else I can trust, because no one else will understand. I need you to keep this secret, from everyone. Even your warlord, or perhaps especially your warlord if the rumors are true, and I know that's not a fair demand."

Mom is quiet again, for longer this time.

"That's right. You knew my last husband. . . well, my

darling son. . . as I hoped, the gift has passed to him." Mom's eyes flash. "Yes, it's a gift. How can you even ask that?" She clenches the phone. "And you know my gift as well. He has both." She snorts. "Of course I've confirmed it. I've got a disaster here to clean up, and not much time, but I'm worried enough to make time. I'm begging for this favor. I doubt Analessa will keep him, in spite of repeated promises that she will. She doesn't like keeping things around that might pose a risk, and Edam is too unique not to threaten her. He's perfectly sweet, bright, kind, and generous, but she won't see any of that. Not once she figures out what he is."

Another pause, this one longer.

"Yes, I know purchasing a child who's nearly four is far outside of the norm, and I know she may have trouble placing him, in spite of his looks and his skill. That's why I want you to promise to buy him if it comes to that. I can't bear the thought of him going anywhere else, since I know you'll recognize his value and understand the need for discretion."

Mom nods, murmurs thanks, and hangs up.

When she comes through the door, she grins at me affectionately. "You still can't wash your own hair." Her laugh sounds sad to me. "Hold still, young man."

I don't want to cry—I want to be big and brave and strong—but when she towels me off, hugging me tightly to her chest, the sobs sneak out anyway. "I'm sorry I made a mess in the living room, and I'm sorry that I'm evil."

Mom only smiles gently at me while she chooses my pajamas and hands them to me. "Do you know what my secret gift is?" She lifts her eyebrows.

I nod. "You heal really, really fast."

Her smile is the biggest I've seen in a long time. "You're such a smart little boy. Yes, ever since Eve gave birth to her fourth daughter, the most blessed scions of Malessa have healed lightning quick. We don't tell anyone else, however. No, we keep the information to ourselves. Not every empress has had this ability, but I have it, and so do you, sweet prince." She kisses my head.

"But when I killed that rat—" I shudder. "Something happened."

"The first time I saw your father, he was fighting twenty-four warriors," Mom says. "It was one of the most glorious things I've ever seen."

"Did you save him?" I ask.

Mom laughs. "He was saving me—he had been tasked to kill me, mind you, but he changed his mind. He couldn't do it, not after seeing me. Because your father was what's called a berserker. It's rare, it's not well understood, and it can be frightening, but it's another gift, the rarest kind. You're not even quite four years old yet, and you just defeated two trained warriors easily. Try and imagine what you can do once you're a trained warrior—when I married your father, everyone thought I had lost my mind. An empress marrying a nobody?" Her eyes aren't even looking at me—she's lost in thought, her sky blue eyes focusing somewhere outside of the one window in our shed.

"Mom?"

She jolts. "Sorry, I was caught up remembering. See, sweetheart, a berserker always has one true mate, one person who fills his or her heart with joy, and only that one person can conquer the terrible hunger inside. Only that person allows the berserker freedom over his or her emotions, and their emotions are the key to controlling the thirst. Or that's what your father called it, the thirst, as if he could never drink enough to satisfy it."

"I'm not even thirsty."

Mom laughs again. "Perhaps you'll come up with your own name, but what I know is that if you find that person, they become your anchor. You'll need them—and with them, you can find balance. With them, you can find peace." She taps my chest. "Once you find them, you won't feel evil anymore. You'll control that rage inside of you, and you'll be able to conquer anyone and anything."

"What if they don't like me back?"

Mom's head tilts, her eyes soft. "How could anyone not love you?"

"Because I'm bad and I hurt people."

Her arms wrap around me, pressing my face against her chest. "You aren't bad, Edam. You're a delight. And you don't hurt people. You react to the overwhelming urges that you don't understand as anyone would—but think of it like this. An elephant is large and powerful, right?"

I nod.

"Well, if it was scared, and it didn't understand what it should do, it might step on people or things and damage them, right?"

"Maybe."

"You're like that, right now. You're no more evil than anything that's large and powerful."

"I'm small."

She laughs. "Small and powerful." She presses a kiss against my forehead. "Perhaps I should have used another analogy. But the point is that, with training and the proper person in your life, you will be a tremendous force for good. No one knows what you might do, who you might save, or to what heights you might climb."

"I could *make* Analessa give you back your place." I scowl my fiercest scowl.

She rubs her hand across my damp hair. "Nothing like that, silly boy. I'm happier here, with you in my arms, than I ever was on that throne."

"You are?"

"I am. Now, Mom isn't feeling very well. Any minute now someone will appear, and they'll ask me a lot of questions. I'm going to lie to them, which is very bad, but no one can ever know, Edam. Every time you kill someone, until you meet this person who will help you to manage things, you'll lose control again, just like you did this time. So you must do your very best, whatever it takes, *not* to kill anyone, not until you meet your soul soother, okay? That's who I was to your father, which is why I allowed him to kill my current husband, who wasn't a very good person in any case. When you find love, like the kind you'll offer someone one day, it's a truly miraculous gift."

Don't kill anyone else, no matter what. Don't let anyone find out what I am. She repeats it three times, as if I won't remember each one. Mom lies a lot in the next few minutes, telling the guards who come that the man and woman tried to kill me, and she defended me.

I know she says that I'm not evil, and I know she says it's a gift, but I must be too young to understand how right now.

Because to me, it seems a lot like a curse, and I seem a lot like a devil.

2

NOAH

The leaves on the tree in front of me are white, but not like snow or ice cream or a blanket. No, they're white like the crystals in a sparkling chandelier, like shards scraped from a giant block of ice, or like the teardrops in Mum's sparkliest earrings.

The leaves shimmer, sparkle, and flutter, almost as if they're alive. The nearly translucent leaves rustle slightly too, as if blown by a gentle wind, but there's no air rushing past me, not here, not now. My toes wiggle in the soft grass —vibrant, deep emerald, and a little bit cool. The tree springs from the ground up ahead, towering at the top of a tall hill, and I'm propelled forward by a surprising need to touch it. I start walking, but quickly begin to jog, and then to run. But no matter how quickly my legs move, the tree never draws any closer.

I need to reach it—I'm desperate to reach it.

My brain scrambles for a logical reason that I'm working so hard to reach the tree. It feels as though it's calling to me, as though it needs me.

I may only be nine years old, but I know that's crazy.

Probably it's because Mum's birthday is in six days, and she would love a few of those leaves. It's really, really hard to make Mum smile on her birthday—she has everything she wants already. Ish says that, and so does Lin, but this year, I'm going to do it. She's going to beam when I hand her my gift.

My legs burn from being pushed too hard, but I think the tree is finally a little bit closer.

A sound like a whimper distracts me, and I stumble. I turn my head, and stop entirely.

The little girl who made the noise is at least a year younger than me, with hair of every color that I've seen hair be. Streaks of red, highlights of gold, bright russet locks, intermixed with strands of the deepest black. I can't see her eyes, but the grace of her movements draws me, and I forget all about the tree. She's wearing an immaculate white pinafore, crisp against her smooth, almost polished skin.

When I creep toward her, careful not to make a sound, I actually grow steadily nearer. She's standing in front of a mirror, a long, tall mirror. It's at least two feet taller than her head, and it stretches as far as I can see in either direction, sloping upward seamlessly toward the top of the hill.

But the strangest part isn't that a mirror or even a little girl popped up where none had been before.

No, the oddest thing is that she has no reflection.

As I approach, she startles, because a reflection of me appears immediately. Dark, nearly black hair, shaggy because it's been too long since I had a haircut, large, dark eyes, and gangly legs. I tower over her, but I've always been tall. Mum says I'm the tallest nine-year-old she's ever seen.

The little girl turns around slowly, her voice clear as a bell. "Who are you?"

I arch one eyebrow and try to talk exactly like my

father. "I should be asking *you* that. You aren't supposed to be here."

"Where is 'here'?" Her huge eyes stare up at me trustingly, bright, deep, astonishingly blue. "And why shouldn't I be asking?"

I swallow, unsure quite why her question annoyed me, now that I'm pressed for a reason. The uncertainty frightens me. "I'm Sh—" I cut off abruptly, embarrassed that I almost told her my real name. I must never share my real name, only the one everyone calls me by. "I'm Noah, and you aren't supposed to be here, not unless Mum says so."

Ignoring me, she spins back around. "I need to get through here." She points at the mirror.

"You need to get *through* it?" Maybe I heard her wrong.

"Of course I do."

Her claim raises the hairs on my arms. She's right—I don't know how I know, but she needs to get through it, or something bad will happen. Something very, very bad. "That's a mirror," I say. "You can't go through it, but you should be able to see yourself in it." I point at myself. "See? I can see what I'm doing." I shift so that I can see her face.

Her lip wobbles. She tilts her head, her eyes widening. "Why can't I see myself?"

I shake my head.

She lifts her arm, but nothing happens. She peers closer, and closer, and closer, her face drawing dangerously near the surface. Before I have time to think, she reaches out, her finger closing the distance between her and the mirror.

"Wait!" But before I can stop her, she touches it.

The surface ripples, like it's made of water, thick water, circles flowing toward the outside, and with them, a blurry and unformed image. As the ripples smooth, her reflection appears and I breathe a silent sigh of relief.

The girl, however, cries out. "Let go of me!"

And I realize that the end of her finger is stuck—inside the mirror.

She shifts her weight, leaning back on her heels, but she can't break free—and her reflection tilts its head at her. That's when I realize it's not a reflection—it doesn't mirror her at all, and it sparkles like the brightest diamond. It looks exactly like her, but it acts nothing like she does. She's leaning, pulling, and clearly distressed. Her exact replica in the mirror is standing utterly still, finger lifted to the mirror where they touch, light refracting from every angle. Her mouth forms a word, and it's as clear as if I could hear the word spoken aloud. "Stop."

Surprisingly, the little girl does stop, her mouth forming a perfect 'O.'

"You need to get your finger free, and we need to get away from here," I say.

"Duh. Thanks for that super smart idea." She yanks her hand to the right, and the not-reflection moves with her. They slide together, one step, then two, and then they're jolting, liltingly, running to the far right, away from the tree, away from me, away from everything.

I should ignore her—it's really not my problem—and head for the tree. Mum's birthday! I almost forgot. I turn toward the tree again, ignoring the mirror and the girl and her stuck finger, but my feet won't move, even when I stare at my left foot and order it to move.

My eyes are drawn against my will to the little girl—disappearing down the hill. I swear under my breath, which Mum would definitely paddle my backside for doing, and sprint off after her. I catch up with her quickly.

"You can't run forever," I say.

She doesn't slow, barely glancing at me over her shoulder. "This stupid mirror has to end at some point, and I'm not stopping until it does." She sets her mouth in a fearful frown, her heart beating steadily. Evian. I mean, I knew she was, but it still surprises me for some reason, because I've met all the evians who live here. Why don't I know her?

"Look ahead of you. Does it end any place you can see?"

She turns her head, and then she stumbles, and finally, stops.

I hate the terrible look of dismay in her eyes. "Then what can I do?"

"No idea."

"I'll break my finger," she whispers, her face contorting in a way I don't like.

"That might not be the best—"

But she's not listening. She sets her feet, and then twists sharply, forcing all her weight into a torque against that one finger.

I hear the crack and grimace.

Then I hear her swear—and I gain a little bit of respect for her. Something about her tiny voice using a word like *that* shocks me. But her finger is still stuck. I lean a little closer, drop my voice and turn my head in case her strange non-reflection can see or hear me. "Let's think this through."

She snarls. "You think it through. My finger is stuck, and even when I break it, I can't get free."

Her finger heals in front of us, the bone straightening as it does. The not-reflection leans closer, her face furious, flashes of light pulsing beneath her skin. She gestures and says a lot of things too quickly for me to have any hope of following.

Then she draws a sword.

Oh, no. "Um, okay, let's think about it fast. It looks like your mirror image is a little sadistic."

"You think?" she asks.

"And she's unhappy with being tied to you as well."

"You're so smart. I'm lucky to have you here helping me." She glances over her shoulder. "Now go away, please." She pulls her free arm back, and slams it against the mirror with impressive force for such a small person. The ripples are much larger this time, distorting the entire surface, sending a shock even through the ground around us. The girl yanks backward, and I'm surprised that the mirror didn't grab her free arm—she's still only tethered with her right arm.

The mirror bows under the force, and the not-reflection shudders with the impact. Her face hardens even more, which I didn't think was possible, and she pulls her sword back, clearly preparing to strike. The flashes of light inside her skin intensify, nearly blinding me.

Unlike the real girl standing beside me, the not-reflection is able to penetrate the mirror barrier—and the blade rips through, quickly, in a terrifying flash, stabbing into the girl's side. Blood pours from her chest where the not-reflection's blade entered.

So much blood—much more than a tiny body should contain. I sink to my knees, desperate to help, and I realize I should have stopped it. I should have blocked the blade, even if I could only have deflected it with my own body.

As the pool of blood expands, I realize that even though we ran from it, the tree is somehow right beside us—the glowing, iridescent tree—inches away, its branches delicately spread above us. It's even more beautiful up close, but it's also fragile, much more breakable than I realized. In fact, tiny cracks run through each leaf, and they snake their way through the branches, forming myriad mazes of cracks and fissures through the trunk, the branches, and the leaves.

The beautiful, iridescent rainbow of glass tree has been shattered somehow and it's dying. I know that truth without knowing *how* I know it. But the girl's blood, spreading even now, sinks into the verdant jade-colored grass at its base. The tree shivers as it does, like it can sense the sacrifice, like it needs the blood to survive, to thrive. And then the tree pulls on the blood, slurping it up, and draining the little girl dry.

Her not-reflection smiles a gruesome smile and wipes her blade on her white pinafore. The tree sighs, the energy from the stolen blood traveling upward, repairing the cracks, smoothing the fissures, and the tree begins to pulse, light and energy spilling out of each leaf, from the ends of the branches, and in a bizarre soft glow from the trunk.

With a gasp, I wake up, completely soaked in sweat. I cry out then. "Help! Mum! Help me!"

A moment later, as I knew she would be, Mum's by my side. Her wide, beautiful eyes are as dark as ever, intent on mine. "What's wrong, darling?"

"I had a dream, a terrible dream."

Her eyelids flutter over her dark eyes. "No."

"There was a girl, and a tree, and a not-reflection."

She shakes her head, pressing my face tight against her chest. "No, my darling, no."

I shove back, forcing her to look at me. "You had the same dream?"

Her lips flatten into a tight line.

"Tell me, Mum. You're a seer. What does it mean?" I gulp in air, desperate not to turn into a hiccuping mess. I'm nine years old—too old to act like a baby. Too old to cry in front of my mum.

But she doesn't explain.

"I know what it means," I say. "Just as you always say you know."

She takes my hand, her fingers closing over mine.

"I failed her—that sweet little girl. She needed me, and I failed her. I should have blocked the blade, I should have saved her from whoever it was, whatever it was, that was trying to harm her. That thing stole her energy, her life force, and it gave it to the tree."

Mum pulls me up against her chest again, her arms so tight that the bones in my arms grind painfully. "You did just what you should have done."

I squirm, but she doesn't let go.

She stands abruptly, and her fingers circle my upper arm like a vise. She drags me to the door, down the hall, and into the central courtyard of our palace. She points at the enormous archway at the entrance to the Garden of Eden. The veined marble columns rise far, far above my head, the precious gems winking in the light from the hallway behind us. The carvings above the columns slash through the stone, stained dark inside each symbol, either from age or a very, very old ink.

Mum squeezes my arm. "You will swear, right now, that when you meet this girl, you will not help her."

I blink and my mouth drops open. Meet her? The girl is real? I assumed it was symbolic.

She releases my arm and lowers her face until she's on level with me. "Did you hear me?"

"I heard you, but if she's real, I can't do it."

"Noah, you will swear. Right now."

If someone told me yesterday that I'd defy my mum, I'd call them a liar, and what's more, I'd have fought them about it. But in the middle of the night, in the light of the shining moon, I shake my head. Nothing could make me swear not to protect her, with the innocent little girl's face still fresh in my mind. "You told me our *duty* is to help those who need us, the weak ones, those who can't help themselves."

Her tone is sharper than I've ever heard. "And how will you do that job, if you *die*?"

I gulp. "Maybe I won't die. I grow stronger every day. I

can help her, and I will. I heal fast—if someone threatens her, I'll defend her and I'll survive."

Mum's lip trembles, and it reminds me of the little girl, except instead of someone I've never met, it's my mum. I thought she'd be proud that I want to do what she taught me. I thought she'd tell me that, of course, I must protect the young girl, the vulnerable, fierce spitfire child.

"You saw her too, right? You saw the same vision?"

Mum sinks to her knees then, her arms wrapping around my waist, her head collapsing against my chest. "You can't possibly understand what it is to be a *mother.* To have the thing you love most in all the world, walking around, taking risks, defying evil, in jeopardy all of his life." Her face lifts, and I realize she's crying, tears carving a path down her perfect, luminous cheeks to drop from her jaw.

"I don't understand being a mother," I admit. "But you've taught me to always do what's right."

"It's not about the girl," Mum says. "The tree needs that sacrifice, and one day, you'll understand what that means."

I swallow, unsure.

"If you trust me, dear one, if you love me at all, then believe me now. Swear—swear under the moon, before God and these arches, that you will not intervene when you meet her. Swear to me that you won't sacrifice yourself for her."

If it was anyone else, anyone other than Mum, I would refuse. But Mum always knows what's right. She always does the good thing. She always knows what to give up, and what to double down to obtain. She's as close to true north as I've ever known, so I do as she says. I swear that when I meet her, when I meet the poor girl with the not-reflection, the girl with bravery and fire and fear in her soul, I won't step in front of the blade when it comes.

I'll save myself instead, so that I can save the world.

Even so, the tightening across my chest as the words

settle against my soul feels like I'm being scalped, like the top of my head is slowly being peeled away from my body and I shudder in the late night air.

"You did the right thing, darling, I promise."

But for the first time in my life, I worry that my mum is wrong.

3

Sometimes, when Judica is being particularly awful, I dress up in all black like she does, and I pretend to be her. This morning, I let her beat me in our morning run, thinking it might put her in a good mood.

That backfired.

She spit in my smoothie when Mom was talking to Larena, and punched me in the stomach after Mom left the room. So after my shower, I pull my hair back into a high ponytail, and I strap daggers onto thigh sheaths, and I lace up the heavy black training boots that I almost never wear.

But when I look in the mirror, it's not enough. The face staring back at me may look exactly like her, but the lips don't curl in contempt. The eyes don't flash with confidence. Everyone who sees me will realize that I don't know what to do with these daggers. I yank them off and hurl them toward the corner of my room, the sheaths careening across the floor and crashing into the trim molding.

The adjoining door to Mom's room opens with a snap. Her eyes are wide, one eyebrow raised. "What was that?"

I shake my head. "Nothing."

She purses her lips. "I have to meet with Kleighton and Henrick to finalize the details of the trade agreement."

I can't quite hide my dismay.

"Would you rather go for a ride?" I wonder whether she saw that upper cut after all—she doesn't usually let me wiggle out of boring things.

I choke back tears and nod.

"Don't go too far, and take a guard or two with you."

Like anyone wants me dead. I'm not a threat to anyone, but if I argue, Mom will change her mind and I'll be stuck listening to them bicker over taxes and tariffs and preferred status. "Will do," I say. "Thanks."

I haven't ridden Midas in almost a week, and the weather today is perfect. I mean, it's almost always perfect in Hawaii, but still. I leave through the courtyard door, boosting myself over the top of the fence instead of bothering with the gate. I nearly kick Holden in the head when I clear the fence pickets—I am so not accustomed to combat boots.

"Careful," he says, catching himself with a start when he takes in what I'm wearing. He swallows and bows deeply.

He thinks I'm my sister. A tiny thrill shoots through me at the thought.

I should correct him, but I don't. We share guards—he should be able to tell us apart. Somehow, being Judica puts an extra swagger in my step, and a sauciness in the tilt of my head that I quite enjoy. "I'm going for a ride, and you're coming."

Holden shoves Osbert, who's staring at me gape-mouthed. "Let's go," he mutters.

They both fall into step behind me.

Osbert clears his throat. "Uh, who's guarding Chancery, if we're going with you?"

I roll my eyes. "I can barely stand Roman and Lionel. I left them there."

"Alright," Holden says. "As long as someone's keeping an eye on her."

My heart softens a little bit. Judica may hate me, but at least some of my guards care about my wellbeing. "It would be a terrible tragedy if something happened to her." I laugh. This is kind of fun.

Neither of the guards contradicts me, but they look sick. That's enough.

I usually chat with the guards on my way to the stables. I ask about their training, their plans, gossip, and so on. But Judica wouldn't do that, I'm sure of it. Stomping along without talking gives me time to appreciate the red-crested cardinal flitting with a splash of brilliant color from behind a cabbage-like leaf of a vulcan palm to the narrow branch of a young almond tree. I tip my head back and marvel a little at the vast expanse of sky overhead. As we approach the stable, I notice the grass on either side is far too long and needs to be cut. But Judica would probably bark at someone if she noticed, so I don't mention it.

When we walk through the large open doors of the main stable, Penelope, who always waves and smiles at me, salutes me and bows her head slightly. "Shall I ready Hades for you?"

I shake my head. "Midas."

She frowns. Bless her for wanting to protect me.

"Is there some kind of problem?" I pin her with my best imitation of the patented Judica stare.

Penelope clears her throat. "Midas is your sister's horse, and I'm not sure—"

"As Heir, I can ride whomever I wish. Your services won't be required," I practically shout. "I'll saddle him up myself." I push past her, striding toward his stall.

She doesn't argue further, and I feel a rush I can't quite explain. I hate upsetting people—I hate stressing them out or causing them distress—but Judica doesn't. She enjoys it, which somehow leaves me free not to care about anyone else either. For the first time, a tiny part of me understands why. It's freeing, not worrying about whether they'll be angry with me, or whether they'll like me. For Judica, it's not about *like*, it's about respect. You don't command respect with kindness.

My guards are busy talking to Penelope about their preferred mounts. It's a good thing too, since Midas isn't the least bit fooled by my clothing. He whinnies the second he sees me, hanging his head out of the space over his feeder and bumping my face when I'm close enough. I wrap my arms around his big golden head and press my face against his fluffy forelock. "No one braided this? You can't even see!"

I don't take as long as I usually do preparing him for his ride, since there's no way Judica would braid her horse's hair, but I do make sure his hooves are picked, his back curried and brushed, and his equipment properly tightened.

And then I tear down the beach, Osbert and Holden barely able to keep up. The ocean air, the rhythmic sounds of horse hooves thundering along, and the calling of swooping birds clear out the end of my funk. Midas and I are having such a great time racing that I forget to cool him down, the stable looming in front of us just as I pull ahead of Holden's leggy bay. I slow Midas enough to avoid crashing into a passing horse, thankfully. But I almost forget to paste a scowl on my face about the whole thing. Smiling apologetically would give me away for sure.

Penelope's practically bouncing on her toes when I arrive, her hand held out the second I dismount. "I'll take him."

"I haven't cooled him down yet," I protest. "I can make a loop."

"I don't mind—I'll cool him down," she says.

Is she worried Judica mistreated Midas? Or that I'll

show up and be upset my twin is riding him? I don't laugh, or smirk, or argue. I hand him off calmly. "Thanks."

But Osbert and Holden still need to cool down their horses, tack them down, and spray them off, so I have some time to kill. I walk up and down the halls, saying hello to Hades, Athena, and Hermes. Mother has always liked using the names of Greek and Roman deities, old fables, and various legends to name our mounts. I think it's kind of funny. I rub Achilles' nose and turn the corner to head back toward the wash rack when something catches my eye.

Or rather, someone.

A guy is hiding in the storage room, judging by the width of the person's shoulders, and I'm dying to know why. I change directions and pivot on my heel toward the tucked away nook. When he looks up at me, deep blue eyes under a shock of golden hair, I almost turn around and run the other direction.

Any other day I would have.

But today, I'm not Chancery. Which means I don't have a crush on the most beautiful guard in Ni'ihau that renders me unable to talk to him. No, today I'm Judica, and I don't care what he thinks of me or how gorgeous he is. It doesn't matter how many times I've watched him train surreptitiously around the corner. Or how many times I've had no idea what to say to him—my brain blanking the second he glances my direction.

"What are you doing in here?" I ask, my voice as haughty as I can manage.

"Sometimes it's hard to find a quiet place to study." He points at the books assembled in front of him. "Anatomy and theory of combat."

"That's quite a pile," I say. "And you're through all the requisite training—so you don't *have* to study anything. What's the purpose?"

"I wish someone would tell Balthasar that." He grimaces. "But in this case, it's not his fault either."

I lift my eyebrows.

Edam's smile is self-effacing. "Let's just say that I've become aware that there's a devil I need to slay."

I sit down on the top of an empty wooden saddle rack, too intrigued to let it go. He's studying anatomy and combat together? Why? "A devil?"

"Nothing you need to worry about," he says stiffly. "But I spent the past few years working in intelligence. You encounter. . . difficult situations and people, and some of them need to be dealt with savagely. Some of them can't be helped and they can't be saved. Some of them must be destroyed."

Pain resonates through his words. I can't quite figure out why or what, but it's authentic. He cares about this monster that needs slaying, and he wishes he didn't need to eliminate it. I swallow. "You're sure you need to kill it, whatever or whoever it is?"

He flinches. "Unfortunately, I've grown increasingly positive."

I inhale slowly. "I'm not saying this is true for you—I don't know you. But I think that often, we don't look quite hard enough for a solution. As a people, evians tend to slice and behead when we should be searching for a better way, for redemption. You'd be surprised how many things can be repaired—can be repurposed or salvaged. But one thing you can't redeem is a corpse."

His gorgeous eyes widen.

"Again, I'm not an expert about this, but I think maybe you ought to revisit the nature of this devil, so called. Maybe you can save him or her. I don't think you should destroy it lightly."

He swallows, his Adam's apple bobbing slightly. His brow relaxes, and he stares at me intently. "You don't?"

"I rarely leave Ni'ihau. I'm sure you know much more of the world out there than I do, and I don't know who or what this threat is. I don't mean to argue with you— honestly, I don't. But in my limited experience, most monsters are really misunderstood people who are injured and hurting."

He inhales sharply.

I reach out and close the book in front of him. *Terminal Combat Forms*. That doesn't sound promising. I place my hand on his boldly, channeling Judica's confidence. "Before you attack this monster, maybe see if there's some way to heal it. Maybe it can be repurposed—perhaps it has some great good it might do, if only it's guided toward it."

His eyes bore into mine, shining and bright, and I realize there's a new emotion there. One I definitely didn't see before.

Hope.

Something runs up my arm then, a little shiver, and pulses through my body. He's so beautiful and so good and so kind. My heart is hammering inside my chest, my fingers trembling against his. The world around me feels different, more alive and more vibrant, somehow, like I never quite saw things until I saw them next to Edam. He opens his mouth then, and fear grips me.

What will he say? Will he ask me to remove my hand? Will he laugh at me? I'm such a child.

I leap to my feet and back up, forestalling whatever he meant to say. "I'm sorry. I've overstepped. What do I know? I'm just a kid."

"I think you spoke with great wisdom," Edam says. "And surprising insight." His eyes don't leave mine, as if he too can't look away.

"There you are, Your Highness. Are you ready to head back? Your mother will expect you when she meets with the Council." Holden stands a few feet behind me, and I was so distracted by Edam's presence that I didn't even hear him approach.

I spin around to face him, noticing that Osbert is standing next to him. "Yes, of course."

When I walk away, I can't keep from glancing back at Edam over my shoulder. He lifts a hand in a salute? A wave? Whatever it is, my heart soars. I almost wish I didn't know that he's as thoughtful as he is beautiful. It's easier to pine from afar when I've only seen him at a distance.

The gardeners have shown up by the time we leave, and they're preparing to mow the overlong grass. We're walking down the path toward the palace when one of the mower motors backfires, and a crash inside the stable pulls my attention.

A crash from the vicinity of Midas' stall.

"What was that?" I ask, alarmed.

Holden and Osbert exchange a glance. "What was what?"

I swallow. It's probably nothing. "Did you hear that loud wham from inside the stalls?"

Osbert frowns. "They're horses, Your Highness. They startle and jump. It's probably Penelope shutting Midas back in his stall."

Probably, but I'll worry until I know. I should have braided his forelock so he could see better. That loud sound came right after the engine backfired—not a familiar sound for Midas. I jog back to the stable, ignoring the irritation plastered all over my guards' faces.

Penelope is shaking when I turn the corner, her face pale as cream.

"What's wrong?"

My eyes are drawn to it immediately, Midas' back left leg is covered in blood. "The motor backfired." Her words are barely loud enough to hear.

I close my eyes. "He kicked the wall of the stall."

She nods.

"Get Wynona. She'll know what to do."

I hold Midas, my hand stroking his face, until Wynona and Penelope return. Our primary vet looks at me sideways, but otherwise doesn't comment. Poor Midas isn't resting any weight on his injured leg. I can't stand here and watch the poking and prodding any more.

"I'll go get Mom."

Penelope quirks one eyebrow at my use of the word Mom. I probably ought to change clothes too. Pretending might be fun, but it's too confusing for everyone else. Osbert and Holden can barely keep up with me when I sprint back to my room.

I'm ducking through the door when Osbert says, "You're not Judica, are you?"

I turn around and press a finger to my lips. "Sometimes it's okay to pretend."

They both smile at me, a little too knowingly perhaps, but with kindness.

"Thanks." I call to Mother from my room, yanking my boots and pants off as I do. I'm tugging a new shirt over my head when she opens the door.

"What's wrong?" She looks me over head to toe.

"Nothing is wrong with me." I can't stop the tears, not this time. "It's Midas."

Mother covers the space between us and pulls me into a hug. "Let's go see what can be done."

She doesn't argue, or tell me she doesn't care about a horse. She doesn't say that she's got important things to do, even though I know it's true. Mom just jogs to the stable with me, no questions asked.

Wynona's expression is grim when we arrive, and I wish I could turn around and run back to my room. Reset that day, reset the last hour at least. But that's not how life works. "What?" I ask. "What's wrong?"

"The impact of his kick shattered the wooden board and there's some localized lacerations to his leg as a result. He also bruised his coffin bone for sure."

That can all be healed, with time.

"But I'm fairly sure there's also DDFT damage." Wynona won't meet my eye—she and Mom exchange a look instead.

Deep digital flexor tendon—it's what allows a horse to position his foot, and it provides support—running from the coffin bone and the heel to the back of the leg. It's not good. "You can fix it, though, right?"

"You'll never race on Midas again, little dove," Mom says.

I should not cry, not in front of all these people. It's not fitting. It's inappropriate. I know that, so I don't, but my voice is too wobbly, too concerned when I say, "I don't care. Can he walk? Will he be sound again?"

"It would take a lot of physical therapy," Wynona says.

"And you love to race," Penelope says.

I lift my nose in the air. "I'll talk to my mom and we'll let you know how to proceed." I may not be Judica, but I can dismiss people when required.

Wynona's jaw drops.

Penelope snorts. "I'll take him to wash the wound off in the meantime."

Once they're gone, I waste no time. "I don't care if I can't race him."

"Chancery, I know this is emotional for you, and I know you care for him, but horses have to work. They have a purpose, like everything in this world. When they can no longer serve their purpose, it's cruel to make them suffer."

"No," I say. "You're wrong. He can be healed, and he can have purpose. You think that the only acceptable purpose is the highest one—which means if he can't race, we should put him down. That's everything that's wrong with evians,

Mom. You all think that if something isn't perfect, it's garbage." This time, I can't quite contain the tear that breaks free and streaks down my cheek.

Mom's expression softens, and her head tilts. She holds her arms out to me.

I step into her embrace and let her hug me.

"You aren't garbage, Chancery."

I sniff. "I know that. I may not be my sister, and I may not be your heir, and I may not be perfect, but I have value."

"That's true, but this isn't the same situation. You're transferring."

I break away and put my hands on my hips. "How is it different? Because he's an animal?"

Mom opens her mouth, but then she closes it with a click.

"I will do whatever it takes—I will work with him, and I will forgo my racing for now, or take another horse when I want to run. But we can't give up on him, Mom. Please."

Mom sighs. "He must fulfill some purpose."

"He will," I say. "I swear that he will. I'll take up dressage, or I'll find someone on the island who needs him."

"Alright."

It's a long road, but with a lot of patience, care, and exercise, Midas does heal. And it turns out that Mom and Wynona and Penelope were wrong. He does run again. He doesn't win any races, but I don't care about that.

No one else on Ni'ihau may agree with me, but winning isn't everything.

Sometimes real joy comes from the process.

❧ 4 ❧

The last time I flew home from facing off against one of the Five, I brought home a persistent wound. Even so, I was so excited to have defeated Adika that I rushed off to the edge of the island to play with my new toy. In joining the first two stones, I managed to shear off the side of a cliff, flinging my friends all over the island and plunging Noah to the bottom of the ocean.

As if I learned nothing from that experience, after I secured Melisania and Analessa's stones, I immediately joined them. Like an idiot, I turned Mount Pānī'au into a volcano, almost melting the island into slag.

This time, I've been careful to keep both of my new stones—one of them cut from Melamecha's finger, and one thrown at me after Lainina watched me *disintegrate* her Consort—in separate pockets, out of contact with the other four that have been joined and set into a ring on my left hand.

The tapping on the door must be Noah, since I called for him. "Come," I say.

He bounces through, his eyes bright. "At first I was

surprised that you were summoning me, Your Most Eminent and Impressive Majesty. I mean, I only barely left your esteemed presence. But I guess once you've been around Noah, you never get enough."

I roll my eyes, and hand my cell phone to Noah. "It's time for you to call your dad."

His eyes widen.

"We're out of time. I need to find the Garden of Eden, and I have a feeling he knows where I should look."

"I can't just call my dad." No one in the world annoys me like Noah Wen.

"Why not? You need an appointment now?" I lift one eyebrow. "I just exploded the last two people who refused to do what I said."

He laughs. "Yeah, you did. Although, to be fair, one of them had a sword about halfway through your neck when you did it."

Usually I appreciate his dumb jokes. They bring a little normalcy to an otherwise unbearably serious sequence of decisions that have been thrust upon me. But right now, I need him to actually do what I'm saying. I don't have time to banter or bicker or cajole. "Why can't you call your dad?" I put one hand on my hip. It seems like a good, queenly way to stand when I'm giving orders.

"Do you not recall the last call I made to him?" Noah frowns.

You'll never be forgiven. Never. His dad's words weren't super encouraging, I'll grant that. "I'm not saying it won't be hard to call him, but it needs to be done."

Noah taps his watch. "Notice the time. It's nine in the morning here, which makes it approximately three a.m. tomorrow where my dad is. If you'd like me to call the man who wants to chop me up in little pieces and then grill those pieces, maybe we should wait until my demands won't wake him."

I sigh. "Fine, we delay a few hours. But get your courage all screwed up and ready, because in five or six hours, you're going to dial that number and poke the bear."

He nods. "Speaking of hard things. Did you plan to touch the staridium from Adora any time soon? It might be nice to know what it does. Or are we waiting until all the humans are clutching their throats and gasping their last breath before we worry about that part?"

"You're on a roll this morning. That nap on the plane must have worked wonders."

He shrugs. "Being a beefy, tough evian, I barely need sleep at all anymore."

I can't believe I ever thought Noah was human. But the dumb staridium stone he has helped him disguise his appearance in ways no one could anticipate. "I need to figure out what it does," I say softly. "But it has been a rough day. I suppose I'm not in such a huge rush." Plus, investigating the breadth of the powers in the stones sort of drives it home: I'm the last empress left. I'm alone. And worse, the danger to the world still isn't entirely clear, but there's no one else who might know the answers—not anymore.

It's all on me.

Noah's brow furrows as if he understands what's weighing on me, now that he's taking the time to think about it. "Maybe I shouldn't rush you. After all, there's no grim reaper at the door—not right this second. I know things are bad, but—"

"Edam did something risky."

"Of course he did. Every time I gain any ground, that guy has to go and, like, pick up a building and smash it to rubble with his bare hands. While shirtless. And flexing. What did he do this time?"

I can't quite help my snort. "I'm not sure, exactly. He wouldn't say. But whatever it was, he advanced fairly quickly with the Sons of Gilgamesh, and now he has discovered their primary goal."

"World domination, obviously." Noah shakes his head. "I swear, sometimes he does risky stuff for no reason at all. Did he do it with his shirt off? Flexing?"

I don't roll my eyes, no matter how hard it is to restrain myself. "They're releasing a new virus. Soon. Unlike SARS-COV-2, this one boasts a 100% death rate."

Noah closes his eyes.

"So maybe we look into the sixth stone sooner rather than later."

I nod.

He steps closer, until only inches separate us. The heat from his body radiates outward. I'm still unaccustomed to this new, stronger, more imposing Noah. It's. . . different. "You can still take a breath. You're not a machine, you know. You're entitled to a break between racing to Tasmania, fighting for your very life, healing from nearly mortal wounds, *exploding* two people you grew up fearing, and then zipping back here."

He's right. I know he's right, but it's like the walls are pressing in on me from every side. I need to assign people to manage each of the families I've taken, reverse the unjust laws and somehow make the evians accept the changes, figure out who I can trust, deal with the Sons of Gilgamesh, join the stones, find the Garden of Eden—my breathing accelerates, my heart racing.

The arms that wrap around me are warm, strong, and capable. The eyes that looks down on mine are compassionate, brilliant, and supportive. The lips that breathe my name are full, parted, and mischievous. "Chancery."

A shudder runs from my neck to my toes.

"You aren't alone in all this."

"No?"

He shakes his head, slowly lowering his mouth toward mine. "No."

I tilt my head toward his, but it's not enough. His mouth is still just out of reach.

"You'll never be alone."

"I'm always alone—always lonely." My words are barely a whisper, more like a lament.

Noah kisses me then, his lips claiming mine, his entire body shifting to shelter me, to shatter me, to destroy me. His broad shoulders roll inward, his hands press firmly against my back, lifting me toward him, driving me mad.

And for the first time in a very long time, I'm *not* alone. I'm supported. I'm safe. I'm protected from the storm.

Far, far too soon, Noah releases me, one hand cupping my jaw, the other at my waist, but firmly creating space between us. "You do not need to make out with me. You do not need to kiss anyone right now. What you need is time to relax, time to think, time to decompress. That's how you'll figure out what you need to do. So I'm going to give you that time." A muscle in his jaw works, but his smile is only a little forced. "I am always here when you need me, but part of that is not being here when you need time without me. Not time *alone,* time for reflection."

He steps backward.

I'm bereft, but I'm also grateful. Like an addict who can't help herself, I needed him to make me stop. "Thanks," I say.

He covers his heart with one hand. "The woman I love has now thanked me for *not* kissing her anymore. I'm clearly irresistible." I'm not sure he's ever sounded more sarcastic. "If he were speaking to me, my father would surely be very, very proud."

"You'll have a chance to tell him yourself soon enough." I appreciate his humor even more now than ever before— with things as awful as they are, it's nice to laugh. Noah seems to sense that, even if the jokes are at his expense. It's an undervalued trait.

"I'll come back around three to reach out to my parents." He ducks out the door, but I notice he's scowling as he goes.

Before the door can even close, Edam's head shoots through. And then the rest of him, followed closely by Balthasar. It takes me a second to realize that Balthasar's holding one of Edam's arms in a very firm grip, as if my Chief Security Officer is actually an errant child.

And even stranger, Edam's letting him.

"What's going on?" I ask.

"I'd like to know the same thing." Balthasar shoves Edam toward me and crosses his arms.

I raise my eyebrows.

"While you were gone—and once this has been settled, I demand to know where you went—Edam killed six of my men."

Killed six men? My eyes widen involuntarily. He did tell me I didn't want to know why his day was bad. And I just killed an empress and a royal consort, so I'm hardly in a position to judge. If his killings got us the information we needed to save the rest of the world. . . "He did it on my orders."

"Excuse me?" Balthasar's voice practically shakes the rafters. "You weren't even here."

"Well, sort of my orders. I told Judica to identify any threats, as you well know. She's my new Inquisitor. She asked to use Edam as an executioner of sorts, whenever required. He was instructed to—" I clear my throat. "Dispose of anyone identified as a threat when Judica didn't want anyone to know why. Perhaps I should be asking you why so many of your men are threats." I cross my arms over my chest in the same way Mom always did.

Balthasar's face flushes bright red. I've never seen him

look quite so upset. Why isn't he even trying to hide it? "I suppose Edam also knew you were leaving and where you went?"

Ah. He's jealous. Why did I trust Edam and not him? For nine centuries, he was Mom's go-to for anything hard. Now twice in a day, he was excluded not only from a decision, but from the execution of major decisions. That can't be an easy displacement.

I make the mistake of glancing at Edam for support. His jaw is set, his fists clenched. Because he wasn't consulted or informed about my latest escapade either. I inhale slowly. "I took a calculated risk." I exhale just as slowly. "I knew the two of you wouldn't approve of it. I knew it was a gamble, and I knew it might be a mistake. But I also knew I had to do something, and that both of you would stop me. You aren't enemies, you know. Not of each other, not of me."

Balthasar steps closer. "There's a reason I don't approve of things—and it's only when they aren't safe for you or there's no chance they'll work. That's my *job* as your warlord."

"I understand your job, and if times were normal, if circumstances weren't extraordinary—" I hold up my hand, the stone flashing angrily as always. "I only told Marselle, Alora, and Noah of my plans, for which I apologize. I knew that neither of you would have approved, and you'd have taken steps to prevent it from happening."

"What exactly would we not have approved of you doing?" Balthasar looks practically apoplectic.

I fish inside my right pocket and withdraw the stone from Shamecha. "I fought Lainina's Consort and Melamecha in a joint challenge. The two of them against me, with blades as the chosen weapon. All or nothing."

Balthasar practically chokes. Edam's hand curls around the hilt of his blade.

"But as you can clearly see, I defeated them both." I pat my left pocket. "I've returned with the last two staridium stones, and I'm finally in a position to fulfill the prophecy."

Neither of them expected that.

"If you had a little more faith in me, like Noah and Alora, I'd clue you in on more of my plans."

Balthasar's shoulders slump, but only slightly. "Well, I'm glad you're alive and that you've returned triumphant. I guess I'll go see to the funeral arrangements for my men." He lifts his chin slightly, his stare defiant. "Unless they're not to be allowed a funeral."

Edam shakes his head. "They should be accorded full rites."

Balthasar nods, pivots on his heel, and leaves, and at least he's no longer stomping. If he closes the door a little louder than strictly necessary, well, it's been a trying few days all around.

Edam's fingers curl around his hilt and release repeatedly, his eyes focused on a single spot on the plush carpet in front of him.

"Are you alright?"

His head snaps up, his eyes pinning mine, an even deeper blue than usual. "You didn't trust that I would support you?"

I open my mouth to deny it, to tell him it was for Balthasar's benefit that I kept quiet, or because of the Sons of Gilgamesh, but I can't lie to him. "You would have tried to stop me."

His boots don't stomp when he closes the space between us, but only because the rug is three inches thick. "You can't keep hurling yourself into the fire. You're not invincible!"

I meet his fury with my own. "I'm not a porcelain doll to be sheltered and protected from the world. I am the

Eldest, and I've got to take risks to save the world. You can't wrap me in a bubble."

"I can't lose you," he says. "I can't."

"Wrong," I say. "I need you to be strong enough to lose me, if that's what it takes. My life hasn't been my own since this stupid rock claimed me, since that prophecy was uttered, since the lives of all the humans on earth came to rest on my completely inadequate shoulders! I can't pick you over all of them, no matter how much I wish that I could! I am *not* more important than every human on earth!" My eyes well with unshed tears.

His hands wrap around my shoulders, gripping me tightly. "I would throw them all away—evians, humans, animals, flora, I don't care. They can all burn if it's necessary. And you need that—you need someone at your back to keep you alive until you can save the stupid, cursed world. If you don't survive long enough, you can't fulfill the prophecy. Even you have to see that."

I shake my head, unable to form words. My hands tremble, my stomach tumbles round and round, and my brain keeps shorting out. It happens every single time he touches me, and I wish I knew why.

"You are more than a lamb to be offered up on an altar," he whispers. "You're more than a prophecy to me. You're not made of porcelain, but you're also *irreplaceable*. If you told me you knew this had to be done, I'd have gone with you, and if you'd have allowed it, I'd have fought them for you."

I wrench my way free, backing away from him slowly. "You can't fight my battles for me! I have to fight them myself!"

Edam stalks me slowly, his eyes intent, his lips pursed, and I tumble backward when my thighs bump against the side of the bed. He smiles then, and something about his expression *melts* me. "You can't fight me. You'd never win."

When he kisses me, I don't even want to fight him, not ever again. I want him to stake his claim and never leave. I want him to burn the world down around us. I'd light the match. No force on earth could quell these flames. Not ever.

His face lifts from mine briefly, and before I can object, he tosses me further up on the bed and follows me himself. His hands wrap around my wrists and yank them up, over my head, behind me, so I couldn't object even if I wanted to.

Which I don't.

One of his hands pins mine in place, and his head lowers toward mine, his free hand brushing against my cheek. "Say you want me with you."

"Edam, I—"

"Say it."

I swallow.

He kisses me again, lightly, gently, and I moan against him. I need more, so much more.

"Say you want me with you in the bedroom. You want me to fight by your side. You want me to stand with you against the world."

"I do want you here, right now," I whisper.

"Say it," he growls. "Say you want me always." He kisses me again, this time harder, more insistent, and it's a good thing I'm lying down because my knees go weak, my heart gives out, my lungs burn, and my resolve weakens. I barely even notice when something heavy drops out of my pocket and settles against my hand.

But when a new well opens up in my head, I yank my hands free, rolling away from him. I'm shaking so hard that my hand knocks the rock sideways, and it hits the floor with a thump.

Edam freezes. "What was that?"

I gulp. "Lainina's staridium."

He sits up slowly. "I was worried that's what it was. Do you know what it does? Is there a chance that touching it just, I don't know, ruined something?"

I laugh. "Doubtful. That was the first time I've actually touched it, and it wasn't long enough for me to try and do anything with it."

Edam closes his eyes and sighs. "I should probably go."

I sit up and cover his hand with mine. "Edam, I know I have a decision to make—one I've put off too long already. You know I care for you a great deal, and—"

He's so fast that I barely have time to react when he yanks my back to his chest, wrapping one arm around my waist and covering my mouth with his other hand. "Shh." He exhales. "I know. I was wrong to try and force you, and I'm sorry. I love you, but you have more than my feelings to consider—and if I'm being fair, you have more than your feelings to consider. A lot more. Sometimes when I'm around you. . . I don't know how to describe it. I forget to breathe. I'm caught off-guard sometimes when you smile, like it's the most beautiful thing I've ever seen. My brain just. . ." He tosses his hands in the air. "It quits working. I wish we could climb on a rocket ship and leave the world behind entirely. I wish the prophecy didn't exist and the world could disappear and nothing but us mattered." His voice drops to a whisper. "But I know that's selfish in a way you never are. I know you'd never forget about the people you care about just because I was close to you."

He's wrong. I feel exactly the same. In fact, I've been pretty sure I loved him for a long time—maybe even since the day he and I first spoke in the stables.

But telling him so would hardly be helpful. Because there is a world to save, and there are other people we both care about. There are things I must do—things I have to prioritize above my own feelings and hopes and dreams.

He drops a kiss on the top of my head, releases me, and stands up. "Thank you for supporting me with the men."

"Did you really have to kill Balthasar's men?"

He nods slowly. "The way to advance within the Sons of Gilgamesh is to complete assignments." He looks like he's been sucking on a lemon.

"Your assignments were to kill Balthasar's men?"

He shakes his head. "The other option—the faster option—is to defeat your assigned handler."

"Whoa." I look into his eyes.

They're haunted.

"You killed *six* handlers? One by one?" My eyes widen as I think about his day.

Edam's always been an excellent warrior, but it takes a toll—I know that as well as anyone. "I now report directly to Nereus in theory, but with Angel dead, I'm not sure who that is. It was apparently a title within the organization, which means—"

"She's been replaced."

Edam nods. "According to the records I found, the last man I killed was waiting to be contacted. That's why I didn't deny that I killed Balthasar's men. It's how they'll know who to contact."

"So the Sons of Gilgamesh and Angel and Mom's death—"

"They're all connected somehow," Edam says. "I'm still working on the details of that part."

"I've been wondering about that. I mean, Mom wasn't part of the prophecy. If they want humanity dead, you'd think they'd prefer Mom ruling to *me*. The Eldest."

"You're in danger," Edam says. "I won't lie and say that their opposition to the salvation of humanity pits them against you—and it made me more willing to kill every member I encountered. One less person to threaten you."

I blink. I hadn't thought of it that way, but clearly

Edam's eager to eliminate anyone who might wish me harm. In a way, he really was serving Judica—who is supposed to be weeding out the same type of people. "Please be careful."

"I'd say the same to you." He bumps the ring on the floor with his toe. "But I have a feeling you won't listen. Promise me you won't join the stones without me around?"

I think about the volcano last time. "It might be safer if I do it alone."

His eyes blaze. "Absolutely not." His fingers lift my chin so my eyes have to meet his. "Promise. You owe me this much at least."

"Fine, I surrender. You win."

Edam goes absolutely still, and I regret using that turn of phrase.

"You can be with me when I join them."

He nods woodenly and leaves, pausing to look at me over his shoulder for a few heartbeats before ducking out.

I lean over and pick the ring back up, careful to only touch the metal band and not the stone, and tuck it into my pocket again. I've got almost six hours before Noah will be ready to call his dad. Plenty of time to take a little nap. I sit back down on the bed, images of Edam tossing me onto it bombarding my exhausted brain.

Someone raps on the door, and I nearly cry with relief at the distraction. "Yes?"

The door opens, and Inara pokes her head through. "Alora tells me you defeated Lainina *and* Melamecha?"

"Technically, I defeated Rothgar, not Lainina."

Inara tilts her head in sympathy. She knows me better than most—she sees right through my joke to the pain that caused me. "I thought you might need to talk."

She's right. I really do.

"**C**an we go for a walk?" I could really use some of the refreshing Kona breeze against my face right about now.

"Of course."

She follows me out my patio door and through the courtyard gate.

"Where are your guards?" She glances sideways at the palace guards following us—all of which I've known forever. They all guarded Mom from before the day of my birth. Georgina, Klayton, Peter, and Icharus.

She's clearly not asking where my guards are. She's commenting on the composition. "You mean the Motherless?"

"Right."

"Almost as soon as we landed, I released them from guard duty and repurposed them. They're preparing to leave for Moscow and for Japan—I need people I trust to secure my rule there, and it worked great with Shenoah to have Moses and a group of Motherless stabilize things. Taking the stone is nice, but the local evians have to accept me as their leader or I'll face one rebellion after another."

"You brought Lainina, Ranana, and Venagra back to the island?"

I nod.

"Well, that will help. They're not there to foment discord, at least."

"Even so, I need powerful regents to handle matters in each location. People I trust."

Inara nods.

"I'm thinking of sending Balthasar to Japan and Job to Moscow," I say.

"Balthasar won't like that idea one bit." Inara smiles. "You'll have to pry him away with a crowbar."

"He's a warlord without a war," I say.

"You did steal the glory from him. I doubt he'll thank you for that."

"Oh, he didn't. But a lot of people would have died," I say. "Melamecha and Lainina were planning to deploy nuclear weapons."

"You shouldn't have risked yourself," Inara says, "but I see why you did, and Mother would have been very proud."

Would she? I spend far too much time wondering about exactly that. We've reached the bluff that overlooks the palace side of the island, and the crashing of the waves is one of the most familiar constants in my life. I sink to the ground, splaying my hands flat against the manicured grass. "I miss her."

"So do I," Inara says.

"Sometimes I wonder how different things would be right now if Angel hadn't killed her."

Inara sits down next to me and crosses her legs, her eyes staring off at the waves as well. "The world turned upside down when she died."

She's right about that, but. . . "For me, it tilted the day before, the first time I tried on Mom's ring."

"You can't blame yourself, you know."

I lift my eyebrows. "No?"

"I'm sure that had nothing to do with Mother dying," she says.

"No way to know."

"I disagree," Inara says. "That was the subject of a prophecy, and you had no control over it. Mom's death had nothing to do with that."

I shrug. "Maybe."

"Why do you think the two were related?"

"Maybe they aren't," I say. "But Mom was pregnant, and if she'd had that little girl, she'd have replaced me. If that had happened." I toss my hands in the air. "I wanted to be freed so badly, but maybe thanks to that dumb prophecy it was never going to happen. Sometimes I wonder whether if Mom hadn't gotten pregnant, if maybe. . ."

"She wouldn't have had to die?" Inara's eyebrows are drawn together. "You could go mad if you continue down that path."

I snort. "I may go mad either way."

"But not before you save us all." She bumps my shoulder. "Right? And I hear you have the last two stones now."

"Yeah, that's true."

"What do they do?"

My laugh is bitter. "Well, one of them controls water."

"Oh?"

"I didn't explain the details to Balthasar, but I was about to die yesterday. I mean, I had high hopes and I had faith and I sort of had a plan, but it fell apart. I was going to die. I knew it, they knew it—and Noah and Alora must have known it too."

"But you clearly didn't." Inara tilts her head, her lips quirking upward. "The prophecy saved you?"

"Hardly," I say. "Melamecha's blade was slicing through my neck, and she would have severed my head from my neck and I'd be gone." I shudder, the shooting pains in my neck echoing through me again now.

"That sounds—" Inara gulps. "How did you—well, not die?"

"Melamecha's pride."

"You may need to be more specific."

I turn to face my sister. "She wore her ring into the fight."

Her eyebrows rise.

"Stupid, right?"

"She must not have believed in the prophecy at all," Inara says.

I shrug. "I hadn't thought about that, but I bet you're right. Her lack of faith saved me, because at the last second, I chopped off her finger, and I grabbed the stone."

"And that's it?"

"When I realized I could sense the ocean behind us, I thought, 'great, now I'm doomed. It's not like I can drown them.' And even if I had been able to knock Melamecha off of me, Rothgar was less than a foot behind her."

"So. . . What did you do?"

I flop back on the grass and close my eyes. "I—"

"You don't have to tell me if you don't want to," Inara says. "But you should know that I've done terrible, grotesque things, so you don't need to worry that I'll judge you."

A chill runs down my spine, in spite of the sun shining brightly overhead. *Terrible, grotesque things?* Maybe she will understand in a way others won't. "Did you know that sixty percent of a human body is made up of water?"

Inara doesn't reply.

"I looked it up when we got home. The brain and heart are higher, like above seventy percent water. Lungs? Above eighty percent. Even the bones are more than thirty percent water." Her claim notwithstanding, I can't bring myself to look at her.

She doesn't say a word.

"As her blade sliced through my spine, I *felt* that water inside each of them," I whisper. "And in my desperation, I *squeezed*."

"Squeezed?"

I sit up then, my eyes fixed on the water in front of me. "Like you might squeeze a water balloon. I applied direct pressure from all sides. . . and they exploded. Completely healthy and standing in front of me, to pink mist in the blink of an eye. It was the single worst thing I've ever done, and I will never do anything like that again."

Inara sighs. "You're young. You'll learn not to ever say 'never.'"

"I think I can safely say that I won't have to use that particularly gory trick again."

"What does the other stone do? I assume you collected Lainina's too?"

I carefully extract the ring from my pocket. "I haven't actually tried to use it yet."

"Excuse me?"

I know, it's pathetic. "I never wanted this job. I hate ruling. I hate having every decision be on me—right or wrong, and it feels like I'm always choosing between two bad things."

"You're actually doing a pretty good job," Inara says.

"But you would've done better, and Judica would have, too."

Inara smiles, but it's bittersweet. "If it helps, I doubt I'd have thought to explode anyone, so that's a little bit of ingenuity that was all you."

I slug her shoulder with my free arm. "Jerk."

"From me," she says, "that's a compliment. But there's no time like the present to try out Lainina's stone."

I hold the Adora stone upward, looking at it in the light. It's still black as pitch, even in full sunlight. "I guess."

"Does it hurt?" Inara asks.

My head snaps toward hers. "Hurt?"

"When it. . .does whatever it does?"

"Not simply putting it on, no." She's wondering why I've delayed. "But the reactions aren't very predictable."

"Last time you sort of broke the island."

"Right," I say. "Although that was when I was joining them."

"I take it you don't mean to do that right away?"

I shake my head. "I'm not sure why that happened, but I also don't think I need them joined, at least, not right now."

"Well, one thing at a time, right? See what that last stone does. Maybe that will give you some ideas. Who knows? Maybe it'll be like a power vacuum stone, and it'll allow you to avoid any issues when you combine them."

"Right," I say. "Because that's how my life operates." I think back on the past few weeks. "Maybe I am a little afraid to use this one at all. I mean, with my luck, it'll be a soul-sucking ring."

"That explains Lainina's permanent moue."

My laugh this time is genuine. "She always looks angry. What's up with that?"

"If your eyebrows were that bushy, you'd be mad too."

I roll my eyes. "Her eyebrows are not bushy."

"They're a *little* bushy."

Suddenly, the ring doesn't seem so scary, not with Mom's mini-me right next to me. When I suspected her of killing Mom—if that had been true it would've been almost as bad as losing Mom. I've needed her by my side more than she realizes, helping me along every step of the way. "I'm ready."

My big sister watches intently as I slide the ring over my finger.

The well pops up almost immediately, and the stone brightens, flashing erratically, but I can't tell what it does.

"And?"

I shake my head. "It's there, but I'm not sure how I might use it."

"If you feel me in your brain in any capacity, do *not* squeeze."

The laughter bubbles out of me, and while I recognize it's not proportionate to the quality of the joke, it might relate to the fear that has taken up seemingly permanent residence in my soul. "Oh, Inara. I would never."

"I'm glad you find me amusing, at least, but that laugh sounded like it was equal parts relief and humor. Is something else wrong?"

I fold my hands in my lap, careful not to even brush the Adora stone against the large one. "Maybe."

"Maybe?" Her eyes are kind.

"It's sort of embarrassing."

"Alright, let's try this on for size." Inara leans back in the grass. "When I was your age, Mother made me attend a negotiation with Senah, you know, Edam's mother."

"Okay."

"And Mother tasked me with the very difficult task of keeping their glasses refilled and jotting down anything upon which they agreed. Other than that, I was just supposed to be observing."

"That doesn't sound bad."

"We wrote with quills back then," Inara says. "And it was hot in the room where we were negotiating."

"Still."

"I ended up smearing ink on my forehead, my cheek, and my jawline. Mother and Senah found it 'adorable' and didn't tell me. They let me go to the dinner and then to a ball right afterward."

"Why didn't anyone mention it?"

"They were all too afraid of me."

"That's funny," I say. "But it has nothing to do with my problem."

"Noah and Edam?"

So she knew what was bothering me and still told me a story about ink smears. "Yep."

"You have been taking your time. I thought you'd have chosen Edam, to be honest. He's the more suitable candidate, and the way you two look at one another. . ."

"I don't care about suitable," I say.

"So you prefer Noah, then."

"That's just it," I wail. "I sound like a stupid teenager, but I like them both."

"You *are* a teenager," Inara says. "Power doesn't change your age or give you the experience of living."

"Don't I know it," I mutter.

"So don't decide yet," she says. "What's the rush?"

"I feel idiotic," I say. "But more than that, it's hurting them."

"And that hurts you."

"This might sound crazy, but I really feel like I *love* them both."

"What exactly do you love about Noah?" Inara asks.

I pick at the grass, tearing off a shiny green blade and splitting it up the middle, then tossing it in front of me and snagging another. "How much time do you have?"

"I've got nowhere to go."

I sigh. "It's hard to articulate, but Noah's always there for me, and not in the way most people think. I mean, Edam's *there* too, it's not like he's jetting around or flaky or worried about his own stuff. He's there, but not in the same way that Noah is. I can't explain this right—but it's like Noah *gets* what I need in a way Edam doesn't."

"Noah does exactly what you need, every time. He knows you well enough to know just what that is and loves you enough to do it, whatever the cost to himself."

My jaw drops. "Yes. That. When I'm upset, I might *think* I need someone to hug me, but really, I need someone to slap me, and he does it. He knows me so well that he knows what I need even when *I* don't."

Inara's eyes are kind, maybe kinder than I've ever seen them.

"He's also funny, so incredibly funny. He makes me laugh harder than anyone ever has, even Mom." A pang of guilt twinges, but it's still true. "No matter how bad things are, no matter how hard my life is, he puts it into perspective. And even when I don't tell anyone what's going on, he just knows. It's like he has Chancery-specific clairvoyance."

"But?"

"Edam."

"But Edam?" Inara laughs. "Like that's all that needs to be said to counter the fact that Noah 'gets' you?"

I sigh. "Edam wants to do the right thing," I say. "And he's willing to do *anything* I want, anything I need. He listens when I talk, always. He's respectful. Sometimes he does things he thinks I want, things he thinks I need to keep me safe, but he's not always right."

"You know that most people are in that boat, right? Mother loved my dad more than the sun loves the moon, but they fought periodically, and the fights were epic when they happened. It was almost always because they didn't agree on what would keep Mother safe—so they disagreed on what she needed."

"But I can't ever imagine fighting with Noah, honestly. Even when I've tried, when I've been angrier than I have ever been, it evaporates. He's that. . . attuned to me? Does that sound as nuts to you as it does to me?"

She shakes her head. "I had someone in my life like that. He never annoyed me, not really, in spite of repeated attempts to do just that. He gave me everything he had, and everything I needed."

I've never heard her talk like this about anyone. I never really thought about the fact that Inara's not married. She's just Inara.

I'm a brat.

"So what happened?" I ask.

Inara sighs. "I was too stupid to see it—and then he died."

"I am so sorry." I put my hand on her knee.

She jolts.

I snatch my hand back. "I'm sorry."

She shakes her head. "No, don't be. You did nothing wrong. You have a lot more insight than I ever did. Sounds like you're about ready to pick Noah."

"Every time I think about being with Noah forever, it feels right. Like, I could totally do that. But."

"But Edam." Inara stares at the ocean again.

"It's as impossible to explain as what draws me to Noah. When I'm around Edam, I feel electric, alive, on fire—like we're drawn together with invisible cords, like we were created with the same matter before we came here, and then separated somehow. My body—this might sound even more insane than anything else I've said."

"Try me," Inara says.

"It's like, it's like when I'm close, my body *craves* him. And beyond that, I like him, too. If I hadn't met Noah, if I hadn't seen how soothing, how supportive, how perfectly we fit, then that fire, the electricity, the. . . inexplicable connection with Edam would have been everything. It's like knowing one of them ruins my ability to choose the other."

Inara wipes a tear from her eye.

Whoa. I thought she'd think I was insane, but . . . "Are you sure you're alright?"

She pins me with an earnest stare. "You know, my dad taught me something once. I haven't thought about it much since, and now I wish I had remembered this a long time ago." She looks around us, eyeing the surrounding foliage critically. Then she scrambles across the ground on her hands and feet.

I stand up and follow her, confused.

She stands up then, too, and trots across the manicured lawn to the edge of the bluff where the ground is punctuated with wide swaths of volcanic rock and rocky dirt. A smile cracks her face. "There. It's a Nohu—the sole member of the creosote family that grows in Hawaii." She leans over and snatches a spiny capsule from a section that isn't covered with the happy yellow flowers. "This is a seed pod."

"Um, okay."

"Bear with me," she says. "This has a point, and I think it will help you."

"Okay."

"Hawaiians, most of them, don't love this plant—they call it a puncture vine. If you step on one barefoot, you'll get why immediately. But it will grow *anywhere*."

"I gathered that when I saw it growing here." I gesture at the rocky, barren ground where nothing else even bothers.

"The sprouting of a seed is practically magical when you think about it." She splits the pod open and plucks a tiny seed from inside. "It starts as this inconsequential thing." She tosses the seed a few feet from the existing Nohu plant. "It's just lying there, innocuously in the dirt. It bothers no one, makes no demands, but then one day, suddenly, it will change. If you add a little water and a little sunlight, something explodes from inside of it."

"Alright."

"That first sprout, that first bit of green, it triples the size of the seed in most cases, or even sometimes quadruples it, stretching, yearning, desperate to *become*."

"You're feeling awfully poetic today." I suppress a smile.

"I wish you knew my dad. He was always poetic. Everything was more beautiful because of his presence."

"I wish I knew him too." I can't imagine his brother Balthasar being poetic—a warrior poet, maybe.

"At the beginning, a seed is pathetically easy to destroy."

"Sure." I cross my arms and look at the tiny speck on the ground.

"A little too much water," she says, "and it will drown. Not enough, and it dries up. Too much sunlight will scorch it—not enough and it starves. A lack of fertile soil, an abundance of wind, a single eager bird—all of those things spell its demise."

"But," I say, "if conditions are just right, the seed takes root, it grows, and it develops—prepared to sting our toes and provide bunches of cheery yellow flowers for years to come."

Inara smiles. "Yes." She points toward the small forest of trees growing on the base of Mount Pānī'au. "Just enough seeds find purchase that there are mighty trees in this world, symbols of strength, durability, and perseverance."

"Okay," I say. "I can see that. In spite of the odds being against each tiny seed, some of them make it through every single mishap, and some of them grow into behemoths."

"And love is exactly like a seed, except perhaps even more complicated—for love to succeed, two seeds must sprout simultaneously."

"Alright," I say. "I get it. A little too much affection from either party, and love drowns."

"Precisely," Inara says. "Not enough from either one and it withers. And when one person does all the work, the imbalance wreaks untold havoc: resentment, regret, recrimination, and retreat. Most of the ramifications may not even be understood until far, far, later. But if you have someone willing to do all the nurturing, someone willing to shield you from the wind and share the sun, someone completely in balance with you like your Noah." She swallows. "An electric connection—I won't lie and say that isn't hard to pass up. But nurturing is vastly underrated."

I think about it, focusing on that tiny seed, contemplating the possibility of choosing Noah. Something strange happens then, something quivers inside my head.

And I realize that I never took off the Adora ring.

Something about that tiny seed calls to me.

I crouch down next to it, my hand hovering in the air above it. "Live," I whisper.

And the sprout explodes from within the seed, doubling and then tripling in size. Roots shoot downward, and the sprout reaches skyward, tiny leaves unfurling and expanding, and more branches and leaves sprouting and quickly seeking, spreading.

The joy that floods my soul as the Nohu grows in fast forward beneath my hand is like nothing I've felt before—except perhaps with Edam. And in spite of Inara's words, I'm just as confused as I was before, because that feeling is the closest I've ever found to how I feel when Edam touches me, as if I'm alive for the first time, the last time, the only time.

"That's amazing," Inara says. "Did you—did you do that with the last stone?"

I nod.

"So it makes things grow?"

I shrug and stand up, releasing the plant now that it's eighteen inches tall, tiny yellow flowers popping into existence in bright flashes. "It encourages things along, at least."

"Astonishing," she says.

I can't disagree with her. The prophecy is the scariest thing that's ever happened to me—from my reaction to the rings to the predictions of utter destruction—but sometimes terrifying things are also the most unbelievably amazing.

"You should join those stones," she says.

"I will," I say. "But not until the time is right." And for maybe the first time, I trust that I'll know when that is.

❧ 6 ❧

Balthasar is just as angry about his assignment as we knew he would be. "You need me here." He fumes as he paces, his large boots clomping on the high-sheen marble tile floor.

"I do."

He stops and spins to face me. "Well, then. We're agreed. I'll stay."

I smile. "Balthasar, I need you and the Motherless, I need Inara, and Alora, and Noah, and Edam. I need Moses, and I need Frederick, and I need Job. I need Marselle—"

His scowl is a little terrifying. "Fine, fine, very clever. I get it. You don't want to send me away, but you will anyway. But I shouldn't worry because you'll be keeping a teenager of unknown origin at your side. I'm sure he'll keep you safe."

I laugh. "I'll have Inara and Marselle, Larena and Frederick, and yes, Judica and Edam and Noah."

He huffs.

"Look, I'm not trying to be irritating or obtuse. I'm trying to be strategic, and I don't know a single person who

58

could do a better job ensuring that Adora is subdued. Do you?"

He won't meet my eye.

"Well, then."

"Fine, but I'm not staying more than a few days. You hear me?" He points at me.

I laugh. "A few days, yes. Or however much time it takes to make sure that we've firmly ensconced Alamecha leadership and rooted out any dissidents who will prevent us from instituting the new laws and protocols. I can't have any ongoing human rights violations."

Balthasar snorts.

I step toward him, my hands clenching at my sides. "You are capable of instituting and upholding *my laws,* are you not?"

His eyes widen and he nods. "Yes, Your Majesty."

I grunt. "Fine."

"I'll need to wrap some things up here," he says.

"Do it fast." I glance at the clock. "The jet leaves in an hour."

Balthasar crushes me to his chest then, surprisingly. "You be safe, and listen to the kid for once. He's doesn't have a wealth of experience, but his skills aren't unimpressive."

Which is about as close to an unqualified recommendation as Balthasar will ever give. "I'll miss you while you're gone."

"Listen," he says. "I know you want to fulfill the prophecy, but you should take a little time to appreciate what you've already done and stabilize things before you do anything hasty in pursuit of the Garden. Okay?"

"Understood." I say.

"Accept the world as it is."

I smile. "Or do something to change it."

An hour later, I stand next to Inara, Alora, and Judica as Job, Balthasar, and the rest of the Motherless leave in two different jets, bound for far-reaching parts of the world. Even though I'm the one who's sending them, I feel strangely bereft now that they're gone.

Judica follows me to my room for a report, listening patiently to what happened as I explain in very general terms. "You could have told me your plan," she says.

"You would have insisted we bring Balthasar in," I say.

Judica lifts one eyebrow. "And he would have told Edam."

"Nuclear bombs would have destroyed a third of Earth."

She doesn't argue the point, which I appreciate. "I wish I'd been there to see it." Her mouth curls into a tiny smile. "Any chance your boyfriend took a video?"

My jaw drops. "Did you hear what I said?"

Her eyes practically spark with excitement, and she shifts eagerly from one foot to the other. "You *exploded* them."

She's deeply damaged. "There's no way he recorded it." I shudder.

"He really is useless."

Noah would be happy to hear Judica say that, although I wonder sometimes whether their mutual animosity is more feigned than real.

"You definitely need to practice that trick," she says.

"Have you lost your mind?"

"Not on people." She rolls her eyes. "Geez. Like, pigs, or something."

"Judica!"

"What? You don't buy a car so you can admire how nicely it sits in the garage. Those stones are weapons, and you're going to need to use them. Soon, maybe."

"They aren't weapons."

"I beg to differ. You have one ring that fires EMPs and

fireballs." She raises her eyebrows. "And another that hurls people and objects through space."

"One is an energy well that somehow amplifies the others," I say. "So that one doesn't do anything aggressive."

"You're right," she says. "The fact that it allows you to hurl more devastating fireballs, EMPs and whatnot is totally benign. I don't know what I was thinking. They're clearly not weapons."

"Another stone fixes and heals things, and the new ones control water and make things grow."

"You used the water one to *explode* people, and I bet there are military applications for the others." She taps her lip.

"If I handed you a bag of marshmallows, you'd see them as mechanisms to induce choking," I say.

"Umm, that's because marshmallows *are* weapons," Judica says. "To literally everyone. They have labels on the bag to protect children."

I laugh. "They're not weapons to *anyone* but you. The humans give piles of them to babies, who drool all over themselves."

Judica curls her lip as if I was telling a story about toxic waste. She's going to make a wonderful mother someday, clearly.

"Remind me that you need therapy once the world settles down," I say. "So much therapy."

"What is therapy?"

I shake my head. Not enough time. "I need to join all the stones," I say. "They pulse when they're near one another, but I'm afraid to do it. Once it's done, I need to find the Garden of Eden and. . . do something. I'm not sure what. I'm sort of hoping there'll be an instruction book, or maybe a sign that says, 'Chancery, press this button right here!'"

"Slamming the stones together can at least be done."

Judica paces at the foot of the bed. "But finding the Garden of Eden. . . Empresses have been looking for millennia. I'm not sure it's even real."

I've been running in the same mental circles, but having her here, acting like slamming the stones together is no issue and pelting me with questions, it's suddenly too much. It's not helping. I know what needs to be done, and she can't do any of it. It's all on me. "You need to get out," I say.

She freezes. "Excuse me?"

Is there no one who won't snap at me? I'm supposed to be the empress of, well, of the whole world, but I don't *feel* any different than I did a month ago, when I was boss of exactly nothing and no one. I wish people would be consistent. Treat me like a real person, or a queen. But I can't navigate which one I am and to whom.

Not that it's Judica's fault I'm struggling.

"I'm sorry. Other than a nap on the plane, I haven't slept in thirty-six hours," I say. "I don't mean to be rude."

Her expression softens. "I get obsessive sometimes. Thanks for telling me what you need." The little wave she throws at me before she ducks out is so unlike anything the old Judica would ever have done that I find myself blinking at the door.

I love this new, more in touch twin, but sometimes I miss the old Judica.

Almost.

I close my eyes and try to sleep. I roll over. I roll back. I breathe in and out slowly. My brain can't seem to wind down—thoughts whirling, fears churning, lists of things to do scrolling past. Finally, I leap to my feet and walk out on the patio, half expecting either Noah or Edam to pop up and try to kiss me again. When no one's there, I'm blessedly relieved. I sink down on the flagstones and pull out both of the new staridium pieces, staring at them one at a time.

Without being in contact with my skin, they're both utterly black. The sun glints on their surface, but doesn't pass through them. It's bizarre. I sense the wells for the Alamecha stone, the Malessa stone, the Shenoah stone, and the Lenora stone—but the other two right in front of me—nothing.

"Are you thinking about joining them?" Inara's face peers over the gate into my courtyard.

I sigh. "Thinking about it."

"Still not the right time?"

"I wish I knew. I'm sick of never having any idea what I'm doing."

"You look like you need another energizing walk. Maybe toward the water this time."

"Sure." I don't bother grabbing my shoes. "That's not a bad idea." We're halfway to the ocean when I realize we don't have guards following us. "We aren't being followed."

Inara laughs. "I suppose Edam needs to figure out a new rotation, now that the Motherless have all been shipped away."

"I'm going to have so much fun telling him how much danger I was in," I say.

"You are sort of exposed," she says. "With no one but me to protect you."

"I guess I'm lucky you're such an accomplished fighter."

"You've never even seen me fight," she says quietly.

"Why is that? You never fight—not in training, not in matches, not in competitions."

Inara's sideways smile is modest. "I'm horrifyingly good. In fact, I often wonder whether I could take Balthasar. It just comes naturally to me, and I don't want anyone to feel bad when they watch, so I don't fight in public. Ever."

Yeah right. She's probably embarrassed. But she's not kidding about everything coming naturally to her. "Sometimes I wish you could take over for me."

Inara freezes.

"You know," I say. "We haven't even tried the stones, not since that first day. Maybe you and Judica could use them."

"I held one when you fought Analessa."

"But you didn't *try* to make it react to you, did you?"

Inara shakes her head.

"Would you like to try?"

Her eyes widen, her hands stretching and closing at her sides.

I felt the same way when I saw Mom's ring that day. Things would be so much easier if she could use them. Oh, I could pass them off and leave the future in her capable hands. "I mean, I'm not, like, trying to shove them on you." But I totally would if I thought that might work.

"Sure," she says. "What can it hurt to try?"

"You have to be careful not to let them all touch," I say. "Unless you fancy melting down the island, that is." I hold out the largest stone—and she slides it on her finger.

We both stare at the stone for a breath, and another. Nothing, and then a soft susurration of color. Her face falls, even though I'm sure she's trying to look apathetic and unconcerned. The stone clearly recognizes that she's Mom's child, but it's not flashing, and I doubt she can feel wells in her head.

"Here, you can try these too." I'm no longer very worried about her touching them. I could be wrong, but I feel like they'll only be rejoined by someone who can use them.

She takes Melamecha's ring carefully, looking it over from the top and bottom before sliding it on her pointer finger. "It's a good thing Melamecha had such meaty hands."

"Stop," I say. "You're ridiculous."

"Mother hated her."

"I didn't like her much myself." For a split second, I'm there again, standing on the beach in Tasmania, the blade slicing through my neck. I shudder.

Inara's lip curls. "I wish I'd seen her explode."

Wow, I don't think I hate anyone enough to want to watch them explode, but first Judica, and now Inara. I really am an anomaly in my own family. "Here, try this one. Maybe with the full set. . ."

Inara's hand pauses, her fingers trembling slightly. I wonder if she's that desperate to react to it. It would be a tremendous relief, but part of me would feel. . *less than* if I was no longer necessary.

I'd get over it, though.

I shove the ring onto her outstretched palm. When she slides it on her unadorned hand, her eyes are more intent than I've ever seen them, as if she can *will* it to react to her. A moment later, I've given up hope. All three rings pulse somewhat, but nothing more than they did on Mother's hand, except eerily in sync with one another.

"That's too bad," I say.

"Do you really think that?" Her voice is sharp, almost reproving.

I walk a few steps into the water, letting it wash over my feet. "I do."

"Would you still pass the throne off to me with such abandon if you discovered that I killed Mother?"

"Excuse me?" My heart skips a beat. My eyesight blurs around the edges. "What are you talking about?"

She's utterly still, not a shiver, not a tremor, not a wobble. "I didn't mean to do it, of course. I only meant to punish her for killing him."

I don't understand. "*You* killed her?" I can still perfectly recall Angel's face when Balthasar walked up behind her—utterly calm. At peace.

I ordered her death.

My hands tremble.

A cold sweat breaks out across my brow.

My stomach churns.

"Mother was poisoning herself, you know. That's why you and Judica and Balthasar failed to figure things out. I had no idea either, not until after I dosed her."

I bite my lip, and then I press harder. As if this is somehow a dream, and pain might wake me up. "You dosed her."

"She was pregnant, and I was the only one who knew. She said she sent the blood test off under a false name so even Job would have no idea. How she managed that, I'm not sure. Mother was never the most tech-savvy. I've wondered for a while whether he knew more than he let on, of course."

"Wait, if you didn't want her to die—"

"I wanted her to *suffer*—" Inara says. "I wanted her to feel what I felt, losing something she wanted desperately."

"But why?" I ask.

"She killed the love of my life, and at the same time, she killed my best friend. Imagine, if you will, discovering that in her jealousy, in her misguided frustration, your mother killed not only one, but both of the men you cared about."

Too many things all at once. Too many revelations, too many layers. Clearly Inara is hurting, and I know she loved Mom. It doesn't make a lot of sense, but I realize what she was saying. She dosed Mom, but she didn't mean to kill her. "You wanted to kill the baby."

"But she was poisoning herself already."

"Wait, why?"

"Turns out you're a freak of nature in more ways than

one," Inara says. "You see, I poisoned Mother another time as well. That's an even longer story, I'm afraid, but again, I meant her no harm. It was an accident."

"That's a lot of accidents." And I realize that she's still wearing the staridium. All of it. I handed it to her, like a dope. It can't be a coincidence that she's telling me all of this now, with those in her possession. "I'd like the rings back."

She laughs, and the sound scares me more than her confessions. It's brittle, it's sharp, and it's. . . almost evil. "I'm afraid I can't give these back to you quite yet."

My heart accelerates. I'm going to have to fight my own sister. "Melina knew? About what you did to Mother?"

"Very good," Inara says. "She figured it out, with Angel's help of course, and she meant to tell you."

"She meant?" I ask, almost too afraid to press her about her use of the past tense. But I owe it to Melina to find out the truth. "Where is she now?"

Inara sighs. "I hoped you might wait a bit longer before asking me that. I'm afraid I had no choice. I didn't mean to kill her either, you must understand."

I close my eyes, which is probably horribly stupid under the circumstances. "All those people, everyone who came with her."

"It's pointless for me to deny that, of course. I had no choice—they meant to turn me in to you."

I force myself to watch her face when I ask, "Why didn't you tell me at the beginning? When it was only Mom? Before you killed anyone else?"

"It hardly seemed likely to help matters then," she says. "And then things sort of, well, they spiraled out of control."

I pull my thigh dagger without another thought, and lunge toward her.

She's gone. I blink. How did she move out of the way

that fast? I spin around, and she's standing behind me, a sorrowful look on her face.

"I take it you're not planning to forgive me?"

"Did you really think I could?"

She shrugs. "I hoped. You forgave Judica."

"You murdered Mom." Tears threaten. "And Melina. And so many others." Tears roll down my face. "I trusted you. I ordered Angel to be killed when you were guilty."

"You did, yes, but I think you can safely lay the blame for that at my feet. No reason to fret that you're a bad person."

"It was your fault." I throw my dagger this time.

And she catches it. By the blade, between two of her fingers. No one can do that. No one. "You thought I was kidding earlier." She steps closer. "But I wasn't. I don't fight because no one else compares to me. That's not bravado or conceit. It's truth."

"Why?" I ask.

"I'm a rare, bizarre anomaly, genetically speaking."

"I don't understand."

"I think you will quite soon, unfortunately. And I'm very sorry for this too, but I don't see any other way. You see, I've been offered a reprieve, figuratively speaking. I've discovered that the love of my life actually survived."

The love of her life. He didn't die. Her anger over his death was the reason she killed Mom. And now she's discovered he's alive. That's why she supported me. . . And why now she doesn't. "Who?" I wrack my brain for someone we presumed dead who wasn't.

"You think he's your father, actually. Eamon—and he was married to your mother when you were conceived, but he didn't father you and Judica, if Mother's journal can be trusted."

She loved Eamon? My *father*, Eamon? "Wait."

This time her laugh sounds terrifyingly normal, as if

she hasn't stolen my staridium stones, as if she's not planning to kill me, and as if she didn't already kill Mom and Melina. "Yes, it turns out that our mother was a bit of a liar."

He wasn't my father? I gulp. Mom lied about who my father was? And Eamon, whom I always thought was my father. . . loved Inara? "You loved Mom's *husband*?"

"If you want to be outraged, maybe aim that indignation her direction. He was my boyfriend before she married him, and if she'd bothered to discover that before she ripped his clothes off—" She shakes her head and inhales slowly. "It doesn't matter. That's all in the past now." She glances at her phone. Taps in a response to some kind of message.

"I'm sorry, am I bothering you at an inconvenient time with my questions about my paternity and all the many murders you committed?"

She laughs again. "Were you always this funny?"

I lunge at her again. This time, instead of evading, she steps to the side, and strikes me, twice. Her right hand hits my elbow, snapping it on the bottom of my humerus. Her left hand strikes my back. It doesn't break any bones, but it sends me facedown in the sand. Before I can rise, her boot presses against my back. "I have something you'll want to watch, I assume."

I grunt.

"I'll let you up, but I warn you. If you attack me again, I'm going to break your face. I'd rather this not get so ugly, but I'll do whatever it takes, as evidenced by my past behavior. Are we clear?"

If she thinks I'm going to sit by idly while she kills me, she's delusional as well as utterly evil. "Clear."

She removes her boot. I turn around to face her, and she extends her phone. It's a FaceTime call.

Edam, Judica, Alora, and Noah are bound, all of them

looking at me through someone else's phone. They struggle, they groan, and then the call ends.

"How?" I ask. "Why?"

"I'm going to need you to join the stones," Inara says, "but if I hand them to you now, you'll get all these ideas. Ideas about tossing me into the air, pelting me with fireballs, and then, I don't know, maybe exploding me into pink mist."

I've already had all those ideas. I can't help my glare.

"Oh, I am a little bit proud of you in this moment, but hang on to that sense of anger. It's the best thing to get you through this next part."

"What part?" I ask, but part of me knows. She showed me the video of Noah and Edam, Judica and Alora, for a reason. She's gathered and incapacitated the people I care about most.

She dials someone and waits. They say something, but I can't make out what. "Go ahead and do it." She pauses. "Absolutely not. Waiting for them to leave is too risky. Sacrifices must be made. Do it now." She hangs up.

Waiting for them to leave? Leave what?

Inara points, and I follow her finger to a ship off the coast. A ship painted cobalt blue, just like the one in the video. "No. Wait. I'll do whatever you want. I'll join the stones and hand them right back to you. I'll abdicate the throne." She can't—she can't do it. Edam, Noah, Judica, Alora. Not them. I crawl toward her on my hands and knees. "Please, no."

And then the ship explodes.

There must be a mistake. They can't have died. They're evian. They can heal from almost anything—I turn to look at Inara.

"I've had this method in mind for quite some time, you know. It's deliciously ironic that yesterday you eliminated

70

Melamecha and Rothgar in almost exactly the same way. Elegant, really."

The image of the bodies I exploded—there and then gone in the blink of an eye—appears in my mind. The thought of the same thing happening to my family, to my friends, to the people I love most in the world—it fractures me—it destroys me. I scream then, louder than I've ever screamed. Rage and horror and terror and futility collide inside of me until my insides melt and disintegrate.

Hands close over my forearm and shake me. "That's enough."

Enough.

I'm still screaming—tears rolling down my face. Incoherency, disbelief, and a fury I can't name well within me, overtaking any sort of logic or rational thinking.

Enora. Alora. Melina. Judica. Aline. Lucas. Paolo. Melina's other people I didn't know. Angel.

Noah.

Edam.

Rage pulses through me like a living thing, and I crouch down on the sand, the desire to shred Inara flooding me—but then I recall that I'm utterly powerless to do a single thing. I can't bring them back. I can't defeat my evil sister. I can't even keep her from killing me, essentially eliminating the last chance of survival for all the humans on earth according to Eve's stupid, garbage prophecy.

I'm utterly useless.

"Normally I don't like holding prisoners, but I may have to make an exception." She sighs. "There must be some way I can force you to join these without putting myself and my new position at risk, but it's a conundrum for sure."

The rings. I blink. They're so close. I've been so intent on killing her, on my anger, on the futility of it all, that I never even thought about any alternatives. For a brief moment, I can almost feel the wells in my head, or at least, echoes of where they should be. The rings aren't touching me—I know it's impossible for me to use them, but—

I shake my head. Can I feel them? Are they there? Or are they truly out of reach? Am I imagining things? Have I gone delusional in my grief?

Something sharp strikes my head, and the world blinks out.

MAHALESH

"They are at war—you were right." Shenoah's eyes meet mine, but almost immediately drop toward her feet. She's scared of my reaction. "Alamecha says the stone is hers by right—she says you were the youngest daughter of Eve, and she's your youngest and therefore your successor by right. Malessa disagrees."

My sister knows it's bad news, no, the worst news. If even Alamecha and Malessa have fallen out—if even they are now waging war on one another. . . I blink, staring at my hands for far too long.

These aren't my hands. Where am I? I don't even have children, so they can't possibly be at war.

"What will you do?" Shenoah's brow is furrowed. She has no answers for me.

"What can I do?" My fingers fly to the stone mounted at the base of my throat—the sting of the metal prongs digging into my chest is a constant reminder of the weight of my decisions. "I wish this horrible stone had never reacted to me in the first place. I have no idea why they're fighting over it—having this rock is a *curse*."

Whoa. I know that feeling, but it's not, this isn't. . . Something's wrong. I'm not Mahalesh. I'm Chancery Alamecha.

"It reacted to you as God's blessing on your rule, as you well know," Shenoah says. "Mother chose you *because* it reacted to you, the same way it reacted to her."

I shake my head. "I don't want it. No single person should have to bear it, and no mother should have to watch as her children attack one another, doing their best to kill off their rivals."

"It's a game to God, clearly."

"No, I don't accept that. The God I know would never want something like this to happen—He gave us our lives, this land, and He gave us powers and a stone to guide us. He wouldn't want us to destroy ourselves, not like this."

"Well then it's your job to work out a solution. Something has to be done soon, or it'll be too late."

She's right. I leave the conference table and close the distance between us, my arms tightening around my best friend, my most faithful ally, my older sister. Her skin is dark against my honey-colored skin, but as different as we look, we've always had the same ideas of right and wrong, the same goals, the same purpose. Her eyes resemble deep pools next to my light, sky blue puddles. The smell of her hair, the strength in her arms, the calm in her demeanor, it settles me as it always has.

"I love you," I whisper. "I always have."

I wish it was Judica I was hugging, but Judica's dead—as dead as Mahalesh and her sister, Shenoah. That pain slices through me as though I had an actual body. Am I dead, too?

Shenoah brushes one hand over my hair. "And I always will."

"Where did I go wrong? Why do my daughters hate one another instead of loving as sisters ought?"

"You can still teach them," she says. "You can lead."

I collapse into the hard wooden chair next to her. "But I can't make them love one another, apparently."

It must be a dream. I'm here, in a dream, somehow watching Mahalesh and her sister, Shenoah. But why?

"There's only one stone," she says. "And you created five mini-Mahaleshes." Shenoah's smile is sad. "You and I work because I never wanted to rule. I never wanted what you have. The responsibility, the doubt, the fear, and the anger that accompanies it all repel me. I'm happy to help you and to smooth over the rough spots, but I find joy in supporting, balancing, and accepting."

"Only one stone." My fingers brush the staridium again. "But it does many things."

Shenoah nods. "Fire, earth, wind, light, water."

"And more, it conceals itself."

Shenoah nods. "From all but allies."

An idea takes hold then, an idea that might solve my problem. . .or spell disaster. "Five powers—five abilities—five daughters just like me. Five daughters who can't get along. Mother always said that the stone would be broken —shattered was her word, I believe."

My sister takes a seat across from me, her eyes wide, her knees bouncing. "I don't like this idea. I was standing right next to you when Mother tasked you to keep all the children of Eve safe, using that stone." She points. "You weren't tasked to subdivide your job—and she certainly never implied *you* would be the one to break it."

"Think about it," I say. "This is all too much for one person."

Shenoah shakes her head so vehemently I worry it'll scramble her brains. "No, you've handled it beautifully."

"Think it through," I say. "As our children have more and more and more children—as we spread, the job will grow. We won't be able to do it all. It makes sense to divide the tasks."

"You're leaping at this because of the pain it causes you to watch your children argue." Shenoah's lips curl. "That's a big mistake—and besides. The stone cannot be split."

"You don't know that," I say. "No one does."

"Mother said—"

"She said one day it would be used to repair the garden, she didn't say it couldn't be separated until then."

Shenoah frowns, but she knows me well enough to quit arguing. I can either do this thing, or I can't. Nothing she says will sway me, not now that I've identified a possible solution. "Convene a meeting. Tell them I've made a decision." Nothing else will stop the fighting—it's the only way to gather everyone here. They'll all believe I'm naming them my successor, so they'll all sheathe their blades long enough to hear themselves be named.

My sister's muscles are tense, the lines around her eyes severe, but she does as I ask.

And they come.

My darling Shamecha, fierce, strong, tall, merciless, arrives first. I'm sitting in my tent when she strides through the door. "The wastelands? Really?"

I stand up and wrap her in a rib-cracking hug. "None of you would have agreed to meet elsewhere."

"Your palace would have been fine," she says. "And no one would dare disobey, knowing Father would carve them up."

"I'll do the same here," Heth says from behind her.

Shamecha grins and abandons me, racing over to hug her father. She stands nearly as tall as him, and I hear the force of their back-smacking hug, smiling in spite of myself. She's always been the child who is most like him. Gruff, unafraid, relentless.

"I need you to promise that you'll accept my decision," I say.

She frowns. "That sounds like something you say to the child you aren't choosing to replace you."

Dad slugs her shoulder. "Stop."

She shoves him back. "What do you know, old man?"

It quickly descends into a hand-to-hand combat session. "Get out of my tent, unless you want me to draw my sword."

They scramble out, laughing as they go.

Alamecha arrives next, which isn't a surprise. Had she not been twice as far away as Shamecha, she'd have been here first. She parts the tent cautiously, smiling when she sees me. "Mother." She slides through gracefully, bowing deeply.

"None of that," I say.

She stands up with a quiet but regal authority. "Why the wastelands instead of calling us home?"

"I couldn't be sure you wouldn't annihilate my beautiful palace," I say. "With the way you've all been behaving."

No one else would have even noticed Alamecha's flinch, but I know her too well. I see right past her ridiculous control to the inferno that rages beneath the surface.

"It broke my heart when I heard that you declared war on Malessa—you two have always been the closest of friends."

She doesn't react to my words at all, not this time. She was prepared for the reprimand. "She vowed to support my claim. She swore it."

"I'm yet alive, am I not?" I ask. "Why are you all fighting over this already?" I slide my cloak aside to show the staridium.

"She's encroaching on my lands. I had no choice but to take action."

"The river's shifting—she has a claim." I throw my arms up in the air. "I didn't actually call you here to argue. I'll make my announcement tomorrow when everyone has arrived." I step closer. "And I expect you to honor my decision, just as I expect the same of every single child of mine."

She lifts her exquisite chin. She always was the most stunning of the granddaughters of Eve—a shining light among a sea of beauty. "As you say, Mother." She bows again—obsessed with rank and power, this one—and glides out. I want to call her back again and force out the compassionate, vulnerable little girl whom I trained in all the basics not long ago. I wish she didn't disguise herself inside such a severe shell—covering her feelings, her fears, her insecurity from the world. It won't help her people to trust her, if she reveals nothing about herself. And perhaps more concerning, when she disguises everything about herself, concealing anything that's less than pristine, how will she remember that no one is perfect all the time?

But my children no longer listen to my advice, it seems.

Adora and Lenora arrive at the same time, and I look on sorrowfully as they both push their horses harder and harder, barely stopping in time to avoid toppling the tent, a dust cloud enveloping us all thanks to their zeal. When they finally dismount, glaring at one another, I realize they're both panting right alongside their horses.

I purse my lips, turn on my heel and disappear through my heavy tent flap.

When they finally enter, they at least have the decency to do it together, cordially walking side by side, as they always should have been.

"That was a disgrace," I say softly.

Adora lifts one eyebrow. She hates being corrected, but she'll never admit it.

Lenora drops into a deep curtsy. "I'm very sorry, Mother. I should never have lowered myself to that spectacle. It was beneath me."

Adora snorts.

"You're both ridiculous. You were inseparable for twenty years, in case you've forgotten. Finished each other's sentences, shared food, dressed alike." Even more than Malessa and Alamecha, they were very nearly twins.

Adora looks out the window in my tent.

Lenora crosses her arms. "Don't remind me."

"Well, tomorrow all this animosity can end. I expect you both to respect my decision—no more squabbling and envy and anger."

Adora's nostrils flare, but she nods.

Lenora curtsies again, even more deeply this time, and I have to work hard not to roll my eyes. Faux respect doesn't make up for their utter lack of comportment in their approach. It certainly doesn't right the wrongs of their behavior toward one another.

"If Malessa comes early," Adora says, "will you make your announcement tonight?"

I shake my head. "Dawn, tomorrow, no exceptions. And anyone who starts any sort of fight before then will be banished. Am I clear?"

Both of them nod woodenly, and I don't bother pointing out that it's the first thing they've done together in over a decade. It wouldn't help—their animosity now runs even deeper than their affection once did.

Malessa doesn't arrive until everyone else has already gone to bed. When she finally sneaks through the tent door, she notices I'm already on my pallet and freezes, ready to duck back out.

I sit up. "I'm not asleep."

"I'm sorry to be late," she says. "I didn't want to cause any unpleasantness."

"Has it gotten so bad that you can't even be around them anymore without fighting?" The crack in my heart deepens yet again.

Malessa sits on the floor next to me, her voice low, noticing Dad's sleeping form at my side. He always could sleep through a battle. "I don't know how to fix it. I've tried, Mom, but Alamecha has changed. She used to be happy, and calm, and kind. She used to care about others, about serving. Not anymore—now she wants to *rule,* not *serve.*"

Ah, my Malessa. If I have to choose one daughter to take my place, it's definitely her. I take her hand. "You can't always fix everything. Some things can't be repaired."

"She wanted to use my troops to subdue everyone else, to conquer her own family, one by one. I realized that if I didn't oppose her, she'd do it. She'd crush the rest of them under her heel, and that can't be the answer. I don't want to fight her—I hate it. But if I didn't make up that stupid reason to face off with her, what happens next? Is it peace when it has been forced at the edge of a blade?"

Tears wells in my eyes, and Malessa leans toward me. Our foreheads meet, and we both close our eyes.

Finally, someone who isn't completely mad.

"I'm going to try something at dawn tomorrow," I say. "Something that will seem insane."

"Insane?" Malessa's laugh is more of a bark. "Isn't that the only thing that makes sense these days?"

"You might be right," I say. "But Shenoah thinks it's a mistake, and I trust her. Maybe trust is the wrong word. I always trust her, but this is worse. In this instance, I *fear* that she's right."

"I've spent the past few weeks wondering whether I've made the wrong decision," Malessa whispers. "Shenoah has followed you, all these years. You wouldn't have been able to rule the other children of Eve, not without her support. And instead of following my sister, instead of supporting her as Shenoah always has you, I denied her—I have raised an army to oppose her. Have I caused this?"

"I always listened to Shenoah's counsel," I say. "Does Alamecha listen to you, sweetheart?"

Malessa swallows.

"Trying to rule the world with an iron fist won't ever work. You must have allies, people you can count on, people you love, people to tell you when you're making a mistake."

"Which is why it bothers you so much that Shenoah thinks your plan might be a mistake."

"Yes."

"Would you like to tell me about it?" Malessa's question is simple, not loaded, not contingent, not fraught with angles.

"Heth supports it."

"Then you don't need anyone else to," Malessa says. "Dad has great judgment."

"Even so, I wish I was going to do this with my daughters' full support, but I don't trust any of them to listen to me."

Malessa covers my hand with hers. "You can trust me."

"I know I can." I close my eyes and review the details in my mind. "There's a chance nothing will happen tomorrow and I'll look senile. Your sisters could decide now is the time to attack—to take the rule away from me. I've overlooked a whole host of small rebellions over the years, and that set the precedent. I've wondered whether any of my daughters might—"

"That's why we're here and not in the palace."

"That's part of it."

And then I tell her my plan. And she listens without comment.

"Well?" I ask.

"I hope it works," she says. "But if it doesn't, I'll have my troops ready. You're not alone, and not all of us want to take anything from you."

Ah, one daughter understands. I suppose it's more than some have, but it doesn't help me sleep. I toss and turn restlessly until Heth shakes me. "It's time. Sheva's outside."

"I'm nine hundred and fifty-four years old," I say. "I'm too old for all this."

He smiles. "That's exactly why we're here—we're both ancient."

At least I have the man I love by my side as I walk out to the center of the camp. My younger brother waits for me with a smile on his face.

I embrace him. "I've missed you."

"All is well at your palace. The people miss you, and they send their best wishes. We are all praying for God to answer your prayer and return peace to the land." My brother's face is calm and peaceful. I never once doubted that he would come to me, bringing good news, and showing his support.

Something occurs to me, embarrassingly, for the first time. "Do you resent me?"

Sheva lifts one eyebrow, and the corner of his mouth twitches. "Resent you? Why?"

"You're younger," I say. "I've always thought that perhaps you should have ruled instead of me."

He snorts. "No thank you."

"You never thought Mother should have left the stone to you?"

He shakes his head slowly. "Not once. Her youngest daughter, to preserve the line. She always said so."

"But you're her youngest *child*. Does it really matter, male or female?"

Sheva smiles, and this time it reaches his eyes. "It does. Life comes from females. Males destroy. You know this. You rule to keep life above death in the balance of all things."

"It doesn't seem to have worked out that way lately." I look around me at the preparations we've made for this gathering. Shenoah and Heth worked diligently to make my vision for this morning come to life. Iron railings run in a wide circle, at least fifty feet across, secured by huge pilings set at eight foot intervals—splitting the gathered onlookers into five distinct camps. They can't be allowed to intermix freely anywhere, because they could break into discord at any time.

Balance? What a joke.

If anything, I've caused a conflagration.

"Why did you spend so much energy making the center so solid?" Sheva asks.

"If this causes the damage I expect it may, I want my children kept as safe as possible."

"We all pray the damage is minimal," Sheva says. "After all, your goal is to restore harmony, right?"

"My goal is to divide in such a way that balance is possible, but division is never clean, and it's never without collateral damage."

I consider this path one last time as the sun creeps nearer to cresting on the horizon, but I still see no other way. "Direct them into their assigned locations," I finally murmur.

Shenoah, Sheva, and Heth don't have to argue with anyone—my daughters all brought their assigned one hundred warriors and not a person more. Each of them stands calmly at the front of her section, eyes trained on me.

"You've been patient with me, waiting to see whom I will name as my successor. Unfortunately, you haven't been as patient with one another. I hoped to find that one of my daughters would show an aptitude for leadership, or that some of you might exhibit wisdom beyond your years."

I pin Shamecha with a stern gaze. "A hundred years old, and still unable to curb your baser desires." I shift slightly. "Adora." I sigh. "You have too much pride. Unchecked, it leaves you blind to your weaknesses, and it forces you to turn on your allies."

Lenora snickers.

I round on her. "You're no better. You two could have supported one another—you could have both been willing to give way to the other, but instead you tear one another down, ensuring that neither of you is strong enough to act alone with success."

Alamecha at least has the decency to look chastened—as if she understands that she and Malessa have fallen prey to the same failing. "You could have had it all," I say softly to my youngest child. "It was yours by right, but I can't give it to you in good conscience."

The four of them stand in nearly identical ways, eyes flashing, lips curled, hands clenched around the iron railing.

"You might all like to know that I offered Malessa everything last night. She alone had altruistic reasons when she stood against her sister. She alone took no joy in the fighting. She alone despaired at the terrible situation into which the four of you have foolishly plunged us."

"So my older sister will rule over me?" Alamecha's knuckles are white on the railing.

I laugh then. "You four are still so blinded by your pride and your greed and your anger that you can't even *listen* to what I'm saying."

"Tell us who you're naming," Shamecha says. "You never speak plainly. As you pointed out, I'm a hundred years old. I don't need lectures or lessons or flourishy speeches—I'm beyond all that nonsense, thankfully."

"Malessa turned me down," I say. "She listened to my heart's desire, and she, like me, hopes for a better answer. As you know, we all live on a giant mass of land—split only by rivers, streams, and lakes. We're surrounded by ocean waves, but all of you are pressed in on one another endlessly, squabbling with the people around you on all sides."

Lenora frowns.

Adora's brow furrows in puzzlement.

"What can you do about that?" Alamecha asks.

"I can do nothing," I say. "As you clearly know."

"But?"

"My mother spoke of a time when the stone would be shattered." I draw a dagger and use it to pry the prongs of the setting from my chest, releasing it to lie on my palm. It flashes angrily in my hand, without my attention focused on concealing it.

Gasps from the gathered masses don't surprise me. There's a reason I usually keep it hidden. It's disturbing to watch a stone pulse and flash and shine as if it's alive.

I lift it up high enough that everyone gathered can see it. It's the size of a lemon, but more than its size, it has a presence. No one speaks, not while they're captivated by the stone. "I've brought you here to witness my request of a higher power. You're God's children, all of you, the children of Eve. He tasked my mother, and then me in her place, to care for each of you. I was asked to ensure that you're safe, strong, bright, moral, and kind."

I pause to let them consider my words, allowing them to murmur in dismay, and to turn and consult with those closest to them.

"I have failed in that task."

Total silence.

"I'm here today to ask God's forgiveness and beg of Him a boon. You'll all observe the answer, and if I'm successful, you'll watch as a new world order is formed."

I kneel in the center of the wasteland, bow my head, and hold my hands into the air, the stone thrust upward. I want to speak the words loudly, clearly, but I can't bring myself to do it. No, the task was given to me, and my plea for forgiveness is similarly personal.

"Forgive me, God," I whisper. "I have failed you in every way. I raised my children, arbitrated between them, taught them right, and taught them wrong. But they are willful, and they are prideful, and they are their own individuals. They make their own choices, often wrong ones.

"The only solution I can think to mitigate our weakness is this: divide this stone into smaller stones that contain the individual powers, and divide the earth in like manner. Allow my children to rule in their respective spheres, separating them from one another, allowing them to watch over and protect their own people without constant battles. I'll know which child to assign which task if each child reacts to the particular stone you intend them to have.

"That is my plea."

When I open my eyes, my daughters stare at me. My sister's eyes are concerned. My brother smiles kindly. My husband bobs his head in a show of support.

But there is no reply.

Perhaps I have failed too terribly to be due any favors. Perhaps I don't deserve to be here at all, dictating to anyone, much less Him. I set the stone down in the center of the ring I created.

And I walk away, ducking under the railing and walking past Malessa and out of the area entirely.

Heth jogs over to my right side, Shenoah falling in on the left. When we reach the edge of the circle, I stop. Sheva has also circled around to take direction. "I thought you were going to pray," he says.

I can't bring myself to admit that I did. Instead, I turn to watch. How will my children react? Is it really all about greed for them? Do they only care that they are better than the others, that they can dictate to them? Are they really that far gone?

"Why did she walk away?" Alamecha asks.

"It's a test," Adora says.

"But of what?" Lenora asks.

"You are all morons," Malessa says. "She's asked God, and now she's waiting. He doesn't operate on our timetable."

"No one made you empress," Shamecha says. "So shut your mouth."

"Are you going to make her?" Alamecha asks. "Because if you so much as raise an axe to try, I'll end you."

Too many people are talking at once then, shouting, arguing, hurling threats. I look skyward in desperation, and I finally notice it. A small but dark cloud hangs over the center of the circle.

And the sun rises on the horizon.

Lightning strikes in the center of the ring, arcing downward from the cloud to the stone.

The sky is lit from without by the sun, and from within by the lightning bolt.

The ground rumbles beneath my feet, spasms rolling outward from the center of the circle we made.

"Go," Heth urges me. "Go now."

"Come with me," I beg.

My husband shakes his head. "This is your birthright, and this is your request."

"Keep the children safe," I beg him.

He nods.

"I'll stand with you," my sister says, her shoulders square.

"And I," Sheva says.

I take their hands in mine and march back through the warriors gathered in Malessa's segment. They part as easily as they can with the ground rumbling beneath us, heaving, shifting, and groaning.

We walk into the center, and I beckon to my daughters. "Approach."

Lightning strikes again, this time less than a foot from where I stand. The tiny hairs on my arms and legs rise, and ozone invades my nostrils. The storm cloud above my head swells and darkens, and I struggle to see the stone, the ground in front of my feet, and my own siblings.

But as thunder booms and lightning strikes, my daughters move toward me as if frozen in flashes of time. With each strike, the stone brightens, light pouring from inside of it in bursts, cracks forming internally, fissures drawing ever nearer to the perfection of its surface.

And then the ground cracks open underneath me with a growl, and I lunge for the stone before it can disappear forever.

When I touch it, pain rolls over me, the heat emanating from it melting the pads of skin at the ends of my fingers immediately. I focus on healing the skin as it burns and holding the stone above my head.

The lightning halts, finally, and the clouds open up above, streaks of sunlight shining across my face. "God has answered my request."

Light or not, cessation of the lightning or not, the pain from the stone builds. My fingers can't heal fast enough, and they begin to melt faster than I can compensate for, but I do not drop the staridium. I asked for this to happen, and there's always a price. Even if it's my life, I accept it.

When the cracks from the inside of the stone reach the outside, the resulting crack is nearly deafening. At the same time, the ground beneath my feet fissures, as if the stone is somehow connected to the land. My daughters lunge backward, scrabbling toward the iron rail as cracks shoot outward along the lines of the circle.

I force the smoking, desecrated remnants of my hands to bring the stone toward my chest, so that I can isolate the largest piece. I extend it outward toward Malessa, but as I do, it darkens. I shift it toward Alamecha's retreating form, and it flashes brightly once, and then again.

"Alamecha," I say.

She turns, her eyes fearful, her hands spread wide.

"You shall rule first among my children, and you shall take the fire stone and guard the lives of all of Eve's children." I hurl it toward her.

In spite of the terror that grips her, that freezes her into place, she snatches the stone from the air, curling it into her chest. The flashes from it diminish, but continue. It's enough.

I fumble until the second chunk of stone separates from the shattered staridium. When I thrust this one toward Malessa, it flares fiercely.

"Malessa," I call.

She walks toward me, unafraid.

I throw her stone. "I bequeath you the stone of earth—and the task to heal and repair Eve's children inasmuch as you can. Teach them to love, to forgive, and to nourish."

The stone settles quickly into her hand, clearly not burning her. A blessing.

As if losing parts of its mass has somehow brought down the energy level, the pain in my hands lowers and my fingers begin to reform, thankfully. I separate out a third chunk and hold it toward Lenora. It goes black. I shift again, offering it to Adora. No change. I spin toward Shamecha, and it flashes repeatedly.

"Shamecha, I offer you this third stone, the water stone. With it, I admonish you to succor those around you, to uplift them, and to cleanse them." I throw it in her direction.

She catches it easily, the wonder clear on her face.

"Thank you, Mother." Her smile is genuine, and my heart warms.

But when I look down at the stone in my hand, it's not split into two remaining pieces, one for Adora and one for Lenora. There are *four* pieces left to give. I blink and try to force them together. There must be some kind of mistake.

They will not rejoin.

But there are only two powers remaining, light and wind. I lift the light stone toward Adora, and it flashes. I call her name and throw it to her. "Adora, I leave you the light stone, with a charge to use it to grow and energize those around you. Light brings wisdom and peace in its wake."

She bows her head.

The last power, the wind stone, I prepare to throw to Lenora, but it goes utterly black. How can this be? Can I leave one of my daughters. . .nothing? I lift it up again, and it remains black. I turn toward Shenoah to ask for her advice and it flares to life, nearly blinding me.

She's only a year younger than me. How can she rule at my death? I don't understand.

But of course, my understanding is irrelevant. I'm not at the helm of this particular ship, so I raise the stone. "Shenoah, for your devoted, unfailing service, I offer you the wind stone. Use it to shift and push in turn, urging growth and change when they're necessary, as you always have with me."

She nearly drops it, but at the last second, with wide, horrified eyes, her hands close around it. She stumbles backward, unprepared to be asked to shoulder this burden.

And then, in my hands, one of the two remaining stones flashes with the force of the sun, almost. That's when I realize that each of the stones, now separated, has diminished. What remains is a power I didn't realize was separate from the others—a spirit stone.

I turn toward Lenora, my stomach twisting at the anger in her face. "My darling Lenora," I say.

Her gaze snaps toward mine.

"I offer you today, the spirit stone, and task you with boosting those around you. Augment their strength, rein in their weakness. In so doing, you will find more power yourself. Your joy is in improvement, in the synergy of all things."

When I throw it toward her, she takes it with a radiant smile. I take that to mean she's forgiven me for overlooking her.

And I glance down at my hands, trembling around one last stone.

My heart races, my muscles shake, and my lungs heave. My hands have healed, but I realize that the cost was a thing I knew from the outset. My life in exchange for the granting of my request. When I pass off this last stone, I will also pass from this world.

The ground beneath me howls and shakes, and the terrifying split widens, breaking into four separate rifts.

"Go," I call. "Take your people and run."

Heth urges our daughters onward, and Shenoah races back toward her tent to locate her own daughter. I stand alone, backing away slowly from the genesis of all of this destruction.

"In order to be reborn, the world must first be destroyed," Sheva says next to me.

He's right.

"When I release this stone, I'll be destroyed too," I whisper.

"What stone?" he frowns.

No one else can see it, and I understand then. The power of concealment, the power of disguise, it was separated. It's also clear to me the reason *why*. Shenoah cannot keep the Garden safe now that I'm leaving, and my daughters will not follow Heth. Not that he'll survive much longer in any case.

But Sheva—I can trust him. He's almost as old as I am, but he has children. He's unfailingly loyal, honest, and forthright.

He should have inherited this whole dumb rock by rights anyway. I don't believe that women are better at maintaining life than men, even if life springs from us. It takes two people to create a child, after all. "God has a plan for you too, brother."

"Excuse me?"

I sigh, but my legs tremble, my knees weakening. I have very little time. "Mother gave me a prophecy before she died."

He lifts both eyebrows.

I can hear her words ringing in my head as I repeat them. "In time of great peril, when the lives of my children shall fail, the Eldest shall survive certain death and unite the families. She comes in a time of blood and horror, in a world overrun with plague and war. She shall command the stone of the mountain in all its forms. Its power shall destroy the vast hosts arrayed against it. With the might and power of God, the Eldest shall conquer all in her path and unite my children as one. Only through her sacrifice can the stone be restored to the mountain. Together with her strongest supporter, she shall repair the Garden of Eden and the miracle of God shall go unto all the Earth to save my children from utter destruction."

"Utter destruction?" Sheva frowns.

"It's dire," I say. "I agree. It sends a chill down my spine every time. And when you consider it with the words from the keystone." I pause. "One day, the Eldest will need to reunite the stones, and she'll need the keystone to succeed. Without that knowledge, she won't be able to prevent that utter destruction."

"You still have a stone," he whispers. "It split seven ways, didn't it?"

I nod and extend my hand.

His eyes focus on my hand where the last stone flashes weakly. And finally, his eyes widen and I know that he can see it—and that's my answer.

"It will keep you and your family safe from my daughters, and in turn you must relocate the Garden and keep it safe until she needs it. Tell Shenoah I need her to spread the lie that she's tasked to watch over the Garden, and no one will think to look for it with you. That's my charge."

He swallows. "But I'm male."

"It doesn't matter. Your youngest child will take on this task in each generation, leading your family in secret, male or female. Promise me."

"I promise," he says slowly.

But he doesn't take the stone from my hand. "Take it," I say.

A tear rolls down his cheek. His voice is rough when he says. "But when I do, you'll die." He's insightful. That will help him.

I nod.

"Keep it."

"It doesn't work like that," I whisper. "Everything has a price."

"This one is too high."

"I agreed to pay it," I say. "Now you do your part and keep this safe until the daughter of my heart needs it. Prevent that utter destruction, and restore the children of Eve to true life."

Sheva's fingers brush against my hand, and the entire world shakes uncontrollably, and then. . .

Darkness.

I sit straight up, trembling. The world around me is pitch black, and I'm cold, shaking so hard that my teeth rattle and my bones ache. I'm underground, and I'm alone, and I'm defenseless, but at least I'm Chancery again.

The irony is that, now that I have no stones, and no power, and I'm about to die, I finally know what I need to do to save the world.

❧ 8 ❧

Something smells terrible.

At first I can't place what it might be. Dead fish? Rat droppings, perhaps?

I force myself to feel around—I'm in a room that's roughly twelve by twelve feet. Calling it a room might be generous. I'm at the bottom of a pit. I can't think of anywhere on island with an earthen pit, so I'm guessing Inara moved me.

The dirt in a six-foot-long section in the center differs from the rest—it's not as evenly packed—it's mounded.

The smell, the mounding of more freshly packed soil. It finally hits me: someone's buried here. Maybe two or three someones, though I'm not especially good at calculating the volume of displacement from decaying corpses.

I shudder.

Inara killed Melina, and we only found Aline's finger. She tossed me here, presumably, wherever I'm being kept. I'm sure she told everyone that I'm dead—some tragic accident. With Judica gone, Melina missing, and me dead, Inara's the next in line for the throne. It's not conclusive proof by any means, but a dread certainty rises within me

95

that the smell is coming from Melina, whom Inara already admitted to killing, albeit by 'accident.' She's probably lying beneath me, alongside her warrior wife.

My heart breaks anew.

Which means there probably *is* an earthen pit somewhere on the island, but I've walked or ridden every inch of the island, and I can't think where it might be. The palace is the only building built high enough that it could possibly have anything underground anywhere near it, and I can't be in the bunker, since I checked there.

Unless I didn't look hard enough. I walked into the main rooms, called out a few times, and then left. Could Melina have been in some kind of storage area, and I just didn't look hard enough? Was I that close... and I failed her?

What if this is a drainage pit? I've wondered how a bunker would withstand the torrential raining during monsoons.

I'm a moron.

Did Melina huddle down here with her wife, waiting? But I was too caught up in my own stuff to notice. Oh, no. "I'm so sorry, Melina," I whisper. "I'm sorry I failed you. I failed everyone."

The Eldest. The stupid rocks chose the wrong person. I'm not strong enough, not good enough, and certainly not smart enough. After seeing my great-great-ancestress, I feel particularly unworthy. Not Alamecha—she was a real brat —but her mother, Mahalesh. She was a warrior, but she was benevolent. It makes sense that Eve chose her, and the strength it took for her to call on God for His help, well, I'm in awe. I can't even ask my friends for help.

My friends.

My family.

All dead.

Leaving me all alone.

I should have relied on them more. I should have listened to their warnings. I trusted all of them, but maybe that's my problem. Too much trust in the wrong people, and too little in the right ones.

Bad judgment.

Sitting in the darkness next to the decaying body of the sister I failed, I realize something. I relied too much on myself—and I'm not strong enough alone. No matter what I do, no matter what I learn, I'll never be enough. In that moment, I surrender. All that I am, all that I was, all that I will be. I'm not enough, and that's okay.

We all require grace.

And that's the moment when I hear the tapping.

It's above me and to the left. When I woke, it must have been night time. It's still *nearly* pitch black, but a tiny bit of light filters through from above me. I blink, and blink, and blink, and I can barely make out that the pit ends, a few dozen feet above my head. The room widens there.

I scramble over the mound above Melina's body. "I'm sorry," I whisper again. "So sorry—but I'm not giving up too early, not this time."

Maybe that's all we can do. No matter how many times we're knocked down, thrown in a pit, fighting against everything, no matter how inadequate we are, keep on swinging.

I will always stand up.

I'll always claw my way out of the pit.

One agonizing pull, one depressing step, one fingernail snapping shove at a time, I do it now. Until I reach the top of the pit. And then I force myself to stand up on my feet and listen again for the tapping.

Nothing.

"Hello?" I call. "Hello!"

I know Edam is dead. He can't save me. I know Noah

was blown up, his staridium sinking to the bottom of the ocean, presumably.

But it will call to me when I'm ready.

And I'll do whatever it takes to recover the other stones and to find his, and to prevent the utter destruction foretold. Inara might have surrendered herself to evil, but I refuse to do the same.

The smallest light still vanquishes darkness.

My personal motto comes to me, in the darkest moment of my life, and it's as though God's speaking to me directly.

I may be small.

I may be inconsequential, but I am still enough.

Because even the smallest light can banish the darkness. Even the smallest acts of good can counteract the wrongs of the world.

And I hear it again—faintly, as if it's further away this time, even though I've moved closer.

"Hello!"

What if it's not a friend? What if the tapping is Inara, testing me? Or some new horror I haven't yet encountered? The tapping stops, and my heart races. I want to leap back down to the bottom of the pit and find some place to hide.

But I can't give in to those thoughts. I pat myself down, casting about in my mind for anything I can use as a weapon, just in case the tapping *does* pose a threat. Nothing but bare hands and feet and a whole room full of dirt.

And hope.

That's its own kind of weapon—to combat helplessness, fear, and self-doubt.

There's a door on the other side of the pit. I circle around slowly, trying my best to make out any details at all. I feel around on the door until I make out the knob, and I twist. It's locked. I wipe my hands on my pants and put my hands around it, squeezing as tightly I can, and then I wrench.

The knob snaps off.

I swear under my breath.

The tapping resumes, but it's opposite me, and up high, higher than I am. Higher than the door. I approach it cautiously, listening intently. It's a pattern. Tap scrape pause. That's an 'a'. Tap scrape tap tap. An 'l.' Tap tap. An 'i.' Tap tap tap scrape. A 'v.' Tap pause. An 'e.' A long pause, and then tap tap scrape scrape tap tap. A question mark.

Alive?

My heart soars. Someone doesn't believe Inara's story. The Motherless are gone, as are Moses, Job, Balthasar, and countless others. Inara killed Judica, Noah, Edam, and Alora. Who's left?

Plenty of people, I suppose. It could be Frederick or anyone else on the council. Marselle. Larena. One of my other guards, Mom's former guards.

Someone is looking for me—someone is hoping, like I am.

Unfortunately there's nothing here with which I can make any noise, not if they can't hear me yelling. But that sound is coming from somewhere, which means it's time to climb again. I pull myself up slowly, painstakingly, handhold over handhold, snapping nails, scraping my arm on roots, covering myself in filth and sweat. I've nearly reached the source of the tapping when a chunk of earth gives way, pulling apart from the wall.

I tumble to the ground, hit the edge of the pit, and flip inside it, falling all the way to the mound at the bottom. The impact against the piled up earth breaks my back. It also causes a cloud of dust, the dank smell from which is overpowering. I feel like crying, but I refuse to waste the time. I stand back up and begin to climb again.

I worry that the tapper will be gone by the time I reach the source of the noise.

I worry that guards are waiting outside for me with orders to remove my head from my body.

I worry that Inara's testing me, and that she'll stop worrying about rejoining the stones and end things once and for all.

And then I cast those worries aside and keep on climbing.

I fall four more times, but never all the way down, never back to the very bottom. Once I touch something metal before the earth into which I've wedged my other hand gives out and I fall. Again.

But finally, I reach the right spot, and my fingers slide through the slats of some kind of vent cover. I break my finger and fall two more times—it's hard to work on something metal when you're sticking to the wall like a deranged Spiderman wannabe—but eventually I succeed in prying off the grate covering the vent. The tapping has long since stopped, but I bang on the side wall of the vent anyway.

I am here. I am here. I am here.

And then I slide, and shift, and shove, and crawl until I'm jammed right up against the square metal vent shaft.

My shoulders are too wide to squeeze through it no matter which way I turn—including sideways. I'm too wide. . .by three inches.

It doesn't stop me from trying. I shove harder, I slam myself into the side, and I twist. But that leads to me falling again, and this time, when I hit the platform in the middle, I cry. Great, heaving sobs, and tears that mix with the grime that now covers every part of me, turning my cheeks into sodden, mucky messes. Not that anyone, myself included, could see it. I can't even wipe anything on my clothing any more, not without making everything even worse—streaky, sticky, caked in soil from my head to my toes.

I climb all the way down to the bottom of the pit, casting around until I find the door knob that fell down here hours ago. Back when I thought this escape might be easy. "I'm going to do something now, Melina, something stupid. I hope it works, and if it does, I'll be leaving you. But I'll come back to bury you properly, I promise. And if you're up in heaven, as I hope you are, I could use a little angelic support. Rally the troops. Tell them I miss them, and tell them I'm not giving up, not ever, no matter what."

I stuff the door knob between the waistband of my pants and my stomach, and I climb again. It's harder to reach the top each time, with so many gouges and loose patches in the walls—held together by tiny, lace like root systems that won't bear weight and cause my fingers to slip —but I do it. Slowly. Methodically. Carefully. And this time, when I reach the vent shaft, I ensure my right hand is firmly anchored before using my left to fish the metal doorknob loose.

I inhale through my nose, and exhale through my mouth, bracing for it. I check my grip one last time tightening my fingers until my knuckles tremble, and then I smash the doorknob against my own collar bone. The pain tears through me, but it's nothing to the raw, pulsing mash of my broken heart that has whammed inside my chest since I saw that boat explode.

Before my collarbone can begin to remodel, the bones fusing back together in their proper place, I force my shoulders together and smash myself into the vent, kicking with my legs, pulling with my arms, my left arm doing most of the work, since my entire right side is fairly unstable. Ten feet. Fifteen. Twenty.

The collar bone stabilizes the body more than I previously gave it credit for doing, but I manage to drag myself along, grotesquely, like an earthworm turned zombie, until my nose slams into another metal plate—a dead end. A thick, heavy iron grate has been welded against a massive metal box. And I know the smell. It's coal, which probably means that I've reached the bunker's air filtration system.

I groan.

I'm not sure how the tapping reached me, or whether I imagined it, but no amount of clawing will remove this grate. I'm stuck here. Tears leak down my face, soaking into the dirt immediately, and I remain still long enough that my collarbone heals in place, with the bones overlapping, deformed and twisted inward.

Part of me doesn't care anymore. My second wind of hopefulness, my stupid thoughts about grace and surrendering and my plan that if I do my part, God will do the rest. . .

Absurd.

Idiotic.

Moronic.

I hallucinated some kind of connection with Mahalesh.

After breaking my collarbone, clawing my way up and down a dirt wall for hours, and stuffing myself into this tiny hole, which I'm not even sure I can reverse inside of in order to slide back down, I'm going to die here. Slowly. Miserably.

Defeated.

How long can an evian live without water? Humans have some rule. Three minutes without air, three days without water, and three weeks without food. I saw that on a show about some people in a snowy plane crash. But evians? I've never heard.

I could be up here, dehydrated, starving, and miserable, for weeks on end. "Why?" I shout at the top of my lungs. "What did I do wrong? Why send me stupid visions and bolster my strength, and then leave me here to desiccate? Why? Do you hate me this much?"

I wish I'd been on that dumb blue boat with everyone else. I lie still long enough that I drift off to sleep—depressed, desolate, desperate. And still desperately alone.

A grinding sound wakes me.

The vent shaft beneath me is vibrating. It's faint, but it's there. I would sit up, if I could. As it is, I simply tense, my body ready.

A huge whoosh of air, followed by a suctioning and grinding noise has me twisting my head around as much as I possibly can. "Hello?"

"Your Majesty!"

I expected Frederick, or Larena, Marselle, or any of a number of people. Warriors. Mother's most trusted advisors.

Bellatrius beams at me, her dark hair flopping forward over her eyes. "I am so sorry it took us so long. Our shift ended and if we had stayed, they would've known something strange was up." I can't help think of the day she first pledged to serve me, back in New York City, back before we knew anything, before I'd done *anything*. If it had been anyone else, I might have trouble trusting them. But not her.

"Our shift?" My voice is raspy, as if I've barely had enough air to breathe. Or as if my lungs are full of junk, which is more likely.

Bellatrius' head disappears, and Arlington's pops into its place. "You have no idea how happy I am to see you," he says, looking for all the world like an eager golden retriever, dark blonde hair sticking straight up all around his face. He's always been this eager, ever since he fled with me and Frederick from the palace when Judica was threatening to kill me. Hours after Mom died.

Not even close to as happy as I am to see him, I imagine.

"I assumed that if someone found me, it would be—"

"Frederick didn't believe Inara, Your Majesty. He called her a liar." Arlington beams at me as if he's just caught a particularly high frisbee.

"And?" I'm scared to ask.

"She said she valued loyalty, but that it was misplaced. She said she knew he was grieving, but didn't have time to deal with it right now. She tossed him in a holding cell down below and said she would circle back around to 'deal with him' when she returned."

"Returned?" I ask.

"She left right after a rushed coronation ceremony," Arlington says. "Everyone's talking about how strange it all was."

All my supporters are gone, and Frederick's in prison for contesting Inara's story. I should probably be thanking my lucky stars that he's not dead. "And what are my chances of retaking the palace?"

Arlington disappears abruptly, as if yanked away by a hook. Bellatrius reappears, her smile forced. "We should focus on getting you out of there. We've got a torch here that can remove that grate, if you can shift back a little."

So she doesn't burn my face off. Good call. "Right."

It takes me a moment, and Bellatrius is clearly horribly nervous at every second's delay, but eventually I wiggle back enough that they can remove the grate, one agonizingly slow inch at a time. While I wait, I wonder at how much time passed between the second I reached the grate, and the time they returned.

I had to have been here, waiting, or their presence wouldn't have helped. They had no way to *know* I was here. Without them, I couldn't have ever gotten out. Both of us had to do our parts, and I did mine.

But then I lost all faith the second I completed my task, that God hadn't figured out the second part. I had to wait here for a while, a few minutes at the shortest, a few hours at the longest, and in that brief time, I abandoned all my hard-won faith.

Timing is tricky—and so often, it's our downfall. I take the chance to say a quiet prayer and apologize for my appallingly threadbare faith. "I'll do better," I whisper. "If you give me a chance."

"Excuse me?" Arlington has replaced Bellatrius and is reaching for me, prepared to help pull me free.

"Nothing," I say. "Thank you." Once I'm out and standing up straight again, more dirt than person, but no longer stuck in an underground box, it's painfully obvious that my right shoulder is hunched and misshapen.

"Are you alright?" Bellatrius asks.

Choosing her as the more levelheaded of the two, I pin her with my weightiest gaze. "I need a favor." When I explain that I need her to rebreak my collar bone, preferably in the exact spot where it fused wrong, her lip curls.

"I'll do it," Arlington says. "I've even worked with Job some. Not recently, but like, a few years ago. I think I can do it. But I may need to cut you open to get the line right. I think he'd perform a full-on surgery, but clearly." He motions around us.

He's right. No time, no place, no tools. A simple slice, a guided break, and some focused healing. Those are my options.

All in all, it goes better than I expect. I manage not to scream, and Arlington doesn't throw up—just a little dry heaving.

"I'm glad I skipped lunch," he says softly.

"Now let's focus," Bellatrius says. "We can't just walk out into the hall with a mud ball and expect no one to notice, no offense."

I laugh. "None taken. But wait, this opens into the hall?"

Arlington nods. "Inara brought your body back—and she rushed a funeral, presumably so she could rush the coronation. She was in a big hurry when she left."

"We visited Frederick. He insisted that if you were alive, the only place Inara could be holding you was in the bunker. He apparently helped with developing the schematics on it, and although it doesn't connect with the palace, they share a utility matrix. Backups only, but it's enough that the ventilation systems are connected in this one spot." Bellatrius points. "Once we pass through, we can reach the palace maintenance area."

"So I'll duck back out," Arlington says. "And Bell will follow, but I'll stay out there, and she'll return."

"My shift has four more hours, and Arlington's has three —which means no one will be watching us too closely right now. I'll go and grab a bucket of water so you can sponge off and change clothing, since I'm a girl."

Thank goodness for that.

"I'll gather some supplies, and once you're through, we'll head straight for the beach," Arlington says.

"What about Frederick?" I ask. "I can't leave him here."

"You need supporters on the island," Arlington says. "He told me that himself—he needs to prepare things here while you regroup. He'll gather people quietly, spreading the truth whenever possible. We'll leave word that you've escaped. We can't risk a pitched battle right now—Inara has some kind of group working for her, people that support her specifically."

I nod. "I know she does. She's Nereus—she killed my mom."

Bellatrius' eyes widen. "That makes a terrible amount of sense." She turns to Arlington. "We need to hurry—and don't grab much in the way of supplies. We can't take a boat."

"We can't?" I ask.

"They're monitoring the water really closely. Anything that large would be spotted immediately."

It makes sense, knowing that Inara used the water to carry out her plan. My heart trembles inside my chest whenever I think of that blue boat, but I can't wallow, not right now. "How are we leaving, if not by water?"

"Oh I didn't say we couldn't leave by water. I said we couldn't leave *by boat*."

"What does that mean?" I ask.

"We'll have to swim from here to Kaua'i," she says.

Fantastic.

I'm grateful, really I am. But maybe next time I should be a little more specific in my prayers. Because it's awfully dark by the time we reach the water, and I'm utterly demoralized, depressed, and bone-wearyingly exhausted.

Swimming forty miles isn't high on my list of things to do. Actually, it's nowhere on the list at all. And yet, here we are.

"At least the current will be working with us part of the way," Arlington says.

I groan. And then, like my friends, I dive into the dark water.

9

At least I'll feel clean again.

That's my first thought, as my arms slide back and forth, pulling and pulling and pulling the dark water, waves splashing against my face. I wish I could at least see the distant island of Kaua'i up ahead.

A few hundred strokes into the journey, salt has replaced grime and I realize it's not much better. Clearly, I'm a moron. God's bluntest instrument. A fool, an idiot, an imbecile.

We haven't gone far when it first occurs to me that if a shark ate me, this would all be over.

Or if I drowned.

But neither thing happens, and I keep paddling along. Bellatrius and Arlington check in with annoying frequency.

My lungs protest at the pace we set.

The saltwater agitates the inside of my nose and throat.

It burns my eyes, which, no matter how much I try, still can't make out Kaua'i.

Inexplicably, my throat is wet and somehow also dry.

The accursed saltwater splashes me in the face every few pulls forward, flooding my nose and mouth. The waves roll me over, knocking me under, confusing up and down. But like the tides, Bellatrius is constant, steady, predictable. She checks on me, and then a moment later, so does Arlington. We're lucky Bellatrius is a champion swimmer, and that she navigates by the stars. Otherwise, we could be halfway across the Pacific right now instead of steadily moving toward Kaua'i.

We swim for what feels like three days, but as the sun hasn't come up, it mustn't be quite that long. And then we just keep swimming. I want to ask Bellatrius every single time she checks in how much further we have to go, but she can't possibly know. There's no sport watch that will tell us how many miles we've swum in the current. And any kind of phone or navigational device could be tracked.

I used to benefit from that, as I was the one looking over every tracker's shoulder. I could keep my tabs, in this day and age, on almost anyone.

Now, on the flip side of the complete control spectrum, it's not quite as wonderful. I feel a little like a bug, skittering away as fast as I can from a kid with a magnifying glass.

"We're getting close," Bellatrius says.

"How do you know?" I shout.

"The water below us isn't as dark."

It looks exactly the same to me.

"And I just saw a reef."

"A reef?" I ask, breathing heavily and splashing around inefficiently in my irritation. "You saw a reef in the dark?" I peer down around us. I see nothing.

"Fine," she splutters. "I saw a weke 'ā 'oama, okay?"

Predators love them, which means my shark fears might be legitimate right now. It's also Inara's favorite fish, which I don't bother pointing out. My heart hammers inside my chest, and I focus on slowing it.

"They don't swim in areas with more than about a

hundred foot depth," Bellatrius continues. "Which means—"

A cloud shifts and the moonlight shines brightly, even though the moon is low in the sky. We've been swimming almost all night. But what it reveals has us all treading water in amazement. The stunning Nā Pali coastline looms in front of us. The current must've dragged us much further north than we meant to go, but it's land. I'll take most any land at this point.

"Any chance the shoes Arlington bagged for us are still dry?" I ask, my voice pathetically hopeful.

Bellatrius laughs, a real feat while floating in active waves. But the waves are finally dragging us the right way— toward shore. "We can certainly hope."

The sun has probably risen by the time we reach the small strip of sandy beach at the edge of the Nā Pali mountains, but we won't see it for another hour or so, not with the tall, craggy giants towering directly in front of us.

"Marselle said she would send someone for us," Arlington says. "We'll know it's her people because they'll have a purple flag hoisted on top of the boat."

"Got it," I say.

Three hours of walking, judging by the rising of the sun, and no boats at all. The shoes were not dry, and even if they had been, we swim around locations where there's no beach at all with enough frequency that we don't bother taking off our shoes each time. After the last few days, squishy shoes are the least of my problems. At least my collarbone seems to have set mostly right. Grief rolls over me in waves, threatening to pull me under, but the urgency of my situation, my need to fight back, and my desire for justice all keep me upright and moving.

"More jerky?" Arlington asks.

There's not much left, and it's kind of him to offer it to me. "You eat it."

He laughs. "I'm fine. We mostly brought the food for you, anyhow. Neither of us was stuffed in a dirt hole and starved for a day and a half, nor are we healing from any injuries." He tosses it at me. "Take it."

I'm chewing on it when I hear the sounds of the first boat. All three of us crouch down, instinctively seeking cover behind a clump of beach cabbage. I peer around the corner of one long and broad, curly leaf.

No purple flag.

My heart sinks. It's not like I expected the very first boat we saw to be the right one. But it would have been nice to catch a break.

"Inara isn't at the palace," I say.

"Right." Bellatrius stands up.

"We're past Barking Sands, almost to Kekaha," I say. "Pretty soon we will look decidedly odd, diving behind clumps of plants or trees or sheds at the sound of a boat."

"True," Arlington says.

"Inara has no reason to believe I could ever escape from the hole where she threw me." I think about Melina, buried in that pit, and shudder. "She won't have sent anyone here —it won't occur to her that I might have left at all."

"And?" Bellatrius asks. "You're saying we shouldn't hide?"

I shake my head. "I'm saying we should be doing a better job of it. If we hide in plain sight, we can keep our eyes out for Marselle without worrying we'll be spotted by any of Inara's people who might be patrolling the area."

"Hide in plain sight?" Arlington frowns. "Do I want to know what that means?"

I smile. "What will be all over the beaches soon, strolling along comfortably, enjoying their natural habitat, so to speak?"

Bellatrius scrunches her nose. "Crabs?"

"Oh my word," I say. "You two are a disaster. I know

that Hawaii is sort of closed right now, what with that horrible virus that Inara's people released." It hits me then that she's been working against me all along. I wish I'd had the presence of mind to ask her about it—to find out her end plan. Why did she leave? Where is she going? Why does she want to kill the humans? It makes no sense. They serve us right now, as horribly unfair as that is. They provide for us. Why doesn't she want to save them, if there's any way to do it?

I shove that back to consider later. "If we want to blend in, we'll need to find some swimsuits."

A few moments later, when Arlington finds an empty house not far from the beach, and we jimmy a window open and crawl through, I regret the idea.

"I think you'll look quite nice in red." Bellatrius barely suppresses her smirk.

"I am not wearing this." I pick up the string bikini with two fingers, not even trying to hide my dismay. "Absolutely not."

"This one isn't much better." She snatches the green polka dot bikini and clutches it to her chest. "But I'm calling it anyway. There's no way I could fill that one out." Her eyes widen, and this time she does smile.

Arlington, the jerk, emerges from the bathroom a moment later in nondescript navy blue swim trunks.

"This is unfair," I complain. But thirty minutes later, no one even notices us walking along the beach. We watch as four more boats fly by, none flying any flags at all.

"Kaua'i is different without any tourists," Bellatrius says. "Kind of sad, somehow, like a schoolyard with no kids."

"I like it," Arlington says. "It's peaceful."

A white powerboat with a bright blue stripe flies by us then, the motor growling. There's definitely no purple flag, but it slows down about a hundred yards past us. My heart accelerates. My hands shake slightly, itching for a weapon of any kind. Plain sight? I'm a moron.

"Look alive." Alrlington shoulders his backpack, knocking his dagger loose.

"Keep that obscured by your leg," I say. "And I want one, too."

The boat turns around and heads back toward us before Arlington has time to pull another weapon free. I struggle to slow my breathing, preparing for the worst. Inara may not be looking for us, or she may. Someone might have checked on me—they may know I'm gone. They may have tortured the information out of Frederick, or Marselle, or someone else entirely.

The boat only holds one person—a tall, broad-shouldered man with steel-grey hair. Hardly a threat. But even if he's alone, this could be very bad—who knows how many other people are standing by? Or whom he might alert to our presence with a radio, or cell phone.

"Princess?" a voice shouts. "Is that you?"

My heart stalls dead in my chest. The man is no one I know, but I know that voice.

I love that voice.

"I know this isn't really the time." Noah's voice coming from the old man's face is disturbing, and also the most beautiful sound I've ever heard. My heart lurches in my chest. "But wow, girl! Red is your color."

$$\maltese \quad 10 \quad \maltese$$

Somehow, Noah survived the explosion.

He's like a cockroach—nothing kills him. I laugh as the boat roars toward the shore, running toward him without thinking, tears streaming freely down my cheeks. Arlington and Bellatrius both try to stop me, their hands grabbing at my shoulders and hands, but I spin and twist and lurch until I'm free.

"How?" Too many thoughts tumble round and round inside my brain.

In answer, the old man drops an anchor and dives over the side of the boat. When his head emerges, it's not the grey-haired man swimming toward me with even movements. It's Noah: strong, broad shouldered, capable, and healthy.

When we collide, the water's too deep to stand, but neither of us cares. His arms wrap around me, and mine circle him. "How?" I ask again.

"Well, if you did survive, which I was sure you did, and you managed to escape, which I hoped you would, this is pretty much the only place you could reach—this side of Kaua'i is a straight shot from Ni'ihau."

His mouth covers mine, and the questions in my mind disappear. He's here. He's alive. I'm not alone.

Unfortunately, no one can really swim *and* hug *and* kiss. Not without sinking. So when we drop below the surface, we both let go. He's smiling when our heads break the surface, and so am I. He kisses my nose. And my forehead. My cheek. My lips. But finally, he tosses his head toward the boat.

Arlington and Bellatrius reach our side then, both scowling at Noah as they tread water. "Where have you been, if you were alive? Why did you disappear?"

"Knowing Noah, it's probably a long story," I say. "But I'm sure he'll fill us in on it."

Noah practically leaps from the water onto the boat, and then offers me a hand, which I gladly take. He helps my two borderline-hostile guards up onto the boat deck and then swings me into a bear hug. "I'm sorry you've been afraid for my life. I've been worried about you too, but I *knew* you had to have survived."

"But I *saw* you explode," I say. "So how are you here?" Did his stone protect him? I still can't believe I handed them over to Inara like an idiot.

Noah sits down in the captain's chair. "Sit, and I'll tell you. We shouldn't just hang around out here, though."

Arlington lifts one eyebrow. "I agree."

Noah spins the boat around, and then shoves the lever forward. I fall back into my seat. "Where are we going?"

He beams back at me. "So, you saw a video of the four of us—Alora, Edam, Judica, and me."

I swallow. Please, please, please have more good news.

"And then two minutes later. . . Kaboom."

I gulp, reliving that moment.

"A lot can happen in two minutes when you can look like anyone at all, but that wouldn't have been enough."

They could never have swum far enough from the boat to escape that blast.

"Inara didn't know about the extent of my *abilities*." He clears his throat. "And she miscalculated something else."

"Just tell us," Arlington says.

"You have no sense of pacing or storytelling basics," Noah grumbles.

"Spit it out," I say.

"If Roman wasn't such a dogged admirer of your psychopathic sister, we would not be here today." Noah frowns.

A smile bursts across my face. "You're just irritated you needed help, and that Judica's boyfriend saved the day."

"To be fair, without me, we would have exploded to bits together—including her overly muscled puppy dog."

"What did you do exactly?" Bellatrius asks.

"When we saw the flip side of that video, we realized who was calling the shots," Noah says. "Which is when I turned myself into Inara and told them to release us."

My jaw drops. "But they could *see* that you were Noah. They bought that?"

"I told them I stole the rings from you, and one of the stones let me teleport." Noah's smile is sly. "And those idiots are so scared of her, they'll do anything she orders."

"But they still blew you up?" I shake my head. "I don't understand."

"They didn't blow anything up," Noah says. "The explosion was initiated remotely."

"Who was on the boat with you?" I ask.

"I didn't know them," Noah says. "Maybe Alora or Edam or Judica did, but by the time I convinced them I really was Inara and they untied me, it was too late to call anyone back."

How close were they when the bomb went off? I can't bring myself to ask the next question. "Did—are—who—"

Noah's eyes are kind. "They're all alive. Roman had just reached us, so once we were free, we leapt into his speedboat and booked it for Kaua'i."

I can hardly believe his words. "Everyone?"

"Edam, Judica, Alora, and even the daring hero, Roman survived," Noah says. "But we aren't really excellent at getting along. It occurred to me that if you *did* escape on your own, you'd likely be headed this way, so while they argued over how to save you, I borrowed this boat to look for you."

"Borrowed?" I lift both eyebrows.

"I stole it," Noah says. "But it's not like the owner would report us to Inara if they find it missing, so. . ."

I lurch across the boat as it skips and leaps and bumps across the waves, and just before I reach his side, the boat comes down hard and I fall into his lap. "Thank you," I whisper.

His heart races, and the wind whips my hair, and I wonder whether I've ever been this happy or this grateful in my entire life.

Which is ironic, because I'm still running from my sister, and I've lost the staridium stones I worked so hard to obtain. A few days ago, I had so much more than I do right now—but I also had no idea who my real friends were. And for the first time in a very long time, I'm surrounded only by people I trust.

What matters in life is the people you love, and those have been miraculously returned to me. For now, it's enough.

"So we're headed. . .where?"

Noah slows the boat, a grin curling up one side of his mouth. "We're nearly there, but I have an idea. How'd you like to do something a little bit fun?"

"No." I raise one eyebrow. "No pranks, not on people who are scared and alone."

"If you had any idea how insufferable they've been. . ." he mutters. "Fine, fine, but for the record, I didn't want to scare them—just surprise them a little."

When we fly toward a tiny, private dock on a bright yellow beach house on the south side of the island, the waves from our wake crash into the wooden pile-ons. "I don't think you're supposed to drive that fast," I say.

"I'm excited," Noah says. "Can you blame me?"

Even though I'm prepared, my hands shake as I leap from the side of the boat onto the rough wooden dock. Arlington and Bellatrius scramble to take up positions on either side, each of them brandishing a dagger.

"Be alert," Arlington whispers, sliding the hilt of a blade into my left hand.

Noah laughs. "I admire your preparation, but it's not a trap."

The back door swings open on creaky hinges, and Judica's eyes widen. "That moron actually found her." She sprints toward me, black boots thwacking against the wooden slats, entirely out of place in this setting—a vacation home on Kaua'i—and I couldn't possibly love the misplaced sight of her more. She barrels into me so hard that I barely swing the dagger out of the way in time.

When Edam runs up behind her, I drop it and it clatters against the dock.

"You were going to attack us?" he asks, eyebrows lifted.

I beam at them all, even Alora who's leaning against the doorframe like a mother dog watching her pups with bemusement. "We're all happy to see you alive."

Roman pokes his head around the corner and throws me the cheesiest thumbs up I've ever seen. I couldn't imagine a more perfect foil for Judica if I tried—and for one split second, her future opens up in front of me. Dozens of kids, a husband who dotes on them, and her face twisted into a scowly frown that none of them believe.

A future I'll never have, but it's good to know that if this works, she'll have it for me.

"You're happy?" I barely manage to wheeze the words. "Even if Judica's welcome cracked a few ribs, I'm overjoyed you survived."

Judica finally releases me, shouldering Edam and then following up with an elbow. "Back off, loverboy. She's my twin. You'll get a turn, but we shared a womb."

Edam's smile never wavers, and as Judica steps aside and he can step into the space she vacated, the air around me thickens and warps, and a thrill runs up my spine. "I can finally breathe again," he whispers into my hair.

"Me too." I'm acutely aware that very little of my body is covered with fabric. Only Edam's cotton t-shirt and cargo pants separate us.

He notices at the same time, his body freezing in place. "How have I never seen you in a bikini before now?" His voice is rough, raw, and deep.

"It's not like we needed to make things any harder," I say.

He grunts.

"Alright, alright," Noah says. "Let's all go inside and we can make a plan for how to get out of this mess. I vote the first thing we do is string Inara up by her toes."

"We're a ways off from that," I say.

"I think we gather some troops and head back over to Ni'ihau right now," Roman says. "We strike before she's solidified anything, before she has time to argue. We can call Balthasar, Job, and Moses—rally your allies. She may have the stones, but that's not enough. Once people know she lied, that's it for her."

"She was smart," I say. "She planned all of this meticulously, and then I stupidly sent my strongest allies away to maintain my recent conquests."

"You're spread thin, but the reasons people supported

you are still there," Alora says. "And everyone believes you're dead. I agree with Roman."

"I'm not sure," Edam says. "The rest of you have no idea quite how many members of the Sons of Gilgamesh have been gathered in Ni'ihau, and if they decide to support her—"

"She's their leader," I grind out. "She's Nereus. She killed Mom."

"How did we not see that?" Judica's lips are compressed into a tight line. As my Inquisitor, she'll take the miss personally.

I need to gather my allies—but I fear that going back to Ni'ihau right now would result in a slaughter. "Everyone thinks I'm dead," I say. "We might be able to use this as an opportunity to discover whom I can actually trust."

Judica frowns. "But the longer you wait, the less people will expect your return. Roman might be—"

"I could spring right back in," I say. "Many of the Alamecha citizens won't know what to make of it—and confusion is never great for the innocent. And Edam knows better than the rest of us quite how many of my citizens are prepared to fight to the death for Inara, no questions asked."

Edam's shoulders droop.

"As the leader of the Sons of Gilgamesh, she was able to leverage a large group of men who would take her side— and that's how she got away with killing Melina's people."

Alora's face crumples. "She really did that?"

I nod. "It's also how she captured the four of you and took over the island so smoothly."

"So she was working against our mother for years?" Judica's lip curls. "I'll kill her myself." Her hands clench and unclench reflexively.

"I doubt you can take her," I say. "I tried to fight her,

and she's fast. There's something not quite normal about her. She said she's a genetic anomaly."

"She can get in line," Judica says. "Because last I checked, anomaly or not, the stones don't respond to her."

I scowl. "That's how she got them away from me."

"She convinced you to let her check whether they respond to her?" Judica's eyes hold too much pity and too much understanding. "You wanted her to take over for you. You just didn't realize she'd do it whether they reacted to her or not."

"I'm an idiot," I say. "Yes."

"No one blames you for her actions," Alora says.

"I think our esteemed empress has learned a valuable lesson here," Noah says, "in not being a chump."

Edam's hand balls up, his lips flattening.

But something inside me that has been festering pops, thanks to Noah's words. Laughter bubbles up from deep down. "You're right." I laugh so hard I can't stop. Tears roll down my cheeks. "I was a complete chump." Something turns then. "How many people will die because I'm so stupid?"

Noah wraps an arm around my shoulders and squeezes. "You'll think of something. You always do." He releases me. "But in the meantime, I think you might have been right about something."

"Oh?" I'd love to hear about something I did right —anything.

"It might be time to call my parents."

"Actually," Alora says. "I called Isamu last night—"

Judica throws her hands into the air. "We agreed we wouldn't contact anyone, and you're calling people and Noah's out stealing boats and trolling the beaches."

"Your boyfriend is here," Alora says. "My husband had flown to Paris to meet me under the belief we'd be running Malessa together."

Noah's eyes widen. "Good old Ish! He's in Paris already?"

"He is," Alora says.

"I hope he's safe," I say.

"I was worried about that too," Alora says. "Which is why I broke the injunction against communication and reached out to him. He believed you to be dead—he said Inara privately sent the heads of the families footage of the boat exploding, and it showed you to be on it, Chancery. They believe the explosion was the result of your attempt to join the stones."

"Wait, what?" I ask.

"It makes sense," Alora says. "Isamu believed that I was on that boat, as well as Edam and Judica."

"What about me?" Noah asks.

"No one cares about you," Edam snaps.

"But Isamu knows now," I say. "Is he still running Malessa?"

Alora shakes her head. "Inara released him, which makes sense. She told him it was so that he could grieve."

Dang. "Who did she install instead?"

"Olivia—Analessa's niece. But Isamu wasn't taken—he's headed for home, for the family estate in China."

Just like Noah. It's so strange that Alora's married to Noah's brother.

"I think we can assume everyone has been told the same lie," Alora says.

"Everyone was told you died," Arlington says. "If Frederick had not insisted you weren't on that boat, we'd have believed it. And we only heard his objections because we were around the corner when he was hauled downstairs."

"Marselle knows?" I ask.

Bellatrius nods. "She does, and Frederick is yet alive. Others may find out."

"My options are to return to Ni'ihau, take the island,

and fight Inara to try to retake the stones, or to turn my attention toward locating something else." I stare at Noah. "Something that, if I returned with the knowledge and proof of it, might rally the troops around me." I've suspected for some time that Noah's family guards the Garden of Eden, but after my vision, I'm virtually certain.

"Oh, no," Noah says. "That's a bad idea. I mean, yes, we should approach my parents, but believe me when I say, we need to approach them from a position of strength."

"You think I need to regain the stones *before* we go there?" He would know.

"Isamu suggested we go for a visit." Alora looks at Noah, her eyes clearly conveying something. "He says we shouldn't call your parents first."

Noah walks toward the window, staring outside.

"He thinks we should—"

Noah shakes his head. "It's too risky. He doesn't know everything."

Only Noah does, and he still can't tell me, not without risking his own life thanks to some stupid vow his parents made him swear. I've never pressed it, but if we did, the seizures could kill him—I'm virtually certain.

"Your brother says that you've always been their favorite," Alora says. "He says that they'll listen to you."

Noah's laugh sounds more like a bark. "Chancery has seen me around my dad. Does that seem true to you?"

"We have a week," Edam says. "Before Inara initiates the plan to release a new virus. A week before the humans of the world die. That was the timeline almost thirty-six hours ago."

"So do we fly to China and ask your parents for help?" I ask. "Or do I gather as many supporters as I can and try and storm the proverbial castle here?"

Noah doesn't move—his shoulders tense, his body utterly still.

Moments tick past, and I'm acutely aware of the hour-glass hanging over our heads, sand trickling through as we deliberate. How long will I spend flying to China? How long to fly back? To confront Inara, who is no one knows where?

We're running out of time.

"Fine." Noah spins on his heel. "There's no way to know who will support you here—and it's better if we let the dust settle anyway, rather than initiating a civil war. We'll leave now—and be at Mom and Dad's by early morning."

Alora smiles. "Isamu already arranged for pick up. Our jet will be here in less than an hour, so it's a lucky break that we've already found Chancery."

Luck? No, this is more than luck. This is grace. I've woken up from a brief nap, and someone is holding a blow torch to the cage, ready to release me.

This is our chance to fulfill the prophecy and save the world, and I won't miss it, not this time. "We better get ready."

Noah inhales and exhales a few times, and then he turns to face me. "I can't believe it."

I blink. Then I blink again. I've just told them that Inara killed my mom, that she runs the Sons of Gilgamesh. What now? "What can't you believe?"

"You're finally going home to meet my parents." He winks.

❧ 11 ❧

"**W**hat exactly can you tell me?" I ask Alora as we board the jet her husband sent.

She frowns. "You mean, what secrets can I share that Noah hasn't already spilled?"

"Dad made me swear on the key before I left." Noah's directly behind me.

"Oh." Alora sits down. I sit next to her. Noah slides into the seat across the aisle from me.

Edam stands in the aisle for a beat, and our eyes meet. His eyes dart to the side, acknowledging that Noah is next to me, and that I need to talk to Alora. He lifts his eyebrows and smiles a half smile and walks past me.

And for maybe the first time, he does exactly what I need him to do in an awkward situation with no fuss, no argument, and no stress. He's learning.

"So what exactly has Noah told you?" Alora asks.

"I know they have a stone," I say. "Staridium, I mean. Inara doesn't know about that one."

"Okay," Alora says.

"Noah has it," I say.

"I figured that out when he transformed into Inara six

inches away from me." Alora shakes her head. "Isamu had mentioned his family—but I had no idea what it could do or that they'd trust this idiot with it. Talk about unnerving."

I laugh. "Quite."

"So, Noah's the youngest child, and he's the descendent of—"

"Sheva," I say.

Noah coughs.

I turn sideways. "They're descended from Eve's youngest son, Mahalesh's little brother."

His mouth hangs open in a very satisfying way. "How could you know that?"

"It was a pretty weird time when Inara threw me in the bottom of the bunker in the dark, to spend who knows how long—"

"You were in there for two days," Arlington's voice carries from behind us.

"Right. Well, while I was stuck down there, alongside what I believe to be the decaying remains of Melina's dead body, I—"

Alora whimpers. "No."

I'm such a jerk. "I'm so sorry. I forgot I hadn't had time to explain. Inara says it was an accident, but that Melina would not agree to help dethrone me and. . ."

Sobs wrack her body—and I wait for them to abate, not pressing, not trying to console her. There's something cathartic about allowing that pain to exist, to pulverize your insides, to do its worst. And then to rise from it, like a phoenix, because you survived and you will survive, and you will not surrender. Sorrow and despair will not defeat you, no matter how debilitating.

I watch as my older sister, my strong, good, kind, loyal sister processes this news. And it occurs to me that Judica might also be struggling. I turn all the way around in my seat until I can see her face.

She's staring straight off. . .I follow her gaze. At nothing. She never knew Melina, by her own choice. Melina threatened her and abused her, but I wonder whether Judica regrets not searching earlier for the will to forgive. She notices I'm watching and shakes her head. Roman hasn't taken her hand, or wrapped an arm around her shoulder. He's giving her space to process. Smart man.

Because she's fine. Right. Of course. Nothing touches her. I don't buy it, but I don't press either.

When I turn back toward her, Alora's face is as stoic as I've ever seen it. "Inara will pay, every last centime."

I nod. "She will."

"Promise me." She grabs my hand, her fingers digging into my wrist. "You won't have mercy, not for her, not after everything she's done."

Part of my heart trembles—there was genuine pain in her eyes. Inara was hurting for a very long time, and she was alone, which is something I understand.

"Chancery." Alora lifts her chin. "No mercy, not for her."

Justice and mercy, two sides of the same coin—both with a place. But in this instance. . . "No mercy." The words settle across my soul, and I realize that I mean it. There are things that can be forgiven, and there are lines that can't be crossed.

Inara has crossed them all.

"And?" Noah nudges. "How did you find out about Sheva?"

"I, um." I look at my hands.

"What is it?" Judica leans forward.

Everyone on the plane can hear me, except maybe Isamu's pilot and co-pilot in the cockpit. Arlington, Bellatrius, Alora, Judica, Roman, Edam, and Noah. And I realize that I don't mind. I know and trust them all. My fear, indecision, and concerns have finally all been resolved.

These people are family. I know it deep down in my toes.

"I had a vision, I suppose," I say. "While I was trapped in the dark. While I was suffering in my own personal crucible, alone, defeated, absolutely without faith. I've been searching for so long, desperate to know what God wanted from me—and I guess He finally decided to show me."

"What happened?" Judica asks.

"In the vision, I was Mahalesh, in the days before she split the stones."

Utter silence.

I wonder how long they'll patiently wait to hear what happened. I wonder how I can possibly explain it to them. "She, um, loved her sister. She loved her husband Heth and her youngest daughters, absolutely, with all her heart. She wanted to do what her mother had tasked her to do—she wanted to serve all of Eve's children. She wanted the world to be peaceful and good, full of joy and promise."

"And did God actually split the stones?" Noah asks.

"He did. In the center of the world at the time, and the process of breaking them down actually fragmented the earth, creating the continents as we know them, I think."

"That's. . .I'm going to need to hear a lot more about what happened," Alora says. "I can't believe. . ."

"Mother would have been over the moon," Judica whispers.

She's right. Wherever she is, I hope she's with Mahalesh right now. I walk them through what happened, step by step.

"So, it sounds like you already knew more than I did," Alora says. "Because I had no idea they had another stone —until none of us could figure out what Noah had done. I knew magic had to be involved somehow."

I think about what Mom would have said about calling it all magic—and for the first time ever, I wonder if she might have agreed.

"I'm the one who figured it out." Edam smirks.

"I couldn't tell anyone anything," Noah says. "And Chancery figured it out way before you did."

I roll my eyes.

"We should all try and sleep," Arlington says. "I have no idea how long it has been since Her Majesty had any decent sleep."

"Too long," Noah says. "I agree. I've been reticent to go home, but everything that you don't know will soon be cleared up—and it'll be a lot easier than trying to guess at the things I can't share, once I'm released from this stupid vow."

"I just hope your family isn't half as irritating as you," Edam says. "Or I might not survive this trip without starting some kind of war."

"Are you making a joke right now?" Noah asks. "Or did the moon and the sun come up together, signaling the apocalypse?"

"When you're not taking up all the space in every room," Edam says, "I frequently make jokes."

Noah and Edam stare at one another for a moment and something strange passes between them that I can't quite fathom, but they aren't arguing, so I don't intervene.

I glance at Alora's phone, resting on her side table. Marselle knows. Isamu knows. Malessa has fallen. Melisania thinks I'm dead—so do Job and Balthasar and Moses. I could call them and tell the leaders the truth, at least. My fingers itch to *do something.* But Inara's tech-savvy in a way Mom never was, and I have no idea what she might hear, or who else she might kill as a result.

I don't know what to do, and I have no idea who I can trust in the far-flung corners of the world. Even if lines aren't tapped, which of them might tell Inara that I'm alive and that I've escaped, or where I've gone? Who might betray me, preventing me from returning and retaking the stones? My perceived death is my greatest protection right now. The only clear path I see leads toward locating and understanding the Garden of Eden.

I hope that when I find it, I'll know what to do with it.

The virus is the critical threat—but the Sons of Gilgamesh have developed it in response to something—to the degradation of the human DNA. Humans are at risk—solar flare or not—of dying out. But what could I do about repairing their critically degraded DNA, even with the stones?

What if I need the stones to do anything at all?

Am I wasting what precious time is left flying to China, only to have to cross the globe and back again? Why couldn't God have been more helpful when I was alone and flailing? A few more specifics, or perhaps a direction or two, would have been really nice.

I'm beginning to suspect that He doesn't work that way, that He cares more about the transformation than the result. If heaven is real, maybe that's true. Maybe we're all just ants racing around—passing time. The thought that we're a giant ant farm to Him is surprisingly funny.

When I finally drift off to sleep, it's with the faith that whatever He wants of me, He helped me to be reunited with the people who care about me and set me on this path. You don't give ants visions. You don't teach them, or guide them, or provide prophecies. In spite of the discomfort of a stiff plane seat and the whirring of the engine, I manage to get the best nap I've had in weeks. Which is probably why I sleep until the plane is preparing to land.

When my eyes finally reopen, Edam and Noah are both missing. I bolt upright. "Where are they?"

Alora laughs. "They went to the back of the plane to talk—closed the partition, even."

"Why?" I ask.

She shrugs. "No idea."

The plane may be descending—I don't care. I unbuckle and jog toward the back, sliding the partition out of the way.

Noah and Edam are staring at one another, but no one is yelling, no weapons are in sight, and no one is bleeding. It's a miracle. "We're landing," I say.

"Right," Noah says. "We were just reviewing Chinese etiquette."

I tilt my head. "Don't you think we all might need to know about that?"

He shrugs. "You guys already have great manners, but this one." He jerks his thumb at Edam. "He's remedial."

Edam rolls his eyes. Noah brushes past him and then, to my shock, past me as well. He ducks through the partition and heads for his seat.

"You coming?" I ask.

Edam leans against the side of a chair. "In a minute."

I take two steps toward him. "Are you alright?"

He nods. "I'm fine."

"Are you sure? You don't look fine."

"I've been thinking about something." Edam sits down.

I sit next to him.

"I was really struggling a while back—four or five years ago."

I frown. He was struggling. . .with what?

"I—" His eyelids flutter. "I had done something terrible, and I wasn't sure—"

"I can't imagine you ever doing something terrible."

He stares me in the eye. "I'm different than everyone else." His voice is low, taut, riddled with guilt.

"You're one of the best people I know."

He laughs, but it sounds sad to me, not happy. "You don't know everything about me, Chancery."

"You don't scare me." Not a bit.

"My father was—" He breaks off again and closes his eyes. "I've been plagued my entire life by this terrible gift."

"A gift has plagued you?" I lift my eyebrows.

He nods.

"Okay."

"It has a steep price," he whispers. "I've always been an exceptionally gifted fighter, but if I kill someone." He shakes his head. "I can't break away from the bloodlust when I do. It's bad."

That makes no sense. "I've seen you kill people to protect me, remember." I think about the time he saved my life at the Ritz Carlton, in Hong Kong.

"A few years ago, after a mission went wrong in the field, Angel sent me back to work with Balthasar. She told me I had things to learn, and that I needed better discipline."

"Okay."

"She was wrong. It wasn't something that could be repaired," Edam says. "When I came home, I began researching ways to solve the problem, and I only came up with one solution." He meets my eyes slowly, his expression dire.

Oh no. "You weren't considering—"

"I'd found several viable methods." His voice is low, pained. "And I was trying to decide between two, when someone I'd never really spoken to before took the time to make a suggestion. Her advice made me reevaluate my plan."

I think about the first time we spoke after his return, when I was dressed as my sister. I would have been too afraid to talk to him as myself, but that day I wasn't myself. Heat rises in my cheeks as I think about that conversation and how I pretended to be my sister. For some reason, I'm afraid to meet his eyes.

"I thought for years it was Judica who saved me that day." His voice is the barest of whispers. "I thought I was in love with her. Every single time I struggled after that, every time the bloodlust snapped into place. . .her face rose up in my mind and I was able to conquer it. I was safe. . .because of the kindness of my soul mate."

Soul mate. My heart slams against my ribcage, painfully loud.

"It took me years to realize that she would never have said the things that the girl that day said. Even after Judica showed an interest in me—I was excited at first—it took weeks and weeks of waiting for the girl I loved to reappear before I realized that somehow, inexplicably, I had been mistaken. It wasn't Judica I loved—it was her twin. And I finally decided that you must have been dressed up as her. You let me believe you were Judica, but it was you all along, wasn't it?" His eyes drill into me, like magnets tugging me into the right place at last.

When our eyes connect, that *feeling* I can't explain snaps into place, and heat pools in my belly. My fingers tingle. My mouth goes dry. "It was me."

"It has always been you," he whispers. "For me, there was never anyone else."

"When I was in that pit, and I thought you were all dead—"

"I thought you might be gone too," Edam says.

I sigh. "I'm so sorry."

"In some ways, it was a good thing," Edam says. "This sort of situation throws things into clear focus, doesn't it?"

"Excuse me?" I ask.

"Here's what I realized."

"You sound like something is wrong." But for the first time in a while, it's almost like everything is right. It always bothered me that Edam cared for Judica—and now I know that it was always predicated on how he felt for me, and his belief that I was my twin. Or that she was me.

"You know that I love you," he says.

I nod.

"It's an inadequate word for what I feel, if I'm being honest. You've known that for a while now."

I open my mouth to tell him that I know how he feels.

He shakes his head. "Not yet, please just listen. I've been afraid to push you, because I didn't want to scare you off. And that should really have been my sign. I realized something though, that day when I thought you were dead." He drags his hand through his hair, his eyes intent on mine, his chest heaving. "I would burn the world to the ground for you. I would kill—" He clears his throat. "I'm not proud of this. I'd kill dogs, cats, pregnant mothers, babies. I'd burn the world to the ground, if I had to, to keep you safe. To keep you with me. When I thought you had died—I began planning how painfully I would kill Inara. I calculated how to call the Motherless to me, how to raise the biggest army that had ever been raised, how to raze her and everything she ever cared for to the ground—not to save you, just to quench the rage that consumed me at the thought of your death."

He's deadly serious.

"I've warned you before that I'm not a very good person, not deep down," Edam says. "And you're my world barometer. Nothing else matters. It's—" He looks away, staring out the window. "I wonder sometimes whether you might have been a perfect match for me at any other time and under any other circumstances, but not these, not now. Like, if you weren't who you are, and if you didn't have a destiny to fulfill, maybe we'd have been perfect for one another."

Maybe we would have been? What's he saying? Why does he look so fatalistic?

His eyes are tender when he turns back toward me. "But that's not the reality. And what I feel for you, it's not healthy because it's not what you need, and more than anything, I want you to have what you need. I want you to be happy. If you really loved me, even a fraction as much as I love you, you wouldn't be agonizing over what to do with Noah." His eyes well with unspent tears. "I don't say any of this as a recrimination. You love him—I can see it—and that's okay. He's right for you. No matter how much he cares for you, he cares as much about doing the right thing. And in this moment, he has a lot to offer you—a path to help you fulfill your destiny. Whereas all I offer you is my blade, and it's powerful, but it's not what you need." His voice cracks. "Perhaps most important of all, it's yours whether you choose me or not."

"I don't understand what you're saying," I say. "Or why."

"I'm bowing out," Edam says. "More than I need to love you, and more than I need you to love me back, I need you to have what you need. I need you to fulfill your destiny and find joy and that means you need the right partner. I realized, in that moment that I thought that you were gone, that I'm not for you who you are for me."

I reach for him, and he flinches. I freeze, because he means it. It's not a ploy—it's not a power play. He's bowing out. To push him further would be cruel.

He's telling me the truth that I've struggled with all this time: Noah is right for me. Noah is what I need.

"But why would God put this connection between us?" I ask. "You can't deny it's there."

A single tear rolls down his perfect face. "I don't deny it."

"Then what? Is God that cruel? Does He hate us?" I think about Inara—she said she did all of this for *the love of her life*. If that's not who Edam is to me, then nothing makes sense. How can I care so deeply for two different men?

"I don't know," Edam says. "But I know that the prophecy is real—your task is real, and Noah can help you achieve it. And as much as I love you—you can't give that up. I won't stand in the way of it anymore. It hurts you, and I would never—could never—do that knowingly."

Edam stands up, swipes the tear off his cheek, inhales and exhales slowly, and then walks back to his seat.

I can't move. My legs tremble, my hands shake, and a splitting ache pounds against the inside of my skull. But most of all, my heart has been split in two—there's too much damage—it can never heal. Even if Noah is the right choice for me, will he want half of a person?

Because that's all that's left of me.

I'm not even close to composed when the plane lands a few moments later. My nerves are frayed, and my mind feels like it's recovering from significant trauma.

Like a nuke just hit my heart.

But as always, my personal life doesn't matter when duty calls. So I sweep the broken pieces of my heart together and dump them in a bucket and shove it in the corner. *Do your job*, I tell my heart. *Beat. Pump blood, and spread enough oxygen that I won't die, at least not until the right time.*

Because that's the one thing about my vision that I didn't share with anyone. Not with Alora, or Judica, or Noah, or even with Edam.

Mahalesh walked into her request knowing the price of her demand. She knew that when she asked for His help in splitting that stone, she would have to pay. God was preparing me with that dream—preparing me that the end of the line is approaching, and like there was for my great-great-great-grandmother, there will be a price.

I'm destined to assemble the final pieces of staridium so that I can save the humans, save all the children of Eve, and restore balance to the earth, but everything comes at a cost. And like Mahalesh before me, only I can pay. It's the nature of sacrifice. It's not a sacrifice unless it's mine to give. At the end of the day, the only things that are really mine are my choices, my time, and my life.

So it doesn't really matter whom I love or whom I'm better with, not really. Because whoever it is—they're in for a lot more pain.

❧ 12 ❧

Edam and I both tell lies much more effectively than we used to. In fact, if I didn't know him so well, I'd have no idea how much desolation hides beneath his forced serenity. I wouldn't notice the tension in his shoulders, or the white lines at the edges of his eyes.

But I do notice them.

Luckily, Alora doesn't see the bucketloads of grief I'm shouldering when I walk past her. Judica doesn't blink when she meets my eye. Or if they do, they blame my despondency on Inara.

And like always, Noah knows just how to interact with me.

He doesn't employ any of his usual jokes—no teasing or banter. He stands next to me, until the space narrows and he can't, and then he gently stops me by holding his left hand out. "I should probably deplane first."

"You sure?"

His eyes are sad, but they're not afraid. "I'm sure."

He's not looking forward to the reckoning he'll surely face, but he doesn't put off hard things. I've learned that much in our time together. He squares his broad shoulders and marches down the stairs, a ghost of a smile haunting his mouth, as if he's rehearsing the role he'll soon slip into, preparing for how to handle his parents, how to keep us all safe, and how to get us what we need.

Not a single cell in my body worries that he's not on my side.

We've all come a long way. I take the steps steadily, easily, secure in the knowledge that if he possibly can, Noah will convince his parents that I'm here for the right reasons, that he'll find the support I desperately need.

Edam flanks me, his hand hovering over the hilt of his sword.

Whereas all I offer you is my blade.

He has a lot more to offer than he gives himself credit for, but I won't think about it right now, not as my head finally drops below the plane fuselage and I can see where we've landed. I may never be able to think about it at all, not without breaking.

I hold my head high, surveying the gathered warriors, row upon row, their expressions made even more severe by the flickering flames from the hundreds of torches that run up and down the runway—and the bright lights of the courtyard in front of the vast palace that lies beyond. My eyes widen in spite of myself as I take in the lines and lines of soldiers. Not the dozens of an honor guard, but the hundreds and hundreds of an army.

So many that they could easily overwhelm us.

"You've returned," a strong voice rings out. I follow the sound until I see Noah's father, but he's not the man I met before. At least, not in any real way. He's the same, and yet entirely different. He must have carefully cultivated a veneer of human frailty before visiting me to demand Noah's release weeks ago.

The man standing at the head of the army amassed on the runway is tall, imposing, and downright terrifying, if

I'm being honest. His features are sharp, and his eyes are bright, predatory even. His arms are folded behind his back, as if he couldn't care less about our arrival—as if he isn't the least bit worried. A few hundred yards behind him, a mountain rises directly upward, massive doors built right into the wall of stone. The top of the mountain is only visible thanks to the light of a nearly full moon.

Presumably, this is the palace fortress of the family of Sheva.

"I've come home with a group of allies." Noah folds his arms and waits patiently while we descend the stairs behind him.

"Allies?" His father laughs. "Don't you mean that you've brought a ragtag bunch of refugees?"

Noah's mouth hardens. "Refugees? Hardly. I bring the queen of queens, the recognized wielder of the stones of Mahalesh, the chosen Mother of the Motherless, the Eldest. I bring to visit the home of the seventh family, finally, pursuant to the terms of the prophecy, Chancery Divinity Alamecha."

And for the first time, I see a side of Noah I haven't ever seen before, not in his full strength. He's confident, poised, and ready to take down Goliath with a single stone, if necessary.

His father is still smiling, but he doesn't look especially amused. "You always were fond of pageantry. I wondered how you would spin this, and frankly, it's not a bad angle. You might have missed your true calling, because obviously you're a terrible *spy*."

"You tasked me to bring her to you, and I have."

"Take them," Noah's father says.

In the blink of an eye, Edam has tossed me a short sword and drawn both of his blades. Where in the world did he have a short sword hidden? And where did he get it from? On the boat, tied up, he had nothing.

I shake my head. Fighting them is futile—we placed ourselves in their hands when we landed here, deep in the middle of nowhere. I won't waste any more lives, especially not his. "Stand down," I say quietly.

Edam's nostrils flare, and his arms tremble. A muscle in his jaw jumps, but he stands down, resheathing his blades and allowing the guards who flow among us to bind his hands behind his back. Judica struggles against her desire to fight as strongly as Edam, but she also falls in line at my command.

And I finally release the breath I've been holding since Noah's father ordered us caught.

"You'd better know what you're doing," Judica mutters.

For once, Noah has no clever reply, and I worry. What if Isamu, and Alora, and Noah are all wrong? What if his father won't support me? What if they trade me back to Inara, trussed like a pig, as a peace offering? What if they don't care any more than she does about the prophecy or the fate of the humans or anything else?

"I don't think all this unpleasantness is really necessary, do you, sweetheart?" A melodious voice travels from somewhere behind Noah's father. Seconds later, a woman with a flowing crimson dress, trimmed in gold and silver, crests the hill. She looks us over one at a time, her gaze stopping with me. "Release them."

I expect the men to look to Noah's father, waiting for him to confirm it, but they don't. They release the others immediately. For the first time, I wonder whether I actually know a single thing about how things work here. "I was told by classmates who had met her that your mother looked like an American model," I say. "In fact, Logan said she was white."

Noah shrugs. "Like most evians, she looks however she wants to look."

"But your father—he rules your family, right?"

His mother has drawn much closer than I realized, or I'd have kept my mouth shut. "Oh, little one, you misunderstand. My husband is a wonderful man, and I appreciate his advice, skill, and counsel in many ways. However, the youngest child always rules our family's line—male or female—and I'm clearly female."

I glare at Noah. He might have figured out a way to prepare me for this one. "It's a real pleasure to meet you, Your Majesty," I grind out.

"You don't ever need to lie, not to me, not here. Notwithstanding the way we sent Noah to find you, we don't appreciate obfuscation, even if it's well intentioned. It has been a requirement for survival for our family for so long, that we eschew anything to do with it within our walls." Her fingers brush the underside of my chin.

I want to smack her hands away, but no one has untied me.

"I'm well aware that desperation has driven you here," she whispers, circling me and untying my hands.

Now that my hands are free, I have to force them to remain at my sides. Punching Noah's mother in the face might not set the right tone. "You're correct that my older sister surprised all of us," I say. "She turned out not to be quite who I thought she was."

"And now my son has brought a plane full of strangers, to whom he has sworn never to divulge our secrets, and he's begging our help on your behalf." She taps her lip with her perfectly manicured finger. "I hope that you're at least engaged to be married, with the broad degree of influence you seem to hold over him?" She lifts her eyebrows expectantly. "We heard that the engagement between you and Edam Malessa was terminated."

"It's Edam *ex'Alamecha*." I've rarely heard Edam sound bristlier.

Noah's mother's lip curls and her eyes sparkle. It was an

intentional jab, then. "Of course it is. My mistake. My sources must have been confused when they reported that you challenged your sister Analessa's rule on the basis of your own legitimate claim to that throne."

Oh man, she likes to dig at people. And she's well informed for being in the middle of nowhere. "I'm not engaged to marry anyone." I square my shoulders and stare her dead in the eye. "Not Noah, not Edam, and certainly not anyone else."

"Well that's a relief." Her lips curl almost maliciously. "I mean, with all those titles, I wondered exactly how many men you'd try to juggle."

I grit my teeth. "I've kept your son at my side for a long time now, and if I were you, I'd probably be just as angry and vindictive."

Noah's mother purses her lips. "You're pretty, but not *that* stunning. Why did he stay with you all this time, if you haven't even agreed to marry him?"

A dozen retorts spring to the tip of my tongue, and judging by the fury on Noah's face, he's got a mouthful to say as well. But his father is faster than either of us. "Oh come, darling. Pettiness is beneath you." Noah's father has made his way over to our side as well. "She's quite jaw-droppingly beautiful."

His mother rolls her eyes. "I suppose she's nice enough to look at."

As if Noah was scouring the earth for the fairest maiden to choose as his bride. I might punch his mother after all. And his father too, for good measure. "Noah hasn't even asked me to marry him," I say. "I'm surprised you think he *could,* seeing as you trusted him so little that you bound him with oaths to keep your secrets and do your bidding. In my family we believe in teaching principles and then allowing individuals to make their own decisions."

His mother lifts her chin slightly. "I'm not sure your family should be touted as a model of familial behavior."

Judica flinches, and I'm sure that I do too.

Her voice, when she speaks again, is soft—deceptively soft. "My father raised me not to criticize those from whom I was begging for aid. I believe the American phrase is something pedestrian, like 'don't bite the hand that feeds you.'"

"Aid? I come to you seeking an alliance," I say, loudly, so everyone gathered can hear. "You may think I'm desperate—but you're only half right. In the past few weeks, I lost a beloved mother and gained a throne I didn't want." I step nearer to her. "And then with nothing more than my mother ever had before me, I attacked and took a second throne and the staridium ring that went with it." I glance around the wide expanse of the front courtyard. Every eye watches me, every ear listening. "After that, I forged alliances when possible—which only worked out in one instance—and then I *took* three more thrones by force, wresting three more stones from the empresses who wore them."

"And where are those stones you took?" Noah's mother asks, clearly already in possession of the answer.

I don't smack that look off her face like I want to—I'm not a child. I'm a queen. "My older sister betrayed me and took them—trust has always been my weakness. But I'm not friendless—and even without the stones that go with them, I still rule the earth. My sister didn't unseat me—she merely lied about whether I was yet alive."

"The world believes you're dead, and you think you still rule any part of it?" Her laugh tinkles, and I hate it.

"I'm saying that there's more to ruling than possession of fancy jewelry." I guess I should have called Melisania and Moses.

"You're more resilient than I expected," Noah's mother

says. She holds out a hand, and when I reach to shake, she clasps my forearm. I follow suit. "Well met, Chancery Alamecha. I'll hear your plea for an alliance—in the morning, at a reasonable hour."

"I'm glad to hear it," I say. "Will you also share your name? I've been thinking of you as 'Noah's mom' in my head, and I doubt that's your preference."

This time her laugh isn't nearly as irritating—she must have been forcing it before. "Not quite, no. I am called Mahakali, but my friends say Kali."

Ah, now she's put me in a delicate position. Do I proclaim myself a friend, which allows her to deny me? Or do I use her formal name, showing her I don't consider her to be a friend? Either way, I leave myself open to offending her, which is likely her gambit. But I know, thanks to my vision, that her ancestor, and consequently her family name, is Sheva. "It's a pleasure to meet you, Your Majesty," I say. "Alamecha is delighted to finally meet the ruler of the Sheva family, after all these years."

Kali's eyes narrow infinitesimally. "My son has not been quite as circumspect as I might have hoped."

"Oh, he didn't tell me a word about your family—its origins, your name, or your purpose. He couldn't have if he wanted to, but I have my own sources."

"And how she gained the knowledge she has isn't of utmost importance at three in the morning." Noah's father shakes his head. "I'm sure the kids are as tired as we are." He turns toward his wife and drops his voice. "Will you see them to their rooms yourself, my darling?"

"Don't be ridiculous." Kali crosses her arms under her chest.

"Then perhaps you should allow the servants to do their jobs." He gestures and liveried servants trot toward us from the front of the palace, clearly prepared to escort us inside.

"My son will stay with me," Kali says.

Noah grunts. "Your son quite likes the Alamecha way of doing things—wherein he's allowed to make his own decisions. If you'd *asked* me to stay in my rooms, I might have agreed, but as it is, I think I'll stay with my *chosen* empress, Chancery."

I worry that Kali's head will explode. Her face flushes, and her hands clench the heavily embroidered fabric of her skirt, but after a heartbeat or two, she flattens her hands and inclines her head gracefully. "In the morning, then."

Even so, I glance over my shoulder every few moments to make sure no spears are headed our way as the servants escort us in style through the front doors and around the corner to the guest suite on the far west side of the palace. It's surprisingly decadent for a fortress carved out of the side of a mountain range.

"You each have your own rooms, as you can see," a tall woman with intricately plaited hair gestures at the rows of ebony-stained, inlaid-wood doors. "You should have most anything you need. As it's quite late here, we haven't prepared a meal, but we're happy to bring you anything you require."

"We appreciate your thoughtfulness," I say.

The servants bow and walk to the end of the hall. They take up positions on either side of the hallway, and I wonder whether they're actually servants. . . or disguised guards.

Arlington glances sideways at them as if he can read my thoughts. "Her Majesty will not sleep alone," he whispers.

Judica frowns. "I agree. In fact, Alora and I can—"

"I'll stay with her," Noah interrupts. "I have some things to explain, now that she has more context."

My twin glances at Edam, expecting an objection, but he merely stares straight ahead.

"Bellatrius and I will stand guard outside the door," Arlington says.

"I'll stand with Arlington," Edam says. "The rest of you should sleep until the next shift."

"Alright," Judica says.

I stare at Edam for several seconds, but when he refuses to turn toward me, I finally duck inside the room. And then I stare. "Wow."

"We have decent resources," Noah says. "And Mum values nice things."

"I can see that." I didn't expect a lot in the guest rooms of a family that has never hosted other empresses—seeing as no one knew they existed. But from the rich, golden carpet, to the textured crimson walls, and the black lacquered hardwood furniture, no expense has been spared on the guest accommodations, or at least not on this one. I collapse into a crimson velvet armchair, which puts my focus on the back half of the room.

It's empty, other than an enormous bed.

"Good thing I'm not actually tired, thanks to a long nap on the plane." I glance pointedly at the single sleeping spot.

"Edam didn't even argue about my coming in here," Noah says. "Wonder why." Noah's never frenetic, never nervous, and always completely at peace within his own skin.

But right now he isn't.

He walks across the room to the bed and touches the lamp on the nightstand, turning it on even though the overhead fixtures provide plenty of light. Then he pivots and walks toward me, turning at the last minute toward the kitchenette against the wall. "Tea?" He glances over his shoulder, but as soon as I meet his eye, he turns back. "Da hong pao is the best tea you've ever had, I promise. If you've heard of the leaves sold from the original trees, well, let's just say they aren't *really* the originals. Whatever you may have had came from watered down grafts off of our family's tree."

"Uh, sure." What's going on with him?

"I expected Edam to demand that only he could keep you safe."

Oh. "He and I had a chat on the plane."

Noah fills a pot with water and sets it above an open flame. I've never seen Noah drink tea, but then, I've never seen Noah at home before. "You did." No questions—just a flat statement.

"Did you happen to overhear it?"

He drops into a chair across from me, but he doesn't meet my eyes. He shakes his head slightly. "I'd never do that."

Which I know.

He finally meets my eye. "What *is* going on? Are you two—" He swallows. "Together? Like, permanently?"

Ah—he knew we had a talk and that things shifted—he just didn't know which direction.

In spite of what he fears, he's been totally supportive, utterly calm, and entirely prepared to step in and fight his parents for me. It's then that I know. Inara's insane, clearly, but she's also as close as I'll ever get to having advice from my mom, and her words have been rattling around in my head ever since our talk.

If you have someone willing to do all the nurturing, someone willing to shield you from the wind and share the sun, someone completely in balance with you like your Noah, well. . . nurturing is vastly underrated.

And after my vision of Mahalesh and the knowledge that the Sons of Gilgamesh are moving against the humans any day, well, I don't have much time left. I need to locate the stones and repair the split—I must prevent the utter destruction.

I know the cost, and I believe Noah can bear it. But I need to know for sure.

"If you could go back right now," I ask, "and you had the

choice to never meet me, would you take it? Have I hurt you badly?"

The wrinkles in Noah's forehead melt away. His eyes widen, his lips part slightly, but he doesn't hesitate, not for a moment. "Never. I'd give up everything I know, everything I have, everything I love, for the chance to know you. Even for a day."

A single day.

He has no idea that may be about what we'll have. Now that I know what I want, it kills me that I'm out of time. But if he wouldn't take any of it back, maybe he won't hate me when I'm gone. Maybe I need to take hold of every single second left to me. At that thought, peace like I've rarely felt steals over me, quieting the ever-present doubts, my anxieties, my fears. For a moment, a brief second in time, it's like my mother's next to me, smiling down on me, and I know this is right.

I drop to my knee, and reach for Noah's hand.

He wraps his fingers around mine without missing a beat, his strong hand curling around my smaller one. "What's wrong?" He looks me up and down. "Are you alright?"

I beam at him then. "Noah Wen Sheva, or whatever your name really is, in the last few weeks, nothing in my life has gone right. A stupid prophecy took over first, and then my mother died, and then I fought my sister to keep her from destroying the world. And then I had to destroy everything to try and save it." My voice cracks, but my certainty never wavers. "In all the ups and downs, only one person never doubted me. Only one person never left my side—except when I plunged him into the ocean on accident. Only one other person reacts to the stupid stones, and if that wasn't enough of a sign, the dumb stones led me to that same person when no one else could find him."

Noah's mouth opens, but he doesn't draw a single breath.

I stand up and pull him to his feet. His arms wrap around my waist, yanking me against his chest, our bodies touching from my knees up to our shoulders. I turn upward and stare into his eyes. "When I need a laugh, you make a joke. When I need a sword to defend me, yours is already drawn. You're a warrior, you're a diplomat. You're a comedian, you're an executioner. You're loyal, you're brave, and you're understanding." His head dips toward mine.

I press one finger to his lips. "Not yet. I need an answer before you kiss me again."

"An answer to what?" Noah's voice is low, deep, and raspy.

"Will you marry me?"

His heart slams against his chest, and his lips curl upward slowly. "You know that you don't have to marry me, right? You could just say you want me for your boyfriend, and once the world either burns or doesn't, we can talk about marriage then. Or even, like, a decade down the road."

Should I tell him? Do I confess?

He'll try and stop me. Like he did on the plane to China. He'll look and look and look for another way. He'll get in the way, if I tell him what I already know deep down in my bones: saving the world will cost my life, just as it cost Mahalesh hers. There's a reason God sent me that vision, to prepare me. I've accepted it, but I don't want to spend my last week on earth fighting about it.

So I keep my secret. "Maybe it's the stakes of the world right now—maybe it's what you and I know is coming, but I don't want to walk around calling you my *boyfriend*. As much as I wish I could have been born somewhere else, or in some easier time, I wasn't. I'm not a normal teenage girl, and I never will be. That's not who I am, and wishing or denying or refusing to accept the truth won't help." I press my hand against his chest, my fingers tracing the valley separating the hard planes of his pectoral muscles. "I want you to be mine in every way. I want you to *marry* me. I want to know that we're facing the future together." I want a partner, someone I know I can always trust, someone to care when I'm gone. And if that's selfish, well, maybe I'm a little selfish after all. "So, will you do it?"

"Chancery Divinity Alamecha."

My name from his mouth lifts my soul.

"I've never wanted anything more than I want to marry you—and that includes the day I discovered that Godiva made its dark chocolate raspberry truffles with real raspberries." He bites his lip. "Since we're getting married, you probably ought to know that my real name isn't actually Noah. It's Sheva—after Mahalesh's little brother, and my ancestor."

"Sheva?" I scrunch up my nose. "The same as your family name?"

He nods.

"So, your name is Sheva Sheva?"

He laughs. "Not that I've ever thought of it like that, but I guess it is."

"Do I have to call you that?"

He laughs. "You can call me whatever you want to call me. I'd even answer to 'hey idiot,' if you're the one saying it." He brushes his lips against mine softly, and then speaks against my mouth. "Not to ruin this moment, but can you tell me. . .why now?"

My hands slide down the twin ridges of his stomach muscles to his waist and around to his back, pulling him closer to me. My fingers curl against the muscles of his lower back, and a thrill runs through me—I'm hugging my fiancé. "Your mother—"

"Whoa." Noah stumbles backward. "Please tell me you

didn't just propose so that my parents will support your claim."

Now it's my turn to laugh. "Of course not. I'm done with all that." I step closer. "But when your mother asked if we were engaged, I realized the only reason I *didn't* want to marry you was that she acted like you'd failed by not securing an engagement." I shrug. "That seemed like a stupid reason not to claim the man I love forever."

Noah blinks. "Love forever." He smiles. "Say it again."

"You're the man whom I love, forever, and I know you love me back, even if I can't regain the stones." I swallow. "Even if we utterly fail."

"I'll still love you," he says. "No matter how pathetic you turn out to be at fulfilling millennia-old prophecies which you never chose for yourself."

"I know that." I lean my head against his chest. "It sounds ridiculous, but that's when I knew. Your mother acted as if you'd failed, and it occurred to me that you're the one person I never need to fear being a failure around —if I fail, you'll still love me exactly the same. I *know* that, deep down."

"I might love you more if you botch things every now and again." Noah grins. "I've always cheered for the underdog."

I roll my eyes.

"But you won't fail." He drops a kiss on my forehead. "Not with me at your side."

The teapot whistles.

His fingers tangle with mine, and he tugs me toward the kitchenette. He starts to make two cups of tea, but when I try to drop his hand so he can pour the water, he squeezes tighter.

"You can't make tea and hold my hand at the same time," I object.

He presses his free hand against his chest. "You clearly

have no idea the caliber of man you're marrying. A lesser man, maybe, would be defeated by such mundane logistics, but not me. I won't surrender your hand to pour this hot beverage, in the face of nearly insurmountable odds."

I laugh, and for the first time since Inara told me she killed Mom, the weight crushing my soul lifts, just a bit. Enough that I can breathe without pain. Noah hands me a cup of tea a moment later, and we walk—hand in hand—toward the chairs we just vacated. Only this time, sitting in them is different. The world around me has shifted.

"So, did you want to talk about bridesmaids' dresses?" Noah asks. "Or would you prefer to discuss the strategy for the meet the parents breakfast first?"

I throw my head back and laugh. I made the right decision—every part of me knows it's true. If you have to choose between the intense guy and the one who makes you laugh, always choose the one who makes you laugh. "Your parents hate me."

He doesn't even bother arguing with me. "They'll come around."

"What if they don't?" I ask.

"Look, tomorrow I'll make Mum release me from my oath, and I'll explain everything—about our family, about what we can offer, and we'll figure out the best way to take out Inara. I'm leaning toward a sniper rifle that shoots ballistic missiles, but I have some fallback plans we can review as well."

"You want to tell your mom and dad, then?" I ask. "That we're getting married? You think that'll help?"

He shrugs. "It can't hurt, right?" He sips his tea. "Ah, I've missed this, so much."

I sip mine too, and he's right. "Wow, that's amazing. I was wondering—I haven't seen you drink tea. . . ever."

"Once you've had this, it's all you'll drink. Nothing else can compare."

"You missed home," I say. "Sometimes I forget what you gave up, all so you could hang out in America to meet me."

"There's something you should know about that," Noah says. "You know that I have this." He touches his chest above where the stone hangs on a cord. He takes another sip, clearly considering how to tell me what he needs to share.

"Right."

"My mum is a s—" His entire body is wracked with a seizure, his cup dropping to the floor, his body following suit.

I set mine on the side table and crawl over to cradle his head until the spasms pass. My hand traces his forehead. "I'll find out tomorrow," I whisper. "It's soon enough."

The tremors fade, becoming twitches, and his taut muscles go slack, his skin so pale I can't help worrying. "You need to know," he whispers. "Before—"

I cover his mouth with my hand. "I'll find out tomorrow, after you've been released. It's fine," I say. "If you're engaged to someone else, some foxy local girl, or if you have an evil twin who will fight you to the death for the stone, or if you're actually only sixteen, we will deal with it." Unless. "Wait, you're not like, my brother or anything, right?"

Noah sits up. "I certainly hope not. That would be horrifying. How could that be?"

I lift one eyebrow. "Inara told me Eamon wasn't really my dad, but she didn't say who my father really is."

He coughs. "You're kidding."

I shake my head. "The fun revelations just keep coming, right?"

"Well." He leans up against the chair and pulls me onto his lap. He whispers in my ear. "I'm quite sure we're not related."

His breath on my ear, his hands around my waist—

something inside me melts into a puddle that pools deep in my belly. "Everything else we can work through."

His laugh is low, deep, possessive. "Fine."

When his mouth dips toward mine, I close my eyes, but he doesn't kiss me. I open my eyes, hungry for the reason.

He's staring at me then—his eyes shining. "I never thought I could be this happy." He kisses me then, his mouth claiming mine. I surrender, my arms twining around his back and up over his shoulders.

He stands up then, as if I weigh nothing, shifting me in his arms and carrying me toward the bed. My heart hammers so loudly in my chest I worry he'll die of laughter. But when I open my eyes to look at him, the eyes that burn into mine don't contain a hint of mocking. He reaches the edge of the bed and pauses, waiting, I think, for some objection.

But he doesn't find any.

He tosses me backward, and I throw my hands back, bracing as I land against a pile of pillows. He bites his lip and I can't stop thinking about his mouth and all the places I want to feel it pressing against me. The pillows surround me as he climbs up onto the base of the bed and crawls toward me.

I blink, and suddenly, my eyelids are heavy. Far too heavy. I wasn't tired before, but exhaustion crashes over me in a wave. I force my eyes open and note that Noah has moved a little closer before my eyes are drawn inexorably closed again. I try to open them, but I can't do it.

I'm so, so exhausted.

My last thought, as I'm pulled under, is *what was in that tea?*

❧ 13 ❧

I claw toward awareness, but it's like swimming to the surface from a depth so deep that there's no light. No bubbles to follow, no guide to help me reach the place where the sky meets the water.

Still, I can't give up. I need to awaken—I know it. I'm desperate for it.

But why?

Every time a thought crystallizes in my brain, it flutters away, out of reach, incoherent. I shake myself, like a terrier climbing out of a lake. And for a moment, a realization hits me that I shouldn't be asleep. I need to be awake!

But *why*?

Dreams crash over me—I'm dressed up for a special day, wearing all white—what day requires all white? A wedding! It's my wedding? But instead of my father, a pig walks me down the aisle. A big pink pig wearing a deep black tuxedo.

I try to shove the pig away, and suddenly, it's Edam.

Walking me down the aisle? No. I revolt against that— not Edam. I love him. He can't walk me down the aisle. Something is *wrong,* so wrong! Where am I? I focus on the source of the blurring, the confusion, the inexplicable fog that chases me, and I *shove*.

And then I scramble upward, upward, upward, until sounds become clearer. Sounds I know, sounds that I've heard before. Noises from. . .the clashing of blades. Grunts of exertion. Something crashing into something else, hard. The splintering of wood.

And then a scream, a scream of complete agony. A scream of betrayal. A scream of horror.

I finally wrench my eyes open, like lifting the lid of an iron box glued all around with industrial strength epoxy. It burns, the light sears my eyes, but I push through it. I blink, and then I blink again, because what I see makes no sense.

Noah's standing in front of the bed I'm on, every muscle in his body taut. I struggle to my elbows so I can see better—because this can't be right. He's holding a woman by the throat, and she's gasping for air.

I can't see her face with the way he's turned, but I know who it is.

"Let her go," I whisper. "Noah."

His hand tightens, choking her out. He shakes his head. "No. I can't."

I force myself all the way up, gaping at the blood—so much blood. The room is covered in it—the bed covers, the carpet, even the sheets right next to me. And there's a hand lying on the floor—a woman's hand with manicured nails that I recognize. Fingers that proprietarily tilted my face upward not too long ago. "What's going on? Why can't you?"

Noah's voice sounds distant, like it belongs to someone else. "My mother tried to kill you. I stopped her just in time."

So it *is* his mother. Part of me hoped that maybe he had a crazy aunt—with as many crazy family members as I have, it feels like a distinct possibility. I close my eyes, and when I reopen them, she's no longer struggling. Lack of air won't kill an evian, but he seems determined. There's no telling what he'll do when she passes out.

And I can't let him kill his own mother, even if she tried to kill me. "Let her go, please."

Noah doesn't acknowledge me.

"As your queen, as your fiancée, and as your friend, Noah, listen to me. I order you to release her." I breathe in, and I breathe out. And he still hasn't let her go. "Noah. Release her. I'm not asking."

Finally, he releases her and she collapses on the ground, instinctively protecting the stub of her hand, pressing it against her chest. Blood smears the front of her dark grey blouse with a dark stain. "I won't thank you for sparing my life—for ordering my son in his own home." Her voice is gravelly and weighted with so much fury—but why? Why does she hate me this much? I don't even know her.

Perhaps more importantly, why would she try and kill me? I've never wronged her. I don't even know her.

My arms and legs are sluggish—she must have poisoned the tea—but I force them to work. I shove to the side of the bed and lurch into a standing position, although I am leaning heavily on the side of the bed. How is Noah functioning so well? He drank far more of that famous tea than I did. So many questions churn in my mind, but only one of them demands an immediate response.

"Why?" I ask. "Why are you trying to kill me?"

Noah's mother scowls. "Did you call him your fiancé?" She practically spits the words.

She asked if Noah and I were *engaged*, as though she *wanted* us to be. As though I'd offended her by not planning to marry her son. Why does she seem angry about it now? "We were hoping to tell you under better circumstances, but yes. We decided last night."

Kali's discarded hand lies grotesquely on the floor, and her blood spatter coats numerous surfaces, yet the news that I'm marrying her son is what causes the look of utter horror to steal across her features.

I do not get her, like, not at all.

"Mother, you need to go, right now, or I will end what you started."

"You would really do that?" She acts like I'm not even here, which I suppose is preferable to actively trying to kill me.

"If you force me to, yes. In case I wasn't clear, I choose her."

"You *swore* to me," she cries. "You swore it before God."

Noah rolls his eyes. "I was a child, and I had no idea what I was doing. You were wrong to make me take that vow, and now you'll release me."

She shakes her head.

"You will release me," he says. "Or I'll do it myself."

She swallows. "It's not that simple."

"What are you talking about?" I ask. "What vow? Release you from what?"

"My son apparently never told you that in addition to being heir to the seventh family, I'm also a seer," Kali says.

"He did not," I say. "But I'm sure you'll pardon him for that oversight, since every time he tried to tell me anything, your idiotic vows caused him to seize violently."

Her eyes soften a little, and she shoves to her feet. The stub of her arm has already healed over, smooth skin covering where her hand previously was. I've never watched a hand regrow, and I'm strangely drawn to it. Again, she ignores me and turns to her son. "I'm sorry I caused you pain, but it was for your own good. Every single thing I've done has been to protect you, always."

To protect *Noah*? "I think you're confused," I say. "There's absolutely no chance that I pose him any threat.

You don't know me, but I swear to you, and I'll swear on anything you bring to me, that I love him. I would never harm him. Never."

She walks toward the door, stepping over the blade of a sword I presume she brought. "She's the girl," Kali says. "You know that as well as I do."

He shrugs. "So what?"

"You know what that means." Her shoulders crumple and lines appear around her eyes and mouth that weren't there a moment ago. It's as though the thought of Noah making his own decisions has aged her centuries. "I suppose if you're old enough to kill your own mother, you're old enough to decide your own future—or lack thereof." Her voice is broken, a ragged whisper when she says, "Fine. I'll release you—it appears that I'll lose you either way." She flings the door open, and Edam and Arlington both draw their swords, their eyes widening as they look inside the room.

How did she get in here, if she didn't dispatch them first? I should have been worrying about them earlier. What's wrong with me? I'm still so groggy, my thoughts careening, my eyesight a little hazy around the edges.

"You don't need to be alarmed," Kali says to my horrified guards. "I'm leaving—and neither of them were harmed." She brandishes the stub of her arm as if it provides ample evidence of her words.

"I would never have chosen to harm you, Mother, but you forced—"

Kali laughs, a broad, open sound. "Were you going to say that I forced your *hand*?" She laughs so hard tears stream down her face. "Well, maybe next time you'll be the one to lose an appendage."

Noah doesn't even smile at her bizarre joke. "I hope there isn't a *next time*."

"And I hoped my son wouldn't choose someone he barely knows over me."

"Chancery would never have made me choose."

"Ah, but I'm not the one forcing that choice on you, as you well know." Kali steps through the doorway. "I hope you don't regret picking your girlfriend over your family."

"My *fiancée*," Noah says. "Not my girlfriend."

"Ah, well, that *is* different." She lowers her arms to her sides, and I can't help looking at the place where her hand should be. "I suppose we can discuss wedding details in an hour or so over breakfast. Won't your father be pleased?" She glides out the door like a dancer, and I breathe a sigh of relief.

"Wait, you're engaged?" Arlington asks. "And where did she come from? And was she missing a hand? I feel like I've taken a hallucinogen of some kind."

Noah groans. "I actually have, but I'm pretty sure she was real. There are hidden tunnels that run from one side of the palace to the other. I should have considered that earlier."

Edam's eyebrows climb his forehead. "You're telling me that—" He bursts through the door and looks around, his eyes widening precipitously. "She came to kill Chancery." His tone is flat, utterly devoid of emotion.

Noah nods. "She did, but I stopped her."

I expect fireworks, drawn blades, and strident words, but none of that happens. The two men look at one another, both of them shifting slightly, some kind of communication taking place that I can't quite fathom, and then Edam nods. He backs slowly toward the door. "I'll be ready for breakfast when you're prepared to leave." He practically shoves Arlington through the door and closes it behind them.

"What is going on between you two?" I round on Noah, one hand on my hip. I need answers.

Noah shakes his head. "I was about to ask you that. Yesterday, he'd have ripped my throat out for putting you in danger, and his eyeballs would have exploded in their sockets at the announcement of our engagement. Today he's bowing out politely and offering to escort us to a wedding planning breakfast with my parents? What on earth did you talk to him about on that plane?"

I crumple onto the base of the bed, my head still woozy, a dull ache throbbing at the base of my skull. "There was something in that tea."

Noah sits next to me and drops his sword on the floor. "There was. I should have thought of that—I'm sorry."

I set my hand over his. "Why does your mother want me dead?"

My fiancé sighs. "My mom's a seer." He blinks. "I can say that now, probably because she already told you. I tried to explain last night—that attempt is what caused the seizure. I had a bizarre dream when I was a child, and she had the exact same one on the same night—she called it a vision. The thing is, she made me promise not to aid the subject of the vision—which was you."

"Wait. You saw me in a vision?"

He nods.

"A long time ago?"

"I was nine years old. You'd have been seven at the time."

"But how could either of you know the little girl was me? I'd never met you."

"I didn't know who you were, of course, but Mum had seen photos of Enora's Heir—and to be fair, she wasn't sure whether the little girl was you or Judica."

I blink. "So you weren't sent to New York to *meet* me, you were sent to. . .what?"

He wraps an arm around my shoulders. "I was sent to determine whether it was you or Judica in my dream. Mom wanted us to kill you both to be safe, but Dad agreed that we needed more information. We were looking for a way to mitigate our exposure to the outside world at the time, and Mom had made me swear not to aid you at all."

Noah was sent to identify me so that his people could kill me. "Why didn't you do it? You knew it was me, I assume."

He swallows. "I think you know why."

"I don't, actually. But before we get into that, I think I need to know what happened in that dream."

"You were young, only seven, and you stood by a mirror, but you didn't have a reflection. . .until you did. But even then, it wasn't a reflection. It looked like you, but it was a demonic version of you, sort of. Your reflection was bent on killing you."

My eyebrows rise. "You saw Judica?"

He bobs his head. "I thought so at first, and so did my mother. That's why she sent me to meet you in New York. We spoke to Alora, long before anyone knew anything about your mother dying or you reacting to rings. She agreed to try and have you out for a visit so that we could meet."

My bruised, sore heart twinges. "Alora said you swore you meant me no harm. She said she wasn't betraying me."

"Dad assured Isamu that we meant no harm to the family. Since no one saw you as being of critical value, she took that to mean you were safe."

At least Alora didn't betray me knowingly.

"So you met me at Trinity, and then what?" My eyebrows draw together. "You don't like Judica, but you never tried to kill her, so you must have known I was the girl from the dream, not her."

He snorts. "I don't like your sister, and I didn't try to kill her. But that's mostly because I realized pretty quickly that you were the sweet girl trying her best to fix things that didn't make sense. And when she failed to kill you in Ni'ihau, I knew that the not-reflection from the dream wasn't your twin. In the dream, you were stuck to that reflection, held hostage by it—and it tried to kill you."

I swallow. "So if it's not Judica. . ."

"I think it's a representation of the prophecy."

Which means, he may already know that the price of fulfilling it will be my life. "But why is your mother trying to kill me now? I can't fulfill the prophecy if I'm dead."

Noah sighs. "Mum's confused. In my dream, I stopped the not-reflection and saved us both, but she doesn't trust me. She still sees me as a little boy."

"Wait." I don't understand. "You stop the not-reflection?" He keeps the prophecy from taking my life?

Noah tugs his hand out from under mine and wraps an arm around my shoulders. "I do, and I think that has been my purpose all along. My mum will eventually trust me too, if you give her time. I know she's not up for mother of the year, but I swear she does love me. We'll get this sorted."

I think about the release of the virus by the Sons of Gilgamesh. "We're running out of time, Noah."

He leans his head against mine. "I know. You want to shower first, or should I?"

"Not to get ready for breakfast." I stand up. "I mean, we're running out of time to save the world."

"Right," he says. "I knew what you meant. Which is why I was thinking it makes sense for us to get married today."

"What?" My mouth dangles open dumbly for a moment. "Today?"

He shrugs. "Don't take this the wrong way, but my parents are both here, and yours aren't going to be able to attend no matter where we go. The two sisters you love most are here. And a short timeline will motivate my parents to hammer out the deal quickly."

"Wait. What deal?"

"Marriage in my family requires an agreement, a give and take from both parties—like a prenuptial, sort of. It really *is* an agreement."

I shake my head. "I know nothing about your family culture or how it works, but we usually have a marriage agreement too. But this isn't a normal—"

Noah takes my hand. "I know," he says. "But you trust me. Right?"

I do.

"I'll negotiate for you. You've done everything up until now, and I've let you, but leave this part to me for once."

"Alright, then you shower first," I say. "It's time I call my brother. I think it's too risky right now to call Melisania, or Balthasar and Job. But I can't go to negotiate for help from my future in-laws and say that I have no idea whether any of the families I ruled two days ago still support me."

Noah frowns. "You aren't going empty-handed—you clearly have support from a huge number of the evians around the globe. The Motherless are evidence of that—and Mum and Dad will see that too."

"I've been thinking about it, and I really think I can trust Moses. I don't worry that he'll tell anyone—he'll understand why we can't let Inara know I'm alive. If we can think of a way to reach him on a clean line, I think I should."

He shrugs. "You're the only one who can make that decision." Noah leans down and picks up his mother's hand off the floor, presumably to dispose of it.

Oh yeah, we're off to a great start.

$$\maltese \ \ 14 \ \ \maltese$$

In the end, I don't call until after Noah and I have both showered and are ready to go to breakfast, because I need him to verify we've got a clean line. And then I have to think of a way to reach out to Moses on an untapped landline on his end.

Sometimes technology is a real pain. I should have paid more attention to Marselle when she went on and on about phone security measures.

Or maybe I'm using all this as an excuse to put off calling. I can't *hope* my brother's still behind me once I *know* whether he is, one way or another. Even though I'm calling from a strange number, and I've essentially summoned him to sit by a clean line until he hears from me without knowing whether he got the message, Moses answers on the third ring.

"Moses?" I ask.

"Chancery!"

"I'm so sorry you thought I was dead for so long," I say.

"I *knew* it couldn't be true," he says. "I knew it."

"Are you safe?"

"I am," he says. "We all are—and everyone will be much better once I share this news."

"You can't," I say. "Not yet, anyway."

"Why not?" he asks. "We had to watch Inara crowned via a video feed. No time to mourn for you, no formal funeral, nothing. I assure you, everyone here will be delighted you're alive. And furious with Inara." His lip curls.

"It's more complicated than that," I say. "I can't explain everything now, but you know about the group that calls themselves the Sons of Gilgamesh."

He grunts.

"Inara is their leader—she's Nereus—and she killed Mom."

He's utterly silent, but I don't even need to imagine the fury he feels at that news. I've been there, times ten.

"She's surely planted more operatives within Shenoah than you dealt with right after I left, which means you need to keep this information very close. I believe she still thinks I'm stuck in the bowels of the bunker Mom built under the island. I'd like her to keep believing that as long as possible. Once she discovers I'm not there, I'd like her to have no idea where I am."

"If that's what's best, I'll do it, but you need to know that Shenoah is with you," Moses says. "And we aren't afraid of the Sons of Gilgamesh. Since we discovered their existence, Katika and I have been working behind the scenes to root them out. We've found dozens, but they've all—"

"Taken a poison pill when you caught them."

"Yes." He swears under his breath, and I can't say I disagree with him.

"It's exceedingly irritating," I say. "How does she inspire such insane loyalty?"

"You inspire more. I'd gladly take a poison pill for you if

a situation required it," Moses says. "We all believe in you here. You're not alone, no matter how you may feel."

I fight back tears. I need to look fresh, poised, and strong for this breakfast. "Also, as a side note, I'm about to get married."

There's some kind of clattering sound, and then a whump. Finally, Moses says, "Wait, what?"

"Is everything okay over there?"

"I dropped the phone."

"Once I realized I wanted to marry Noah," I say, "I didn't want to wait."

"I wish I could be there," Moses says. "And I'm happy for you. You deserve some joy, especially right now. Huge congratulations for both of you from me."

"Thanks."

"No, thank you. Chancery, anyone else on earth would have stuck me in a straightjacket after my wife was killed. I was struggling and you knew that, but you also knew that I needed to *do* something. No other empress on earth in the past six thousand years has put a man in charge—that matters to us too. You have more supporters than you know."

He doesn't know that Mahalesh put her brother in charge of one of the stones, and as much as I'd like to tell him, it's not my secret to share. I think about my barely older brother, teetering on a knife's edge after Adika killed his wife. I had no business asking him to do what I did, and I'm lucky that he didn't crack under the pressure. "I should probably be apologizing to you."

"Without having a purpose, I would have curled up and died." Moses is quiet on the other end. "I haven't had many people believe in me, but you did from the start. My biggest regret is that I didn't get to grow up with you. Every day when I pray, I thank God that my little sister is someone I can look up to, someone I can be proud of, someone who is doing His will."

My heart swells. I hope he's right.

"Tell me what you need, and I'll be there, without fail." The phone clicks, and my connection to my brother is gone. I miss him more than I would have thought possible for someone I barely know.

Noah's hands drop on my shoulders and squeeze lightly. "See? You're not a supplicant. You're here as an ally, and my parents will see that too. It will be fine."

"Should I call Job? Balthasar?" I look up at him, needing someone else to tell me what to do for once—and for the first time in a long time, I have someone to ask, someone I can rely on.

Noah circles around and sits down in front of me. "Job will be safe, and Balthasar too, as long as they believe the story she's telling. We need to formulate a plan, and then once we have one, we'll be ready to delve for more allies."

"I wish I knew where she was right now," I say.

He shakes his head. "She doesn't know where you are, and that's enough."

"What if she has her people attack? I should warn Melisania, at least."

He shakes his head. "She told everyone you were dead—and she went through most of the proper protocols. As far as anyone else is concerned, you're gone. Leave it for now."

"I have trouble letting things go," I say.

"I noticed that." He smirks. "But today we'll do all we can, and then we'll let go of the rest."

"That's a good wedding theme," I say. "We could have butterflies and a crown made of flowers for me. Just *let it go*. What kind of stupid monarch *lets things go*?"

Noah laughs. "Well, I can think of an icy one who did, but that's beside the point."

I frown. "An icy one? Are you talking about the cartoon movie for children?"

"Don't act too cool for school. When this is all over, I'm making you watch *Frozen*. It might do you some good to channel your inner Elsa, but for right now, we actually have a wedding to plan. You've got Shenoah behind you for sure. And you have every reason to believe that Balthasar will come through for you in India, and that Melisania will honor your deal once she knows you're still alive."

"Inara is his niece," I say. "Whereas I'm not related to him at all. And Melisania is an opportunist. I'm not sure I can count on her for anything."

"Melisania handed that ring over—no fighting, no arguments—because she believed you were the queen from the prophecy. If I had to guess, I'd say she might not even believe Inara's lie." Noah grabs me around my waist and swings me in a huge circle. When he sets me down, I feel freer, somehow. "You need to try and relax a bit, because panicking will not help you, not right now. Balthasar loves you, and he loved your mother, and your mother would *not* have approved of Inara stepping in and trying to kill you and Judica, just after you were finally getting along. He won't side with her."

I wish I were more sure of that, but Noah's right that I might have a chance—assuming Balthasar can hold a newly conquered family against an uprising. Gah, I hate not knowing anything about anyone. "Sitting and waiting is the worst thing in the world."

Noah leans back in one of the bright red chairs, miraculously clean of blood spatter—or maybe it just blends in better. Not an encouraging thought. "I can think of things worse than that, and some things in your life are great right now. Let's focus on those, and make a plan for fixing the bad things one at a time."

"You're right," I say.

"Speaking of," Noah says. "We should head to breakfast—and we need to bring our game faces."

I lift my eyebrows. "I've been thinking about that. Shouldn't I negotiate for myself and you negotiate for your family?"

Noah laughs. "Typically our parents would handle it, but seeing as I am one hundred percent devoted to you, I think I'll do as a stand-in for the absent Enora."

Every time I think I'm over Mom's death. . .something brings it right back. And it's like a knee in my gut, an elbow in my nose, a fork through my hand, every time. Sometimes it feels like a thousand years have passed since she died. Sometimes it feels like a blink.

Noah leans forward and takes one of my hands. "I'm sorry."

I shake my head. "Not your fault."

"I really will take care of it—you can pick your dress or something while I use the techniques Mum and Dad taught me against them." He smirks.

"Pick my dress? Like it's that simple? I'll simply waltz through a room in your Mother's palace, full of gowns in my size, and then I'll just select one." I roll my eyes. "Let's face it." I look down at the beach shorts and tank top we swiped from the vacation home. "I'll be getting married in this if we go through with this 'let's get married today' plan."

"My mother tried to kill you, and she's pretty hard to deal with sometimes, but if I know her at all, when we go to breakfast, she'll have an entire cart full of dresses waiting as an apology."

"Will they be saturated with a slow-release toxin?"

Noah grins. "No. Probably not."

"Probably?" I roll my eyes. "You can't possibly think she'll soon be offering me chocolate croissants with a side of a wedding gown. She was trying to stab me through the heart an hour ago."

He shrugs. "More like dòujiāng, yóutiáo, and bāozi with a side of wedding gown, but close enough. What would you like to wager?"

"Wager?" I tap my lip. "I can't think of a thing I want that you wouldn't already give me."

"That's no fun," Noah says. "How about, if I win, I claim the right side of the bed."

My jaw drops. "You don't play fair. Are you kidding right now?"

He shrugs. "Because if the wedding is today, that makes tonight. . .the wedding night." He lifts his eyebrows.

My stomach does a somersault, and I can't tell if I'm excited or nervous or giddy or terrified.

Noah squeezes my hand, and a shiver shoots up my spine. Okay, giddy? Yes. Nervous? Maybe. But not terrified.

"Hey, I just want to make sure you don't think you're going to hog all the covers *and* get the right side."

"Hog the covers?" I sit back, feigning irritation.

"You look like a cover hog, that's all I'm saying."

"What exactly does a cover hog look like?" I lift my eyebrows.

"You have a tendency to snatch the last roll right out of the basket," Noah says, "when you notice that I'm eyeing it." He shrugs. "It's alright, I don't mind. Much."

For a split second, I imagine a world where my biggest problem is someone taking my covers in the middle of the night—no, not someone. *Noah.* My heart is so full of joy and light and happiness at that thought that I can't articulate it. I long for that life—for the time to steal Noah's rolls, for the chance to roll across the bed, squishing up against him, breathing silly thoughts against his ear.

I want an entire life—but I know I can't have it—not if things go badly, and probably not if they go right.

Somehow, knowing our time will be so short makes it more precious. I want to cherish every single second before the end comes. I stand up and step toward him, leaving me right in front of where Noah's sitting.

His arms wrap around my waist, and his head turns upward. I sink onto his lap, and he doesn't miss a beat. His lips capture mine immediately. He cups my face with both hands gently, kissing me softly, gently, achingly. It's as though he knows it too—this perfect moment can't last.

I'm not sure how long someone's banging on the door before I notice and tug my mouth free with a smile. "Someone wants to talk to us."

He shrugs. "Ignore them."

"We have a wedding to plan—and now we want to do it in one day," I say. "Maybe we'd better. . ."

"Oh, fine." He kisses me one last time, lightly, airily, but I sense that it's not light or airy, not to him. It's everything.

The banging intensifies. I jog across the room, my flip-flops thwapping against the carpet, and swing the door open.

Judica's hand freezes in mid-air, and she and Alora both glare—but not at me. At Noah. "Married?" Judica practically shouts. "Have you lost your ever-loving mind?"

Alora shoves past me and rounds on both of us. "You can't get married, not right now."

"Why not?" I ask.

Judica shakes her head.

"The world is ending," Alora says. "You can't get married when the world is ending."

"Are you sure?" I pin Judica with a stare. "You should get married, too. Think about it. We were born the same day—why not get shackled the same day, too?"

Judica blinks. Then she stumbles back one step. "Married?"

"I think it's the perfect time," I say softly. "The material point is, I'm empress, so neither of you can stop me." And now I sound like a recalcitrant teenager. Which, admittedly, is what I am.

"While we're getting things out in the open here," Noah says, "you may as well know we're planning to have the ceremony tonight."

Judica spears him with a look, one hip cocked, hand caressing the hilt of her sword. "You, get out."

Noah doesn't argue or posture or appeal to me. He walks right out the door and down the hall.

Chicken.

"Look," I say.

"No," Judica says. "This isn't where you tell us off, or where you convince us that you're old enough and you know your own mind. Because a few days ago, you fell through a window—while making out with Edam."

My guards are all fired. If they're still alive—they're definitely fired. I huff.

Alora lifts one eyebrow and glares at Judica. Then she turns to me, her face entreating. "We just want to make sure that you're *positive* that this is the right move for you."

"I haven't told anyone this," I say. "But you two may as well know. God sent me a vision, and He did it to prepare me. There's a price attached to what I'll need to do once I find the Garden of Eden."

Judica swallows, her face shifting, her jaw set. Her fingers grip the hilt. "No."

My heart swells at just how far we've come in the past few weeks. Mom would be so proud of us, of both of us. "It's not your decision," I say. "And I've already made it. I should already have realized—the papers we found that Melina left are pretty clear. 'Only death shall satisfy the renewal of life, and it must be given freely or all will pay the final price.'"

"Those prophecies can mean anything," Alora says.

"Which is why I wasn't positive, not until I had the vision. Separating the stones took Mahalesh's life," I say. "And my job is to repair the damage her children have done afterward. She fractured the stones, but they failed to care for the children of Eve. The stones have the power to fix the damage, but it won't be easy. I'm sure everything will be clearer once I find the Garden, but somehow I'll need to use them—and I think part of that will be the power that's created when they're joined. The more I think about it, the more I believe that we'll need that power to do what needs to be done."

"You think this needs to happen before the Sons release their virus," Alora says.

I nod. "I do, yes, which means we don't have much time."

"You think the Garden is *here*," Judica says. "In China. Guarded by Noah's insane family."

I kind of figured Judica would be taking notes—Noah's mother is the first person I've met who seems to care less about what other people think than she does. "I do."

"But you don't have the stones." Alora bites her lip. "Right?"

I shake my head. "I don't have them, no. It's not ideal. Believe me, I get that. I'm eternally struck at the irony of how things play out. I finally get the stones—and then I lose them to someone I trusted—someone whose life I spared. I executed Angel for no reason, as far as I can tell."

"She didn't blame you," Alora says, "for what that's worth. She told me as much before you issued your ruling."

"I've done a lot of things wrong. Too many things. I shouldn't have trusted Inara, clearly, but I'm not sure I'd change who I am, even now, because I was right to trust both of you. And I'm right to trust Noah. I love him—and I love Edam too, and you've observed that. But Edam and I had a heart to heart on the plane. He gets it—he understands that while I love him, Noah is what I *need.*"

"You're sure you don't need a warrior by your side when you return to fight Inara for the stones?" Judica asks. "Because I actually like Noah more than I expected, but he's no Edam."

"He's not quite the warrior Edam is," I say. "But Edam said he'll be by my side even though we're not together."

Alora frowns, but she holds her tongue.

"Speaking of that," I say. "I had a weird dream, and I'd like to talk to Edam. Is he still outside?"

Judica and Alora exchange a glance. Alora asks, "Uh, you had another dream?"

"It's not a vision, okay? I've only had one of those."

"Well," Judica says. "One. Or possibly two."

Right, the dream of Noah drowning. "But this one wasn't of me and Edam—you know what? It doesn't matter. If you two have decided to *allow* me to do what I've already made up my mind to do, then maybe you'll clear out for a minute."

Alora steps toward me and yanks me against her for a slightly-too-tight hug. "Mother would be proud of you— and how you and Judica have worked through things. I'm proud of you. You need to know that."

"Thank you," I say. And I mean it.

Alora finally releases me, and Judica shifts slightly. "All that stuff Alora said," Judica says. "I agree with it."

I laugh. Judica has changed a lot, but she's still Judica. "Thanks—and think about that double wedding thing. If I can throw together a ceremony in a day, you may as well tag along."

The deer-in-the-headlights bewilderment returns, but Alora tugs her out the door. I follow them out and turn to the right where Edam's standing at attention. I clear my throat. "Can we talk?"

He frowns, but he follows me inside without an argument.

"I know it can't have been great for you to hear—"

"I expected it." Edam stares at the floor.

I blink. "Oh."

"I wish you both well."

"You're not mad?"

He lifts his face, his eyes burning into mine. "I'll never be mad at you. I could never."

Why is this so hard? "I wanted to ask—" I had that dream of him walking me down the aisle, but now with him standing next to me—I can't be touching him all the way down the aisle while walking toward Noah. I just can't. "I guess I wanted to ask whether it would be too hard for you to be there, at the wedding."

He shakes his head. "I'll be there. I'll always be there, whether it's hard or not."

I swallow back my tears and nod numbly. "Okay, great."

He bows and walks back out. I head out immediately too, trotting as quickly as possible, and I catch up to Alora and Judica halfway down the long hall. "Any chance one of you wants to walk me down the aisle?"

Alora laughs. "I'd be happy to do it."

"Thank goodness," Judica says. "And I need to be clear on something. If I did this, would I have to wear a dress?"

I wrap one arm around each my sisters. "You should both know how lucky I feel that you're going to be here with me."

And I really mean it.

❧ 15 ❧

In the past eighteen years, Judica has always been prepared for every task placed before her. She trained daily in healing, torture, weaponry, hand-to-hand, diplomacy, deportment, and on and on. I, on the other hand, was regularly late, distracted, or otherwise unprepared.

There are very few things for which I am uniquely qualified over my twin sister—however, I may have discovered one area in which I surpass her. My lack of preparation may have actually prepared me for this.

As I walk into a dining room the size of an American football stadium with walls of stained glass depicting what appear to be the story of their family, my blood-spattered flip-flops thwack loudly against the smooth marble floor. My tattered tank top and Daisy Duke shorts couldn't look more out of place, but I hold my head high and think of all the times I was improperly attired, utterly outgunned, and totally unprepared back at home.

And I smile.

I doubt Judica could do the same.

"Good morning," Kali says in Cantonese. She's show-

178

ered and changed into a white silk sheath dress, and her hand has already begun to regrow, the progress fairly impressive. Even so, the mass of bright pink tissue where the bones are regrowing and the skin is stretching to cover is hard to stomach. I focus on her face instead.

"White, Mum? Really?" Noah asks in English. "As if the huge vases full of yellow and white chrysanthemums on the tables weren't bad enough."

Kali presses her lips together. "My son would never have acted as you have."

I expect Noah to flinch—that his mother is wearing what amount to funeral colors here, and decorating the tables with funeral flowers. It's almost as if she's decrying him as her son. Instead, he rolls his eyes and laughs heartily. "You're so melodramatic. I'd almost forgotten."

His father, standing beside his mother in a very Western suit, joins him, laughing warmly. "We've missed you. Things always tilt toward the overly severe when you're gone."

Kali arches one eyebrow imperiously. "She hasn't changed you so much, then."

"She hasn't changed me at all," Noah says. "Other than helping me grow up a little, I suppose."

"Shall we sit?" His father gestures at the thirty-foot-long banquet table. On either side of the flowers, it's laden with dozens and dozens of platters piled high with food. "We're looking forward to getting to know your fiancée, and I would like to extend my congratulations to you both, and my welcome to Chancery."

I smile and walk toward the table.

Noah's father smiles back, and I finally see a little of his son in his face—notably, the crinkling eyes and the broad smile.

"This is my sister—my twin, as you can see." I incline my head to Judica. "And my older sister, Alora."

They both curtsy, although Judica's is more of an exaggerated head bob. "Well met," they murmur.

"Noah may not have mentioned," Kali says, "that we traditionally negotiate an agreement prior to a marriage."

"We do the same," I say. "When someone is marrying an empress or her heir."

"Wonderful." Kali sits down and points at a chair, presumably inviting me to sit across from her. "It sounds like we have quite a bit of common ground."

"I hope so," I say. "And your son has graciously offered to negotiate on my behalf."

Kali's mouth drops.

"But I've decided not to take him up on that. After all, I don't need an awful lot from you—and as you've been tasked by Mahalesh herself to help me with most of what I need, I'm sure you won't feel the need to bargain for that aid."

Kali's eyes widen.

"You're going to fit in nicely," Noah's father says with a barely suppressed smirk.

"I hope that's the case," I say. "And in light of that, I'd really love to know your name—so I can stop referring to you as Noah's dad in my head. I forgot to ask Noah earlier —but with the vow-imposed restraints still binding him, I'm not at all sure he could have answered anyway."

"I'm Gareth," Noah's father says. "Which isn't a very Eastern name, but I was born in Europe."

Sometimes I forget that evians have so much control over their own appearance. I wave my hands at Alora, Noah, and Judica. "Sit, everyone, please."

"Yes," Kali says. "Do."

"Thank you for preparing such a wonderful meal," I say.

"And when you're done eating," Kali says, "I've taken the liberty of having my designers bring a variety of gowns for you to look at—they'll be in the sunroom over there."

She points. "I wanted to apologize for my misguided attempt earlier." She's talking to me, but she's staring at her son.

My fiancé takes my hand, twining our fingers and placing them on the table so that his parents have to look at them. "I'm glad you've warmed to the idea—Chancery and I have decided it's best if we marry today."

His mother's mouth hangs open in a very satisfying manner.

So, probably, this is good timing. "While we're discussing timetables—I'll go ahead and let you know my number one condition to the marriage. I'll need you to immediately remove all binding vows from my fiancé, and I'll expect immediate access to the Garden of Eden, of which I am aware you've been the caretakers."

Noah beams next to me, as if he couldn't possibly be prouder.

"What makes you believe we have any knowledge of the location of the Garden of Eden?" Kali lifts one eyebrow.

"Mahalesh told me that she tasked Sheva with its care," I say, boldly meeting her eyes. "I'm assuming you didn't mess up so badly that you've *lost* it since that task fell to your family."

This time, it's Judica who laughs. "You're scarier than me," she says. "*Mahalesh* told me." Her laughter is sharp, staccato.

"You speak to Mahalesh, do you?" Gareth asks.

"I receive the occasional vision," I say. "But I didn't think a *seer* would struggle with the source of my knowledge."

Kali sighs. "Is that all you need from us? *Just* the Garden of Eden?"

"It's a start," I say. "But I'll also need a little military support. Unfortunately, I recently lost control of the staridium stones I'd gathered."

"Lost control?" Kali lifts one eyebrow. "I'd say your sister nearly killing you, kicking you out of your own home, and crowning herself empress qualifies as losing control."

"I won't apologize for trusting someone I loved," I say. "It's who I am. It's the only reason, in fact, that I was able to trust your son—even after you tossed him in my path without an ability to share the truth with me. It's the reason I was able to love him—in spite of his inability to be honest and forthright." I lower my chin a little—since I'd like to project confidence, but not arrogance. "You raised him to be a wonderful, strong, confident, supportive warrior, so clearly you know the value of familial bonds."

"What kind of military support do you anticipate needing?" Gareth asks.

"You're the Sheva warlord?" I ask.

He nods.

"My current plan is to scout the Garden and try and figure out exactly what I'll need to do in order to fulfill the prophecy, and then I'll locate Inara. Once I know where she is, my head of security, Edam ne'Malessa ex'Alamecha, will develop a strike plan that will put me within close quarters of my sister. I won't be sure what force I'll need until I know where she's located."

"We can assume it will be substantial," Kali says.

"And also that whatever it is," Noah says, "you'll do it, because we all know the alternative if the prophecy isn't fulfilled."

Utter destruction.

The words hang in the air between us, unspoken, unacknowledged, and nevertheless, oppressive. Heavy. Ominous.

"We don't have much time," I say.

Noah explains about the Sons of Gilgamesh.

"We've been blamed for Covid-19," Kali says, "but we

weren't the ones who released that virus. We certainly didn't develop it in a lab in order to harm our own people."

"We know," I say. "And I wish that was the largest problem we're facing."

"Even if they don't release a second virus," Gareth says. "We're on a fairly short timeline as it is."

"Eat," Kali says. "And we'll honor your first request."

I tilt my head sideways. "My first request?"

"We'll take you to the Garden." She wipes her mouth on a white linen napkin, as if it's nothing. As if she's offering to show me her newly remodeled bathroom.

My heart races inside my chest. "I'm ready now." I jump to my feet.

Everyone with me does the same, except Noah.

"Only you for now," Kali says.

"Hold on now," Judica says.

"I'm going," Alora says.

"She's not going anywhere without me accompanying her," Edam practically shouts.

I hold up my hands. "It's fine. For now, I'll go with them alone." I look to my right, leveling my most withering glare, and Judica folds her arms across her chest. Alora drops back into her seat with a huff. I turn left next, hoping Edam will fold. He sets his jaw, staring right back at me.

"Oh, fine," Gareth says. "Your head of security can follow us."

A door near the back of the room opens abruptly. All our heads whip toward it. A tall man with black hair and flashing golden eyes practically jogs toward us. Edam unsheathes his blade in a split second, standing at the ready.

Noah opens his arms. "Isamu!"

Alora's husband. My sister sprints across the room and leaps into his arms. He spins her round and round, and then they're kissing. My reserved, quiet sister is basically making out with some guy in the middle of a banquet hall.

"So, about the Garden?" I decide to refocus.

"Right." Kali points at the door on the opposite side of the room. "You can follow us."

"What exactly am I supposed to do?" Judica asks. "Edam can go, and I'm just supposed to stand around here by myself?"

"Shouldn't you be finding Roman right about now?" I wink at her. "Tonight is coming up quickly."

She blushes—bright red. My insane sister *blushes* at the idea of talking to Roman about a wedding. I think that's a good sign. A very good sign.

We follow Gareth and Kali through broad double doors, opened by servants with bowed heads, and then we follow them down a long hallway.

"Is this close?" I whisper to Noah.

He shakes his head. "Not really."

"So we're in for a long walk."

He nods.

Great. Like today wasn't already awkward, now I'm on a field trip with my fiancé and my ex, and my future in-laws, who happen to hate me. Noah doesn't even try to hold my hand, not right in front of Edam. I focus on putting one practically bare foot in front of the other, and not allowing my flip-flops to whap too loudly on the hard marble tiles.

Isn't it interesting that even here, across the world from my palace, the floors and walls and decor are somewhat similar? We leave the palace and step out onto a broad, cobblestone courtyard—bounded on either side by the rocky walls of two mountains. We stare out into a small valley between two vast peaks—a strange place for a palace, let alone a garden.

I've spent a lot of time over the past few weeks imagining what the Garden of Eden might look like, how it might feel, where it could be located, and how it could have remained hidden. After my dream, I knew that it was likely located on a portion of the earth that was shattered with the breaking of the stones, and that it has shifted quite a long way from where it first began. But I assumed it must be located in a lush, stunningly beautiful locale. How can it receive enough light and rain to survive between these two rocky, inhospitable mountains?

Large archways loom not far ahead.

Our steps slow, as if something monumental, something that requires reverence, lies in front of us. The air thickens —but not from humidity. It's something else, as if gravity's pull is a little stronger here. I'm not the only one who senses it. Edam's heart rate accelerates. Noah's shoulders tense. Kali's head lifts slightly, and Gareth's steps drag against the cobblestone pathway.

We pause in front of the archway, only a few dozen steps separating us, but when I look past it, I notice there are more just like it. A total of four large archways form the sides of a square. The one directly in front of us is slightly larger than the others, but a few hundred yards away there's another, and there are two framing the square boundaries of the garden, the two side archways jammed right up against the mountainside.

And inside of the archways is a sprawling cacophony of greenery. Vines, trees, and heaps and heaps of flowers abound. Butterflies swoop and swirl. A vibrant blue bird turns its head slowly toward me, intelligent eyes locked on mine. It takes wing then, and flies over the archway toward the castle behind us.

"This is the Garden," Kali says. "Exactly as it was when my father passed rule of our people to me."

I look up at the keystone above the heavy wooden archway. An inscription is carved across it, in a language I don't know. Possibly Adamic—Mom hadn't bothered to teach it to me yet.

But the words blur together in front of me, and suddenly, I can read it. I blink, and then I blink again. Somehow, as if an Internet translator rejumbled the words before my eyes, they make perfect sense. I read aloud. "My children, the pure, the precious, a task I set before you, the price of your power. The strength of my children shall fail, but it must be restored or all shall perish. The Eldest shall ascend, in spite of the might and rage of her enemies, with the help of the Lost. The Lost and the Eldest, opposed in past but in sync to the end. After the Lost is found, the Eldest must trust. Together the Lost and the Eldest may enter the Garden. Only death shall satisfy the renewal of life, and it must be given freely or all will pay the final price. The rift must be well and truly healed before the bisection in convergence of the ringed with the largest and smallest in the seventh generation, or the time is past and the end begins, never to renew."

They're the Lost, Sheva's family. I'm the Eldest. I must enter the Garden, with the Lost at my side. I take Noah's hand in mine—he doesn't waver—and walk toward the entrance.

"Wait," Kali shouts. "You can't enter. No one can."

I stop. "Why not?"

"You'll die." Her eyes are wide, her mouth open. She believes what she's saying.

"Who cares for the garden?" I ask.

She shakes her head. "No one. It never rains in this place, and the sun never shines full upon it. We moved it, after the sundering of the land, as Mahalesh told Sheva to do. We hid it here, and no one has entered, other than birds and bugs, ever since."

"Together the Lost and the Eldest may enter the Garden." I smile at Noah. "Let's go."

"No one has entered, because everyone who tries. . .explodes." Gareth's voice is grim. "I've seen it myself." Gareth grabs Noah's arm, and Kali grabs mine.

Edam draws his sword.

"Look," I say. "We won't explode. It's written right there on the keystone. Obviously Noah's the Lost, and I'm the Eldest."

"No one knows what that says," Kali says. "No one can read it."

"It must be Adamic," I say.

Gareth shakes his head. "It's not. It's unintelligible."

I frown. "My sister translated it fairly closely, before she died. But I can read it plainly."

"Perhaps it's because of your vision," Noah whispers. "You can read it when no one else can. Perhaps it's a gift from Mahalesh."

"I don't know, but I believe it's safe." I drop my voice to a whisper too. "Do you trust me?"

He bites his lip and tilts his head. "Do birds fly? Does the sun shine? Do the waves crash? I'll always trust you."

I glance at Edam. "It's fine. They won't stop us."

A large tear wells in Kali's eye and rolls down her cheek. "Please don't." Her breathing hitches.

"We've both seen it," Gareth says. "Don't force us to watch our son attempt to enter."

I close my eyes and listen to my heart. Peace, calm, surety. The first time the ring reacted to me, it took me by complete surprise. I wasn't ready—I had to be dragged every single step of the way. But not now, not anymore.

I'm listening, God. I'm here, and I'll do what you need.

I step forward, Noah by my side, and walk through the open walkway.

The weight I felt outside dissipates, my fear gone. When I turn around, I can't see anyone beyond the archway. It's as though they disappeared, as though we're outside of time and space in here.

I blink. "Noah?"

He nods his head, his eyes wide. "Yeah, I can't see them anymore either."

"Okay, just checking," I say.

"My mum is, like, totally flipping out right now."

"I really hope she doesn't kill Edam," I say.

"Your boy is pretty tough. I think he'll be okay."

"Two to one," I say.

Noah shakes his head. "Edam's different. I'm sure he's fine."

I love that he doesn't get offended that I'm asking about Edam, that I'm worried about him, even now, on the day we're supposed to get married. "Shall we see what exactly is in here that matters so much?"

Noah smiles at me. "Abso-freaking-lutely."

❀ 16 ❀

A monarch butterfly lands on my shoulder. "Um, there aren't supposed to be monarch butterflies in China," I say.

"I guess no one told him." Noah leans closer and the butterfly startles, winging above our heads and toward a brilliantly blooming tree. "What kind of tree is that?"

I follow his line of sight past a Chinese ginkgo, which I assume he would recognize, and a heavily laden Narangi orange tree, to an enormous tree with a breathtaking array of vibrant leaf colors beyond them. "Is it a Japanese maple?"

"The leaves are like a Japanese maple," Noah says. "Russett, green, crimson, gold, but look at the trunk—it shoots straight up in the air, like a thin version of a baobab tree— which only grows in Madagascar as far as I know."

"I know what they look like," I say.

"So, maybe the weird tree we don't recognize is significant," he says. "Maybe we should go check it out."

I spin in a circle, noting several plants I've never seen. Orchids with fluttery petals and no column. Pine trees with flowering pinecones. Apple trees with fruit that more closely resembles purple bananas hanging in long, dangling

189

cascades rather than the usual bunches. "I don't think it's hard to find something here that we can't recognize. It feels like time stopped here on the day Mahalesh shattered the stones, as if it's been in some kind of living stasis since then."

"Then what are we supposed to be doing in here?"

I'm not sure. "Let's walk around until we figure it out."

He takes my hand again, and we walk through the paradisiacal garden together. We pass under enormous trees that clearly wouldn't have fit in the space we saw from outside the archways. We meander past a stream that definitely didn't exist beyond the boundaries of the fence. Birds flutter across our path. A fuzzy. . . something scurries right in front of us, pausing to stare at us with wide violet eyes.

"Boo," Noah says with a half smile.

It squeaks and runs away, its fluffy tail flaring to reveal downy feathers. "What was that?"

Noah shakes his head, his eyes wider than the critter's.

"I'm not sure we'll determine our purpose by wandering around," I say.

"What then?" Noah asks.

I open my mouth to tell him I don't know when I see something over his shoulder, a smallish tree, relative to the full-size trees all around us, but different.

Because it's planted in a stunning blue and green enameled pot.

"That," I say.

He turns to follow my gaze, and he's as struck by it as me, judging by the slack position of his jaw and the separation of his lips.

"Is it a bonsai?" It looks like a bonsai, sort of, but it's glowing.

"If so, it's the largest bonsai I've ever seen," Noah says. "But it *is* in a pot, in a garden no one has entered in thousands of years. Then again, bonsais require near constant care and pruning."

"Mom told me that humans think they originated in Japan, but they actually came from China, over a thousand years ago." I run through the typical types of bonsai trees. "It's not a pine or a juniper."

"It's not." Noah smiles. "I don't know what it is—and your mom was right that the art of bonsai came from China, but it didn't start a thousand years ago—it began much further back than that. We've always practiced the art of careful and consistent pruning—it's one of the first tasks we're set as children. We must learn that life thrives by *not* being allowed to grow unchecked. Adversity is the most beautiful shaper of a life well lived."

I step closer, studying the details of the potted tree. "Is it glowing?"

Noah doesn't answer me.

"It's curved downward," I say. "The branches and leaves sprout below the level of the pot. If it wasn't raised on that enormous cabinet, the leaves would be brushing the ground."

"That's called a cascading bonsai," Noah says. "It represents perseverance and change through suffering or trial."

"This is essentially at the center of the garden," I say.

Noah shakes his head. "We're definitely a little to the left of center."

I smack his shoulder. "I mean, this is in the heart of the Garden of Eden."

"Mom said Sheva moved it," Noah says. "I wonder if this is what they moved—this and the archways."

"Nothing about that in my vision," I say. "Unfortunately."

"What are we supposed to do with it?" Noah asks. "I hate how unclear everything is."

"Life is unclear," I say, as something occurs to me,

slowly, as if the understanding has to unfold within my mind, like the text on the archways. "We have to learn as we go, as we make mistakes and do things right, we learn. But the rift—the rift must be healed." I walk toward the tree, my resolve strengthening. "Something about this tree will help heal it."

Noah hasn't moved.

I stop and glance back at him. "What?"

He shakes his head. "Nothing. I'm going to go for help if that thing, like, zaps you, or something."

I laugh as I approach the tree. It's not going to zap me —it's been waiting on us. Patient, calm, growing exactly as it should while the world around it changed, while it endured the suffering of being forgotten. Closer now, I can see that it's not a tree alone, bereft. Ants circle the bottom. A lizard runs up the trunk before racing back down over the branches that drape in an arching curve over the cabinet and run toward the ground.

A bee zooms away from the tree in a jerky, wonky path, bobbling up and over my shoulder. This tree is alive—it's teeming with life. Amid it all, it has grown, shifted, and endured. It may not be perfection, but it's perfect in its harmony with the things around it, with the changes it has made as life shifted and transformed.

I reach for it, my fingers splayed before me, and I know in that moment before my fingers connect, that this tree *is* the Garden of Eden.

And it's not.

Because the Garden isn't a place. The Garden is balance and harmony and peace. It's change through life. It's cultivation and nurture. It's all the principles we've ignored as we've spread across the earth, taking whatever we want whenever we want it. Shoving others into boxes, making them serve, using without thought or care as to what we need or what the ramifications of our actions will be.

I've been taught my entire life that I'm better than a human because my DNA is more pure. I'm not corrupt—I'm perfect. That's the evian claim to prominence, to preeminence.

It's true that as DNA breaks down, the human bodies don't work quite right. The brain chemistry, the biological processes, they don't behave as they should. But our souls—those are free of the restraints of the body. But like this tree, one thing impacts the others.

My fingers touch the tree and the light from it—it *is* glowing—envelops me. When I close my eyes, I'm entirely subsumed, my body gone.

I'm aware that Noah is screaming, shouting, and terrified behind me. I worry for him, and also. . .

I don't.

Because I'm a part of the tree—and it's connected to the entire world. The animals, the plants, every living thing.

And the humans, they pulse somehow—like a warning light that a battery is running low. Nearly eight billion blinking lights—calling to me—begging me for help. The tree has curled downward, closer and closer to touching the ground. In the very near future, a large portion of the life-force on earth will die. The prophecy isn't wrong. These lights are barely hanging on, and I finally understand how to fix them.

The Garden is this tree—but it's also more than a tree. It's a connection to life across the planet. It's the key to saving all of them. I wait a beat, basking in the glow, basking in the love I can feel from an all-powerful creator who made this, a method by which the living things all over the earth can be tended. And then I step backward, peeling away from the Tree of Life.

Noah stumbles back and then surges forward and wraps me in his arms. His grip is so tight, my bones nearly creak.

"I'm okay. It's okay. I finally know what we need to do,"
I say. "I know how to stop the utter destruction."

"When you disappeared," Noah says. "I thought—" He
leans toward me, his forehead pressing against mine, our
noses touching, our eyes in line.

"I'm so sorry," I say. "I imagine Edam is similarly
freaking out beyond the archway."

"Maybe we'd better get back," he says.

"Oh, we can't." I bite my lip. "You aren't going to love
this part, but we need to somehow get *this* cabinet through
that archway." I point a few hundred yards ahead, through a
tangle of limbs and undergrowth.

"Are you kidding?" Noah's face falls. "How are we going
to do that?"

I shrug. "No one else can come in, so. . ."

Noah curses under his breath.

I glance around, hoping we won't be struck by lightning.
"Maybe ease up on the profanity in the *Garden of Eden*."

He rolls his eyes. "Oh please. God knows exactly what a
miserably rusty tool he has in me. A few bad words won't
scare Him off now. I'm not called the *Lost* for nothing."

I laugh, and we set to work. Unfortunately, it takes us
about ten minutes to drag the billion pound cabinet five
feet.

Noah wipes his brow. "Here's a thought."

I lift my eyebrows. "Let's go plan a wedding, and then
get married, and *then* come back tomorrow with a furniture
dolly."

"Um, I was going to suggest we try lugging Edam in to
help, but that's an even better idea. I really love you," he
says. "Have I said that lately?" He wraps his arms around
my waist and lowers his head over mine.

"Not nearly enough." I whisper the words back to him.
"I love you too, Noah Sheva soon to be ex'Alamecha." He
kisses me then, and with the butterflies fluttering all

around us, it's about perfect. When he finally releases me, I sigh. "It's too bad we can't be married in here."

"It really is," he says. "But unless you want your guests exploded into bits, we might be wise to choose a less exclusive location."

"You're such a downer," I say.

We walk back out, and when we emerge, there are dozens of people waiting outside the gates. Judica, Alora, Roman, Isamu, Arlington, and Bellatrius. Edam's face is tear-streaked, which I just cannot imagine.

"Thank goodness," Alora says. "Your insane head of security was about to charge in there and probably be blown to bits."

Ah, Edam. My sweet, brave Edam. My heart contracts a bit. I long to close the space between us and hug him, but I don't. His shoulders relax, and he smiles at me. "I'm glad you're okay," he mouths.

"I'm sorry you worried," I mouth back.

And then Judica barrels into me, knocking Noah aside to hug me. "You are a real brat."

"I am," I say.

"Don't ever do that again." She lets me go so that she can punch me—right on the nose.

Blood streams down my face, leaving a metallic taste in my mouth. Half a dozen soldiers draw swords, but I wave them down and use the bottom of my tank top to wipe the blood off my face. "It's fine. Honestly. That's just Judica."

Alora laughs. "We're all relieved. We thought. . ."

"I know," I say. "We should have come back out right away, but we were busy in there. And the good news is that we've found exactly what we need to fulfill the prophecy."

Kali steps closer to the Garden.

"But to be on the safe side, I think we probably ought to assume it's not safe for anyone to enter but Noah and me."

Her eyes narrow, but she doesn't move closer. I'm glad —an exploded mother-in-law would not be a great omen for our wedding.

"We are going to need a huge furniture dolly," Noah says to Gareth. They walk down the path toward the palace, Noah gesturing to him about the size.

"So wait," Alora says. "What's the dolly for?"

"We're going to steal a tree from the Garden," I say, "and take it with us. Once I take the stones back, I finally know what to do with them."

"What?" Edam asks.

I wish I could explain it. "I'm not sure I can put it into words, but I need to *heal* the human DNA somehow."

Every evian within hearing distance makes an identical face, reflecting bafflement, horror, and disbelief.

At least I'm not supposed to do the impossible. "But for today, my biggest plan is to prepare for a wedding." Time to get Judica back. "And if I'm not mistaken, my darling twin is going to be joining me."

All the color drains from her face.

"Helping you plan a wedding?" Roman laughs. "That will be fun to watch. I'll make sure she doesn't decorate with black crepe, skulls, and spider webs."

"No." I shake my head. "She's going to get married right alongside me."

Every muscle in Roman's body stiffens. "Excuse me?"

"She hasn't had the guts to ask you yet," I say. "But I thought I might help her out, you know, since she just gave me such a kind love pat." I blow her a kiss. "And you two are already engaged, right? Ever since that weird dinner where I killed Analessa?"

Roman turns toward my twin sharply, his carved jawline thrown into sharp relief against the backdrop of the mountain behind him. "What's she talking about?"

"I, uh, well, you said that you wanted to. . ." Judica swallows and looks at her feet.

"My sister likes you," I nudge. "And you got engaged in front of two million royal evians, remember? So it's too late to back out now."

Roman laughs. "Two million might be a slight exaggeration."

Judica still hasn't moved.

"Your sister loves me. I'm the best thing that has ever happened to her." Roman reaches out and takes her hands in his. "She's not good with the verbalizing, but I know it's true."

"I told her we should get married today—together."

Roman's eyes light up. "Yes. I want to do that. Absolutely we should."

Judica looks upward sharply. "You do?"

"Of course I do!"

"You never mentioned it again, not after you were sort of forced into it—"

"Forced into it?" Roman growls and yanks my sister toward him.

I need to look anywhere but at the two of them. Watching their interactions is. . . bizarre. Like watching a shark hug a dolphin. Or a rabbit kissing a porcupine. But there's nowhere else to look, and I can't quite force myself to walk off and leave them. What if Judica drops the ball again?

"I lost the tiara," she whispers.

"You didn't lose it, *krygsman*." He kisses her then, fast and hard. "We will take it back, but you don't need it."

Krygsman? What in the world does that mean? Actually, I probably don't want to know. "Alright, so that's a yes?"

They're kissing now, and they aren't paying any attention to me. I scrunch my nose. "Okay. . ." I jog around them, and back toward the palace. A few dozen yards down the way, Kali catches up. I didn't realize she was still near us.

"Thank you," she says.

"For what?"

"For bringing my son back out safely."

I pause and turn toward her. "I'll always keep him safe."

She nods. "You see that you do that."

"Of course." I start to walk again, the ridiculous flipping and flopping of my shoes the only sound. "I do have a favor to ask."

"Oh?"

"My sister and I both need wedding dresses." I clear my throat. "And my older sister, and my other people will need suitable attire too."

Kali smiles. "Of course. I wasn't jesting before. I have a number of gowns assembled for you to consider. I might not have been a huge proponent of this match, but my son has clearly made up his mind, and I can see that you care for him. I appreciate the opportunity to host the nuptials."

Something inside me relaxes. So far this day is going much better than I anticipated, given that I was drugged and then awakened by a sword fight in my bedroom that ended with a severed hand. The back of the palace looms in front of us.

"However."

Something about her tone sets off warning bells, and I freeze. "Yes?"

"We haven't concluded our negotiations." She lifts her eyebrows.

"Right." Duh. I asked to see the Garden, or rather, demanded, and then we went. "Well, what did you have in mind?"

"We are providing the Garden, and the groom, and the military force."

She's right.

She glances around us, noting that no one else is especially close to where we're standing. Even Edam is far enough behind us to afford us some modicum of privacy. "I am aware that my son can use the staridium as well as you. It's been a carefully guarded secret that we even possess a stone, but he reacted to it when he was a small child."

I nod.

"I'm unsure exactly what you bring to this match." She lifts her nose and sniffs pointedly at me, as if I smell.

I can't even argue with her. I don't bring much to the table, not when you look at it that way. We can both use the staridium. We can both enter the Garden. He's bringing the military force and, well, everything else. "So you're opposed to the marriage?"

She purses her lips. "My son is quite set on it."

"Alright," I say. "What do you want?"

Her smile, when it spreads across her face, completely transforms her features. "Oh, only everything."

"I don't understand."

"My son will not take your name—you'll take his. He'll be the ruler, the king of kings, the supreme emperor of the world, after the marriage."

I blink a few times, processing her request. A man to rule. All the decisions taken from me and placed in his arms instead. It's everything I have ever wanted. "Sure, I'll agree," I say. "With one condition."

Kali lifts one eyebrow. "Yes?"

"You pass your rule off to him just before his marriage. He's emperor of literally every single thing—not every family *but yours*."

She purses her lips. "He wasn't wrong about you. You seem disarmingly simple, relaxed, and almost naive. But when it matters, you're sharp." She nods. "Done—your entire claim passes to my son, as does my leadership of this family when the two of you are wed."

17

"I did not expect to be wearing this for my wedding." Judica scowls at the mirror.

Even her sour expression doesn't change the fact that she looks stunning. "You don't have to wear that," I say. "I'm sure they can find you some black pants to go with those combat boots."

"They wear white to funerals here," Judica says. "Right?"

I nod.

"Then I guess it's fine." Judica smooths down the already flat skirt on her pristine, snowy dress.

"If you're not careful, you'll pull the lace overlay, and then you'll have no choice but to wear black pants." In spite of my teasing, I absolutely love that my dark, macabre sister chose a traditional wedding gown. The dress itself is a beautiful sleeveless sheath that hugs her bust and runs straight to the floor. The delicate lace overlay looks like it was made by a bevy of focused nuns. It covers the better part of her upper arms, and then flares slightly from the figure hugging underdress, but it's not flared. And underneath it all, with signature Judica flare, she's wearing Gianvitto Rossi, knee-high, lace-up black combat boots. If the dress were any tighter, it might not work, but as it is, you can't see them until she walks.

It's *so* perfectly Judica. Perfectly lovely and exactly what you expect, until there's a knife pressed to your throat.

"You look like the perfect Chinese bride." Judica turns toward me. "And *I* was the one who wanted to conquer China."

"Actually." I smile. "China has conquered me." I tell her about the deal Kali and I struck.

"I would have taken her head off." Judica's eyes flash. "You're the Eldest. You're the one who united the families and gathered the stones. How dare she imply you bring nothing to this bargain."

I hold my hands toward her, palms out. "And I lost them."

"That's not the point."

"I don't care," I say. "I've never cared. And Noah won't care either."

"You shouldn't have to give up a thing," she says. "Not a single thing. You've given up enough already."

My eyes well with tears, but not prompted by sorrow or sadness. Caused by joy. "This is what I want—to stand beside you, to walk down the aisle together, and to know we're walking toward men who love us and will take care of us. And we'll take care of them in turn." I shake my head. "Mom would be so happy. She wouldn't care whether my dress was the pure crimson silk worn by royalty and wives, or a hugely puffy white cupcake like yours." I bump her hip. "And I don't care either. I was fine with the idea of flopping down the aisle in my beachwear. Our appearances don't matter to me." I think about wearing flip-flops down the aisle and cringe a little. "Not much, anyway."

"You've always cared so much less about the things that

don't matter." Judica wipes a tear off my cheek. "Which is good. I need you to keep me on the right path."

"I might not always be here for that—"

She presses her finger to my mouth. "Stop. You have no idea what you're saying, and you don't know what will happen. So promise me that you'll fight this until the end of the line, doing everything you can to stay with us, just like you'd fight for me."

"I can do that."

"I love you, Chancery, and I still need you. Remember that when you're eagerly running toward your glorious demise. It's harder to stick around and do the hard work than to make some kind of flashy swan dive."

"I think the phrase is a swan *song*," I say.

"What?" Judica blinks.

"Never mind."

"Are you ready?"

I shrug. "As ready as I'll ever be." I stop to look in the mirror for a moment, curious what the world outside will see when they look at Judica's twin. At the empress who lost everything.

The strapless crimson silk dress wraps around my chest and follows my curves like shrink wrap, until it flares out at my knees. Beautiful gold silk peonies flare across the bodice on the upper right and flow downward, tapering off in size and quantity as they near my waist. The same 3D flowers climb upward from the bottom left, leaving only the middle of my dress bare. Golden strappy sandals expose my freshly painted red toenails with each step.

"He's a lucky guy," Judica says. "But if I'm being honest, I feel pretty bad for Edam."

I shake my head. "I can't think about that. You understand why?"

Judica takes my hand and squeezes. "I'm sorry."

"We're getting married."

She bobs her head. "Yes, we are."

We finally walk out the door and into the hall. Alora's wearing a black and white chiffon dress with the most beautiful onyx detailing across the bodice. Isamu's wearing a white tux with a black vest, and he really pulls it off.

Edam's standing just behind them in a black tux and sapphire vest, and when he looks up at me, his eyes are such a bright blue they nearly knock me over. His smile is genuine, not even pained. "You look stunning."

"I thought you might assume I was—" I toss my head over at Miss Traditional White dress.

Edam shakes his head. "Never."

I almost tease him about taking so long to figure out when Judica and I switched places, but I figure he doesn't need any extra poking or prodding today. "Thanks."

"Are we going?" Arlington asks. He's wearing a deep navy tux, and he cut his hair short. It suits him.

Bellatrius tugs at the bodice on her silver silk gown, trying to pull it up.

"It looks great," I say. "Don't worry."

Her eyes widen.

"Yes," Judica says. "Let's go."

The servants lead us to a ballroom that's at least as large as ours back on Ni'ihau.

"Mom likes to entertain," Isamu says, looking somewhat sheepish. "She always said we had to stay concealed but that didn't mean we had to hide."

"I guess not."

A bower drapes across the entry doorway—white wisteria, deep red roses, and black lilies. I have no idea where Kali found all these flowers on such short notice, but for once, it wasn't my problem. I like not being in charge. Although we're mixing Eastern and Western, when the music begins, it's the wedding march I'm accustomed to hearing.

Alora lines up in the center of the aisle, offering an arm to both Judica and me. She glances at Judica, and then at me, beaming at both of us in turn. Isamu and Edam, Arlington and Bellatrius, fall into step behind us. I walk through the door, head held high, eyes ahead, prepared to face the future with a partner by my side.

I walk slowly, calmly, with my two sisters next to me and my supporters behind. Mom died. Inara betrayed me. Lark is gone. But through it all, I kept going. I think about how much I've grown since I met Noah—as a wide-eyed, confused, lost little girl.

I wonder briefly whether I might be the Lost referred to instead of the Eldest.

But even if I am, I've been found. I look up at the raised platform at the front of the path we're on, and Noah's staring right at me. My heart lifts at the sight of him, his large dark eyes, his jagged black hair, and a black tux with a red vest and a gold tie.

It's right—my decision, my place, my efforts—I'm at peace with it all.

Noah's dad stands next to him, also in a black tux but with a gold vest and a red tie. A few feet away, at the bottom of the steps, Alora stops. She lifts both arms, and Judica and I walk up the stairs alone. For the first time, I notice Roman standing on the other side of Gareth.

He's wearing a black tux too, but with a white vest and tie. I don't feel too bad about not noticing him when I notice how intently he's staring at Judica. It warms my heart.

"Friends, enemies," Gareth says. "We're gathered here today for a very exciting double wedding."

His bizarre opening line startles a laugh out of me. He's more like his son than I realized. And I'm not the only one who laughs.

"Of course I'm kidding. We're all very pleased that our

son is marrying Chancery Alamecha, and that her twin sister, Judica Alamecha, has decided to be married here among us. New friends, but fast friends nonetheless, and soon-to-be allies in the fight ahead."

Noah reaches for me, taking my hands in his.

"As you can see, the kids are eager to move along with this," Gareth says. "But first I get to prattle on and on—sharing my wisdom with them. Preparing them for the ups and downs of marriage."

A few chuckles.

"But again, you're in luck. For better or worse, I don't have a lot of wisdom that I haven't already shared, at length, with my son, so this will be brief. I just want to warn both couples that you'll be angry with your spouse. Sometimes you might want to shake them or even punch them in the nose. That's why it's so important to remember that marriage isn't about promises or feelings or even nego-tiations. It's not about compatible visions or plans for the future. Plans fall apart. Visions change. Feelings fade or shift."

The audience murmurs uncomfortably. Gareth is nearly as bad at pep talks as Noah.

"Marriage, successful marriage, is about sacrifice. It's about putting someone else above you. It's about service. If you will serve your spouse, if you care for everything they need, then nothing you do will ever feel onerous. And you'll change together, synergistically becoming more than you ever could have been apart." He tilts his head and looks at Noah and me for a moment. Then he sighs. "Do you have vows you'd like to exchange?"

Oh, no. How did I not think about vows?

Noah nods eagerly. Of course he does.

My stomach lurches. "You can go first," I say.

Noah's grin nearly splits his face. "I called you 'princess' when we first met as a joke. I knew who you were, and I was so positive you had no idea who I was that I couldn't help but poke at the secret." He pauses, looking into my eyes. "For a while, I worried that you wouldn't be able to forgive me for how we met. It was a lie, and for that, I'm deeply sorry. And then after that, I couldn't tell you, well, anything really. I wanted to tell you who I was, where I came from, and what we stood for. I wanted to proclaim our purpose, and talk to you about the future, but I couldn't do it. I spent hours praying, cursing my situation, and worrying how you'd take it."

I had no idea. I squeeze his hands.

"But you're such a shining light that you didn't hold any of it against me. I thought I knew you from the start, but really, you knew me. You always watch what people do and take them at face value. Since the day we met, I've felt encouraged to make the right decision because I didn't want to let you down. You've made me the best version of who I could be every single day since we met. I wasn't good enough for you then, and I'm still not. But you make me *almost* good enough, and if that's enough for you, it's enough for me. I promise that for every single day that my heart beats next to yours, I'll do my very best to be better than I was the day before."

And now it's my turn. Even if I'd planned something to say, I'd be at a loss now. My heart swells inside of me, but I have no idea how to share what I feel, especially with all these people watching. How did I not realize this was coming?

"Just talk to me," Noah whispers. "And know that I don't care what your vows are. You can recite the ABCs, and that's fine. We'll tell everyone it was a symbol of how you're sticking with the basics in our relationship, because they're the things that work."

I laugh then, and words suddenly come to me. "Life has been tumultuous the past few weeks. Actually, that might be an understatement. I was utterly unprepared for the waves that would crash over me, one after another, with no relief between them. I lost my mother." My voice breaks. I look at the ceiling and breathe slowly a few rounds to stem the tears that threaten. "I lost my best friend, Lark." I won't sob, not at my wedding. "And I lost my older sister whom I'd looked up to for my entire life." Oh, Inara.

Noah wraps his arms around me then, pressing my cheek against his chest.

I finally lean back and continue. "I tried to fling myself like a kamikaze," I say. "More than once." The bomb. The challenges. The double challenge. "I wanted everything to be over and the waves to stop crashing over me, but every single time, you were there. Making jokes, leaping in front of me to take a bullet or a blade, and advising me without bias or judgment. You never tried to take my tasks away from me, but you lifted me up, helping me see that the strength I needed was already inside of me. You said I make you the best version of yourself, but before you, I had no idea who that really was. You managed to help me find myself, without suppressing or changing who I am. I have no idea how you did it then, or how you do it now, but you're everything I need, everything I love, and you see in me everything that I hope to become. If God had to tear away everything from me one at a time, at least he compensated me in return with you. If it's not a fair trade, it's awfully close."

Noah leans toward me then, his lips drawing inexorably closer, one millimeter at a time. My entire world shrinks until the only thing that matters is his mouth and the way mine is pressed against it.

"I think I'll go ahead and pronounce the two of you husband and wife, with the power vested in me," Gareth says. "And suggest that my son kiss his bride."

Noah's lips press even harder against mine, and his

hands grab my waist, pulling every part of me closer against him. "Mine," he whispers against my mouth.

"Yours," I whisper back. And then I'm lost entirely, less and more. Sheltered and destroyed. Made and unmade.

Gareth clears his throat. Then he does it again, and I realize he's telling us to stop kissing. I don't want to, but I remember how many people are gathered around, watching. I finally pull away. Noah nips at my lips as I pull back, his eyes still hungry.

"Double wedding," I hiss.

His eyes widen, and he swings me around to stand at his side, his arm slung around my hip. "Forgot. Sorry."

Judica rolls her eyes. "Ridiculous."

"I'd like to invite Judica and Roman to exchange vows too, if they'd like."

"Sure," Judica says. "I mean, who wouldn't want to follow that sappy pile of . .." She mutters the rest under her breath and bobs her head at me and Noah with a wry smirk.

"I want to follow them," Roman says. "I'm not good at words, at expressing how I feel. But I'm very good at loving you." He turns to face the gathered audience. "Most of you don't know us at all, but I'll tell you the very first time I knew I loved this woman, right here."

This should be good.

Roman's lip curls on the side. "We were at her mother's birthday ball, and Judica was sixteen years old."

And now I know exactly what he's going to say.

"A royal nephew of Adika—a first cousin of mine—said that Judica looked hot. I won't bore you with the exact phrase he used, but she heard him. He expected her to take it as a compliment. I think he meant to catch her attention, but he didn't know her at all."

Heat rises in Judica's face. I wonder how wise it is for

Roman to share this with everyone gathered. Judica's pretty private.

"Judica shoved Esabis against the wall, pressed a dagger to his throat, and asked him whether she still looked hot." Roman stares Judica in the eyes. "My warrior is never afraid, never nervous, and never fearful. She faces every single problem head on. She never dissembles, and she never gives up. She was tossed into a stormy sea at an early age, and she's never stopped swimming. Every time I think that she can't do anything else to impress me, she grows and learns and turns over a new leaf and I have to step back in wonder again."

Judica frowns. "You—"

Roman puts a finger against her lips. "I'm not quite done, not yet."

She bites his finger.

I snort, but I cover it up with a cough pretty well, I think.

"Your fire, your fight, your passion—they've drawn me like a lovestruck moth to a flame for years, but I never dreamed you might love me back." Roman strokes the side of her face. "The day you told me you loved me, everything in my life shifted. Every bad thing that had happened to me —" He waves his hand through the air. "None of it mattered. You healed it all in a blink. I'd walk through fire for you. I'd drown a battalion for you. But I won't have to— because you'd do the same too, and you'll be right there with me, at my side, sword drawn, leaping into the fray. I can't think of a single person I'd ever be happier to race through life beside."

Judica lifts her chin. "You say you're not a warrior, and that you're not good with words. The only thing you're not good with is seeing yourself clearly. You're brave. You're strong. And you're the least afraid person I know. You love with ferocity, you trust with abandon, and you lift me up. That's why, even though the idea of getting married to someone I'll be with for a thousand years should terrify me, I'm smiling up at you like a complete fluff-brained moron. Because marrying you isn't scary. It's the best decision I've ever made, Roman. I'd do it again tomorrow, even if I had to wear the same dumb dress all over again."

And to her, that probably is the ultimate pledge of love.

He kisses her then, his hands digging so hard into her lower back that he lifts her off the ground, her black combat boots dangling in the air.

The audience cheers and hoots, and I wonder whether they did that when Noah and I kissed. Part of me wishes I remembered, and part of me doesn't care. Because after they finally tear themselves apart, and after we endure an amazing meal that means very little to me, and after we accept congratulations from a million people I've never met, and after Noah's mother formally passes her throne off to her son in an agonizingly long ceremony, Noah finally tells the entire room that he's tired.

He ignores the jokes, and the jabs, and the well wishes, and he leads me firmly, gently, and eagerly down the hall to his room. Not the guest quarters, not the outsider part of the palace.

To his room.

And for the first time, I walk through a door into Noah's real home—the first place we've been where he is utterly himself. He releases my hand and backs into the room. I walk behind him, my eyes on his face. "Your room. Part of me didn't think this really existed, and part of me wondered if you'd have a red racecar bed."

His grin nearly splits his face, and he shifts sideways.

A large enameled black bed looms behind him. "No racecars—sorry to disappoint."

"Not disappointed, not exactly," I say. "I had no idea

what to expect, honestly." I spin around, realizing it's smaller than I expected. Much smaller.

An enormous picture window overlooks the back court-yard, and if I squint I can barely make out a speck that I know is the Garden of Eden. There's a black desk, papers neatly stacked, books lined up against the wall, a huge bookcase that covers one wall, and a red and gold embroi-dered sofa. None of it tells me much, not until I notice the decorations.

There aren't photographs, and there aren't paintings.

More than a dozen sketches, framed in black lacquered wooden frames, rest in various places around the room. His dresser. The top of the bookcase. The windowsill and his nightstand. Something about them tips me off. The angle, the shading? I'm not sure. "Did you draw these?"

Noah swallows and nods.

I walk across the room and pick up the one resting on his nightstand. It's a girl—no more than six or seven. I turn it around to face him. "How?"

He shrugs. "I said my mom's a seer. I'm not, but after I had the dream, I couldn't think about anyone else."

"You can talk about it now?"

He nods. "Something about going inside the Garden appears to have released me from my vows—probably because I made them on the keystone outside the Garden to begin with."

I turn the sketch around again—it's uncanny. The sketch is of me.

"Did you know it was me the moment we met?" I ask. "Or did you still think it might be my sister?"

He walks toward me and gently takes the sketch. He sets it on his nightstand and takes my hands in his. "I knew you were important to me. I knew I needed to help you. I had no idea then that you would transform everything about me, that you were my past, my present, and my future. I knew that I cared about you, but I had no idea what love was, not until I watched how you did it. You've taught me almost everything that matters."

"I love you too, Noah." I smile at him.

And this time, when his lips meet mine, I don't hold anything back. I surrender everything to Noah—because I know I'm completely safe with him. Now and forever.

18

S unlight streams across my face and I blink. The first thing I see is my arm, but it's hairy. Much, much hairier than it ever has been before.

What is wrong with my arm?

I sit up, alarmed that my arm doesn't shift when the rest of me does. That's when I realize it's not *my* arm. I snatch the sheets up and gasp.

I'm married.

I was asleep next to my husband, and he's still asleep. His arm tightens around me, and drags me back next to him. His words are muffled against the blanket pressed to his face. "Go back to sleep."

"We have a lot of work to do," I say. "And a rather large tree to move."

He groans. "Oh, fine." Noah sits up, but he's not in a huge rush to go down for breakfast.

I'm almost embarrassed when we finally show up around ten a.m. Judica and Roman are already there, but they're still eating so they didn't beat us by much. I'm surprised to find his parents are there, and Isamu and Alora. Why are they all here? Were they waiting for us?

"I can't tell you how happy I am to see all of you gathered together." Noah spins in a circle, taking in the dozens of people gathered for brunch in the banquet hall—including the rest of my friends. Arlington, Bellatrius, Edam. "Because as your esteemed and very powerful emperor, I have a declaration to make."

Kali frowns. She opens her mouth to speak, but Noah holds up his hand.

"First, I'd like to say how very satisfying it is, to know that I basically rule the world. I'd like to thank my mother for negotiating all this power and importance on my behalf. I've always felt that I would do a wonderful job as the supreme ruler of the earth."

Gareth's lips are pressed together, almost as if he's trying not to laugh.

Alora and Isamu share a glance I can't interpret.

Judica, however, is scowling heartily.

"I know this will be a very devastating decree for many of you to stomach." He nods slowly, with mirth I don't quite understand. "But I've come to the conclusion, after spending some time with Chancery ne'Alamecha ex'Sheva, that she will do a better job at, well, if I'm being honest, at every single thing that a ruler does." He reaches inside his shirt and drags a black leather thong over his head, a dark black stone hanging from it. He extends it toward me, and then he drops to one knee. "So it's with a heavy heart that I surrender my throne to Chancery, and beg her to let me take her name, and agree to take this heavy burden from me."

Kali practically snarls.

Noah turns his head slightly. "Are my ears working? Or is someone questioning my absolute authority and ability to pass my rule to whomever I see fit, as grand supreme most excellent emperor of the entire world?"

Gareth laughs.

"Eleven hours," Kali mutters. "Eleven hours before he tosses it all out the window."

"You knew what would happen," Gareth says. "You raised him."

When I don't react, Noah steps closer and drops the cord holding the stone over my head. "What do you say, princess?"

I shake my head. "I don't want it."

"Too late. I already called 'not it.'"

Judica laughs. "You two are truly the most ridiculous pair of idiots I've ever seen."

"I'm not sure that's how you should be addressing her grand royal supreme most excellent Majesty," Noah says. "Because if she doesn't like your tone. . ." Noah shrugs. "Well, she might really glare at you. And I swear, when she does that to me, it's about the most adorable thing I've ever seen."

Judica shakes her head. "I'm just glad I don't have to call her Chancery ne'Alamecha ex'Sheva anymore."

"Like you ever would have done that," I say.

"I would've heard it used plenty," Judica says, "which would have been bad enough."

"Having this stone does give me an idea." A well opens up in my head, the power inside puddling up nicely. I focus on it, dipping inside it, spreading the power out and stretching it around a little. "We've been working on combinations of options for cornering Inara—forcing our way into her inner circle."

"We have," Kali says. "What did you have in mind?"

"What if we approach her as an ally," I say. "Then instead of trying to retake the stones in an honorable way, we snatch them, like she did?"

"There's a problem," Judica says. "You said the way she fights, you can't take her."

She's right. Inara's freaky fast. "I can't." I shake my

head. "There's no way. So when it came down to it, unless she willingly handed them over to me. . ."

"Who would she hand them over to—hypothetically?" Noah asks.

I shrug. "No one comes to mind."

But it would save so many lives if we could reach her without a full scale attack.

"What do you mean 'the way she fights?'" Edam asks.

"She's fast," I say. "Like, faster than anyone I've ever seen. She moved fast enough I didn't realize she had moved at all until she was behind me."

Edam swallows.

"Do you know how?" I ask.

He shrugs. "Maybe."

"What is it?"

Edam sighs. "I could defeat her, I think."

"You think?" Noah asks. "That's not exactly a resounding confirmation."

"I get faster," Edam says, "when I'm around fast people. I've never met anyone I couldn't best."

"I think there's a reason Inara never fought in front of anyone," I say. "I think she has some kind of power we don't understand."

Edam shrugs. "I'm willing to risk it if you are."

"We can circle back around to this," I say. "But first we need to figure out where she is."

"How do we do that?" Judica asks.

"I think it's time for me to start calling some people," I say.

"Let's get the tree out first," Noah says. "And we need to keep in mind that we're a pretty long flight away from most places."

"Are you sure it's wise to remove this tree from the Garden?" Gareth asks. "If it's important, maybe it should stay there."

"It's a risk," I admit. "But with the virus the Sons plan to release—"

"I think you should leave it with us," Kali says. "You can always return here once you have the stones."

"Your Majesty," a wide-eyed servant says from the doorway.

"Yes?" I ask.

"What?" Kali asks.

"Yeah?" Noah asks.

I meet Noah's eyes and we laugh. "Too many cooks," I say.

Noah shrugs, and we turn to face the servant. "What's the news?"

He glances at Kali for confirmation.

"Go ahead," she says.

"There are concerning reports from news outlets." He extends a tablet.

Kali takes it and taps the screen. A tinny sound blares from the small speakers. "The DOW plunged yesterday, with reports of hundreds of deaths in Rio de Janeiro. At first, reporters believed the deaths were related to the novel coronavirus, but the government is now confirming that these deaths are related to a new virus, similar, but far more deadly. The local government is calling this the reinavirus— a much more deadly cousin to the coronavirus."

My heart stops in my chest. "We remove the tree and take it with us."

This time, no one argues. Far more people follow us to the entrance to the Garden this time, a large furniture dolly prepared and dragged to the area directly behind us. I stop in front of the archway and look up at the inscription again —still clear as day to my eyes.

"You can't read that?" I ask.

Alora shakes her head.

Judica shrugs. "Not a word."

"What about you?" I squeeze Noah's hand.

He shakes his head. "I mean, we've spent a lot of time working on the symbols—it's not Adamic. There was a record we had of what Sheva said that it said, but that's recorded in a *sprachbund*—a mixture of Sumerian and Amorite. But as far as I know, no one has ever been able to make sense of it."

Kali nods next to him.

"So the pictures Melina left?" I lift one eyebrow.

Noah fills his mother in on what we found shoved up inside the fireplace of my sister's cottage after she disappeared.

"We had some dissenters some years ago," Kali says, "before my time. They wanted to create another garden, and they felt the key was in the archways. They did not get along with the current leadership and were asked to leave, but it's my understanding that they replicated the archway keystones in several places throughout the world. They used the alleged translation in some places, and a direct replication of the symbols of these keystones in others. As far as I know, none of them ever resulted in anything even remotely close to this."

A living garden that exists independent of actual sunlight, precipitation, and seasons? I'd say not.

"Are you nervous to enter again?" Noah whispers.

"No." But I'm nervous about stealing the tree. What if it dies the second we remove it? What if I can't get it out? The new virus has been released, and I've lost the stones. Am I about to risk the portal that connects me to the light within each of the humans on earth? How can I be sure this is the right move? Maybe I should leave it here, safe, and bring the stones back.

But it has been moved before.

"Let's go," Noah says.

My grip tightens on his, and we duck inside the garden

together. We turn and look over our shoulders at the same time—and just as before, everyone standing past the archway has disappeared. Birds flit overhead—butterflies flutter, but all else is quiet and still. I wonder whether an avalanche or an earthquake could damage this place. I'm guessing they can't, since it's been here for thousands of years now. Miraculous.

We wind our way toward the tree, faster this time in spite of Noah dragging the large, modified furniture dolly, and when it comes into view, seemingly unharmed from the five foot shift yesterday, I breathe a little more easily. "Do you think we need to move the archways?" I ask.

Noah freezes. "You aren't really sure what to do?"

My shoulders slump. "I have no idea what I'm doing."

He sits down on the ground, his hands sinking into the lush, verdant green grass. A lizard runs up and onto the top of his knee, staring at him with a cocked head. "Tell me what happened when you touched it."

I drop down next to him, squatting with bent knees, my hands digging past the grass and into the moist, dark soil below. "I disappeared," I whisper. "And became *more than* myself. It was like I was floating amid the entire earth— points of light flickering all around me. Bright white spots for evians. Weaker yellow lights for the humans."

"They were close to you or far, geographically?"

I close my eyes and remember. "Well, it was nothing like what we usually feel as close and far. Or I don't think so. There weren't any lights directly next to me for instance, and you stood only a few feet away. It was more that I could sense everyone around me, not crowding, not racing away, just *floating*. And yet, I knew you were there, beside me, corporeal. If I would step out of the tree." I drop backward onto my bum. "This sounds insane."

He points at the glowing tree. "This *is* insane. We're sitting in front of a tree that has sustained this entire garden for thousands of years, letting no one enter. Except for you and me. No guidebook, no mentor, nothing but guesses and feelings and intuition."

"I don't think it allowed us entry per se," I say. "I think it was more that the people who entered would have harmed it, so it protected itself."

"Which means your impulses for it are good ones," Noah says.

"Yours too, I guess," I say. "But the more I think about it, I don't think the tree would wish to harm anyone, even someone who meant it harm. Whoever had that idea about the keystones, it feels right. They're a shield, and this is the treasure." I crawl across the grass, my knees sinking with each shift, my hands pulling me forward until the shining wooden cabinet is only inches away. The lowest branches, their shiny, green, heart-shaped leaves barely clear the ground. My fingers move toward them again, slowly, incrementally, willing it to know that I mean it no harm. And then the tip of my finger brushes one small, lighter-than-the-rest leaf and I *disappear* again, and reappear within the boundless force of the tree.

Again, lights blink into existence around me, softly, brightly, flickering. And as I sink into it, opening further to the sensation, more and more and more lights appear in bursts—both near and far. But I was wrong before. They are based on location, sort of. All of them are accessible, but one light, a brilliant one, pulses just behind me. It must be Noah's... and another bunch of lights are congregated just behind it. The evians waiting at the entrance.

I have no fingers here, no hands, no body at all, but I brush against the lights, and they pulse once, then twice, as if in recognition. They're beautiful, so indescribably beautiful. I reach out then, expanding, pushing, unfurling, and I begin to accept the vast scope of what lies within this bonsai—animals, sea creatures, evians, and humans. The weaker yellow lights still feel *wrong* somehow, as if they're sick. And then I notice swaths of them flickering and going dark.

My heart stutters in my nonexistent chest.

Another cluster goes black. And then another. Winking out—and I know it's forever.

I yank away as quickly as I can. "It's happening," I gasp.

"What is?" Noah jumps to his feet.

"Something is killing them."

"The virus?"

I shrug, feeling more helpless than ever before. I wonder whether the tree feels it, whether it suffers. "I'm not sure, but humans are dying in batches. We should hurry."

Noah points wordlessly. I follow his finger to the lowest branches of the tree, where the leaves nearly touch the earth. They're blackened on the end, and curling under. Oh, no. No, no, no.

"I'd like to touch it," Noah says. "Does that sound like a mistake to you?"

We don't have much time, but this might be important. "If you feel drawn to it, you should do it."

He holds out his hand for mine. "Just in case." His half smile may be the most endearing thing I've ever seen.

I twist our fingers together, my heart soaring at the knowledge that he trusts me, loves me, and believes in me. And then he reaches his free hand toward the tree, and I'm absorbed again, but this time, I'm larger —stronger.

I'm not alone.

A shiver runs through me—and not me—I don't exist in this place, not in the same way that I do on earth.

You're with me.

I am.

And I'm suddenly out again, my heart thumping hard in

my chest, my eyes burning in their sockets. "Whoa, you went in and out fast."

"That was strange," Noah says. "Like I didn't exist, like I was floating in a chamber of empty nothing. Except for the twinkle lights."

I laugh. "Something like that, yeah. But it's a little more disorienting to go inside with you—out of body, out of mind, and out of control."

"You're saying I did it the hard way?"

I nod. "Try again, without me this time."

And he does. Watching his body disappear, sucked away into the tree, is terrifying, even though I know what's happening. Where does his body go? Panic pulses through me—what if he doesn't return? What if the tree keeps him? What if, somehow, I'm protected, but he's not? I almost grab the tree myself, but I don't know what would happen if I did, so I wait.

A moment or two later, his body flickers back into existence. I wonder what would've happened if I had moved into the space he occupied before he was sucked inside—when he reappears in that same place. If someone inside the tree was spit out—would it happen on top of someone else occupying that space currently? I shudder at the thought. This entire thing is bizarre in the extreme.

And our lack of knowledge is dangerous.

"All those lights," Noah says. "It's. . ." He shakes his head. "There's no way you can help that many humans."

"There are a lot," I admit.

"You think you know what you need to do?" Disbelief is plain on his face.

"Not quite, but I think I'll know when it's time—like I figured out how to reach the tree and then how to enter it. I think I'll be guided through the parts I don't understand." I shrug. "Does that sound insane?"

"Not to me," he says.

"Which is why *we* work." I circle his wrist with my hand and tug him closer.

He doesn't need much encouragement. His mouth covers mine, and my arms wrap around him automatically. I sigh against his lips, happy to be with him, next to him, spending time with him.

But we don't have a lot of time—not right now. So, reluctantly, I pull away. "We need to move this out and get on our way."

He scrunches his nose. "We still feel good about moving it?" He tosses his head at the glowing tree.

I sigh. "I'm worried about the spread of the virus. The human lights are flickering—there's something wrong with them. The Sons of Gilgamesh aren't incorrect about that, but now that they've begun releasing the new virus, we don't have much time to figure out how to fix it."

"Alright." Noah's hands encircle my waist and he swings me around so I'm several feet away. Then he stretches, flexing his fingers. "Here goes nothing." Before I can stop him, his arms circle the base of the large cabinet and he lifts.

I leap forward as the pot tilts, steadying it, but his muscles bulge and he grunts and the entire thing lifts up more than a foot in the air. I slide the dolly underneath, and help him lower it steadily. After that, we have to move a few plants out of the way, but we mostly just roll it to the exit.

Noah eyes me cautiously. "You still feel good about it? About rolling out of here with the plant you identified as the heart of the garden?"

I close my eyes and inhale slowly, listening for any kind of warning, stress, or anxiety. I can't sense any—not here, not now, not at all. "I do."

"Alright." Noah positions himself behind the tree and shoves.

I jog through right after him, blinking at the tree on top of the furniture dolly. The Tree of Life was at least six feet tall, resting on a heavy cabinet on the other side of the archway, but now it's two feet tall at the most, and the cabinet looks like a medicine cabinet.

Edam glances from Noah to me and back again. "You couldn't carry *that*? Seriously?"

I laugh.

"It was way bigger on the other side," Noah says.

Edam's eyebrows draw together in doubt. "Okay."

Judica and Roman can't stop laughing.

"You want to see what things look like in there?" Noah asks, gesturing at the archway. "Be my guest."

I follow his gesture toward the archway, so I'm watching when everything in the garden, which admittedly looks far less impressive from this side, withers and dies.

The gathered onlookers gasp, almost in unison.

"That's ominous," Kali says.

I turn back toward the now tiny Tree of Life, but it's still healthy—a variety of vibrant greens comprising its shiny, albeit smaller, leaves. I lean forward and touch it, and in a blink, I'm sucked inside again. Not a second later, Noah's beside me—not physically, but I can feel him with me. His shining light wraps around mine, and I relax against him.

We may have collapsed the garden here, but the sea of lights, and our connection to it, is intact. I step backward and reappear beside the tiny bonsai tree sitting on the huge furniture dolly.

"Do *not* do that again," Judica huffs.

"You gave us all a heart attack," Edam says.

"Sorry," I say. "I'm so sorry. When the garden withered like that, I worried."

"A little warning," Noah says, "might help us all navigate more peacefully in the future."

"Right," I say. "Of course."

"Disappearing into trees," Alora mutters. "What's next? Flying horses?"

"I would *really* like to sign up for that next," Noah says. "Where do we fill out request forms?"

Gareth smiles. "I always knew you were different, son, but..." He shakes his head. "I'm glad I was here to see that with my own eyes—sliding in and out of a tree you dragged from the Garden of Eden."

"I'm not sure how fast this virus spreads," I say. "But I think it's urgent for us to recover those stones."

"Right," Alora says. "Agreed. How do you propose we go about locating Inara without immediately notifying her that we're en route?"

I sit on the corner of the furniture dolly. "I need just a moment to consider."

Noah perches next to me.

"You could call Moses and see what he knows," Judica says. "Since he's loyal."

"I need to think of who would be the best person to emulate," I say. "Someone Inara will trust."

She and Balthasar always got along well—and he's her uncle. Job was also close to her, but I think she'd be more afraid of Balthasar's tactical skill. He might be the safer choice, if I want her to respect the ability of the person I'm pretending to be as a fighter at all.

"Let's get the tree back to the palace and ready to ship," I say. "And then I need some time with Noah."

Judica rolls her eyes. "I'm a newlywed too, but you don't see me—"

"To teach me to use this stone," I say. "Come on, Judica. Geez. Eww."

"Eww?" Noah lifts one eyebrow. "That's not what you—"

I shove him and he almost falls off the side of the furniture dolly.

Edam looks like he might puke, but I brush past all of them and head toward the palace. I'm already back at Noah's room, where I realize the door is locked.

"You are in a mood," my new husband says, when he rounds the corner.

"Figure everything out, Chancery, and do it quick, and don't put one foot wrong or everyone dies," I say in a high falsetto.

He laughs, takes my hand, and then turns his knob. He bumps it with his hip and the door opens.

"That was locked," I say.

"Not locked," he says softly. "It just jams sometimes. And life is like that too—sometimes we think something is a roadblock, when really it's only a bump in the pavement."

I sigh. "You think I'm overreacting."

He shakes his head. "No, I don't. But I think that this next step, learning to use my stone, will be a snap compared to what you've already faced." He points at a mirror on the far wall. "Come over here."

I follow him over.

"Now, pull that stone out."

I fish the cord out from under my shirt and hold it out in front of me.

"Wrap your hand around it."

I obey.

"You feel the well of power."

I nod.

"Okay, then pull a little of that, and use it to cover yourself with a cape—that looks like Balthasar."

"A cape that *looks like Balthasar?*" I laugh. "That's bizarre."

He shrugs. "Fine, then you figure it out."

I turn back toward the mirror and imagine I've got a

cape that looks like my Warlord. . .and then I drop it over my head. My body ripples and grows—taller, broader, older, and scarier. I am suddenly Balthasar. I swear, loudly.

"That may be the first time I've heard you use any kind of profanity, princess." Noah swallows. "I'd chalk it up to your new disguise, but that sounded exactly like you."

"How am I supposed to disguise my voice?" I startle at the disconnect between my voice coming from Balthasar's mouth in the mirror.

He grins. "Same idea. Think about coating the inside of your throat with Balthasar juice—"

"Gross, what?" My entire face scrunches up. "How about covering my mouth with a voice modulator set to Balthasar?"

Noah laughs. "Better. Good job."

"I can't really credit my teacher," I say. But my voice suddenly sounds lower, much lower, and gruff. It worked.

"See? I told you—this part is easy."

"Wow, all I needed was that rock all along."

"It's holding the illusion that's tricky," Noah says. "It took me weeks and weeks of practice before I stopped dropping it occasionally."

Uh, that would be really bad.

"And you might consider calling Balthasar to locate Inara."

"Why?" I ask. "I doubt he'll take my side, and even if he says he does, how can I trust him?"

"I never met them, but by all counts he was very devoted to his brother and your mother—and remember, Inara killed her. I did watch the fury with which he beheaded Angel. I think if you share the truth about your sister with him, he'll quickly get on board with doing whatever needs to be done."

He might be right—and I'd bet a bundle that he knows where Inara is right now, since I sent him to manage Adora.

Inara would have had to check in with him at some point, right.

"You think I should just call and say, 'Hey Balthasar, it's me. I'm not dead'?"

Noah shrugs. "Maybe not in that voice, but yeah, I'd tell him the truth and see how he reacts."

"It'll give away that I'm still alive," I say.

"So you call him *as* someone else."

Noah's brilliant. I could call him *as Inara*, or as my mom, or really, as *anyone at all*. I grab Noah with both hands and kiss him full on the mouth.

His arms pinwheel around, he backs away from me so fast. Like he's repulsed. "I'm sorry." He splutters and wipes his mouth. "I mean, I know it's you, but I just *cannot* kiss Balthasar in any form."

I'm laughing when I drop the disguise, and this time when I kiss him, he doesn't protest. Not at all.

❧ 19 ❧

"I'm calling him as Alora," I say.

"Why not as me?" Judica asks. "Balthasar loves me."

"You realize I'm right here," Alora says. "I can *actually call* him."

"I need to see how he reacts, and try to figure out where he is," I say, "and then I'll be able to make a determination about how much to reveal. Plus, it'll be a trial run for me on how well this weird power works—'voice only' version, before I have to do voice and appearance at the same time."

Noah rolls his eyes, but he doesn't argue with me, and neither does anyone else. We've all gathered in the guest room where Noah's mother tried to kill me. It's as neutral a spot as we've got here. Technically, Noah's mother passed the rule of the family off to him, and he passed it to me, but I don't really want to press the point while I'm on my honeymoon.

Some honeymoon.

I dial the number that will hopefully ring my mother's

brother-in-law, hoping that he'll be on my side, and not his niece's. Ugh, what a tangle.

Balthasar picks up on the second ring. "Hello?"

"I'm glad you answered," I say, focusing on the words and the cadence of my sister's voice. It's bizarre how the dumb stone shoves my voice and inflection into the same pattern, the same vibration and intonation, and the same grammatical behaviors of my much older sister.

"Alora?" There's a muffled shifting and bumping. "Is that really you?"

"Rumors of my death were greatly exaggerated," I say.

"What about Chancery?" he asks, urgency in his tone. "She's with you? Or Judica?"

"Where are you Balthasar? Who else is with you?"

The line goes silent.

"Are you still there?"

"Inara tried to kill you, and killed the twins. You're worried I might support her still?"

"She's the youngest," I say. "That makes her the rightful ruler."

"She wasn't Heir," Balthasar practically growls. "Murdering Chancery was an act of treason."

"Not if she killed Judica first—and then killed Chancery. She would have been Heir by then," I say. "And that's certainly what she'll argue if you press the matter."

"I don't want to bring her up on charges," he says. "There's no Five left to prosecute the case, even if I did. Chancery saw to that—and Inara waited until she was done. I think she's been planning this for some time."

"You're in Ni'ihau, then?" I ask.

"Of course not," Balthasar says. "I secured Adora for Chancery the second I heard, hoping against hope that she survived."

"Does Inara know you're working against her?"

Balthasar's laugh is bitter. "I'm pretty sure she does. She

executed Lainina and Ranana, but only after she used that as a threat to try and force their people to rise up against me."

"Who would you be holding Adora for, if I hadn't survived?" I ask, reminding myself I'm speaking as Alora. "Are you sure that you haven't decided to seize control for yourself?"

"Me?" He laughs. "Please. I reached out to Rivena, but she and I are both hoping it doesn't come to that. Frederick was thrown in prison, not killed outright. That gave me hope."

"Hope of what?"

"That Inara isn't as awful as I fear she is. And now I can't help thinking that if you survived, maybe Chancery isn't dead like Inara said. It seemed like something Enora's youngest might do, floating off on a boat alone to try and join the stones without risking the island, but why would doing what the prophecy directed destroy *her*?" He grunts. "That part of the story doesn't add up."

"Does Inara say what happened to the stones?" I assumed she was wearing them openly, but perhaps not, if she's claiming that trying to join them destroyed me.

"She says they're lost at the bottom of the ocean."

I snort.

"Alora?"

I sigh. "Chancery survived, Balthasar, as did Edam and Judica."

"I knew it," he says. "What a relief. It's about time there's some kind of good news. Did you hear there's a new virus circulating? It's worse than the one before, although it still only affects humans, so far."

"We heard," I say. Then I drop the vocal modification. "Where are you?"

"Chancery?" The relief in his voice is plain.

"Yes, it's me."

"I haven't been able to figure out where you're hiding," he says. "Hopefully you're with Moses—I've called him more times than you can imagine, but he denies knowing anything about your whereabouts or well-being. I took heart in my inability to find you, however, since it means Inara probably can't locate you either."

"I'm not with Moses," I say. "But I can't hide—not anymore."

"You're worried about the humans being harmed by the new virus." His voice is flat.

"I'm not worried," I say. "I'm devastated, as you should be. And even without this latest threat, from what the prophecy says, they're running out of time anyway. Something is supposed to happen near the end of this year—something that will accelerate the decay of their already damaged DNA."

"You can't save the entire world, Chancery. You're not all powerful, and some things can't be fixed."

I'm not going to argue with him, not here, but his resistance is so familiar that I welcome it. I've missed him. "I'm going back to Ni'ihau."

"You can't do that," he says. "It's not safe, not even close to safe."

"I don't have a choice," I say. "The stones are there. She took them from me. They need to be joined for real this time; the prophecy must be fulfilled."

"Come to me first," he says. "We'll lure her to us."

I almost turn him down. But when I glance around the room, Noah, Edam, Alora, Judica, Roman, and even Arlington are all nodding. Since when do they want to turn control over to someone else?

"She knows I haven't surrendered yet, but I can do it. She'll believe me," he says. "I promise I can bring her here. She'll come to me, expecting a welcome, and she'll bring the stones. They're not something she'd leave lying around. She'll keep them with her."

"I don't know." Sneaking in and taking them as someone else still seems like the safest play. And if I didn't trust Balthasar before the call, why should I trust him now?

"Never let the enemy dictate the terms of engagement," Balthasar says. "That's offensive plays 101."

We certainly can't invite Inara here—but if we could wrench home court advantage away from her, and I'd have Balthasar on my side. . . He's the best fighter Alamecha has seen in a millennium. Between Balthasar *and* Edam—the two of them might be able to take her, no matter how fast she is.

"I'll consider it," I say. "Where are you?"

"Lainina's palace outside of Bombay," he says. "Near the Hiradevi Temple—her north palace."

"It's called Mumbai, now," I say.

He scoffs. "Okay. Whatever you say."

Some things never change. I'm only holding out because Inara left me gun-shy. But I can't live my life hamstrung by my past mistakes. And it's not fair to mistrust Balthasar because of her actions.

"Do you have access to a jet? Or do I need to send one?"

"I'll call Rivena. If your story checks out, I'll come in the middle of the night," I say. "Make sure we're cleared to land."

"We'll be waiting to welcome you." Balthasar's voice drops. "Chancery, I'm glad you're alright."

"Thanks." I hang up before I can start bawling.

And Rivena backs up everything. She offers to meet me in Mumbai with her personal guard. I decline, but it's nice to know that not everyone has betrayed me.

"That was well played," Alora says. "Bringing Inara to us will be much better than trying to attack her back home where she's told everyone who knows what. There's no chance we could lure her here, especially since she'll know that you're free by now. She'll be expecting something."

"This might not work, then."

"If anyone can pull it off, it's Balthasar," Edam says. "In fact, maybe he can use Rivena to do it."

We spend the next half hour discussing options, and then I call Balthasar and Rivena back, instructing them on how to play things. Rivena, sick at the discord between Althuselah's daughter and brother, brokers a peace talk. She's positive she can get Inara to fly out to meet him.

Even so, the whole thing ties my stomach in knots.

"This is the right call," Judica says. "Not taking the fight to Ni'ihau will also keep Frederick and your other supporters back home much safer."

I hope she's right. "We leave in ninety minutes." Everyone disperses immediately—Alora ordering Isamu around like a footman, Judica and Roman racing out the door to head for their room. What they possibly need to pack, I have no idea.

"I need to say goodbye to my parents," Noah says.

"Should I come?" I ask.

He shakes his head. "Go make sure the tree's being properly loaded," he says. "I'm sure they'll want to gush and sob and bawl, and Mum won't want to do that in front of her new boss."

I roll my eyes. "Tell her that I expect regular updates on how my new Chinese holdings are doing— and that there will be some significant changes coming down the pipeline. Once the world is safe, anyway."

"Oh good," Noah says. "She'll be delighted to hear that. Did I mention? Mum *loves* being told what to do." He ruffles my hair and jogs out the door.

"You're happy." Edam's standing alone amid the chaos, and I realize that he's not.

I wrap my arms around myself, suddenly a little chilly. "I am."

His smile is genuine, at least. "I'm glad."

"I'm sorry, Edam. I know this has all been really hard for you."

He shakes his head. "It hasn't."

I tilt my head. So much for his *I'll love you forever and ever and then some.*

"I realized at your wedding that I never cared much about whether *I* got to have you. I just wanted you to be happy. Seeing you joyful brings me peace."

Something large inside me breaks then, and I begin to cry.

His entire face falls, horrified. He rushes toward me, his hands reaching out and then snapping back. "I—I don't know what to do right now."

I shake my head, and drop my face in my hands. "It's nothing you did, and there's nothing you can do. The world is just so monstrously unfair, that's all."

"That's true." Edam's expression is grim. "I wish there was more we could do to fix things, but sometimes I think it's the injustice that teaches us—that forces us to grow."

Was he this wise last week? Why didn't I listen to him more? "That's true—we grow when we're forced. Otherwise we're complacent."

His smile is comforting and calm, and I realize he meant every word—he's not suffering, and he's not in pain, not as long as I'm happy.

"This would be much easier on me if you were a jerk," I whisper.

He laughs. "Then I'll endeavor to be a loser in the future, whenever feasible."

"Thanks," I say.

He walks me down the hall, and we inspect the bonsai tree together. "You disappeared into that." He nearly chokes. "I'm not sure why it scared me more than when you disappeared into the garden."

"They said I'd explode if I wasn't allowed in there," I say. "Maybe you were prepared for something violent, so a disappearance seemed like a positive change."

He shrugs. "Probably so, yeah. But when you puffed out of existence, for a heartbeat, I thought I'd lost you."

I'm married to someone else, but he doesn't already think he's lost me? "I'll always be here for you," I lie. I thought it would make things easier for him when I die, that I chose Noah, but now I'm beginning to wonder. I don't want to hurt anyone, but when you weigh it in the balance: the people I love versus all of humanity, well, there's no contest.

"Don't sacrifice yourself." His words are barely more than a whisper.

How can he possibly know what I'm planning? My eyes meet his, and I see that somehow, he does know. "I don't have a choice, Edam. I didn't write that prophecy, but it is what it is."

He clenches his hands. "I hate that phrase. What does it even mean? It *is* what it *is?*" He fumes. "An orange is an orange. The sky is above me. Those statements all mean more than 'it is what it is,' and they mean nothing at all. They're just statements of fact. People say 'it is what it is' when they mean to say 'what you want doesn't matter.'"

I laugh then. I wish I could reach for his hand, but I can't offer him that, not anymore. "Oh, Edam, some things just have to be the way that they are. I could bash my head against a wall, wishing Mom had lived, wishing Lark was here, wishing Inara had chosen to love *me* more than her ambition. I could spend the next few weeks hoping and praying that she'll come around and see the error of her ways. But all that wishing will never change what *was*, what *is*, or what *must be*."

"No." He shakes his head. "I don't accept that. Your dying isn't the only way to save the broken humans. There must be another way—something you can do for them that isn't this monstrously unfair. Sometimes the world is just. Sometimes it's good and right and wonderful. I want you to find that path."

How can everyone have figured out my secret?

"You thought it was the end when you went to China too, remember? That time you ditched me?"

I do.

"And again, you were ready to sacrifice yourself when you went to fight Adika. None of those were the end." He steps so close that his breath mixes with mine. "Promise me—promise me, please. You owe me this much. Promise if there's *any* way that you can survive this, you'll take it."

My eyes flutter. "I can't do that," I say. "If the cost is too great, if the damage will be too high—you already said that you'd burn the world down to save me. Your estimation of what's too much. . .I can't trust it."

The muscle in his jaw is twitching when Noah clears his throat in the doorway of the jet. "Is everything okay?"

"I told Edam he couldn't touch the tree." The lie just slips out.

"You really shouldn't do that, man," Noah says. "For reals. I have no idea what would happen to someone who can't use the stones—someone who isn't mentioned in the prophecy. And if I'm not mistaken, we may need your sword arm yet before this is over."

Edam grunts and stomps toward the back of the jet.

My husband walks toward me, stopping right next to me, his eyes gentle. "Do I want to know what really just happened?" Noah asks softly.

I shrug. "Probably not."

"Alright." He squeezes my shoulder and takes a seat.

I sink gratefully next to him and take a nap on his

shoulder almost the second the jet takes off. When he shakes me awake, I rub my eyes and look around. Pitch black outside—which means we're likely close. I peer through the window, the bright lights of Mumbai glowing in the distance up ahead.

"You ready to be 'on' again?" Noah asks.

I shrug. "Does it matter?"

He wraps an arm around my shoulders. "It matters to me."

I pull the stone out of my shirt. "You could take over."

He laughs. "There's a reason I abdicated to you."

"You're an introvert, and ruling was too hard on you?"

This time his laugh rings out so loudly that people all around us turn to see what's going on. "Yes. You've figured it out. I'm a closet introvert."

"But seriously, I hope I made the right call." I lean my head against his chest. "Because I've been thinking about this. You're older than I am, and I never know *what* to do. I think there's a pretty decent case to be made that I'm the Lost and you're the Eldest."

"And the 'she' and 'her' pronouns in reference to the Eldest?" He brushes my hair back from my face. "What about that part?"

"Pronouns are confused all the time," I say. "In fact, I think that's a little sexist of you, to fixate on those."

"I love you," he says.

I turn my head to look up at him. "That was out of the blue."

He kisses me lightly. "Not really. We're hurtling into the unknown, and in case we're too busy to talk much, I wanted you to remember that—never forget it. You're brilliant and capable and kind and generous and funny and I love you—everything about you."

It has nothing to do with whether I made the right call

in flying to Mumbai, but somehow, it's exactly what I needed to hear. "Thanks."

"Oh good. I've always hoped that I would tell the girl of my dreams 'I love you' and she would reply with a tepid 'thanks.'"

I jab my elbow into his ribs. "I love you, too."

"Finally." His arms wrap around me tightly as the landing gear deploys and we touch down on Lainina's private runway outside her overblown palace. True to Balthasar's word, we land safely. That's promising. Being shot down out of the sky is never a wonderful surprise, even if evians often survive the initial crash.

"That's a gloomy face," Judica says. "Shouldn't you be, I don't know, beaming right now? You're a newlywed, and we actually landed without incident."

"You're a newlywed too. Why isn't your face dewy?" I cock one eyebrow.

She rolls her eyes.

I glance back at the Tree of Life, a gentle light emanating from its branches in the back of the jet. "Luckily, I think that bonsai is doing enough glowing for all of us."

"It creeps me out," Judica says.

I swear, if a fat baby angel dropped out of the sky with a lute, she'd shoot it between the eyes. "You're creepy," I say.

She shrugs. "Alright," Judica says. "Let's do this." She draws her sword before heading down the steps of the plane.

I hope Balthasar isn't offended that we're all armed and ready when we arrive on his doorstep, because Edam, Arlington, and even Noah all follow suit.

Balthasar's waiting a few dozen yards away on the steps of the entrance to the palace. "I see you had a lot of faith in my word. It's touching, really."

"You trained me, old man," Edam says with a smile.

"Well, come inside," Balthasar says. "Eat. And if you want to keep your swords out, well, try not to stab anyone who doesn't attack you first."

I laugh, but I'm the only one. We might all be a little too much on edge.

"Is that a tree?" Balthasar looks over my shoulder at where two of Noah's people are unloading the bonsai.

I beam at him. "I found the Garden of Eden."

"It's *glowing*." His mouth forms a satisfyingly round 'o.'

"That's what I'll use, once I recover the stones, to save humanity."

Balthasar crosses the courtyard and the side of the landing strip, pausing to squeeze my arm. "I really am glad you're alright."

Edam sheathes his sword, and the others follow suit.

Balthasar walks slowly, almost reverently, a few more steps until he's inches from the tree.

"Be careful," I say. "When I touch it, it kind of. . .sucks me into it."

He turns around and gapes at me over his shoulder. "So you're sure that this is the key to the fulfillment of Eve's prophecy?"

I nod. "I am. All I need to do is recover the stones, and I believe I can repair the damage to the human DNA—I think I can save them from this virus, from all of it, by using the interface, for lack of a better word, built into that bonsai."

He straightens and waves at his people, calling them over to help transport it. Then he pulls something out of his pocket and flicks his wrist. By the time I realize that he's holding a lighter, there's no time to stop him. The second the flame from the tossed lighter touches the leaves of the tree, the flame explodes upward, consuming it.

I leap toward him, desperate to put it out. "What are you doing?"

Balthasar grabs my wrists easily, twisting them around behind my back and pressing a blade against my throat. He's smiling when he turns me around so that I can face him. "Thank you—for flying to me, confessing your plans, and then racing right over just now—you've made everything *so* much easier."

❧ 20 ❧

Balthasar's blade slices into the skin of my neck until blood trickles down the line of my throat. Judica, Edam, Noah, and Alora are all frozen in place. Balthasar's warriors surround us, blades drawn.

"I challenge you," Edam shouts. "To the death."

Balthasar laughs. "You think I care about all that nonsense?" He shakes his head. "I would have shot your plane down if I'd been one hundred percent sure you were all inside. I haven't survived this long by being a complete idiot. It's unfortunate that it's come to this, but I can't take any risk of that prophecy being fulfilled—the only path to evian greatness lies through the utter destruction of the dregs that humanity has become. You've seen it as some kind of dire prediction to prevent, but it's not. Their demise will set us free."

"Wait," I whisper. "Are *you* Nereus? I don't understand."

The knife digs deeper, blood running down the front of my shirt in a rush. "Nereus?" He snarls. "I would never have harmed your mother. Never. The worst part about beheading Angel is that she should have paid far more for her betrayal. I still can't believe she thought she could use a name from *my* organization to cover her misdeeds."

Wait, he still thinks Angel was Nereus? He doesn't know that Inara killed Mom? I suppose that's not something Inara would have confessed to him, and I didn't have the chance to tell him on the phone. Our conversation took a much different path than I intended.

Noah's eyes flash. "You may not care about honor or challenges, but you should know that my parents will avenge mine and my brother's deaths—and they won't hesitate to destroy you and everyone you care about." Noah turns his head sideways and glares at the warrior standing beside him.

"Your parents?" Balthasar sighs. "The family of outcasts who have haunted China for centuries? They're going to come out of hiding and do what? Kick me? Pelt me with chopsticks?"

"Moses is with me," I say.

"Wrong again." Balthasar lifts me up until my feet dangle, knife still pressed to my throat. "I hold all the cards here—none of you can best me physically, and I command zealously devoted troops in every single family, in every nation. And best of all, the virus has already been released. Even now, if you turn on the television, you'll see reports of humans overwhelming hospitals and medical centers, doctors and nurses who can't help, and governments that are already succumbing in terrifying numbers. The end is already upon them."

"Why?" I ask. "You could at least tell me that much before you slice my throat."

"My parents have nuclear weapons and they know just where we've flown," Noah says. "And exactly who we trusted when we came here. I'd love to see you withstand a direct hit from that—because if the humans are dying anyway, they won't hesitate to bomb you and your supporters out of existence."

Balthasar lowers me until my feet are touching the ground again, and his hands dig into the skin and muscle of my shoulders. "Perhaps you merit further questioning." He narrows his eyes at Noah, and then looks down at me. "Which means I may yet need leverage." He turns to his people. "Tranq them all. Double the dose on Edam."

Edam brings his blade in a wide circle, taking out three warriors near him, but then a dart hits my arm and the world around me goes dark.

I swim in blackness.

Not even sure whether I want to wake up.

I'm tired.

So tired of all of it.

Maybe this time, I surrender to it.

Maybe this time, I don't climb the pit, or break my collarbone and crawl through the air tunnel. Or reverse the plane and fly away from the bomb. Maybe this time, I give up.

But all those lights.

And the deep eyes of someone I love, begging me to try. And the dark blue eyes of someone else. Calling to me. Entreating me not to give up. The urge me onward, forward, upward. And I begin to claw.

As I rise, a great buzzing fills my ears—but from the other side of the tremendous sound vibrating through every cell of my body, I sense something else. Something I recognize.

Words.

It's a tumble of nonsense at first—nothing I can interpret. And then I realize that it's simply another language. One that I don't use easily. Russian. Balthasar's mother tongue. Once that piece of information clicks in place, I'm able to pick phrases from the chaos of white noise that blankets my muzzy mind.

The first from a rough voice, gravelly, full of anger. "—thirteen men and it took four tranquilizer darts before he dropped. We should kill him for that alone." A slamming sound, followed by a splatter, like water against pavement.

"Admit it," Balthasar says. "Just say the words."

"Go. To. H—" Edam. That's Edam's voice, speaking in English.

Another slam, and then a pained exhalation.

I need to see what's going on. I try to open my eyes, but everything's still black. Except a speck of light on the far right of my vision—near the top. Something is pressing against my face. A blindfold, it must be. I wiggle and my head pounds like someone banging on a bass drum. I scrunch my nose and face and then stretch it out, and slowly, one shift, one wiggle, one move at a time, the speck of light widens. I can almost make out the toe of my black boot, although I can't move it. I'm sitting up in some kind of concrete chair, my hands and legs both shackled, my neck enclosed in a metal collar. He doesn't mess around with the restraints. No leisurely cell for Balthasar, no.

"I already know what you are," Balthasar says. "You can admit it."

"Coming from a lying, traitorous—"

Another slam and a grunt.

"This grows tedious," Balthasar says. "Maybe I *should* just kill him."

"If you kill anyone, I won't tell you a thing." Noah. "And you want to know where Mum and Dad keep their nukes. It's the only way you can escape from this without losing your people and perhaps even your own life."

Balthasar laughs again. "You have quite the knack for overstating your position."

"Sir," someone from far behind me calls. "Inara is hailing. She's requesting permission to land."

"Wonderful news," Balthasar says. "Has she agreed to the trade?"

"She has, Warlord."

"Excellent. Bring her to me when she arrives. She might be able to help—she always had more aptitude for torture than I did. Or perhaps she just has more patience with it."

What trade? I can't believe he wants to *oppose* the prophecy—why? And why did he destroy the tree? Just the thought of that ancient tree burning causes despair to surge within me. It's too late now—even if we escape, even if we regain the stones, even if he doesn't kill us all, I can't save them. I can't prevent the utter destruction.

I have well and truly failed.

Edam was worried about me sacrificing myself, but now I'll die along with everyone else, for no reason at all. Tears leak from the corners of my eyes. What's the point in negotiating? Noah's wasting his time—which means they're torturing them for nothing.

I try to shout, but my words come out as more of a wheeze. "Just kill us."

Footsteps move toward me. I shove against the restraints pitifully, but nothing happens. Whoever set these up has experience holding evians. "You're awake."

"Stop playing with us," I mutter. "Man up and just do it."

A blade presses against the side of my neck. "If you're sure."

"I had no idea you were such a coward," I whisper. "I wonder whether Mom knew."

"Excuse me?" The blade disappears and Balthasar crouches next to me. "A coward?"

"You'd kill me like this? Bound, restrained, and blindfolded?"

I can almost hear the smile in his tone. "How would you prefer to die?"

"You should look me in the eye," I rasp. "So that when you do die, and you're old enough that it won't be too long before that happens, and you look my mother in the eye and tell her you murdered me, at least you can tell her that I wasn't trussed like an animal."

He tears my blindfold off, his eyes sad. "I don't want to kill you, Chancery. Do you think I'm a sociopath?"

If I could spit on him, I would. "I was thinking psychopath, actually."

He chuckles soundlessly. "You've always been the funniest of all her daughters."

A tear leaks from my eye and rolls down my cheek. "Why, then? If you don't hate me, if you cared for my mother at all, how can you do this?"

Balthasar frowns. "If I cared for your mother?" He turns toward the wall. "She's the only person on earth I ever truly loved."

The last piece fits together suddenly, and I realize that he must have been Sotiris' father. "It was your baby."

He sniffs and then inhales deeply. "I wasn't able to confirm it. That moron Tristan was so worried that he incinerated the body. Before I could even confront him about whether there was a sample, he killed himself." He grunts. "It's impossible to find competent help—even the zealots. Hopeless devotion doesn't cure extreme stupidity, unfortunately."

"Wait. *You* stole her body?" I shake my head as much as I can with a cuff around my neck. "Why?"

His hand trembles against his knee. "I had to know whether the baby was mine."

"If you thought Mom was capable of being unfaithful—"

He stands then. "Your mother was a magnificent and

complex individual. The finest woman to ever live, by a wide margin. But to assume you understand her motivations and actions is always a mistake."

It hits me then. Inara is here—coming to broker some kind of deal. He plans to use her to torture Noah's information out of him. And I want them both to burn if we all die. I want them all to roast from whatever nuclear weapons Noah's parents may be able to fire off.

My only play is to share the truth with Balthasar. If he loved Mom like he says, it'll unhinge him. "You should know the facts before you do anything else that can't be undone."

"What's that?" When he turns toward me, his expression is relaxed, his eyebrow raised in disbelief.

"Angel didn't kill Mom. I made a major error there—and you executed the wrong person. Mom's killer is still walking around free."

Balthasar freezes, the relaxation in his body replaced with taut fury.

"I'm assuming you'd like to know who really killed her."

He spins around, his face contorted and flushed. He's angrier than I've ever seen him. "You will tell me. Now."

"One of the hardest lessons Mom taught me was to never give away something for nothing," I say. "She drilled that in to me, over and over. I always felt that the truth was its own reward, but Mom disagreed. Vehemently."

"What do you want?" he grinds out.

"At least free me," I say. "Let me stand next to you and look you in the eye when you kill me. Give me that much at least, and I'll tell you the truth."

He releases my neck binding, and I roll my head back and forth, stretching the muscles of my neck. He frees my hands next, and I take my first good look around. The room is much, much larger than I expected. It's as large as Mom's throne room.

"Lainina punished people regularly," Balthasar says. "She felt that before any trial, the torture and information extraction process should be public whenever feasible. That meant she needed room for the victims and the audience. It's the reason this wonderfully large room exists."

Edam's next to me, only a few feet away. His head is down, shackled in iron as mine was. His chest rests on an iron riser, leaving most of his body free—to be beaten and kicked and cut, it appears. His clothing is covered in blood, but of course, his perfect evian body has healed everything—so he's straining against the restraints at full strength. And he can't even meet my eye.

Noah's next to him, and Judica's just past him. Judging by her lack of movement, she's not conscious. Alora and Isamu are beyond him. No Arlington, Roman, or Bellatrius. "Where are the others?"

Balthasar shrugs. "I killed them."

Oh, no. No, no, no. I hope Judica doesn't wake up and discover Roman's gone. Although, if she doesn't wake up, I guess that's worse.

"How many pressure points did you think I needed to pry a little information out of your cagey boyfriend?" Balthasar stands. "Besides, there were only seven restraint chairs."

Seven? I turn the opposite direction, where Roman's behind me, bound and unmoving. Since we're all dying, it's ridiculous that I care about him being alive, but I do. Maybe I haven't given up all hope. Although, Arlington and Bellatrius. I stifle back a sob. I can't afford to cry, not right now.

"I did it. Now tell me."

"Are you going to release my feet so I can stand?"

Balthasar rolls his eyes. "You can stand now, you just can't move. Now tell me who really killed Enora, and how you know it this time."

"You invite me to visit," Inara says from the doorway. "And offer to let me kill Chancery and Judica, and then when I arrive, you're freeing her?"

Balthasar lifts one eyebrow. "I'm not freeing her. She and I have struck a bargain that will be complete shortly."

Inara walks through the doorway, surveying the row of bound and shackled prisoners. "Pathetic."

My hands begin to tremble at my side. How can she and Balthasar both be this *broken*? And how did I fail to see it, with as much time as I spent with them?

"I find that I've changed my mind," Inara says. "I don't want Chancery and Judica dead after all."

Excuse me?

"What?" Balthasar asks.

"I brought the stones, as promised. I have no need of them, since they won't do a thing for me, but I find that I've had a change of heart. I want Chancery freed."

I look up at her from my stupid concrete and iron seat, baffled. What is she saying? What's her bizarre angle now? She must have heard what I was telling Balthasar. She's playing an angle, but I can't figure out what.

But when she meets my stare, there's something in her expression I don't expect: regret.

She thinks she can walk in and apologize and I'll forgive her? It's too late for that—she killed Mom. Melina. Melina's people. She essentially killed Angel. The list goes on and on. She can't walk in now and offer to spare me and think all will be forgiven.

The tree is burned.

The prophecy can't be fulfilled.

Utter destruction is now inevitable.

"I'm afraid I can't agree to that deal," Balthasar says. "As much as I wish I could. I understand your desire to spare her, believe me, but I can't take any chances on her fulfilling that stupid prophecy. Even without the tree."

"It's the only way I'll give you the stones." Inara crosses her arms under her chest.

"You think I care about those rocks?" Balthasar laughs.

"You're the one who called and offered me a trade," Inara says.

"Loose ends," he says. "I figured I'd do something I meant to do anyway, and tie up some loose ends in the process."

"Why do you care about the prophecy?" Inara asks. "You don't want to rule. You supported my bid for the throne utterly and completely."

Wait, he did what? Was everything he told me a lie then? I'm such an idiot. So if he never wanted the throne, did he lie to Rivena? What's going on?

"None of you have spent time around them, the humans." Balthasar stares at the dark window on the back wall. "They're a plague. They rape and murder and squabble and maim. They're greedy and selfish, vile and foul. The only solution to the problem they present is a reset, just as it was in the time of the flood."

"You do run the Sons of Gilgamesh," Inara says. "Gideon was right."

Balthasar smiles, slightly. "So he did tell you he reported to me? I didn't think he'd have the guts to share that with you—but if you suspected, why didn't you ever approach me?"

"He didn't tell me anything," Inara says. "He left me a box of letters, and I pieced things out from small clues."

"But then how did you—"

"You had a loose end that wasn't dealt with," Inara says. "And I found it myself."

His brow furrows. "What?"

"Although I suppose if you want to be technical, he found me."

Balthasar swallows, his eyes shadowed. "Who?"

"He didn't die, you know." She tilts her head. "Melamecha was digging into those insurgents, and she found your men. She discovered your plans, and she saved him at the last second."

I've never seen Mom's warlord quite so nervous. "Eamon didn't die?"

Oh my—what? My dad is alive? Or, I guess, not my dad, but the man Inara loved? The man she blamed Mom for killing? I'm so confused.

Inara's lips twist.

Balthasar rests his hand on the hilt of his sword. "Tell me what happened."

My sister's face shifts from angry to deranged. "Two birds with one stone, was that it?"

He shifts from the ball of one foot to the next, excitement in his eyes. "Something like that."

"Remove the competition for Mother and the eager lieutenant who was gathering too many loyal followers at the same time." Inara steps closer to him. "You couldn't resist the chance."

"Your mother wanted Eamon gone—she said as much. I did her a favor."

Inara snarls. "He was leaving her, you idiot! You killed him for *nothing*."

Balthasar's face falls. "You loved him."

She trembles, and I feel sorry for her in spite of myself. "I love him still, and you *killed* him. But Gideon, whom I also loved, survived." A corner of her mouth turns up. "Surprise."

"Gideon's alive?" Balthasar looks around. "Where is he?"

Inara shakes her head. "Nice try. I wouldn't bring him to you so you could finish what you started."

"Why are you here?" he asks. "Are you thinking that if you save Chancery, she'll forgive you for trying to kill her and everyone else she loves? That will never happen."

"I'm not delusional," Inara says.

"You sure?" Balthasar steps toward her. "Because I know for a fact you don't care about the humans, not like Chancery, and not like her insanely zealous human-loving father Eamon did."

"You know nothing," Inara says. "But you always thought you knew everything. That's your downfall. Pride." She draws her sword with a snick. "I'm here to challenge you. You've had a good run. For nine hundred years, no one could defeat you, because you never played on a level field."

"You're challenging me?" he asks. "For what? I'm not your enemy. I had no idea how much you loved Eamon—and I had no idea he was leaving your mother." He shakes his head, a demented laugh escaping his lips. "That sounds so twisted."

"You're not my enemy?" Inara's eyebrows rise.

"I don't need to be." Balthasar sheathes his sword. "Let's take this down a notch. You and I can still be on the same side. You can still rule. Bygones can be bygones."

"Only because you don't already know the piece of information that Chancery was bargaining with a moment ago."

Balthasar's hand goes back to his hilt, his eyes wary.

"You see, a few weeks ago, through a bizarre sequence of events, I discovered that my mother had either killed, or at the very least basked in the pleasure of the death of the love of my life."

"No." Mom's brother-in-law shakes his head. "No. You didn't."

"Oh, but I did." Inara blithely hands him the information I meant to wield as a weapon. "I poisoned her."

No excuses, no regret, no apologies.

"I threw suspicion onto Angel rather successfully, but at this point, there's no use in denying it. It was me." She leans toward him. "I stole her from you—and in the process, I killed your unborn child too."

Balthasar unsheathes his sword for a second time with a roar. "You want to fight me? Fine."

He brings his sword down against her hard and fast, but she blocks him easily. He parries again, but she blocks and then with a dagger that comes seemingly out of mid-air, she stabs him in the side, growling like a feral animal. He slams his hand into her wrist, breaking her hold on the dagger, but worsening the damage to himself precipitously.

He spins away and yanks her dagger out of his own side. In a blur, he swings after her with a sword and the stolen blade. His side is nearly healed, and soon the only evidence of his vulnerability will be the bloody gash on his dark blue shirt.

"You're fast," he says.

"Your brother really never told you?" she asks.

His eyes are wounded. "Told me what?"

"*I'm like you.*" She advances with another flurry of blows, almost too fast to track.

Balthasar blocks and swipes, spins and slashes, finally backing far enough away to hiss, "Berserker."

"You should have known when I snapped you out of the haze after Dad died. You were too stupid to realize what I was." She laughs then, and attacks again, even faster this time. She scores his shoulder. He tags her calf. She climbs the wall and flips over on top of him, and he ducks and slides away.

It's like watching a battle scene in fast forward—times ten. I'm not even sure who I want to win or to lose. Inara kicks Balthasar in the knee, and then slashes at him with a second dagger, but he deflects with his sword and the dagger clatters away, sliding in my direction. They're so occupied that I wonder whether I might. . .

I'm still bound around my ankles, but I crouch down

and then rock forward toward the dagger, desperate for anything I might use to free my feet. I fall forward, my knees slamming against the concrete floor and reach as far as I can—but it's still not far enough. Several inches still separate me from the discarded dagger.

Steps to my right side alert me to a problem, but I don't have time to scramble back to my feet. "You should not be reaching for weapons." I recognize Phillip, one of Mom's old guards, and clearly an acolyte of Balthasar's. His sword edge presses against my lower back.

"I thought Balthasar might need it." I smile.

"He wants you dead." Phillip's blade presses harder.

"I think that's still up for debate," I say.

"No." He shakes his head. "He was very clear. Only Inara wanted to keep you alive."

"Well, in a moment I'm sure he'll set things all straight." I scramble backward, away from Phillip and his stupid back-slicing sword.

He follows me doggedly, ignoring the battle still raging behind him. "I should take care of this loose end for him now, while his hands are full. He'll thank me for it when he finally beats her." He tosses his head toward the edge of the room where Inara is using the back of a chair to deflect his strokes until she can reach her dropped blade.

"I don't think Balthasar likes anyone to do things he doesn't explicitly tell him to do. Didn't you hear him talking about the idiocy of his people?"

Phillip presses his blade against the place between my second and third ribs. "You're calling me an idiot? Is that wise?"

"If you draw a single drop of her blood, I'll slice you into pieces and feed them to your stupid lizard," Edam growls. "And if you do more than nick her skin, I'll flay you alive."

Phillip drops the blade from my side and circles my

seat, bringing his sword up against Edam instead. "You always thought you were better than the rest of us, from the day you showed up."

Oh, no.

"Phillip, you should probably be paying attention to your boss," I say. "He might need your help."

"Need my help?" He laughs, and the sound sends a shiver up my spine. "You know very little if you think Balthasar might need my help. He's so far ahead of everyone else, no one can touch him." He stabs Edam in the side, piercing a kidney unless I'm way off. "This guy, on the other hand. He's not ahead of anyone, he just *thinks* he is."

Edam doesn't even flinch. "But everyone was ahead of you, Phillip, you ponce."

Phillip stabs him again, this time harder and deeper.

Edam still doesn't flinch, but when he coughs, blood spatters the ground.

"You're not so tough when you're restrained, are you?" Phillip yanks his sword out of Edam's side and presses it against his throat. "And I know for sure you're not going to survive this. No one's asking anyone to spare your life."

"I am," I say.

But he doesn't care what I think—clearly. Phillip pulls the sword back, and swings it around, and I realize he's going to decapitate him. Right here, right now. I can feel the useless well of power in my head that means Balthasar didn't search me for my last stone, but in that moment, I can *almost* feel the others. Shimmering like mirages, a shadow of the wells that should be there.

Noah's words from before echo through my mind. *I think it's your power somehow, princess, and they're mere focal points or something akin to that. They may amplify the power inside of you, but I believe that it ultimately comes from you.*

I'm powerless.

I'm bound.

I've already failed.

I'm no Mahalesh, no all-powerful matriarch.

I'm not Enora, a wise and terrible empress.

I'm not Judica, a warrior for the ages.

I'm not even Inara—doggedly devoted to the pursuit of what matters to me.

I'm only Chancery, and the only power I have is the desire to do what's right. At any cost.

I shove at those mirage wells of power, desperate to access anything that might allow me to save Edam's life in this moment. The pain that streaks through me nearly splits my head in half, but I writhe past it. Searing agony—blinding, shredding, horrifying torture, as if the lobes of my brain are being shoved through a juicer, and yet I press forward, clawing for those wells of power. The stones must be close—Inara brought them with her.

And like I've torn through a wall of fire, the power explodes inside my mind and I seize it, flinging Phillip across the room. I use the same power, the same kinetic force, to release the bands around my own feet, the iron bands encircling them snapping and twisting in front of my eyes.

It's not enough. Not quite yet. I can't just fling Phillip away and then leave Edam prone. He'll come back and finish what he started. He'll kill Edam in front of me. With the last bit of power I wrested through that wall, I shatter the resistance of the bands holding Edam in place, the bands around his neck, his wrists, and his ankles all twisting until he's free.

Only then do I collapse to the ground, shuddering, my hard-fought power gone, dissipated and depleted. Leaving me empty and shattered. Edam rushes to my side, lifting me off the ground, his face close. "Chancery, are you alright?"

My mouth won't form any words. It's not working at all.

He squeezes me. "Your hair—" He grunts and spins, dropping me abruptly to the ground. I watch, frozen by the aftershocks of the pain from seizing the power of the stone without possessing the stone, while he turns to face half a dozen guards, Phillip included, without any weapons. He drops beneath Phillip's guard and slams the hilt of his sword, knocking it up in the air, and snatches it away, beheading Phillip with his own weapon.

Before the other attackers have processed what happened, he's on them, slicing, gutting, eviscerating.

"Psst," Noah says. "Princess."

I turn my head. It's the first movement I've been able to force from my body since I freed Edam.

"Can you free me?" His head is still restrained, but his eyes are turned sharply in my direction.

I fumble around in my head for the mirages again and groan at even that attempt. Not via that route. I turn my attention to my hands, willing them to work. It takes me a moment, but I use them to shove myself up to a seated position, and then I straighten all the way. My legs don't seem to be working, but I flog my hands until they drag me across the floor, one slow pull at a time.

From the corner of my eye, I realize that Balthasar and Inara are still fighting, but neither of them looks very good. And in that second, Inara's eyes lock on mine.

Balthasar takes advantage of the distraction to slide his sword under her ribs, severing her spine. Her legs go slack. Her eyes widen, and she whispers. "I'm so sorry—from the depths of my gut."

He yanks the sword free and uses it to behead her before her body has the time to sink to the ground.

And I'm officially out of time. I scramble forward, lurching around Edam's empty chair and dragging myself toward Noah. I reach his side with just enough time to claw at one arm restraint before Balthasar bellows, "To my aid."

Edam was eliminating the last guard when a dozen more pour through the door. No, no, no, he needs help. I redouble my efforts to free Noah, but my fingers aren't strong enough to even approach prying iron bindings open.

"In front of me," Judica hisses.

Oh good, she's awake. And my legs are working, sort of. I fumble my way forward and grab the discarded dagger. I use it to pry the bindings from Judica's hands and then feet, and finally her neck. She snatches it from my hand, clearly unhappy with my speed, and uses it to free Noah. Admittedly, she moves far more quickly than I was. She practically leaps Edam's and my restraint seats in one bound to reach Roman. She and Noah and Roman join the fray, helping Edam.

Which is good, because Balthasar has joined the fight. Even Edam can't take on a dozen men and Balthasar at the same time. I'm scanning the room for a weapon I might use to lend a hand when I see my sister's mangled body. Even with the betrayal, even knowing what Inara has done, my heart splits open inside my chest. She did apologize at the end. From the bottom of her gut.

Which was an exceedingly strange thing to say. I walk toward her.

The one well of power in my head pulses, and I wonder. Was it some kind of message? Did she know she was going to lose? Was she telling me something? I glance back at the fighting.

Noah and Judica are handling the influx of new guards, and Roman's bent over, freeing Alora and Isamu. Edam and Balthasar are locked in the same kind of battle that Inara just lost. I should help—I need to do something.

But if Inara was telling me something, it might be important. I stumble toward her body. Her head is at my feet, surrounded by a terrifyingly large pool of blood. I lean down and close her eyes. Even in death, they look so terribly similar to Mom's. I think about the life she led, and how twisted it all became.

Oh, Inara.

Why would she change her mind at the end? Why plan to kill me, and then shift? She said Eamon wasn't alive after all—Gideon was. Was he her nurturer? Her Noah? Did he help her to see the evil in her actions? He worked for Balthasar. Maybe he told her. . .what Balthasar planned? Or perhaps without the prospect of saving Eamon to justify her actions, she realized that she'd gone too far. I scramble toward her body, the pulsing in my head growing stronger.

She loved me from the bottom of her heart. She loved me with her whole soul. Those are things that people say. Her gut—it's not. . .But she said she brought the stones with her. . .Balthasar might simply take them. Unless.

If she swallowed them, they could be hidden in her gut.

If not, I'm desecrating her corpse.

But if I had the stones, I could end this. Spare Edam, spare Noah, and Judica, and Alora, and Roman. With trembling hands, I check her boot for a dagger. Nothing in the right, but when my hand slides inside her left boot, there's a small, ruby-handled dagger. I tug it free and use it to slice her abdomen open, from the wound Balthasar made that she couldn't heal, downward.

The dagger catches on something, something stiffer than human flesh. I reach inside my sister's body, every single part of me revolting against the task, and withdraw a bag. I tug the drawstrings open and. . .two rings with small stones and one with a large one tumble out onto my hand,

And there's something else in the bag, something stiff. I slide the rings on my fingers, ignoring the pulsing from the stones demanding that I reunite them, and free the damp letter, folded and refolded, from inside the bag.

It's brief, but I read the hastily scrawled words twice.

Balthasar is your father.

He killed Eamon—Mother didn't. I had so many things very, very wrong.

I deserve to die, so if you're finding this, don't blame yourself.

Redemption is impossible for me, I know, but I hope you can learn from my mistakes and do better.

No, I know you can. You always were the best of us.

Eamon may not have been your biological father, but he'd have been very proud of who you've become.

I'm proud too.

I

The world around me shudders somehow, as if time has inexplicably slowed. As if control of the future now rests in my hands. I glance down at the blood-streaked stones settled in place again on my fingers and realize that it sort of does.

The wells of power yawn open in my mind easily, now that I'm touching the focal stones. I glance around the room and thrust my hands outward, sending Balthasar's guards flying into the walls.

Edam's still fighting, unaware of what has happened. Unaware of the truth of whom he's actually fighting.

My father.

I slam the door to the room closed with another wave of my hand.

Edam slices the backs of Balthasar's legs, and then drives his sword upward, separating Balthasar's spinal column in a way that's eerily similar to how my father just killed Inara.

"Stop," I say, doubtful that Edam will hear me.

As if he was standing right next to me, as if he's attuned to the very timbre of my voice, Edam freezes. Balthasar turns toward me, his eyes widening just as Inara's did at the end.

I know exactly how this scene will play out. Edam will behead Balthasar, just as Balthasar recently terminated Inara's life.

That cannot be.

"No." My words aren't bold and clear and confident like I wanted them to be. And unlike the moment when I wheeled the bonsai out of the Garden, I have no idea whether this is the right thing to do. Clearly that feeling of calm peace was nothing more than my own hubris.

But one truth I know: there has been far, far too much death. Too much burning. Too much elimination. Not enough joy. Not nearly enough peace. No under-standing or forgiveness. And no new life, not here. Not lately.

And I can't handle any more ugliness. The world is already at capacity for monstrosity.

"Thank you, Edam; you've saved us all." I walk slowly toward them, trusting that Edam will listen and obey.

Thankfully, he withdraws his sword from Balthasar's neck, who sinks to his knees. Unlike Inara, Balthasar's still alive in this critical moment.

"You're the only person who could have defeated him." I reach them, and I look down into my father's eyes. "As you already know, my father is quite a fighter."

Balthasar chokes, and then coughs blood all over the floor and my boots.

"He almost killed me and his other daughter, Judica." I turn back toward her. "But I wonder whether he would have done the same thing if he knew the truth of who we are."

My father blinks.

"How could you not have known we were your daughters?" I extend the paper from Inara.

"Enora swore I wasn't." He takes the paper and scans the words. "She showed me DNA evidence that you were Eamon's children when I pressed her about it."

"Looks like Mom lied as much as the rest of us," I say. "I doubt Inara got it wrong, not this time."

"No." Balthasar sits down. "No, not something we can easily verify, thanks to Job and Judica's genetic testing. Inara would have those results at her fingertips back in Ni'ihau. She would have confirmed it."

"He burned the tree," Noah says behind me, warning in his tone.

"He killed Inara," Judica says flatly.

"Who killed Melina, and Mom, and caused me to kill Angel. Not to mention all Melina's people." I shake my head. "Where does it all end? An eye for an eye is the most rubbish law I've ever heard. You just end up with a million maimed or blind people when you're through, and no one is any better off."

"You want to forgive him?" Edam's chest heaves from the exertion—and probably his fury.

I hold out my hand to my father. "I don't even know whether he wants forgiveness."

Balthasar stares at his hands for a long time. "Why didn't she tell me?"

I can't begin to fathom what kind of bizarre relationship he and Mom shared—both of them guilty over whatever happened between them after his brother died. I have no idea what prompted Mom to do what she did, but I hope he will let it go. I'd love to have one parent, even if he's remedial, vengeful, and misguided. Even if he might have doomed humanity with the flick of a Zippo.

Oh, the tree. The virus. Murdering Eamon.

He has a lot to atone for. I'm not sure if he can ever do it.

Balthasar turns his head upward, his eyes meeting mine. "I didn't know."

"I'm aware." He almost killed me, too. He would have, if Inara had been a bit later. It's a lot to forgive. "And I don't promise I'll ever forgive you for any of it, Dad. Most of the things you did aren't even within my power to forgive."

He bursts into tears then, ugly crying in front of all of us.

"Why bother?" Judica's boot taps. "He deserves to die." No one argues with her, not even me.

"But once we kill him, that can't be undone," I say. "Perhaps for now, a little time in one of the chairs he shoved us into."

I'm surprised when Judica doesn't argue. She wrenches Balthasar up by one shoulder and shoves him toward the chair that recently held her. He doesn't resist. He doesn't even look like he's paying attention to the world around him as she shoves his hands into place and clicks the restraints closed.

The window at the back of the room shatters and guards leap inside, one after another, weapons drawn—guns presumably loaded with ballistic bullets, swords, and even a few spears. Balthasar's head whips as far sideways as it can. His voice is firm. It's the voice of someone who has commanded armies for nine centuries. "Stand down."

The woman with dreads who was the first through the window opens her mouth to argue.

"I said *stand down*," Balthasar bellows. "We're going a new direction—and you'll acknowledge Chancery Alamecha as your empress and my absolute successor. Am I clear?"

"You're under duress." She tosses her head toward the man on her left and then toward the woman on her right. "Nothing you say means anything."

Balthasar pops the restraints on his hands as if they're made of marzipan. I'm going to assume it's because we'd already fiddled with them when we broke Judica free. I hope that's the reason, because otherwise I'm even more pathetic than I thought.

He squares his shoulders, his eyes fiery and fierce. "Do I look like I'm under duress?" He gestures back at me. "You'll bow to my daughter and swear to serve her, as will every single Son and Daughter of Gilgamesh, or I will shove your necks on the chopping block myself."

Guards are still leaping through the window, but the one perched on the windowsill freezes. And as I glance from one end of the room to the other, it's clear that they're all shocked—mouths open, eyes wide, unnaturally still.

"I, too, was surprised," Balthasar says. "But if I've learned anything in a thousand years, it's that sometimes it's the things we *don't* know that change everything. I've been so sure that I knew it all, that I understood what was right and what was wrong, and now I realize I've been standing on the wrong side for years, and I've dragged all of you down with me."

The shoulders of the dreadlock warrior standing in front sag. "They're not forcing you to say this?"

My father shakes his head. "No, although I have a lot to repay, and even more to atone for—if they even allow me to try."

He killed Inara and Eamon, and released not one, but two viruses.

And he burned the tree—the only method I had of fixing his most egregious error.

"I need to see the tree I brought immediately," I say. "Or at least, whatever's left of it."

Balthasar grimaces. "It's not in good shape."

Probably the understatement of the century, but. . . "I have a stone that repairs things. It set the island back to rights after the volcano. I hope it will be helpful with this too."

My father turns back and looks over his shoulder at Judica. "Did you want me in the chair right now? Or should I return after I've taken Chancery to the tree?"

She rolls her eyes. "Tree. Then we'll talk."

He strides quickly toward the door, but he can't pull it open. "What happened here?"

I scrunch my nose. "I might have used a little too much force when I slammed it shut."

Edam crouches in front of it. "You shoved the metal door against the frame, smashing them together. I'm not sure how we can get this open again."

"I can—"

"Nope," Noah says at the same time Edam says, "We'll take it from here." When they both agree on something, it's better not to belabor the point.

The door being jammed explains why the guards were pouring through the window. It takes Balthasar, Isamu, and Edam to remove the hinges and force the door backward far enough that we can leave. I fall into step next to my father, with Noah by my side, and Edam walking on the other side of Balthasar. Judging by the looks Edam keeps shooting my way, he doesn't trust Balthasar as far as he can throw him.

I don't blame him.

We reach the tree quickly. It's still sitting in a charred pot on the edge of the small private runway. My heart sinks. I had hoped I could salvage it, encouraging new growth from the old.

But there's nothing to salvage. The tree is now an ash-covered black lump, glistening softly. I dip into the pool of power from the Malessa stone to try and heal or repair it, but no matter what I shove at it, nothing happens.

Because there's nothing left to heal.

"I'm sorry," Balthasar says softly. "You have no idea how sorry."

Nothing he says, no remorse he feels, can fix this. Some things, no matter how hard we try, can't be repaired. I spin on my heel and walk inside, leaving Judica to deal with him however she wants.

❧ 2 2 ❧

"**Y**our Majesty," Larena says. "There are human leaders requesting to speak with you."

More human leaders. Of course there are. It's all our fault that they're dying, and I have no idea what to do about it.

"You've ordered the blood draws?" I lift my head from where I laid it on the desk in despair, the deep ebony lock of hair that shifted in Mumbai sliding across my face and obscuring my vision. I tuck it behind my ear absently.

Her expression is grim. "Evians all over the world are volunteering—your broadcast was effective—but it's a drop of water on a sizzling pan. No matter how many humans we inject, more are dying. Thousands more."

I spin in Mom's chair and look at the charred stump of the tree I insisted we bring back with us to Ni'ihau. I've tried to use the power in the Malessa stone over and over and over and it never works. Humans have been dying by the hundreds of thousands for nearly a week, and even pumping out as much of our blood as we can, it's not making a dent.

So much for thinking that my dad hadn't killed many people.

"They would be dying in a few months either way," Noah says. "I know you're blaming yourself, or maybe Balthasar again, but it's not entirely fair. All he did was speed things along."

"And would you not want a few extra months?" I stand up and pace. "The solar flare that will break their DNA down the rest of the way is theoretical. This is happening right in front of my eyes, while I'm their leader, and I'm supposed to be preventing exactly this!"

"Your father did help us prevent the release of the virus in a dozen more locations. He contacted every one of his operatives and countermanded his earlier orders."

"Yes, yes, he's basically the poster child for reformation, which doesn't help us at all!" I spin around and kick the charred pot, sending it hurtling across the room to smash into the wall.

Larena clears her throat and extends a stack of papers toward me.

I can't read another casualty report. I can't. I shake my head.

"This is the list of human leaders requesting a conference, as well as the daily numbers for—"

"Chancy," Noah says.

"I know that this isn't good news." Larena huffs. "But this is my job and yours too."

In the eighteen years I've been alive, I've never heard Larena huff. She's the most constant, the most capable, the most steady person in Ni'ihau. I take a moment to really look at her, and I notice that she's fraying around the edges. This is taking its toll on all of us. "I'm sorry, Larena." I take the papers.

"Chancery Divinity," Noah says. "Love of my life, *pay attention to me.*"

I whip my head around. "What?"

"You're going to want to take a look at this."

I force myself to my feet. *What now?* I drag myself across the room. Is he actually concerned that I might have stained Mom's ivory carpet? Because I don't care whether—

The pot dented the wall where it crashed, but it didn't break. The corpse of the tree must have made contact pretty hard too, because the base of the blackened trunk split open.

A tiny speck of something glows softly inside the rift. I lean over, squinting at the speck. It brightens, and then grows dim. Brightens and then grows dim.

A pool inside my head shivers.

It's not the power of the Earth stone, Malessa's stone, which heals and repairs.

The power trembling inside of me comes from the Light stone, Adora's stone, the one that has the power to foster new growth. It's the power that I discovered alongside Inara, on the day she betrayed me. I'd almost forgotten about it—but seeing as there was no seed, no life at all inside of the charred tree, I don't hold myself too much to blame for the oversight.

I crouch down and lift the tiny glowing particle from the remains on the tip of my index finger.

"What is that?" Larena asks.

"I think it's the hope we all lost," I say. "Convene the Council, but tell them to meet me outside in the courtyard under the big banyan tree."

She ducks out of the room with a spring that's been missing from her step since my return.

"Do you think you can regrow the tree?" Noah asks.

I turn to meet his eyes, dragging my focus away from the tiny speck that I desperately hope is a seed. "I really, really hope that I can."

"And then what?" His eyebrows draw together.

I hold out my free hand, and he takes it immediately. "And then we pray that the seed takes after its parent."

We walk, hand in hand, through the door to the back courtyard and all the way across it to the base of the huge banyan tree. I played under this as a child—and Mom built her bunker underneath it. Melina's still buried there. I haven't had the heart to move her. I've considered burying Inara in the same place, but I'm not sure whether Melina would want that.

In my heart of hearts, I hope that they're together, free of pain and anger, frolicking up in heaven. I doubt it, but a girl can hope. It's what Mom would want, too. And I hope she's up there with Althuselah, and that Inara is finally reunited with Eamon. I like the idea that heaven is like Earth, free of thorns and misunderstandings and wrinkles. Full of forgiveness and redemption and peace.

Marselle and Larena arrive first, with Edam close on their heels. Then Judica, Alora (and Isamu, who isn't technically part of the Council, but insists on accompanying his wife everywhere), Maxmillian, Job (who survived his time under Inara's rule just fine), Frederick, and Franco appear. Finally, lagging behind all the others, Gideon shuffles up. He doesn't come through the gate into the courtyard—he stands near it, but doesn't walk through.

"Are you coming?" I lift my eyebrows.

"I wasn't sure whether you wanted me." I asked Gideon to take Inara's place, since he helped her to see that she should try and make things right. He's also the one who encouraged me not to replace Balthasar as my Warlord. I'm still unsure whether that was the right move. My feelings change by the day, or sometimes the minute, but until I'm positive what I want to do, Balthasar waits in the holding cells below the palace.

"I want the entire Council present," I say. "I've made a discovery, and I'd like you all here to witness my attempt to repair what was damaged." I hold my finger up high, somewhat nervous about the Kona wind, given the size of this speck-that-I-hope-is-a-seed. "This was resting inside the desiccated trunk of the tree we brought from the Garden of Eden."

Judica's eyes light up. Alora and Isamu clasp hands and share a glance before turning absurdly hopeful expressions my direction. Edam's lips flatten into a white line for some reason, and Gideon frowns.

"You all know that we're on a timeline here. For every second we delay, the cost is unbearable. So I'm going to try and expedite its growth." An idea strikes me then—something I might never have thought about, except for my location. "The tree from which this seed came is dead, but the entire planet is full of life. In fact, this banyan tree in front of us is a thriving example."

I move forward, Marselle and Alora shifting so I can pass them. I lean toward the base of the banyan tree and carefully shift the speck from my finger to a crevice between the exposed top of two of the strong roots. "You probably haven't heard much about the Light stone—I acquired it recently when I defeated Rothgar on behalf of Lainina. On the very day that Inara betrayed me and stole the stones, I discovered it has the power to speed the growth of things—in front of her, I turned a Nohu seed pried from a tiny pod into a large, thriving puncture vine, complete with bright yellow blooms."

It's time to make good on my grand claim. Now isn't the time for false hope—we've all been hit too hard. I stand up and focus on the well of power that connects to the Adora stone. I pull on it, sucking every speck of energy that I can. If I were using the Alamecha stone, I'd have pulled enough to shape a fireball that could take out half the palace.

I direct every single bit of it at that speck, begging, encouraging, cajoling, and entreating it to *grow*.

Nothing happens.

A nervous knot forms inside my belly. What if it wasn't a seed at all? What if it's some kind of bug, like a mite or a parasite? Or maybe it was just a tiny leftover filament?

A pressure starts in my ears then, building, shifting, pressing, and then I realize that I can't just shove energy, not at a seed. It needs more. The power is there, hovering near that speck, but it needs shape. It needs form. It needs direction. When I sprouted the Nohu seed, I was thinking about the possibility of loving Noah. It was that love, that hope, that future that gave it shape and form and life.

I imagine Noah's and my future now—sunny mornings, strolls along the beach, afternoons reading, sitting elbow to elbow and hearing petitions, children racing between our legs. Then I call to the speck and offer it a purpose— brighten the future, little speck, improve our world, tiny sprout, *live, little sapling*.

Like Red Bull with his tongue lolling out, like a bird launching from the branch of the Banyan, like Midas trotting toward me with a whicker, energy and excitement and brilliance erupts from inside of that seed and unfurls, encountering the life and strength of the enormous banyan.

It could shy away, growing only against the powerful life-force already occupying its space, but no. I push them toward one another, *stronger together*. And somehow, the seed merges with the beating heart of the banyan, pulsing and glowing and unfurling into the shell of the trunk and exploding outward. What once was a bonsai now soars overhead, spreading, growing, expanding, covering us all in shade. Enormous white and blue blossoms explode at the end of the branches, drenching us in a delicate, fresh scent I've never experienced before.

Melon and mint and citrus somehow mix together with

the fresh ocean air to brighten a space enveloped in sorrow since Mom's and Melina's and Aline's deaths.

When I look around the circle of my Council this time, every face smiles. "It's indescribably beautiful," Gideon says.

We all take a moment, circling the tree, leaning toward the blooms and breathing in the intoxicating scent. But the weight of the world presses on me, and I can't enjoy the moment as much as I'd like.

"Let's go inside," I say. "When Larena brought me today's numbers, I didn't have the heart to look at them. But now, with an opportunity before us, I think it's time for us to prepare to do what Eve prophesied from the beginning."

No one says a word, which among this group, is a small miracle. I point at the door to my room, and they filter past me one at a time. Noah's still standing near the tree. He tugs at one of the blossoms, pulling it off.

My mouth drops. "What are you doing?"

He walks toward me and holds the bloom out. "Life and death go hand in hand, you know."

"They each have their time and place," I say. "But you're right."

Noah takes my hand in his and entwines our fingers. He tugs me toward the door, and when I begin to walk, he tucks the bloom above my ear. It's far too large for something like that, but somehow, it stays put. "That white and blue, against the dark streak." His breath catches. "I don't tell you enough how beautiful you are."

A thick lock of my hair turned raven black when I used the power without the use of the stones, and I haven't been able to turn it back. At least it doesn't bother Noah. He appreciates every aspect of my appearance and tells me daily. "I didn't earn this face," I say. "It was a genetic gift."

He stops dead, his fingers tracing from my temple to

my jaw. "I wasn't talking about your face. It's stunning, but it's your soul that calls to me. You're brilliant and fierce, but you're also humble enough to listen. You take risks if they are only to yourself, and you'll do anything to shelter those who are hurting. I couldn't possibly love you more, mirror girl."

"Mirror girl?" I frown. "What does that mean?"

"Never mind."

He must be talking about the vision he had when he was a child. "I'm all grown up now. I'm not the helpless child you saw."

"Don't I know it? You pulled a lot of power back there in Mumbai," Noah says. "And that always takes a toll."

My free hand rises to touch my reminder—the black streak on the right side of my face.

"You're about to do more heroic stuff," he whispers. "And no matter what happens, don't forget that you're beautiful—inside even more than out."

I don't deserve Noah, but I'm grateful for him all the same. I kiss him quickly, and we hurry inside.

"Seven hundred thousand dead," Marselle says. "But each day we lose double the number of the day before."

We're running out of time. Too many lights have already blinked out before they should have. "I need to address the humans of the world."

Franco gulps. "To say what?"

"They deserve to know what's happening, and who we are." And if my plan works, they deserve to know what is changing. "How can we make that happen?"

"Well, we'll need to arrange for translation and distribution," Larena says.

I shake my head. "I know that every delay costs lives, but I really think that they need to hear from me directly, in their language wherever possible. I'll record the first broadcast in English, and the bulk of the others I can give myself as well. But I'll need translators to work up my speech and help me with each."

"And then what?" Alora asks. "What's the plan?"

"The rift must be healed," I say, unable to explain my plan better than that. "And I plan to heal it."

❊ 23 ❊

"**I**s it on?" I ask.

Dmitrius shakes his head. "You'll see a red light here." He taps the side of the camera.

I've spent years talking to people, including the human leaders of the world like the American President and British Prime Minister, but I've never been on television. Mom never was either, not since the day it was invented.

I'm strangely nervous.

The red light blinks on. I insisted on a live feed to all English speaking countries—so it's my fault I'm in this situation. It should have occurred to me that I might be nervous, knowing that millions and millions of people I don't know and have never met would be watching, judging, and blaming me. All of us, really, but mostly me.

"My name is Chancery Divinity Alamecha. My mother should have killed me the day I was born."

The red light blinks onward, regardless of how anyone watching reacts. Regardless of whether I reach them at all. But there are real people on the other side of this. Real people who have been told that the world government's response to the crisis is being broadcast live.

"For nearly nine hundred years, my mother ruled over most of those of you who are watching this broadcast. She held your lives in her hands. Your belief that you elected your own officials was, largely, a lie. You felt like you had control over your life, and thanks to some dramatic changes by my mother, you did, at least to a degree. But a lot of what you have always been taught is a lie, and although I didn't fashion it, I've benefitted from it. For that, I am sorry."

I bite my lip. "My people have always felt justified in their positions, ruling over the rest of you. You're *human* and we are *evian*, a distinction that I believed my entire life meant *everything*. But what does it actually mean? I'm sure you're wondering. Many of you have grown up believing that all of us descended from the first man and the first woman. Most of you call them Adam and Eve. Some other cultures call them something else. God placed them here, and the rest of us descended from the two of them."

"We believe the same thing, but something we haven't made common knowledge is that the Bible is right when it reports that they lived nearly a thousand years—and that their descendants did the same. One of the few characters in the Bible who is mentioned by name and assigned an age is Methuselah. He lived nine-hundred and sixty-nine years. That age, according to my records, is accurate. And you'll note that he was seven generations removed from his ancestors, Adam and Eve."

"Like Methuselah, I am seven generations removed from those first parents. My mother should have killed me because I was the earlier birth of an identical twin pregnancy. My younger sister should have been preserved, while Mom should have killed me. You see, the youngest daughter of Eve has been the ruler of a chunk of the world since the beginning—with our nearly perfect DNA, we heal almost immediately. We're fast, smart, strong, and free of illness and disease."

"I'm sure you've surmised by now what that may mean to you: we're immune to the spreading virus that many call the reinavirus. But I need to confess a more terrifying truth. A rogue element of my people, the evians, those of us who are less than fifty generations removed from Adam and Eve, believed that humans should be eliminated. They felt that, given the significant deletions that have occurred over the generations to your DNA, deletions that have resulted in cancer, cystic fibrosis, Huntington's, muscular dystrophy, a susceptibility to all sorts of bacterial infections and viruses—I could go on, but the point is that a dissident group of my own people created the virus that's currently damaging all of you."

"I'm sure you're throwing something at the screen right now, wishing you could attack me in person. I would be, in your place. But I'm here today to do more than confess our culpability in your danger. I'm also here to tell you that I've found what I hope is a solution, and not just to the virus that threatens you right now. You see, my great-great-great-great grandmother Eve tasked her daughter Mahalesh with an important task: to protect and safeguard all of you. We failed you—for generation after generation, worrying more about our own pride, our own power, and our own greed than about the well-being of those whom we should have been serving."

I lift my hands toward the screen, rotating them to display the rings pulsing on my fingers. "Part of my legacy was these stones. Stones that all came from the same rock in the beginning. I was also given a way I can reach out to each and every one of you. If you've seen the X-Men movie, where Professor Xavier uses the mind helmet machine to see human life, then you have some idea how this might work. It's the closest comparison I've been able to draw.

Very soon now I will begin the process of locating each and every one of you, and I intend to repair the beautiful, fractured lights that compose your souls."

I swallow and look upward, silently praying that they'll trust me in spite of all evidence that contradicts what I'm asking of them. "I think I can repair your DNA and set things right. I'm not sure exactly how that will happen, but I've come to believe in the past few weeks that there may be a divine creator out there, wanting good things for us. Even if he or she isn't actively involved, I believe some force for good is watching over us. I believe that we can all be saved, one way or another. So I'm asking you today to pray to whomever or whatever you believe in. If you don't believe, that's alright too. I don't blame you. Meditate for me, if you will. Offer up positive energy and calm your mind. In three hours, once I've had the chance to communicate with as many humans as I possibly can, I'm going to begin to try and fix this mess my people have caused."

I step closer to the screen. "Because I believe that my people are your people. I believe you're all my people. We all share the same lineage, and although we may have neglected you, we're the same in our hearts. I'm begging you to trust me right now. Hold and hug your loved ones and try to have a little faith. You're not alone out there, and I firmly believe that we're stronger together."

I nod at Dmitrius, and he cuts the communication.

After I've recorded it, I prepare to do the languages I speak.

"You do realize that there are more than six thousand languages in the world," Noah says.

"I didn't know it was quite that high," I say.

"With nearly a hundred and forty people dying a minute," he says. "I'm not sure there's real benefit to recording each one yourself."

"Agreed," I say. "So we'll do as many as we possibly can in two hours."

"Assume ten minutes per broadcast," Noah says. "You can hit the top twelve. Hindi, Spanish, French, Bengali, Russian, Portuguese, Urdu, German, Mandarin, Arabic, Indonesian."

"Maybe Japanese and Swahili too," I say. "Since I've already done English."

He nods and walks off, presumably to organize translators for the rest. The two hours pass in a blur, and by the end, my tongue feels like jelly and my eyes struggle to focus on anything but that little red light.

"You're done," Noah says.

"I could do Marathi, maybe," I say. "I took a conversational class on that, so it wouldn't be as hard for me—"

Noah wraps his arms around me. "I've got an hour with my wife before we dive headfirst into trying to repair the DNA damage of six thousand years." He kisses my nose. "I call a halt."

I lean my face against his chest. "I'll be thinking about the humans dying every single minute of the next hour."

His hand strokes my hair. "I know you will. It's one of the things I love about you."

"And also hate." I laugh.

"I could never hate you," he whispers near my ear.

I let him drag me back to my room, but once we reach the inside and I collapse against the billowy comforter, he wraps me in his arms and holds me. Nothing more.

And it's exactly what I need. No one on earth knows me quite as well as Noah. My head presses against the steady beating of his heart. His arms tighten around me, his warmth and strength buoying me up. His breath against my ear comforts me in a way nothing else does.

Somehow an hour passes in a blink, and it's not enough.

But it would never be enough. A thousand years

wouldn't be enough. So when the clock on the wall chimes noon, I press a kiss against Noah's jaw, and he releases me. I stand up and pull the tools I've had waiting to pry the stones free out of my drawer. The largest includes the Fire, Earth, Spirit, and Wind stones, and I pry it loose first and slip it into my right pants pocket. The heavy gold prongs of Lainina's ring bend easily, and I slide the Light stone into my left pants pocket. The platinum tension setting around Melamecha's Water stone looks the least secure but is actually the hardest to pry apart. I drop it into the back pocket on my pants. Finally I tug the stone Noah gave me after our wedding out of my shirt and use my fingernails to pry the clasp apart, freeing the Binding stone. I slide it into my other back pocket.

Noah and I walk into my courtyard hand in hand.

My Council's already there, with the exception of Balthasar who is locked up below. A small part of me wishes he was here, that I'd have a chance to say goodbye. But it's too late for me to call him up here. After all, it's his fault all these humans are dying right now, today, so soon.

The rest of my Council stands in a circle around the enormous banyan-not-banyan tree, which now boasts even more blooms than it did this morning. Clearly the Hawaiian sunshine and breeze agrees with it.

I thank Larena and Marselle for their devoted service and loyalty. I do the same for Maxmillian and Franco. And then Job is standing in front of me. I might have doubted him at times, but that fear was misplaced. Job loved my mom and me, and served us well. "I'm so glad you're here still, safe and strong. You've been a blessing in my life."

Job shakes his head. "You've been the blessing—a light in the darkness, truly. I'll be praying for you."

Gideon looks utterly changed from the man I met on the day Inara died. His shoulders and face have filled out. His eyes are bright, and his face has color. But his eyes are just as haunted. "She would be proud of you," he says. "So very proud."

I squeeze his hand. "I'm sorry she's not here to see it."

"Could you have forgiven her?" he asks.

"I'm not sure there's any way to know for sure," I say. "But I would have tried."

I reach Alora and Isamu next. Alora's eyes dart almost immediately away from my face. "No," she says.

"No?"

Her head shakes so vehemently she almost can't speak. "I won't do it."

I grab her hand. "Do what? What's wrong?"

"You're walking around this circle all solemn and earnest. You're clearly saying goodbye."

My throat closes off and tears well in my eyes.

"I won't say goodbye to you. You aren't going to die today." She grabs my arms with both of her hands and shakes. "Do you hear me, Chancery Divinity Alamecha? You are not dying. You are going to save the world like you always do, and then you're going to step away from that tree all fresh-faced and innocent and smile at me. Then I'll say 'I told you so.'"

I hope she's right. I nod, wipe my eyes, and move past her. Noah's already hugging Isamu like he's a barnacle and his brother is a barge, so I step around him to where Judica's practically scowling at me. "Uh oh," I say. "You don't have a fork behind your back, do you?"

She laughs and then immediately scowls at me. "Alora already lectured you, which is unfair. She stole my thing. I'm the angry one."

I hug her against me as tightly as I can. But after a moment, I let go. Every minute I delay has a cost, as I am well aware. "I love you," I say. "What more is there to say?"

"You have taught me more than I thought possible,"

Judica says, "but I'm not done learning. So I need you to come back out of that tree, alright?"

I lean close again and whisper. "Nevertheless, if it comes to that, you'll make an excellent empress. You always would have."

I step away before she can object, and come face-to-face with Edam. He's last, and I still have no idea what to say.

"Remember your promise," he says. *If there's any way that you can survive this, you'll take it.*

"I didn't promise," I say.

He looks me in the eye and lifts his chin slightly, as if to disagree with me.

But I can't promise anyone anything, because I have no idea what to expect. No words I can offer will help my loved ones—but we all know I have to do whatever I can. My entire life has been the flight of an arrow, streaming toward this moment.

Utter destruction.

I'm finally here, standing right in the middle of it. I walk toward the tree, Noah by my side, and I close my eyes. Mom's face appears in front of me. *Accept the world as it is, or do something to change it.*

I'm doing it, Mom, just like you taught me. No matter the price, no matter the pain, I will change it.

I pull the largest stone from my pocket and balance it carefully on the end of the fingers on my left hand. Then I remove the Light stone, placing it a few millimeters away from the biggest one. The Water stone goes next to it, and finally, I tug the Binding stone from my back pocket.

"What's the plan here?" Noah asks.

"Joining the stones releases a lot of energy," I say. "And this time, I know just what to do with that force. I think. We'll need every bit of whatever this creates and then some."

Noah nods.

"I'm not sure quite what you should do," I say.

"I've got some ideas," Noah says. "You worry about your part and let me handle mine."

I look up at him then, his face somehow bright under the shade of the dense tree branches. I realize that he's glowing—and so is the tree. He leans toward me and his lips meet mine. My heart lurches in my chest. I nearly forgot to say the most important goodbye. "Thank you for being patient with me, always."

His head tilts sideways. "I'm not patient with you. I'm in awe."

"I love you," I say. "Not in a giant, unmanageable conflagration. I love you in the moonlight. I love you in the between times. I love you in the pain of loss and the agony of waiting. I love you in the space between one heartbeat and the next—and I love you from now until forever."

Noah kisses me again, gently, slowly, and I'm lost. I'm in free fall—and my hand shifts just a centimeter. I try to right it with my free hand, and the Binding stone touches the Water stone, and then they roll forward, pulling the others like magnets together.

A sonic boom that somehow makes no sound, a burning heat that melts nothing, and then my hand disappears in an explosion of light. Noah and I reach forward together, the Lost and the Eldest, and our hands touch the smooth bark of the banyan-not-banyan. And just like before with the bonsai, we're sucked inside.

I'm here and I'm nowhere. I'm alone and inextricably entwined. The vastness of the earth overwhelms me until I feel a pull, something anchoring me to now, to here, to the task before us: *prevent the utter destruction.*

Noah's presence is strong, even without our bodies. I calm my mind, release my fears, and reach for him. He's there, and he loves me.

I can do this.

The lights around me pulse—bright, beautiful, clear lights nearby, with only the tiniest cracks inside their depths. The wells of power in my head have expanded and now we're swimming in them without arms or legs. We're drowning without water or air.

I approach a nearby light—it's Judica. I'm not sure how I can tell, but I can. It's almost the same as mine, but slightly different. A tiny hairline crack runs along the center—a teensy genetic error. A single deletion, or maybe two. I pull on the enormous well of power, the light, the fire, the earth, the spirit, the water, and the wind. I spool them all together and bind them into the tiny crack.

And light explodes from inside of it, like a sun going supernova.

I know what to do for the humans now, times a billion, into infinity. The vastness of the task laid at my feet engulfs me and I spin downward, untethered, sinking.

Arms that aren't there lift me up, hands stroking my face. *You can do it*. The words whisper across my soul. *I believe in you*.

With a soundless sob, I set to work. I gather up the shining lights and the few dim ones nearest to me and I begin spinning, improving my process as I go, using less energy each time. The shining explosions when I succeed nearly blind me to the other lights, but I learn to move away quickly once I've repaired the cracks, perfected the DNA. I move along before I can be delayed.

I gather more lights each time. Ten. Twenty. Thirty. Fifty. Two hundred. A thousand.

Fifty thousand.

My shoulders can't ache, because I don't have any. But they do anyway. My back throbs, even though I have no back. My temples pound against my skull, although they don't exist.

A hundred thousand human lights, and then two hundred. Five hundred thousand and I notice that the pool of energy is shrinking.

Terror flares inside of me, but Noah calms me. It will be enough. I gather the lights in batches of a few hundred thousand at a time, spinning, spinning, repairing, healing, and then racing away from the explosion of sparkling light.

I want to rest, but there's no resting, not here. Lights blink out all around me as I gather, and I panic, increasing my speed, straining and pushing against my limits, my own weakness. Arms that aren't arms surround me. *Consistent, careful, methodical.* I sigh against him, because he's right. Panic isn't helping me or anyone else.

I drop to smaller batches, more manageable with my waning power. Fifty thousand. Then thirty. Thirty more. And then twenty thousand. The lights seemingly never end, but the pool of power keeps shrinking. How many can I save?

How many won't make it?

The pain begins so slowly that I almost don't notice at first. It started as aching in limbs I don't have. But it grows, oh it grows. When I gather up the lights this time, only fifteen thousand or so, I have to let some go. They'll have to wait for the next round. Burning pressure runs through me, rocks me, and knocks me back.

I spin and repair and spin and repair, but then I have to pause. The well is nearly empty. And there are still so many, many lights. A billion? Maybe more. I gather a smaller group—ten thousand. And I spin, but there's no power left. The vast pool from the joining of the stones is gone and the pain explodes inside my head that isn't a head.

If I want to save them, if I want to heal them, I'm left pulling on my own strength—my own life force.

That's the pain—that's the agony. It's the same thing that turned my hair black in Mumbai. It's the price I must pay. I could stop, sure. I could allow all of those lights, those humans, those evians, to die. To blink out.

But why am I worth more than them? Why does my pain justify their loss? It doesn't, and if I really believe that, I can't stop. Not until there's nothing left inside of me to give.

If there's any way that you can survive this, you'll take it.

Accept the world as it is.

Or do something to change it.

My bones that aren't bones shake. My muscles that aren't muscles tremble. And my heart that isn't a heart contracts. I'm not worth more than any of them. In fact, I might be worth less. I was tasked to save them. It's my entire purpose for *being*. If I could trade my life right now for Melina's, I'd do it. If I could trade my life for Mom's, I would, without hesitation. If I could trade my life for Inara's, to give her another chance to redeem herself, I'd take it.

And so I surrender, letting go of the power that holds my body-not-body together, that keeps me as *me*, releasing who I *am* to become instead a source of power that can be shaped, spun, and utilized.

But the same arms that have lifted me, the same arms that have held me together, they won't allow it.

Down, down, down, they press. Until I look at my belly that isn't a belly, my womb that isn't a womb. And I see two tiny sparks within me. *Pregnant*.

What? It's not only me—I'm growing children inside of myself. Even so, how can I choose the three us over all those people, all those lives? But then the power trickles back into the wells, the pools surrounding me, flooding me with the strength that I need to spin all the lights that float around me, cracked and breaking, and I know.

It's Noah.

He knew it all along—he is the Lost. I thought it meant

that his family was lost to the world, that their purpose had been hidden. But it's not that kind of lost. It's the loss I feel when he leaves me, leaves us. He is lost so that the others can be saved. He was always meant to be here as a sacrifice.

No! The word tears from deep inside of me through the vast measures of empty space, through the darkness of the void, *NO!*

Tell them I love them. Don't let them forget me. And don't forget me yourself. I'll love you outside of space, outside of time, into forever.

And then he's gone.

I float there for a moment, watching the flickering human lights wink out, too numb to react. Because the light that mattered most to me in all the world is gone. The arms that lifted me up are no more.

And I no longer want to change the world. I'm tired of all of it. So tired. I can't continue. Not alone, not without him. Not now. How will I ever explain this to our children? It's unfair! I want to rend and tear and destroy in my rage at the injustice of fate. At the horror of the sacrifice that's asked of me. I was willing to give myself, but not him, not Noah.

Failure is a choice.

I hated Mom's personal motto. I've always hated it. I don't choose to fail—it happens when I'm not good enough. And I'm not enough now. I can't do it, not without him. I can't raise children alone. I can't live in a world where he isn't.

I don't want to, either. I want to let go.

But that would negate his sacrifice.

The smallest light still vanquishes darkness.

My own motto. Did I know, even then? Did I realize it would come to this point, and I wouldn't be strong enough alone? The smallest light. And I have two to care for now. I look down with my eyes that aren't eyes at the two perfect, beautifully bright lights inside of me. The lights that Noah and I made together. The lights that will live inside of this world, thanks to his sacrifice. Thanks to his death.

And I begin to gather the lights again. And I spin, and I repair. I spin and repair and I spin and I repair until there are only a few thousand lights left.

There's no power left, but there are still three thousand lights.

What do I do now?

What else can I do? I pull on myself, drawing, spinning, and pulling past the agony, spinning, shoving along until I can't pull more, and then I pull a little more and repair the last of the lights. I watch as the last one explodes into supernova.

And then I close my eyes that aren't eyes, and I send my love toward Noah in case he can sense it.

I'll never forget you—the world won't ever forget you. Your sacrifice saved so many.

I plunge backward then, my back slamming into the ground, my hair flying up in front of me. I'm able to recognize only two things before the world around me blinks out.

Noah isn't with me. I knew he wouldn't be, but it still hurts.

And my hair is black as pitch, every single strand of it that I can see.

Something cold and sharp is pressed against my throat. I blink my eyes, and realize I'm lying in my bed—formerly my mom's bed. The sunlight has barely begun to stream through the windows, which means it's very early in the morning.

"You're finally awake," Kali whispers.

Noah.

My heart breaks all over again, and I can't even bring myself to care that she's clearly here, threatening my life. "Do it."

"You want me to kill you?" Kali frowns. She tenses then, every muscle in her body freezing.

"It would be the last mistake you ever made," Edam's deep voice rumbles from behind her.

"Your guard was asleep." Kali smirks. "You might need to fire him and find a better one."

"Back away from her right now." Edam's voice is tight, and I can imagine the set of his jaw, even if I can't see it.

Red Bull barks behind Edam, my very impressive guard puppy, finally awake. "If you don't step away from me, my dog will very likely piddle all over your shoes."

Kali's mouth twists. "It's good that your sense of humor is still intact—Noah would like that." She swallows. "Where is my son?"

I close my eyes.

The sword slides across my throat, barely grazing my skin, and then the pressure is gone.

I open my eyes and watch the tip of her blade drop to the floor, the hilt barely retained by Kali's limp hands. Her shoulders slump. "Where is he? Why won't anyone tell me?"

"We don't know where he is," Edam says. "We did tell you that."

"You said the last time he was seen, he entered the tree with *her*."

I sit up in bed, scooting back against the headboard. No one bothered to change my clothes, it appears, since I'm still wearing the same jeans and navy blue blouse I was wearing when I touched the tree yesterday. "Your son—" My voice breaks and my eyes well with tears. I can't say the words. I know what I need to tell her, but I can't make the words emerge.

"My son, what?" Kali's eyes spark. "Say it."

"Noah went with me into the tree yesterday."

Edam clears his throat. "Actually, you entered the tree thirteen days ago."

Almost two weeks? How can that be? I shake my head. "No." I blink and look at the window, as if somehow that might tell me something. I couldn't possibly have been inside the tree that long—but without sky or earth, without sun or moon, how would I know? All I remember is pain, and aching, and power, and spinning, spinning, spinning to repair the cracks, to save the lights. "Thirteen days? Really?"

"My son disappeared with you into that tree," Kali says,

"and then all over the world, geriatric patients on their deathbed grew younger in front of the eyes of onlookers. People dying of that stupid reinavirus healed. People in wheelchairs stood up and walked."

Edam steps closer, and seeing his face is like seeing the sunshine again. "There have been a lot of miraculous—"

"I don't care about the miracles," Kali says. "I don't care that all the *humans* are now genetically unidentifiably different from us." She steps nearer, her hand clenched so tightly around the hilt of her sword that her fingers are white. "*You* reappeared last night. *You're* here. *You're* healthy. So where the hell is my son?"

Tears streak down my cheeks, and I realize she already knows, but she can't accept it, not until I she hears it from me. "I ran out of the power from rejoining the stones and there were so many lights left—so many people who were still dying. I saw the lights blinking out in front of my eyes." I drag in a huge breath. "I was going to heal them anyway."

"Using your own life force," Edam says.

I nod my head.

"And my son wouldn't let you." Kali pins me with a glare. "Say it."

I shake my head. "He wouldn't let me, no. He—he gave his life force to save the remaining lights, and in the process, he saved me." I glance at Edam. "He never came back out?"

He shakes his head tightly. He gave up every speck of energy that made him who he was—which means there's not even a body to bury.

"You could have simply come back, both of you." Kali wipes at her cheeks fiercely, one side and then the other. "You should have exited the tree and gone back when you had figured out another way."

"If you think she could have done that, then you don't know Chancery at all." Edam crosses his arms. "No one forced Noah into that tree."

"Chancery did," Kali says, rounding on me. "You're selfish and you swore that you would keep him safe, but that was a lie." She lifts the sword again.

"Selfish?" Edam laughs. "For planning to sacrifice her life to save so many others?" He whacks her sword so fast that she drops it, and it slides across the floor. He steps closer, his sword down, but his eyes threatening. "You're grieving, so I'm going to give you a pass. One single pass. Talk to her that way again, and I will end you. Do you understand me?"

Kali's eyes flash.

"She is already broken," Edam says. "*Destroyed* over this. You want to hurt someone, be my guest. Go fight anyone you'd like. But ask yourself whether your son would want you to be in here, threatening his wife. He made his choice, and you're cheapening it."

Noah's mother sinks to her knees and drops her face into her hands. I know just how she feels. I curl onto my side and bawl right alongside her. I wish I could hug her, but there's absolutely zero chance she'd allow that. I'm not quite sure how long we stay that way, me sobbing on the bed, Noah's mother bawling on the floor, and Edam watching it all like a statue carved of stone.

A loud rap at the door startles me, and I sit up and wipe my eyes. "Come in."

The door opens a crack and Job's head pokes through. "Is she awake?"

"I am."

Job flings the door open and runs across the room, nearly tripping over Kali. His eyes widen, and he moves around her. "I am unbelievably happy to see you." He reaches for my hand.

I yank him toward me and hug him tightly.

"I'm supposed to be doing a physical exam," he says. "Whether you're awake or not."

"That sounds like an order from Alora," I say.

He nods. "She'll be here any minute, too. She only left your room a few hours ago. You gave us all quite a scare. How do you feel?"

I haven't taken a second to consider that. "I'm alright, but there's a sort of pressure on my chest." My hands come up to the area where my collarbones meet and I freeze.

"It was most strange," Job says. "When you exploded out of that tree, Edam sounded the alarm. No one else was there at the time—thirteen days is a long time to wait—and I rushed to your side, but you were already unconscious."

I look down at my chest, where the staridium stone is set inside my skin, flashing and pulsing. Oh, no. What in the world?

"It was there, just like that, when the tree spit you out." Job's eyes are sad. "I wasn't sure what to do, so I left it that way."

"Do you think we should cut it out?" I ask. "It's stuck inside my body."

"Absolutely not," Edam says.

Job turns toward him. "Why not?"

"Who knows what might happen to her if you do that." Edam shakes his head. "It's not worth the risk."

Kali stands up and crosses toward the back wall to pick up her sword. "As exciting as all of this is, I'd better be going."

"I won't take long," Job says.

"That's alright," Kali says. "We were through." She turns toward the door, clearly sick of looking at me. "I brought something for you—something else you broke beyond repair."

"What?" I ask.

"I've left them in your courtyard." She glares at me. "The archways for the Garden you killed."

Edam steps toward her.

"I imagine we'll be leaving in the next few hours." She strides toward the door.

"Wait," I whisper. I don't want to share. I want to hold this secret against my heart, my only consolation in the wake of Noah's death. I'm not ready to tell anyone, not yet. But keeping it from his mother isn't fair—and worse, it's selfish. She deserves to know.

She looks back over her shoulder, one eyebrow raised in irritation. "What?"

I almost say *never mind* when she looks at me like that. But she's hurting as badly as me. "You might be happy to know that your son made his decision for a good reason, at least. Not just out of love for me."

"Excuse me?" She pivots on her heel so she can scowl at me more completely.

"When you go inside the tree." I choke and clear my throat. Job is listening to my heart and poking at me. "Can I have just a second?"

His eyes widen and he nods and steps back.

"There aren't bodies and people inside. Everything is lights—it's hard to explain. It's like a giant floating. . .jar. Each light represents a person, and Noah and I spent a lot of time using the power from the stones to repair the lights—evian, human, both."

She purses her lips and cocks her hip to one side. "And?"

"It apparently took quite a while to do it," I say. "Probably partially because I had no idea what I was doing at first. Only one person can direct the actual use of the power, but Noah was there all the time, supporting me, lifting me up, and even communicating with me sometimes.

It's difficult to talk in there, and I can't really explain how it works, other than to say that you can send a message if you try hard enough." I shake my head. "This isn't coming out right."

But for the first time since she entered, her face softens. "It was a great thing you did." Her lower lip trembles. "I do see that."

"No, that's not what I'm saying." I look at the ceiling, trying to suppress the tears that threaten again. "What I'm trying to say is that when Noah realized what I meant to do, that I would keep healing the lights, the humans, the evians, their DNA, even once the well of power was gone, he stopped me."

She looks away. "I know that."

"But I didn't tell you *why* I let him."

Her head whips back to mine, her eyes intent. "What?"

"I could have refused to use his energy—I could have saved him."

Fury, white and hot, radiates from her, all of it directed at me. She steps forward, her eyes burning. "Why—"

"Noah directed my attention downward, for lack of a better word. There's no up and down there, not like we have it here, but he made me *look*, and I realized that within my own light. . .there were two more."

She blinks several times. "What?"

"I'm pregnant," I say. "With twins. Noah's children. He wanted to save them."

Kali covers her mouth with her hand. When she finally drops it, her eyes glistening again, she addresses Job. "Is she? Is it true?"

Job shrugs. "This is the first I'm hearing of it, but she's only been married three and a half weeks, so. . ."

"Check," she orders.

When Job looks at me, there's a question on his face.

"Do it," I say. "I'm positive I'm right, but confirmation won't hurt."

"We could do a blood test, or it might show up on ultrasound—just the gestational sac, but if you have a preference—"

"I want to see it," Kali says.

I almost argue with her—it's not her body, after all. But it was her son, so I nod. Job leaves to grab the ultrasound machine, and Kali stares out the window the entire time. I have no idea whether she's upset or excited. Maybe a little of both.

"Um." Edam swallows. "I should get Judica and Alora. They'll want to be here for this." And he's desperate to leave. Of course he is.

"Right," I say. "Yes, of course."

He could have sent the guards at the door to fetch them, but he leaves instead. I understand why, at least.

Alora and Judica practically burst into the room together, both of them bright-eyed. "You're awake?" Judica jogs across to the bed and then stops abruptly, as if she's unsure what to do. Red Bull whines and licks her hand, and a deep growl from near the door causes him to whimper and hop up on the bed next to me.

"Keep away from me, mutt," she says. "Or Death will eat you." But her eyes aren't angry. She perches on the edge of the bed, one hand stroking Red Bull's head. "I'm so glad you're awake."

Alora sits at the foot of the bed. "I'm also beyond pleased to hear your voice. It's been a harrowing two weeks."

I still can't believe it has been that long. I run my hand through my hair. . .and realize my last memory is correct—it's entirely black. "That's. . .different."

"Eh, you can grow it out any color you'd like once you're totally recovered," Judica says.

I'm not so sure, but I don't argue with her.

Job arrives then, wheeling a cart inside. "I'm going to have to do what's called a transvaginal ultrasound. It's the only one we might have a chance at seeing the babies with —but it's a little more invasive." He glances at me to see whether I understand.

Ugh. Vaginal. Got it.

"Typically, any visitors would stand up there." He points toward the back wall. "They'll be able to see the ultrasound screen here, but not the rest of you. And I've told the guards not to let anyone through."

I nod. Letting my sisters and mother-in-law see my lady parts is the least of my problems right now. "Go ahead."

I'm a little surprised at how quickly Judica and Kali scramble for the back wall. Alora glides over and stands beside me, taking my hand. "A baby is always a blessing," she says softly. "And two is double the blessing."

Job points at the screen. "And there are definitely two sacs there."

Kali's tears this time drip down her cheeks and across smiling lips. Definitely happy then.

"Oh man," Judica says. "Wait until this news gets out. I can already see the headlines. Goddess Chancery to Give Birth to Twin Demigods."

My mouth falls open. "Excuse me?"

Judica's eyes light up. "Whoa, no one told you yet?"

"Told me what?"

Job's finally removing the probe, and I don't waste any time pulling my pants back on.

Alora glances from Judica to Job and back. "So, I guess as you did the thing that you did." She pauses. "I can only really speak for myself. But I knew when you were healing me, or whatever. It was a light, bright warmth that spread through my body, and then I saw your face, smiling down on me, like a benevolent angel or something. It was strange."

Judica laughs. "Same here, except from what I hear for the humans, it was a lot stronger."

I blink. "They *saw* me?"

"And now," Alora says, "they're all worshipping you."

❊ 25 ❊

I barely have time to grieve—the world is such a mess. "You'd think that saving them would have made things better," I complain.

"Only if you were very naive." Alora ruffles my hair affectionately and then takes her seat. "Most of our problems are of our own making. It has always been that way."

My Council has been more important than ever. I'd need to be an octopus to handle even a fraction of what needs to be done all by myself. "Alright, let's review. Although the global economy is enormously complex, there are several substantial industries that are now, if not entirely obsolete, close. The most obvious is healthcare."

Franco stands. "I provided a report on this, and if you'll flip to page two, you'll see the main ones. The global economy is made up of twenty main sectors. You know most of them already, I'm sure, but they include things like energy, development, technology, agriculture, etc. The industries most impacted by the recent, ahem, prophecy, are healthcare, obviously, and eldercare. Also things like the prison system, which are large but not quite as vast."

Prisoners didn't take long to realize that they couldn't

be contained by regular old iron bars anymore. But many of them previously suffered from mental health issues and genetic disorders, as well as dependency issues and with those eliminated. . . "Speaking of prisons, are the committees we set up for the processing of criminals in our clean sweep program working well together?"

Gideon nods. "The last time——"

Franco clears his throat loudly. "I wasn't done."

I sigh. "I'm sorry. I never seem to be able to finish anything before something else demands my attention."

"Nevertheless, I was unable to finish this report at our last meeting, and it's critical that we begin the process of repurposing resources. Entertainment has shifted dramatically, both in terms of what consumers now desire and in terms of the provision of——"

I'm grateful for Franco, but sometimes he's so boring I can barely make myself focus on his reports. I nod and listen to the litany of issues that I caused by healing all the degrading DNA worldwide.

"The real danger," Judica whispers, "is that now that everyone is as strong, as beautiful, and as healthy as us, they may not listen to us anymore."

I actually wish the humans would listen a little less to me. I tried to hold a press conference yesterday and riots broke out all over the world as people mobbed anyone blocking them from seeing my face on the television. There have been a rash of private boats and ships attempting to reach Ni'ihau. Poor Edam has had his hands full coming up with acceptable ways to keep our island safe now that I've announced our existence to the world.

"One of the largest issues we face," Franco continues, "with the newly expanded length of life, is that of overpopulation and production of sufficient agricultural commodities to feed and house the expected population going forward."

Governments all over the world are crumbling as the people realize they were merely shams for our leadership. It has made things easier and also harder. Many of the empresses from whom I took the reins of leadership were not kind, generous, or just. Their past actions have created an understandable lack of trust between the people and the evian leadership.

"Luckily, Chancery's complete and total popularity will make that particular solution possible," Alora says.

I really need to pay better attention. What solution? I clear my throat. "I'm sorry. Can we recap? What issue?"

A year ago, my daydreaming would have earned me a lecture from Mom. Now my entire Council shoots looks of pity and understanding my way.

"I'm not broken, you know." I mean, I am, but they can't see that, not just from looking at me. I know that for sure—I've spent far too much time staring at my new hair in the mirror. Despite all my attempts to regrow it the way it was, it always grows back the deepest black.

My hair reflects the state of my heart.

Three hours grind by, problem after problem after problem cropping up. And then I record another broadcast to inform the general public of our solutions. And I've had about enough of the ridiculous misconceptions. I decide to go off script and address that at the end of the broadcast.

"It has been brought to my attention that many of you saw me when I used the staridium to heal your DNA. I'm glad that the task was accomplished, and I'm happy it wasn't miserable or painful for you. However, I need to be very clear on something. I am not a deity, nor am I godlike. I was given a task to perform, and until we're able to establish reasonable, well-planned local governments for each region around the globe, I'm filling in as your leader. But I urge you—please do not pray to me. Don't mistake my actions as an instrument for a higher power as an indication that I *am* a higher power. I believe there *is* a God—but I'm not her or him or it."

I think about the advice Mom gave me via a letter right after I first ascended the Alamecha throne. *As a queen, you can never make any mistakes.* Except that's not possible, and covering up the truth only makes matters worse. I think about Inara and Eamon, and Enora and Balthasar. How much heartache, how many murders, and how much pain could have been avoided with a little honesty?

I stare intently at the screen. "I stumble. I make mistakes. I get angry when things go wrong. I'm as imperfect as all of you, and I don't want to ever represent myself falsely. The time of lies and deception is behind us, I hope. We need to move forward together, and that means you need to be able to trust me. When I make mistakes over the coming weeks and months, I'll tell you, and then I'll do my best to fix them and do better going forward. I'm going to ask the same of you. When you mess up, admit it, and then ask for help."

"And when you pray, don't pray to me. Pray to the God who gave me the power to heal a broken world. Ask God to help us accept the world as it is, or do the right things to change it for the better. That's my prayer for all of you. Have gratitude for what we've been given, and then work hard by my side to repair the things that are wrong. If we all do that, if we look at the world for the truth that's all around us, we can make this world into the one we all want."

Once the red button stops blinking, I head immediately for my room. Judica falls into step beside me.

"You know," I say. "You could grow your hair out black and do some of these for me."

She laughs. "Nice try. There's no way I could fake your general air of concern and love for all those morons out there. You've given them the world's greatest gift, at significant personal cost, and they're all sh—, uh, they're pooping the bed."

"Language," I say. "Mom would be furious."

Judica smiles. "Mother would be ecstatic right now. You fulfilled the prophecy, you're *pregnant*, and you have all the stones. She would love that the humans are literally worshipping you."

"I have all the stones alright—they're imbedded in my chest." I groan. "That's the first thing we need to fix," I say. "And the next is the worshipping thing. I think that once everyone realizes I'm a person like any other, they'll—"

"Oh please," Judica says. "They need someone to listen to, someone to believe in, and we need someone who can convince everyone else to create this new world order you're so keen to direct."

"Imagine it," I say. "Evenly split societies full of healthy, strong people working hard, improving things together, and taking care of one another."

My twin rolls her eyes. "People are still people, even when they're so-called perfect people."

"Agree to disagree," I say.

"Oh, I hope you're right," she says. "But I'm pretty sure you're not."

I duck into my own room and lie down on the bed. I could really use a nap. I'm not sure whether it's the babies, or the extended time I spent inside that tree, but I'm exhausted all the time. When I look through my back window at the beautifully flowering banyan-not-banyan, I notice that the framework for the archways has nearly been finished.

I'm not even surprised when Kali starts banging at my door. "Are you ready?"

I wave her past and follow her into the courtyard. We watch as the workers lift the heavy chunks of carved stone and place them in the inset wooden beams around the tree.

I'm not sure what I expected to have happen, but I'm a little disappointed when nothing does.

"Maybe it's too small," Kali says. "We should have followed the dimensions from the old Garden."

"That wouldn't have fit in the space," I say. "We'd have needed the palace torn down to replicate—"

"Palaces can be rebuilt," she says. "But this—"

A bird swoops by my face, and I turn to see where it came from. And I realize we might have been a little too hasty. Even though the tree is only a dozen yards ahead of me, I can't see it anymore. A vibrant palm, a towering willow, and a banana tree are visible through the archway, as well as azaleas, hibiscus, and birds of paradise, but no banyan-not-banyans.

I smile. "What was that you were saying?"

"I wish I could go inside," Kali says. "That's what I was saying. But since I can't, I'm glad I was able to see the tree before it disappeared."

The tree that absorbed her son. I step toward the archway, and she grabs my arm. "What?"

"Maybe you better wait," she says.

"Until?"

"Until you're only risking your own life by walking through those pillars."

"You're the one who insisted we set them up again," I say.

"It was my family's task."

"I think that time has passed," I say.

"Old habits." Kali walks toward the garden herself and reaches her hand out toward the entrance, but she stops a few inches short. "Once I've met them, I might try walking through myself."

Met them. I place my hand over my belly. "I'm sorry Noah will never meet them. Sorrier than I can articulate."

Kali turns around, her lips soft, her eyes kind. "I know you are."

"Thank you."

The next months pass in a blur of meetings, broadcasts, and visits to various locations to vet existing leaders and make decisions about new ones.

When I return from four days of nonstop meetings in India, tasks have piled up for me here.

"Education remains the top priority," I say to the Council. "It's the best way to prevent every possible issue we've encountered." One of the babies kicks hard, and I shift to give it more room. Not that any position is great when you're more than eight months pregnant with twins. And I'm so hot all the time—like monstrously hot. I never wore dresses before, but now I wear them all the time—for air flow. I smooth it down over my belly and shift in the hard chair. "You know that the locations with properly structured primary and secondary schools are transitioning the best."

"But education can't solve the issues of minimal resources and arid land," Maxmillian says. "The world aquifers are being depleted faster than they can be replenished, especially around large cities. So when we start talking about equitable division of resources into the formation of new countries, we can't ignore the fact that many of these locations aren't ideal. They won't support future population growth since they can't support themselves as is."

The issue of water comes up over and over, and it's vexing to say the least. We need water for actual use—drinking, cleaning, recreation—but we also need it for crops and cooling and animal husbandry. With a world so covered in water, you'd think it wouldn't present such complications. "Pull up the resource map again," I say.

"Which area?" Maxmilllian asks.

"I want to see the areas that are worst."

"Africa, if we're talking access for human consumption, but we immediately began to rectify infrastructure," he says. "But once it's all complete, they'll still struggle with having enough for everyone. And the Middle East and India have the same issues, as well as the central areas in the United States, and vast tracts of land in South America. There's just not enough fresh water to go around."

"Can you zoom out the entire map?" I ask.

He frowns, but he does it, pressing the clicker over and over to display it on the screen. At first I'm distracted by the names and places, the location of cities, and population figures. But then I blur my eyes, focusing not on the data, but on the topography. "The land," I say. "The earth."

"Yes?" Maxmillian looks at me as if I've lost my mind.

But Mahalesh's vision crashes over me then. When the stones shattered, at her request, the land broke too, spreading and changing. It was as fractured as the stones— and it has suffered along with the humans' DNA.

For the first time I realize that the land was also broken and requires repair.

I stand up. "I need to excuse myself."

Job leaps to his feet. He's still not an official part of the Council, though I should add him. He's been instrumental in preparing the educational materials for the humans around the world about what their bodies can now do, and how to treat them, how to optimize their performance.

But he has also followed me around like a bodyguard, watching for any sign of distress or concern. I think that Mom's death might have broken his brain. "I'm fine, Job."

"I'll come along just to make sure."

I don't scream at him, or fume, or even punch him in the nose, but I consider each in turn.

"How about I walk with her," Edam says. "I'll be sure to call for you at the slightest sign of trouble."

Job frowns. "Well, I suppose—"

I grab Edam's arm and practically sprint out the door. There's absolutely zero chance that Job will approve of my plan. Less than zero. Edam's unlikely to be pleased, but he doesn't fight me very often. At least, not anymore. I don't exactly sprint down the hall, as that has become harder and harder to do gracefully as my stomach has grown increasingly rotund, but I move quickly.

"Where's the fire?" Edam asks.

"Oh." I slow down. "No fire. I just needed a break."

He lifts one eyebrow dubiously. "You need a break from a Council session after asking Maxmillian to do something strange with a map, having an 'aha' moment, and then bugging out about Job following you?"

"What's an 'aha' moment?"

"When something amazing occurs to you, your breathing always hitches and the corners of your lips shift, not into a smile, but upward."

Edam pays far too much attention. I open my door and barrel through, shaking my head when another guard, Ulysses, tries to follow. He takes up a position outside, and I slam the door closed. "I'm sick of everyone dogging my moves like I'm an invalid. My pregnancy is healthy, and I haven't broken down sobbing in months."

"Not in public, anyway," Edam says.

The door to the hall is soundproof, but I found out recently that he can hear me through the window. "I am fine." I fold my arms over my belly.

"Define 'fine,'" he says.

What's his problem today? Usually he leaves me be— almost avoids me. I'm not sure we've been alone together since the day I woke up after being spit out of the tree. My hands spread out over my belly. Even if I'm totally off base, at least this might get him out of here. "Are you angry?"

"Angry?" Edam has never looked less angry.

"That I'm pregnant."

Once I caught Edam eating Cocoa Pebbles late at night, in the kitchen, alone. He has that same look on his face right now. Embarrassed, and maybe also hurt. He shakes his head. "Of course not."

"You're totally fine with it?" I look down at my stomach. "The fact that I'm going to be having two babies soon—Noah's babies—doesn't bother you? At all?"

"Of course not," he says.

I don't argue with him, I just stare at him. Because I know him well enough to know he's not really telling me how he feels, and I'm tired of ignoring it. "You haven't been in the same room alone with me in seven months."

His Adam's apple bobs up and down when he swallows. "You chose him, Chancery."

I did choose Noah. What did I think? That somehow, now that he's gone, Edam would just swoop in? Maybe I did think that, a little bit. "I did. I know I did."

"Do you know? I'm not sure you do. You've never been rejected—no one has ever picked someone else in your place. And now Noah has died, and you're all alone, and you're doing all these hard things without anyone else to rely on, but I can't be that person for you."

Because I injured him too badly. I get it, actually. I told him he's second best, and Edam's not someone who can ever accept second best. "You don't have to stay here," I say. "The world is full of perfection and beauty. You literally have billions of people from whom to choose. I wouldn't object if you wanted to make a new life elsewhere." And frankly, if he's going to be dating someone new, I'd rather not watch. It's monstrously unfair, given that he's had to stand guard at my wedding, and then watch day in and day out as my belly swells with Noah's babies, but there it is.

"This is who I am, and this is where I belong." He looks at his feet. "Have you been dissatisfied with my work?"

"Not at all." He has been the backbone of my Council, executing my plans immediately and flawlessly. In fact, he's proven to be far more resourceful and efficient than I expected, and versatile too. He's helped Maxmillian and even Franco on several occasions.

He bows. "Then I'll continue."

"Alright." I glance at the door, willing him to leave.

"But the largest part of my job is keeping you safe," he says softly.

"Great," I say. "Well, as you can see, I'm safe."

"You won't be in a moment, when you sneak through that door into the courtyard turned Garden."

"How—"

Edam touches my arm and a jolt of heat runs up my arm. We both jump away. "I know you, Chancy. I've always known you. You had that 'aha' look and decided to run back to your room." He lifts one eyebrow. "You've been wanting to go inside and see the tree for months, and no matter what idea you had, it's still a bad plan."

"I realized that the earth is broken, just like the DNA was," I say. "And I think I can fix it. Think about what that could mean! If the vast deserts could be farmed? If the areas without arable land could suddenly produce crops? And what about the weather? What if some of the destructive weather patterns—hurricanes, tornadoes, earthquakes—what if they're the result of the same damage?"

"What does that have to do with the tree?" He looks pointedly at the stone set in my chest. "Can't you test your theory with that?"

"It's connected somehow," I say. "I know it is."

"Well," he says. "In a few weeks, once you've had those babies, I'll go with you."

"No," I say.

"You let him walk through."

"He was mentioned in the prophecy," I say. "He could use at least one of the stones. I knew he'd be alright."

Edam shakes his head. "You let him give his life for you, and you won't even let me risk mine."

"It's not about that," I say. "I—"

A splash of water on the ground beneath me causes us both to pause. "Uh, what's that?" Edam asks.

"I think my water just broke."

26

"I'm, uh, I'll go get Job, then." Edam's still staring at the floor. "Is that normal?"

I laugh. If I hadn't done so much reading lately on what to expect, I'd be asking the same thing. "It is."

He nods a little too much. "Right. Okay, well, great." His eyes shoot up toward mine. "Is it too early?"

"I'm having twins, so they usually come early. But even so, two or three weeks early is fine."

"That's a relief. Okay, I'll go get Job."

I reach for his arm and stop short. "Judica too? And maybe Alora?"

"Should we call Noah's parents?"

I mutter under my breath. "I think we have to."

"Maybe she'll be a little. . .nicer," Edam says. "Since you're about to give birth."

"We can hope," I say.

Edam jogs to the door and then stops, his back still to me. "I'm excited for you," he whispers. "I think babies will help you with the grief."

My heart contracts—not just because he's right. But

because he still cares whether I'm grieving, even if it's for Noah. "Thank you."

I sit on the edge of my bed and place both hands on my stomach. "Well, babies, you're in for a rough few hours, but then there's a lot to look forward to—and I can't wait to see you for the first time." I lean toward my belly. "Mom loves you. No matter how you look, or how well you can use a sword."

Judica opens the door at that moment, suppressing a smile at finding me talking to my stomach.

"You can't tell me you aren't doing the same thing." I eye her stomach pointedly.

"I promise you, I have not had a single conversation of any kind with my whelp." She hates that I'm having *two* babies to her one. I bet she's annoyed that I'm already in labor, too. She's *so* competitive.

"Roman does all the talking, then?" I raise both eyebrows.

Judica groans. "He *sings to him*. It's so ridiculous. Like the baby has any idea what he's saying, or even who is saying it."

"I bet he loves Roman more," I say. "They say the babies can listen to us while they're in there."

Judica's nose goes up in the air. "Pah. He won't be such a wuss that he's swayed by singing, trust me. My son is going to be fierce. He'll come out swinging."

Movement from her belly draws my eye.

"See? He's already kicking." Judica winces.

"Uh, is he kicking? Or was that a contraction?" Judica's due two days after me—which kind of makes sense. We did get married at the same time.

"Please. If I was contracting, I'd know it." She walks toward me easily. "He just kicks hard." She sits next to me. "Does it hurt?"

"I'm not sure. I haven't felt a contraction yet," I say.

Judica scowls. "Edam just sprinted down the hall like a drama queen saying you were about to have the baby."

"My water broke," I say. "So technically he's right, but it might be a few hours."

"Excuse me?" Judica asks. "What in the world does that mean—your *water*?" She looks me up and down critically.

I arch one eyebrow. "Please tell me you read something to prepare you for having a baby?"

She frowns.

"Anything at all?"

She shrugs. "Why would I spend hours preparing for something that takes no time to do?"

"You spent years training for a challenge and they can take minutes."

She scowls at me. "That's not the same."

"Okay, but you read up on how to take care of a newborn. Right?"

"They have nannies for that," Judica says. "Honestly, Chancery, what kind of empress reads books on caring for babies when the world is in turmoil?"

Ohmygosh. "How are you going to feed yours?"

She twitches. "If you think I'm going to let a baby stick its face on my boob and eat from my body. . ." Her nose scrunches. "Pass."

The palace turns into a kicked hornets' nest moments later, Alora and Job descending together. Job keeps pressing his ear to my belly. "Is that really necessary?" I ask.

"You can hear their heartbeats," he says. "Right?"

I nod.

"But they're a bit of a jumble, mixing with yours and one another."

I shrug. I guess so.

"I'm just checking to make sure that there's no distress."

Of course everyone's super duper nervous, but it's

starting to annoy me, and that makes me snappy. "Will you all chill? Everything is fine."

"If you die, the humans-turned-evians will freak out," Alora says.

"What's the incidence of death of the mother in childbirth for evians?" I ask. "Less than one thousandth of one percent?"

"According to the records, it has only happened twice," Job says.

"In more than six millennia?" I laugh. "You guys need to calm the crap down."

"How regal you sound," Alora says. "Perhaps we should live stream this beautiful process for your concerned citizens worldwide."

Larena knocks and enters without waiting for my permission. "Your mother-in-law is en route."

Judica grimaces.

"I didn't realize you disliked her," I say.

My twin shrugs. "I don't really care. I never have to deal with her."

Then why the sour face? I glance at her belly, where her hand is pressed against it. "Are you in labor?"

"No way."

"How bad do you think these contractions I'm having feel?" I ask.

"I've heard people describe it," Judica says. "Childbirth is the worst thing ever."

I laugh then. "*Humans* describe it that way. They don't stab one another and walk across coals as part of their normal educational training. I'd describe my contractions, which are increasing in strength I might add, as mildly uncomfortable. Somewhere between a punch in the jaw and a broken elbow."

Judica's eyes go round.

"Are you contracting too?" Job leaves my side and

crowds Judica, who's clearly horrified. He presses his hand against her belly. "That's definitely the end of a contraction. Do you want me to find you another room?"

Judica shakes her head.

"You'd better go grab Roman," Alora says. I've never seen her look quite this entertained. "It's shaping up to be a very exciting day."

But of course, as if she predicted it, Roman races over, and then. . .nothing happens. In fact, after half an hour, I doze off.

Someone shakes me awake, gently. "Your contractions are worsening," Job says. "I'm not sure I've ever seen anyone sleep during this—without any kind of pain control."

I shift him aside and climb off the bed.

"You really should stay seated," Job says. "I think you're close to delivering, and this shouldn't surprise me, but Judica's almost ready too. I may need to have Alora catch one while I catch the others if you keep this up."

Judica beams at me. "I bet I beat her. I always was faster."

I walk toward the back door.

"Stop," Alora and Job say at the same time.

But I don't care what they say. I felt like I ought to go into the Garden earlier, and now the knowledge is like a weight on my chest. "Noah," I say. "He should be here for this."

"Get Edam," Alora whispers. "She's acting crazy."

Job runs toward the front entrance, but I'm nearly out the back door to the courtyard. No one is going to stop me, not this time. Noah disappeared into that tree, and I'm going to give birth to my babies next to it. I felt this morning like this was somehow connected to healing the world, and now my babies are coming. I've learned that coincidences, true coincidences, rarely exist. Not in my life, anyway.

"It won't bring him back." Alora grabs my arm.

"I know that," I say. "You think I'm insane?"

Judica follows me out the door, huffing through her nose. "Please come back inside, Chancy. You can't risk the babies, remember?"

I understand why they're worried, but I'm not. The stone in my chest is flashing, and there's a tug in my heart, pulling me toward the tree. I'm not sure why, but I've learned to trust it when I know something needs to be done.

I walk slowly toward the archway—staring at the variety of vegetation beyond the stone entry. It changes nearly every week. Right now, a vibrant lemon tree laden with bright yellow lemons, a lush magnolia with heavy, fragrant white blooms, and a riotous hot pink rhododendron lie just beyond the doorway. Butterflies and bees fly from one flower to the next, and a bluebird chirps at me.

Inviting me inside, maybe.

Edam races past Alora and Judica and grabs both my arms, his fingers circling my wrists, his grip gentle but entirely firm. "No."

"Yes," I say tightly, my throat dry as a contraction ripples across my belly.

"If for no other reason, you can't deliver your children alone."

Somehow I have to. I'll figure it out. Certainty fills every cell in my body.

"Then I'm coming with you," Edam says.

I turn to face him. "Absolutely not."

"It's safe for you?" he asks. "Then it's safe for me."

"And me," Judica says.

"If you're going, then I am too," Roman says.

"And me," Job intones. "I'm delivering these babies, or

I'm dying in the effort." He's holding a stack of white cloth in his hands, though what he needs that for, I have no idea.

Edam releases me, but he points at the archway. "You tell us. Are we all going inside? The days of Chancery the lone warrior against the forces of darkness are past. If you're in, we're all in with you."

"Not me," Alora says. "I don't want to explode into a million bits."

I laugh. Trust Alora to lighten the tension. Can I risk all their lives? I know I'll be fine—I know it in my bones. I also know there's something I need to see, or something I need to do, and it's related to the tree. I step closer, inches away now.

Edam mirrors me, his eyes flashing, his shoulders square.

I pull on the well of power inside of me and shove him back, just a few inches. "I could keep you all right here."

A muscle in Edam's jaw pulses, the one I love so much. "You won't do that. Not now. Trust goes both ways." The words he spoke earlier echo in my ears. *You let him give his life for you, and you won't even let me risk mine.* Why? Why was I alright with Noah walking into the Garden, but not Edam? Why did I accept Noah's sacrifices, and not Edam's?

I'm not ready to analyze that, not right now, not while another contraction grips me, and my babies are ready to arrive. Right now is the time for growth, for trust, and for healing. "Fine," I say. I either trust that this is safe, or I don't. "But I step through first."

Edam grabs my hand. "Together—I won't risk being locked out. And you need to know that you're not alone."

Judica circles and takes my hand on the other side. "You aren't alone." She squeezes my hand a little too hard, and I realize she's contracting too. We need to hurry.

"What about me?" Job complains. "You three all get to walk inside together, and I'm what? Your little helper?"

"Hello," Roman says. "I'm right here."

I laugh. "You are the most infuriating family in the world."

"Oh for the love," Alora says. "Fine. I'll come. Isamu is going to kill me—"

"Not if you explode," Judica says. "That's the beauty of this plan. If it doesn't work, kaboom, no more pain, no whiny relatives."

I'm smiling when we step through.

Judica's hand is still firm inside mine and so is Edam's. I walk one step and then another, leaving room for Job and Roman and Alora, who step through right behind us. Their gasps fill me with delight and wonder. Not a single snap, crackle, or pop.

And just like before, the entire landscape has changed, expanded, and shifted from what we saw before we crossed the boundary. No lemons or rhododendron blossoms spread out in front of me. There aren't a million bushes and flowering plants like the Chinese Garden, either. Maybe there hasn't been enough time. I feel like the inside of the garden is less illusion and more alternate reality.

The banyan-not-banyan rises before us, at least twenty feet taller than it was before, enormous white and blue blossoms scattered across its branches—but alongside those blooms, there are large buds in clusters of two.

"It's so big inside," Alora says, looking upward at the peacock blue sky and the outrageously large branches. "And is it just me, or is the grass almost unbearably green?"

Now that she mentions it, I notice that it *is* brighter, almost sparkly, like the sparkling facet of an emerald. Perfect down to every last blade, and evenly cut, as though someone rides a lawnmower as large as the island past, leaving no lines of any kind.

As a contraction grips me, I release Judica and Edam and walk closer.

"Don't touch it," Job says. "Remember what happens when you touch it."

"I need to touch it," I say.

"You're about to deliver," Job says. "What you need to do is lie down."

I can't stop moving, not yet. I walk toward the base of the tree, finding a smooth spot, free of roots and bumps, and I sit down next to it. "Here," I say. "I'll deliver right here."

Surprisingly, no one argues with me. Judica chooses a place a few feet away, and Alora sits next to her just as Job sits next to me. Edam takes a spot on the other side of me, and Roman sits on Judica's other side. It should be strange and twisted and bizarre, but like everything in this place, it's simply beautiful.

"When you feel like you need to push," Job says. "Do it."

I lean my head back against the grass, and Job shifts with Alora, downward so he can see what he needs to do. "You're at a ten, for sure," he says.

"So is Judica," Alora says.

And then it happens. My babies are coming—my arms twine upward, pressing against the base of the tree trunk. But this time, I don't blink out of existence. I don't disappear into the tree, and when I push, power surges, and as my baby is born, power explodes from inside of me and from the stones, into the tree.

"It's a girl," Job says, just as Alora says, "Your baby boy is so big!"

Alora hands Judica's baby to a beaming Roman and takes my little girl from Job.

"And again?" Job says. "I know you're tired, but you'll need to push again for the second baby."

But I'm not tired, not at all. I feel like I've just reached the top of a mountain, and I'm admiring the view. I bear down again, and Job catches my second child, and another well of power pulses from me into the tree.

"Whoa!" Edam's looking upward, and I focus on the tree above my head. "It's blooming!"

He's right. The twin bud clusters have all unfurled, one dark purple, one deep sapphire blue, and inside of each bloom is a glowing speck. Just like the seed inside of the charred bonsai that I fused with the ancient banyan.

Job creeps toward me, and he holds out a squirming baby, wrapped in white cloth. Duh—that's what it's for. Babies can't regulate their temperature well. I shove up to a seated position and take my son in my arms, staring into his alert face—eyes that are almost black staring at me from perfect, burnished copper skin. "His name is Noah," I say. "For sure." Because his father's real name may have been Sheva, but to me he'll always be Noah.

Edam moves out of the way as Alora walks toward me and places my daughter in my other arm. Her face is as light as baby Noah's is dark. Sky blue eyes and whitish blond hair, with squirmy baby legs and arms. "What about her?" Alora asks. "Name ideas?"

"Melina Inara," I say. "Because I think they both deserved better than they got, and this little girl is going to have *everything*."

A strange noise beside me, like an inhale that slurps pulls my gaze to the left.

Roman's arms are wrapped around Judica, and their baby son is nursing with Judica smiling down at him. I should be laughing right now, but I'm not.

Because even if my sister is doing everything she said she never would, all is right with the world.

27

Nine-hundred and forty-six glowing seeds sprang forth from the banyan-not-banyan on the day my twins were born. Nine hundred and forty-six chances to heal a cracked and bleeding world. It should be enough—more than enough.

I'm holding one on the tip of my finger, carefully balanced, with two dozen cameras pointed at me, but no red lights are blinking, not yet. "This is strange," I whisper. "I'm not sure whether it will work to record it."

"Why wouldn't it?" Alora asks, Melina sound asleep in her arms.

"Mom would say that it's not magic," I say. "But it sure felt like magic to me before, when I planted that first glowing speck and it fused to that banyan."

"Mother didn't know everything." Judica's son, Constantin, is strapped to her chest. Contrary to everyone's expectations, she has taken to motherhood like a pig to slop. She will hate that comparison. I'll have to remember it for later.

"She knew a lot," I say, "but not everything, no. I just hope this works—not only so that I don't look like an idiot, but because, look around."

Arid dirt mounded in erratic piles with very little in the way of plant or animal life spreads as far as even an evian eye can see. I chose Nevada to plant the first seed, in part because it was Mom's territory and I feel less bad experimenting on it, and in part because we own eighty percent of the state, so if I screw something up, I'm not damaging anyone in particular. The only real beauty out here is in the sunset. Well, that and the tiny details. The small miracles of life are beautiful everywhere.

An agile gecko darts behind a rock at the call of a golden eagle overhead. A sage grouse with its fluffy white collar forages in the sagebrush, and Joshua trees rise in various places near and far, their spiky arms entreating the sky, whether for rain or sun, I don't know.

"Why Warm Springs, Nevada?" one of the men operating a camera asks. "It's diabolically hot here, even in February."

I laugh. "You're not wrong, but that's kind of the point. If we're to heal the land, we need to start with the places that are the most broken, don't we?"

He shrugs.

Time to begin. "I'm ready," I say. "You can start recording."

Red lights blink and blink and blink. "I'm a little nervous," I say. "This is new ground for me—trying to allow all of you to witness my efforts live." I tap my chest where my white blouse frames the stone stuck half-inside my chest. "You've seen the rejoined staridium before, but you've never seen me use it. When it was shattered, thousands of years ago, it broke into several distinct parts— parts that now work in harmony to help heal, nourish, repair, shift, grow, and boost as necessary." I lift my finger in the air, the speck clinging to my fingertip in spite of the gusty, dusty wind tearing across the desert. "This seed came from the tree in my garden, the tree I used to restore the

DNA of people all around the world. I believe it's a gift meant to help restore the earth so that it can support an ever-increasing and longer-lived population. As we aid one another, as we work to heal our society, I believe that we can heal the whole world."

"Which is why I'm here, in Warm Springs, Nevada, a ghost town that used to be a stopover point for stagecoaches. There are some mostly dry springs that provided a bit of water, but certainly not enough to generate a consistent, sustainable ecosystem. We're pretty far from anything resembling successful farmland, and Nevada is the driest state in the United States of America, year round."

I shift and drop to my knee in front of the enormous Joshua tree behind me, carefully lowering the seed until it's nestled in the base of the Joshua tree. "A seed is a miracle in and of itself," I say. "It takes a tiny, inconsequential thing and from the inside of it explodes a mountain of growth and new life that didn't exist before. It takes a series of things—water, air, nutrients from the soil, and energy from the sun—and then that seed improves the world around it by cleaning the air and providing food and cover for animals and bugs. Sometimes we take these miracles all around us for granted, but we shouldn't. Each of them is a gift. They're reminders of the larger miracles in our lives like family and friends."

I place both hands over the seed and close my eyes, weaving the power inside my head into a blanket and dropping it onto the seed. At first, I feel resistance, like a barrier prevents me from reaching the seed, but I funnel more power and weave a larger blanket.

Then the stone flares, nearly blinding me, and the power the seed pulls is tremendous. Much more than a single seed anywhere would or could take. It pulls, and it pulls, and in seconds, I'm utterly drained and straining. I stumble forward, my face bumping into the rough, down-ward-pointing bristles of the trunk of the Joshua tree.

The ground beneath me trembles and clouds gather overhead, and I'm terrified that I've mistaken everything. Noah's tiny wail slaps my ears like a clap of thunder from where Isamu is holding him next to Alora.

And then the world goes deadly silent, and I smell ozone. The rainfall is sudden, the heavy drops pelting all of us, including the camera equipment. The camera people throw jackets and shirts up above them to keep filming. In the midst of the chaos and shouting, I almost don't notice the Joshua tree behind me, trembling slightly, as if it's buffeted by wind we can't feel.

I scramble away from it, waving Alora and Isamu back-ward as well.

If I'd waited a moment longer, I'm not sure what would have happened to me. The bark of the Joshua tree shifts, flaking away, and the trunk surges upward, colors exploding outward—as the Joshua tree transforms into something that resembles a rainbow eucalyptus, its branches soaring outward, its colorful trunk expanding.

"We need to move!" I shout.

Greenery springs away from the ground around the tree, leaves unfurling, branches expanding, and blossoms exploding.

The camera people, the onlookers, and my family all jog as quickly as we can from the epicenter where I planted the seed. Almost as quickly as we scramble away, the circumfer-ence of the rainstorm expands, and the vegetation aggres-sively sprouts.

"Throw it all in the jeeps," I shout.

My guards spring into action helping the camera crews, which are still filming, to load their gear. Edam practically tosses me into the biggest vehicle—a huge, open-topped Defender. Isamu passes Noah to me, who calms almost immediately when placed in my arms. Alora passes me Melina next, and they hop into the back of the Jeep. Edam floors it, but we're still soaked in the process, pelted by tempestuous gusts of rain. Newly sprouted plants growing underneath the wheels cause the vehicle to shudder and jolt as we drive.

"That was exciting." Alora's eyes are wide.

I turn my head sharply to the left, relieved to see that Judica and Roman and little Constantin are in a rugged jeep next to us, also flying over the expanding circle of greenery with a little difficulty.

"I'm voting we use helicopters next time," Edam says. "This is a little too exciting for me."

The earth splits with a crack next to us, water flowing upward from the dry dirt. "Hold on," Edam shouts. Roman and Edam both hang a hard right, flying across the undergrowth until they reach the highway. We drive at close to max speed for nearly two hours before leaving the rain behind.

"Petrified Forest National Park tomorrow?" I ask.

Alora and Edam groan, but I smile. Because it's working—we're changing the things about the world that need repair, one step at a time. And oh, the world we're going to create. It's staggeringly beautiful.

❧ 28 ❧

"I need a day off," I say.

"You should have taken a week off long before this," Judica says. "Three days after giving birth we started planting seeds all over the world. It's been a month, and we've already planted twenty-four."

"We have so many left to do," I say. "So much left to heal."

"This effort is a marathon," Judica says, "but you've been sprinting. Have you even taken the twins to meet their grandfather yet?"

I suppress the twinge of guilt—their grandfather murdered Eamon, the first Melina's father. Because he was jealous. It's not an easy thing to forgive, even for me. I'm saved from answering by a knock at the door.

"Come in," I say.

"You have a visitor." Frederick's eye twitches.

I suppress a groan. No one makes him look this ragged except Kali. I know exactly how he feels. I wish from the bottom of my toes to the top of my head that she'd head back to China. It's been a month of her visiting, which is about twenty-nine days too long.

"Where are those delicious little widdle babies?" Her eyes light up.

Judica mumbles some kind of excuse and slips out the door. Freaking coward.

"Oh! My bitty bitty Noah!" She lifts him from where he was sound asleep in his crib and rocks him back and forth.

I actually miss when she was trying to slice me up. The baby talk is going to *kill* me; either that, or I'm going to behead Noah's mother. Like, straight up. Oh, Noah. Why aren't you here for me to complain to? The grief washes over me, tearing into my heart like a starving hyena at the most inconvenient times. I wipe away a tear and turn to face Kali. I will not scream at my mother-in-law. I will not scream at my mother-in-law.

I will not scream at my mother-in-law.

"He was asleep," I say through gritted teeth.

She rolls her eyes. "Those rules don't apply to grand-mothers. They simply don't."

I clamp my jaw together so tightly that my teeth grind.

Kali's eyes widen, as if she's caught a scent and can smell an upcoming kill. "You've been crying."

How can she always tell?

"But you're not crying about my son, not now. He's been gone nearly a year."

As if there's a statute of limitations on grief. "I'm fine, Kali. Don't worry about me."

"Oh, I'm not worried." She turns back around, walking toward the window. "Frankly, I'm shocked it has taken this long."

"Excuse me?"

"Well, you've had the babies, and heaven knows you look like you've never had any."

Irritation snakes its way up my spine. "I'm evian."

"Of course you are, and you've seen to it that everyone is."

I sigh. "What are you saying, Kali? I'm too tired to argue with you right now."

She spins around, her eyebrow arched imperiously. "I'm ready, you know. I've prepared myself for you to—" She waves her hand in the air. "Have a new boyfriend, or marry him even, I guess. That seems more your style anyway."

I choke.

"Oh, please, like anyone will be surprised."

I can barely breathe.

She rolls her eyes. "Don't ever say I'm the one who held you back. Every week you wait is a surprise to me."

"I don't need your permission to do *anything*," I say softly, but a little too bitterly. "But you do need mine."

"What does that mean?" She narrows her eyes. "Is that a threat?"

"It's a reminder," I say. "That you're here, holding your grandson, on my grace."

"I think that perhaps the throne is finally going to your head."

"Unfortunately you can only stay for about five more minutes," I say. "I'm taking *my* children to see their grandfather."

"Gareth is—"

"*My* father," I say. "Balthasar."

I almost regret my rash words after Kali leaves—because now I'm pretty much stuck going to see him. It turns out forgiveness is harder than I thought. Once Kali's gone, Noah bawling, I nurse the babies. And then Melina spits up all over herself, so I change her.

Twenty minutes later, I've almost convinced myself that I don't actually have to do what I said I was going to do. Then Noah yawns and his mouth and nose are the cutest things I've ever seen.

A month—and Balthasar still hasn't seen them.

It's time.

I tuck one under each arm and head for the door. I've gotten much better at doing things while carrying them both—but I also always have more help than I need. I'm spoiled, but at least I know it.

"Where are you going?" Frederick asks.

"I'm heading down to the holding cells. It's time for the twins to meet their grandfather."

Frederick shifts slightly, his boots scraping the ground. If I didn't know him so well, I wouldn't realize he was nervous. "Can I hold one for you?"

I don't argue—I pass off Melina. She's happy no matter who holds her. Whereas Noah can't settle down without me most of the time. Frederick walks alongside me, waving two guards to fall in behind us. I don't think so many guards are necessary now that the rival families are gone—there's been not a single death threat or attack since I cleansed the DNA—but no one seems to listen. I got sick of arguing.

"Did you know?" I'm careful on the stairs down to the holding cells. I don't want to drop little Noah.

Frederick stills. "Know what?"

"That Mom and Balthasar—"

"I knew he loved her." Frederick's voice is sad. "He wasn't the only one."

That doesn't surprise me—I always thought maybe Frederick did. He certainly acted more like a father to me than anyone else. Why couldn't it have been him?

"But did I know that he was your father?" He shakes his head. "Enora was intensely private—no one knew her until she invited them in, and she certainly never acted any differently around him."

At least I wasn't the only one shocked by the revelation. The temperature drops precipitously down here and I shiver, squeezing Noah more tightly. I'm glad he's swaddled and tucked in well. We round the bend, and I see the one occupied cell, my heart racing. With all that's been going on, I've been able to avoid thinking about the fact that I still have a parent alive in the palace.

Each step is difficult, but I force my feet to keep moving until I'm standing in front of the cell bars.

Balthasar leaps to his feet and starts for the bars—then stills like he's worried he'll startle his dinner. I shouldn't think of him as a threat, but I can't help it, not now that I know what he is. Strangely, I never think of Edam in that way, as thought he might pose a threat.

"I'll be right here," Frederick says, handing me Melina and falling into line with the two dozen men standing guard.

Even so, I know that if my father got out, he'd mow through them all. Berserker. I shiver. It's in my bloodline—it could have been passed to either of these two angels. That's probably reason enough for me to learn what I can.

"I brought your grandchildren," I say tightly. "I thought I might trade a little time with them for a little information."

His brow furrows. "You don't need to trade with me. I'll tell you anything you want to know."

I will not feel sorry for him. I'm too soft as it is. "Nevertheless. Do you agree?"

He taps the bars. "These aren't necessary. I told you—I won't try and escape. I'll sit here and wait for as long as you ask. Or you can execute me and I won't resist. I understand. I was in the wrong, and I see that now. I'm many things, but I've never, ever been someone who can't admit when he's wrong and accept the consequences."

As far as I know, that's true. But what do I really know about him? Alora has told me that the bars aren't necessary, but how much does she really know?

I toss my head and a guard unlocks the door and swings it open for me.

Balthasar's eyes soften as he looks down at Melina and Noah. "They're stunning."

"Thank you." I don't want to care what he thinks, but I can't help it. I'm pleased.

"May I hold one?"

I shift Noah toward him, knowing that he'll cry the second he's taken from my arms. It's mean, but part of me is still so angry. I love him, and I hate him. I want to see him smile, and I want to stab him in the neck.

Balthasar's beefy hands, his fingers still blunted and calloused, even after almost a year in a cell, close around Noah, and I wait for the bawling to begin. But his dark eyes turn upward and when they lock on Balthasar's dark eyes, he beams, his entire face crinkling.

I've always thought Noah was a clone of his father, but for the first time ever, I realize he looks a startling amount like his grandfather, skin coloring aside. I want to snatch him back.

"He's the most beautiful thing I've ever seen." Balthasar, Warlord to Alamecha for nine centuries, cries then, tears rolling freely down his face. "I don't deserve this, but I'm grateful." His face turns toward mine. "Thank you. What can I tell you?"

"I'm afraid," I say. "For my children."

He sits down on the edge of his cot, snuggling Noah against his chest. "That they'll be like me." His expression is grim.

I nod.

"They might be, but it's exceptionally rare. I hadn't met another or heard of one, not in nine centuries. The last before me was my father. There were rumors that Edam's father. . .and at this point, given what we know, I'm guessing those were true. That makes only five of us in more than two thousand years."

"Which means it's unlikely that they'll be—"

"Like me," he says. "Correct. And I hope for their sake they aren't."

"Is it that bad?" I ask.

He shudders. "Yes and no."

"No one can defeat you," I say. "You're faster, stronger, and you heal faster."

He shakes his head. "We don't heal faster, that's just Edam. It's why he beat me."

"Then you're faster and stronger," I say. "Those don't sound bad to me."

"No." When he smiles, I see what Enora saw in him. Affection and a little bit of self-effacing humility. "That part isn't bad, especially if you have the heart of a warrior."

"What about it is so bad?" I ask.

"Berserkers only ever love one person with their whole heart," he says. "It's really helpful if they love others—it's important that they're surrounded by family. I only ever had my brother."

"Althuselah."

He nods. "He was the only one who ever cared for me, and I would have done anything for him."

"And that helped?"

"When we kill something, someone, something happens to us, a frenzy of fury. We can't stop ourselves—we attack everything we come into contact with, until we're left alone, or until someone we love can get through to us."

"Your brother did that for you?"

"He did, until I fell in love, anyway. Then it was much easier."

"With Mom," I say.

His voice is gruff. "Yes."

"After Althuselah died?"

He closes his eyes, his hands tightening on Noah.

"Before."

"I loved her from the moment I saw her," he whispers.

"But she married your brother," I say.

He shrugs. "I loved them both, so I never did anything to stop it. The adoration of a berserker only works one way. From what I hear, it's frequently unrequited." He pauses to let those words sink in.

Ah, poor Edam. And Inara. I fear anew for my children.

"Even though she loved my brother, I loved your mother every day that I knew her. And I loved my brother, too. Those feelings never twisted. When Althuselah died, it gutted me—and your mother. It killed us both. But then, something that was far worse happened."

Worse than his brother dying? Worse than his brother marrying the woman he loved? "What?"

"I hoped."

"Mom didn't ever want to remarry," I say. "Alora told me she said that."

"I was okay with that," he says. "It was as if something died inside her, and while it broke my heart to see it, I understood. You see, something died inside of me when he passed too."

"Until she met Eamon."

He stands up, and so do I, carefully taking Noah from him. "I'm sorry," he says. "It agitates me, talking about it, even now."

"And Inara was a berserker, too."

"From my father, yes, and Althuselah never told me." He winces. "That stings, but I understand why. As much as I loved Enora, we were all commodities to be used in her eyes. She loved Althuselah more than the world, but she'd have thrown him under the bus to save Alamecha if she had to. The family was always her one true love."

"You don't even sound angry about that," I say.

He sits again, staring at his hands. "I could never be angry at her, never, no matter what."

"You loved her that much?"

He laughs, but it's a hollow sound. "I'm not sure if it's even my choice, honestly. It seems, from what Gideon has told me, that Inara was the same. Those two cared for one another deeply and they meant to get married, until Eamon showed up. After that, she was—" He throws his hands into the air. "It's not the same for us." He stands up and looks me in the eye. "We love once, no more, no less, and it's absolute."

"That sounds like torture."

He closes his eyes and a smile spreads across his face. "It's not, or at least, it doesn't have to be. It's pure, it's consuming, and it's overwhelming, and that's freeing somehow. I've never been angry at your mother, and I never would be. I'd have done anything, killed anyone, and burned the world to the ground if she asked me."

"You very nearly did."

His face falls. "Yes, I nearly did. And I made some grave errors out of jealousy and misunderstanding, as you know. I wish I could take those back, and I know I can't." He brushes one finger down Melina's face. "I am sorry— terribly sorry. But I never would have killed Eamon had I not believed in my bones that Enora wanted him gone. You should believe that, not because I want you to think less of her, but because you should know the truth of it, at last."

Mom wanted Eamon gone—I don't even doubt it. Isn't that what spurred Inara to murder her? What a mess.

"I'll come back," I promise. "Sooner and more often this time." But I can't stay here, not anymore. Not right now.

"I hear you're doing amazing things—healing the world, from the center of the earth out. I want you to know that I couldn't possibly be more proud of you. As blind as both your parents were, it's a miracle that you see so very much."

"I prefer to think of you as star-crossed," I whisper. I lean up on my toes and press a kiss against his cheek. And then I dart out of the cell with my babies and jog up the stairs toward my room.

Looks like I won't be taking that break after all—because after today, I really need to get back to doing something helpful in the world.

❧ 29 ❧

I climb the steps to the raised platform quickly—it took forever to pry Melina away from my leg. If Balthasar hadn't offered her a lollipop, I might be making this address with her on my hip.

Warm Springs isn't even recognizable, not now, almost two years after I first planted the seed. The platform is fifty feet off the ground, and the stands expand hundreds and hundreds of yards away from it in carefully shaped rows. Beyond that, everything in Warm Springs is comprised of hundreds of shades of green, as far as the eye can see. For now, the area around the rainbow eucalyptus tree is still a public park. We may need it in centuries that come for cropland, but we're making far, far more food than we need right now. Saving excess crops in the frozen tundra up north was a stroke of brilliance by Maxmillian that I hope we'll never need.

"I am Chancery Alamecha, and I am delighted to welcome all of you to the very first World United Games!" I shout, almost as soon as I reach the microphone.

The cheering is practically deafening.

"I've chosen to do the opening ceremonies here, in

Warm Springs, within a few hundred yards of where I planted the first seed from the Garden, in the lush embrace of a verdant new park that we dedicated last year. Until recently, the evians held our own games, while the humans held the Olympics. I can't tell you how delighted I am to combine the best parts of both things in celebration of the new world we're creating together."

More cheering, and this time, the large screens behind me show footage from gathered crowds across the world. "Thanks to the amazing technological advances of this century, we're able to share this in high-definition 3D with citizens around the globe. I hope we'll all approach these games with excitement and benevolence. The lines of many nations have been redrawn, balancing populations, resources, cultures and world religions to optimize both standards of living, and harmony in co-habitation. Over the next few years, each of your new countries will begin to elect their local leaders, and my hope is that very soon, I won't be needed to do much of anything at all. I want you to trade and grow and share and learn together, as neighbors, family, and friends. And as I think we've proven in the past few years, we're all so much better together."

"Synergy is a funny thing. In the world before, everyone was trying to grab the biggest piece of pie and shove it in their mouth, but now, as we share, the pie only grows. That's why this year, our games will focus on team sports above all else. Team combat, team rowing, team dance, and team races, many of them relays. I want each of you—here and at home—to think how you can work with others to improve the world for all of us."

I pass off the entire presentation to Annabelle, a human turned evian with a flair for presentation and engagement. She announces the various sports and activities and the schedule for each, and then each new nation is able to present its flag, followed by its competitors. We stole that from the Olympics. It's a wonderful way to allow each to feel pride in their accomplishments while still being part of a greater whole. Colors, symbols, mottos, they all help us appreciate and understand those around us.

"That went well," Alora says.

Noah stiffens against her until she finally releases him and he runs toward me as quickly as his short legs can carry him. I swing him up on my hip without thinking—a toddler on my side has become such a fixture in my life.

The bigger surprise is that Melina has fallen asleep on Balthasar's shoulder. "I think she was tired," he rumbles softly.

She loves her grandpa, and he adores her too. It was the kids' begging that finally forced me to free him almost a year ago. They're really hard to deny, if I'm even one percent unsure about my course of action.

"Let's get them to bed," I say.

"Holding this two hours before sunset was a stroke of brilliance," Edam says. "These things always drag on for far too long."

I smile. "We've still got the ball to attend."

Judica groans. "Do we have to go?"

"Yes," Roman says. "Because you look amazing in that gold dress, and you promised me." Constantin leans over his father's shoulder, using Roman's ears as handles, and tries to grab a flower off a rhododendron. Its bright magenta blooms are toxic, however. They wouldn't kill him, but he wouldn't feel great for a while.

"Don't let him put that in his mouth," I say. "It'll make him sick."

Roman bounces a few times and races forward, Constantin squealing with joy. "Last one to the state house gets to change all the diapers!"

That's enough to put a spring in my step, and Roman and I beat everyone else to our row of rooms. Not that I really mind a little poop—not really. It's almost cathartic, doing such mundane things after the past few years of the bizarre, tragic, and scarring.

Judica complains about it, but I know she secretly loves the bedtime routine as much as me. Cranky, whiny children are fed, bathed, dressed, snuggled, and rocked off to sleep. My favorite role in the world is parent. But once they're asleep it's time to dress and transform into Chancery Alamecha, empress of the world.

When there's a knock at the door, I rush to answer it. I don't want Varvara to wake the babies, or I'll be late.

Except it's not Varvara.

It's Kali.

The last person I really wanted to see right now, if I'm being honest.

"Can I come inside?" She pushes past me, because as always, asking is a courtesy, but not really a request for permission.

"Make yourself at home," I say softly, "but please don't make much noise. The twins are asleep, and I've got a gala so I don't have time to—"

She waves her hand through the air as if I'm a child myself, prattling on about nothing important. I hate how idiotic she always makes me feel.

"I won't take much time," she says. "I promise."

"Is anything wrong?" Now I'm actually worried.

She draws in a tortured breath. "Not for you—not with you. No, nothing is wrong."

Okaaaay.

She twists her hands together. "I'll never forget the moment you first arrived on the front steps of our palace, tugging my son along on a silken cord."

I did no such thing, but of course she knows that.

"I resented you for the hold you had over him. I hated that he valued your opinion and cared for you so much more than he did for me—I had given birth to him, after all. I had taught him everything, sacrificed everything, and even trusted him with my birthright." She glances pointedly at my stone.

I wonder whether all the empresses still resent me for this. My hand brushes against it involuntarily. It's a part of me—it's not like I can give it back.

"But that's not why I'm here," she says. "In fact, it has taken me far too long to come to you and confess this."

Confess?

"When you arrived, it was in my son Isamu's jet."

I remember that.

"After you left, in a jet we provided, I was upset, drowning really. Furious and jealous, hurt and scared."

She's never been this emotive, even with her own grandchildren. I'm genuinely worried about what she might say.

"I watched the security feed from your flight the day you left. Most of it was, as you would expect, quite boring, but part of it was eye-opening."

"Please tell me I don't drool when I sleep."

For some reason she turns her head away sharply and wipes away a tear. "There's a lot of his playfulness in you, you know. It's clear that you were made for each other, which must be some kind of twisted cosmic joke. Why God would create the two of you, and also *him*, and then destroy my son—" She brushes her cheeks and straightens her shoulders. "Also not the point."

Also him? "What is your point?"

"I have behaved poorly. I'm positive my son is seething. Well, either that, or he's terribly disappointed in me. I've known this since right after he left, and I've allowed you to writhe anyway. Perhaps I hoped that you'd betray him—his memory anyway. I hoped you'd prove yourself to be unworthy of him, but no. You haven't. You've been the best mother—" Her voice cracks, and she thrusts a jump drive at me. "Watch this. It will explain better than I possibly can. I'm not sure exactly what complications are holding you back, but if one of them is something I said, or the memory of my son, well." She covers the bottom of her face with her hands for a moment.

I take the jump drive.

"If it's Noah's memory, or if it's something I said that's causing you to do everything alone, I'm sorry."

I have no idea what it cost her to say that. A lot, I'm sure.

"He's been gone for three years," she says.

Three years, two weeks ago.

"You've proven to be a far more adept, insightful, and skilled ruler than any of us could have hoped. Noah made the right decision. You have made me proud." She spins and races out the door before I can object, and I'm left staring at a tiny metal jump drive.

I walk quickly to my laptop—Varvara will be here any moment. I stick it into the port and wait while it pops up on my screen. The image is grainy, but it's clearly a video of Edam and Noah, walking down the aisle in the back of the plane. Right before Edam bowed out—just moments before he told me that Noah was the one for me.

"She loves you," Noah says.

My heart breaks a little, looking at his face, so resigned, so defeated.

"She does," Edam says.

"That's not the right phrase," Noah says. "She *loves* me. She *burns* for you."

Edam smiles, and it's so beautiful that it cuts like a knife.

"You could beat me," Noah says.

"I will. When she's pressed, she'll choose me."

"And I hate that I have to ask this," Noah says. "You have no idea how badly I hate it."

"Ask what?" Edam's hand grips a seat, compressing the top so hard that the plastic audibly creaks.

"You've heard the prophecy," Noah says. "What you may not know is that she'll save the world, but she'll die doing it."

Edam blurs on the screen, his hand suddenly at Noah's throat. "She will not die."

Noah chokes, but his head nods. "Will," he barely spits out.

Edam's hand tightens and Noah's face correspondingly whitens. "I'll never allow it."

Noah goes limp, and Edam drops him abruptly as if he wasn't even aware of what he was doing. Noah hits the ground, but revives quickly, rubbing his neck with both hands. "You're a scary dude, for real. But that won't save her, not from what she faces." Noah stands up and stares Edam in the eyes. "Only I can save her."

"No." Edam shakes his head and backs up. "I can save her."

Noah frowns. "Believe me, I wish you could. You have no idea how badly I wish you were the Lost and I was the heartthrob with the biggest sword." His wry smile kills me.

"What are you saying?"

"I had a vision when I was a kid." Noah blinks, as if he's surprised he can say the words. "I haven't been able to tell her, but for some reason, I seem to be able to form the words for you. You'll find out more, and this will make more sense, but I've known for a very long time that I had a choice to make. The Eldest will save the world with or without me—and I can help her, or I can let her do it alone. But if I don't help her, she will most certainly die."

Edam's eyes are full of such rage and such pain and such helplessness that I wish I could reach through the video and hug him.

"You want that task," Noah says. "And it's so stupidly ironic—because you have the *best* job here. Don't you see that? Loving me and choosing me, and then losing me when she saves the world, it's going to *wreck* her. She'll need you then, more than she's ever needed anyone—and you'll get to spend the next nine centuries with her." Noah steps closer, his voice low and urgent. "I'll get her for a week. You get her forever."

"You'll break her," Edam says, his eyes full of tears. "That will kill me. I can't watch it."

Noah smiles then. "But you didn't say that it'll kill you for her to choose me." He drags in a terribly ragged breath, and looks upward. "That's what I needed to know. I needed you to care more about how she would feel than about your own pain."

Edam's fists clench at his sides. "Of course I care more about her."

"Good, then we can save her together. If you break her heart, if you end things with her today, I'm confident that she'll pick me. And I'll keep her alive as she saves the world." Noah whispers. "You just have to hang on until she's ready for you, because if you make your move too fast, guilt will eat her alive until she's only a shell. That's the biggest problem with someone as *good* as her. Can you do that?"

"I can do whatever she needs," Edam says. "Always."

Noah claps him on the shoulder. "Good man."

It's strange to watch myself burst through the door from the front of the plane. "We're landing," the naive Chancery-frozen-in-time says.

"Right," Noah says. "We were just reviewing Chinese etiquette."

I freeze the video on his face. How could Noah have known me so well? How could he have realized what would happen and how, and have been willing to walk into the fire, his head held high, knowing exactly how badly he would burn?

Varvara arrives then, completely oblivious to what I've just learned. It helps me—to have to react to someone else, to act as though my heart hasn't been sundered in two and sewn back together with dental floss.

"Why does Judica get a simple silk shift?" I complain.

Varvara's smile suffuses her entire face. "You're not only a mother, a friend, an enemy, and a lover. You're the queen of the world, the saver of all the children of Eve, the bearer of the stones, the mother of a new earth, and the healer of the broken."

"Oh come on," I say. "Don't be ridiculous."

"This dress says all of that and more." She smooths down the ridiculously full burgundy silk skirt that bells outward from my waist.

"What part of that list requires me to be naked from the waist up?" I arch one eyebrow.

She laughs. "You're ridiculous." She turns me toward the mirror. "Naked." She snorts.

I may not be naked, but it's far closer than I like. Deep crimson flowers snake upward, crawling over the gauzy illusion bodice that covers me from my wrists to my shoulders and down to my waist. I may technically be covered, but the illusion bodice truly covers nothing. If not for some very carefully placed flowers, I'd be horrifying a lot of people worldwide.

"I think—"

Vavara presses a finger against my lips. "You've been the ingénue. You've been the mother. Now it's time for you to be a *woman*."

I don't like the sound of that, but she silences all my protests and shoves me into a chair. After a stupidly long amount of time spent brushing and curling my boring ebony hair, she brushes gloss across my lips.

"You may ask Judica and Alora. If either of them recommends that you change your gown, then fine. We'll look for something else. But look at how the deep red offsets your skin, your eyes, and your ebony hair." She points at the plunge in the bodice. "And how expertly Marchesa framed your stone. It's even flashing with more red than usual, as if it approves."

Don't personify it, Mom would have said. Magic isn't real. Oh, how I miss her, still. "Alright," I finally agree. "We'll see what they have to say."

Marselle arrives then, to watch the twins, and she freezes in the doorway. "That's—you're—wow."

I can't tolerate another second of Varvara's gloating, so I don't dally. "I'm meeting everyone in the courtyard."

"Have fun," Varvara says. "And no going morose, you hear me?"

"I'm never morose."

Neither of them argue, but they don't meet my eye either. Are they right? Have I been depressing? Well, not tonight. I'm resolved.

Alora, Isamu, Judica, and Roman all love it, and their gushing irritates me. "Where's Balthasar?" I ask, because I'm too big a chicken to ask what I really want to know.

"He and Edam are there already, hammering out last-minute security protocols," Roman says. "Frederick and his crew will run point to get us there."

My skirt takes up almost the entire seat in the suburban on the way to the Event Center in Nouveau, the city that sprung up almost overnight, not far from Warm Springs. Alora waves Isamu off. "There's barely room for me. Go with them."

He frowns, but he climbs in with Roman and Judica without voicing any complaints.

"You look nervous to me," Alora says.

I shake my head, the red ruby earrings Varvara insisted on adding at the last second swinging. "I'm fine."

"You're so used to being around adoring masses that I wonder what could have your heart pounding like that." The corner of her lip turns up. If she says anything else, I'm going to turn around and head back to my room and claim that Noah wouldn't let me leave.

Ah, Noah.

I've grown so accustomed to thinking of Noah as my *son* that when I remember *Noah*, sometimes it takes me by surprise, wrenching something inside of me.

"It's okay," Alora says, "for you to be excited."

Guilt. And horror. And fear. And yes, a thrill of excitement. Too many emotions—I should really skip this stupid celebration.

Frederick turns his head back toward us. "We're here."

My heart accelerates, and the stone flashes with something I swear resembles excitement. The door to the suburban opens, and a hand drops down in front of me. I'm used to being helped out of cars when I'm dressed for events, so I take it without thinking.

Heat rockets from my fingers to my arm and slides up toward my racing heart, and *I know*. It's not a guard. It's not one of Balthasar's people.

It's Edam.

It's been years now, the better part of three, that we've taken great pains not to touch. He almost avoids me like I carry the plague. I don't even blame him. I hurt him—I know that. But now I wonder if it wasn't more than that. Was he waiting all this time. . .for me to be ready? For my heart to heal and the guilt to recede?

I step out, my crimson painted toenails encased in silvery Louboutin sandals poking out underneath the billowing skirts, and Edam lifts me smoothly to my feet, his eyes sliding from my face to my chest and downward. His hand tightens on mine, and my entire world narrows to slowing the hammering of my heart in my chest.

When I look up at him, he smiles his devilish smile, an expression I haven't seen in years.

Alora must be dying—or maybe not.

Maybe no one else can feel what I feel, the searing heat, the shivering excitement, like the world is turning too fast, like time is sliding down, down, down a yawning chasm, never to be recovered. Like I want to fast forward and pause the same scene and play it over and over until the whole thing glitches and the television explodes.

"I've never seen anything so stunning in my life," Edam whispers, his breath against my ear. Then he straightens and guides me toward the entrance, moving smoothly into place behind Judica and Roman.

I'm aware that Alora joins Isamu, and they circle around to stand behind us. I'm aware that others mill around us, nodding and waving and welcoming me. I'm aware and my body reacts as it ought, my mouth expelling words that people expect, but it's as if I'm operating on autopilot. My entire focus, all my attention, narrows to the place where Edam's hand touches mine. The world rotates on its axis like normal, but we don't turn with it. No, we're in some kind of free fall, a place outside of space and time.

"Would you be opposed to dancing with me tonight?" he asks.

I don't dare meet his eyes. I'll incinerate, I know it. I nod numbly.

"Chancery?" Edam's voice is light, warm, playful almost. "Look at me."

No, I won't, I can't, I shouldn't. But my chin rises anyway, my eyes trailing up his black tux from his knees to his flat waist, where I know a washboard stomach hides, and sliding past his powerful chest, to his chiseled jaw and

the shimmery bit of golden stubble he never quite elimi-
nates, to his angled cheekbones and finally, to his eyes.

They're a deep, fiery sapphire blue. They burn into me,
a shiver running from my shoulders to my toes. "What?"
My lips move, but I have no idea what I'm even saying.
Why did he want me to meet his gaze? What does he want
from me? "I'm looking."

And for the first time, I am. Like the tree in the
Garden, he practically glows. A smile starts in his eyes, and
travels to his mouth, revealing shiny white teeth underneath full, smirking lips. My own lips part, and I sigh.

"Let's dance." His voice is low, rough, hypnotic.

I bite my lip, and he tugs me toward the dance floor.
Only then do I realize it's entirely empty. With steady, sure
steps, he leads me to the very center. The symphony plays
the opening notes of Beethoven's fifth. My eyes fly to his—
it's the first song I ever queued up on the computer that
first time we trained. That was the first time we were alone,
other than the moments I spent as Judica talking to him in
the stable. It's not a very good song for partner dances, but
it doesn't matter. Not with Edam.

His breath against my ear as he rests his hands on my
waist combines with the pounding of his heart, and I know.
I couldn't hear his melody then, not in the early days, and I
haven't been training, not in melodics, not for a long time,
but I open my mind to listen now, to the song around us, to
the melody inside Edam, and we move together. He backs
up, and I press forward. His hands fall back and mine move
with them. He spins and I pivot, and in an unchoreo-
graphed performance, we undulate, completely in sync.

At first, it's the sheer joy of dancing, the delight in
reading a melody, and then it's the thrill of performing. But
then, as the song crescendos, I realize that it's more than
that. For the first time maybe since I fought Judica, I hear
my own melody. It rises, it falls, complex and with great

depth. Mother, sister, daughter, friend. Warrior, empress, healer, supplicant. Grace, hope, peace, and forgiveness combine within me to show me that I can do this, I can move past the soul-rending wound I was dealt, the sacrifice demanded as payment of the great good I was able to accomplish.

And I let go of the guilt.

When the song ends, Edam and I are both out of breath, his hand resting against my cheek, our bodies pressed from my chest down to our knees.

The audience cheers loudly, and it frees me from the spell that has fallen over me. He takes my hand in his and we bow together, and then we walk off the dance floor while others flood it. More era-appropriate music begins, a mixture of the before and the now.

"We need to talk," Edam says, his hand at my waist.

"Yes." It's all I can manage to say, but I follow him out of the main event area and around the corner. He winds up a stairwell and steps out onto a balcony overlooking Nouveau's downtown skyline. "How did we escape without guards?"

Edam laughs. "Frederick will suffer a cardiac event any moment and that will distract them a few more minutes. I'd say we have five minutes before Balthasar pulls the feed and finds us here."

"Five?" I lift both eyebrows.

"Probably an optimistic estimate." His hands tighten around my waist. "Which means we don't have much time."

"We've already wasted too much," I whisper.

His mouth opens and his eyes widen, hope shimmering in their depths.

"I have a question." I press one hand against his chest, my fingers curling against his warmth.

"Anything."

I force myself to look up at him. I need to know the

answer—maybe more than I've ever needed anything. "Balthasar and I spoke," I say. "About berserkers."

He swallows. "Okay, but that's not a question."

"My father loved my mother for nine centuries. She never—they didn't—" This is hard to articulate. "Inara loved Eamon, Melina's father. And he—" I shake my head. "She loved him anyway. In spite of his betrayal. There was so much pain and so much damage and so much raw—"

Edam touches my lips with one finger and need arcs through me. I sway against him. The connection is real. I have no idea how Mom and Eamon could possibly have resisted the connection with Balthasar and Inara. I have no idea how *I* did. "You're worried that you hurt me, but I'm fine. I'm better than fine."

I scramble backward. I can't think when I'm touching him. "That's not it." I blink. "I mean, yes, I do worry about that. But what I want to know—my father told me that he didn't have a *choice*. He said that no matter what she did, no matter how she treated him or anyone else, he would have loved my mom. I think maybe Inara was the same with Eamon, and I don't want that for you and me. I don't want someone who's dragged through the gutter, forced across hot coals, and shoved into loving me against what would have been his will if he was allowed to have it."

His smile is radiant—like sunlight after the ravages of a hurricane. "You've never done anything that tortured me— except for loving him, and you couldn't help that. You had less choice than me when the prophecy stole your life. But unlike Inara, unlike Enora, you shone brightly through it all. You chose goodness, purity, and all that is right and true. You've been a beacon to the world, but also to me, standing tall as you plowed through all opposition. You have embodied your family's motto at every turn. You've been the change in the world."

"But you may only think that—"

"Enough." He steps toward me, his hands gathering me against his chest. "You're looking for reasons because you're scared. Without this connection, a connection I've ignored and denied for years and years now, I still long for you. When you're nowhere near, when you're miles away, I still pine. You're all I want, all I care about, and all that matters, and it's my *choice*, as it was my choice to watch you save the world arm in arm with Noah." He drops a kiss on my forehead. "I *choose* to love you every single day. It's the singular joy of my life, loving you."

He leans toward me, his lips drawing nearer with each breath. "Noah made me a promise, and he fulfilled his end of that deal. I stepped aside for him, and he kept you alive for me. *Forever*, that's what he promised me. So you asked me before whether I minded that you had children with him, whether it bothered me that you loved him. And the answer is that I will never mind. I'll always be grateful for him and for the gift of my life with you. Those children bring you joy, and it's my chosen duty to protect and prolong and cherish every single thing that makes you smile. I love them as I love you—unerringly, unwaveringly, and without condition."

His mouth covers mine then, and my heart soars. Up, up, up. Gone.

A heavy metal door bangs open behind us. "Are you kidding me?"

Edam releases me with a heavy sigh. "To be continued," he whispers.

I can't suppress the smile. "Promise?"

Balthasar bellows. "You two aren't children. You can't run and hide in stairwells. No one thinks it's cute."

"I do," Edam whispers against my mouth with a smile. "I think it's irresistible. Marry me. Be mine forever."

"Yes," I say. "I will."

Edam's unworldly strong arms lift me up and throw me

into the air, hundreds of feet above the ground, the stars twinkling above our heads.

My father shouts, but I don't care. It's nice to feel young for a moment, to feel reckless and wild and free. And when I fall back down toward the earth, Edam's arms catch me.

They always will.

❧ 30 ❧

"**W**hy is that dress so weird?" Melina asks, her head tilted sideways.

Varvara frowns. "This dress belonged to your grandmother." She tsks. "It was Enora's wedding dress."

Noah tugs on the long, draping sleeves that split open along my forearms and then fall nearly to the floor. "You can't get a new one?" He scrunches his nose. "Because if you can't, I still wouldn't wear this. I would wear the sparkly blue one." He points at my closet.

"You're being very rude," Varvara says.

"It's fine," I say. "They're not even three years old yet." I crouch down and gather them next to me, their inquisitive eyes wide, their minds receptive and curious. "Your grandmother Enora was stunningly beautiful."

"Like you?" Melina asks.

I touch the underside of her chin. "Like you."

She beams.

"And she met two men a very long time ago."

"Two strong men," Noah says.

I nod. "Indeed. Althuselah and Balthasar. They were

355

brothers."

"Grandpa?" Noah frowns. "But he's still alive."

"That's a long story," I say. "And I'll share it with you sometime. But when she met the brothers, she first fell in love with Althuselah, and they were married for more than eight hundred years."

Both of their mouths drop.

"It's a lot of tens." They're familiar with ten, as they regularly count their fingers. "But my mom can't be here. There was a lot of confusion, and some really big mistakes were made, and she died." They've both seen me crying over Mom being gone, so this isn't new to them. "I decided that since she can't be here, and to honor the marriage she had with Althuselah, I'll wear her old dress today."

"It's all those tens of years old?" Noah strokes the sleeve. "It doesn't seem crumbly and old."

I laugh. "Well, to be perfectly honest, the actual dress is still in her vault." I point at the locked door. "It's not in the best shape, precisely because it's so many, many tens of years old. But this one was recreated as close to hers as we could get." I touch the exposed stone in my sternum. "With a few modifications."

"So she can't come, but you feel like she's here." Melina smiles. "That's a good idea. Is our Daddy coming too?"

Oh, my heart. "He can't," I say. "That's why we're using all the flowers from the banyan-not-banyan." I brush the hair out of her eyes. "Your Dad wishes he could be here so bad, and he wishes he could pick you two up and carry you and hug and kiss you."

"But he can't," Noah says. "So Edam's going to love us and take care of us for him."

"That's true," Kali says from the doorway. I wonder when she ducked inside. "And I can't think of anyone I'd trust to take care of my treasures more." Her arched eyebrow tells me that it pains her to say it, but that she's speaking the truth. "And of course, grandpa and I are here too."

The kids run over to their grandmother. "I'll take them and keep them entertained until you're ready." She looks me over head to toe. "You look very beautiful. An enchanting mix of past and future."

"Thank you." I mean it. It's very generous of her, to come and to support us. Supporting my wedding to Edam must have been a nightmare of hers for quite some time, and yet here she is. She has grown a lot in the past few years.

A few moments later, Varvara has tied the laces in the back of my deep sapphire silk gown, and positioned the simple gold circlet the way she wanted it in the mound of black hair she prepared on top of my head. "Those accent flowers are perfect," she says. "Where did you get them?"

The tiny blooms also came from the banyan-not-banyan. It continues to bloom with the large, fragrant blue and white blooms that are often the size of dinner plates, but it also occasionally blossoms with the tiny flowers that provided nearly a thousand glowing speck seeds—the seeds that healed the earth and made all the dry and arid valleys and mountains fertile again. "They came from Noah."

She frowns, but she doesn't press. "You're ready."

When I open the door, Balthasar is standing outside, fidgeting with his tuxedo. "Oh." His eyes fly wide. "You're wearing—"

It didn't occur to me that he'd be outside my door. "You're, why are you, I mean—"

"I asked Frederick if I could steal a word," he says. "I know I haven't earned it, and it's fine if this isn't—"

"You can walk me down the aisle," I say. "That would make me happy."

He freezes, and then a smile spreads across his face slowly. He opens his arms and I walk into them. They tighten around me, his head dipping toward my hair. "You have brought me more joy than I ever imagined, certainly far more than I deserve."

"I'm sorry you missed my first wedding," I say. "And Judica's too."

"Your twin is just like me," he says. "Too much like me. I doubt she'll ever forgive me."

"It just takes her longer to warm up to things," I say. "But her heart is as big as Texas. She'll eventually come around."

He releases me. "I hope you're right, but even if you're not, I've been granted more grace than I deserve."

"Thank you," I say.

"For what?"

"For loving my mom, and for being willing to accept when you were wrong. And for wanting to walk me down the aisle today."

He tucks my arm into his elbow and starts down the hallway for the main palace entrance. "You deserve this, and the universe needs it. Two happy love stories instead of only one. That must be a blessing. And a man whose heart is big enough to love you all."

I know exactly what he means—me and my beautiful children. Noah's legacy. I can't think of many people who would be that strong. We've reached the heavy wooden doors, always so at odds with the entire vibe of an island palace. But standing in this dress, I finally understand them. Mom picked a modern island—in a beautiful string of islands—to make her new home. But she brought with her the weight and wisdom of her past. And now I'm carrying it forward too, into a future that none of us can predict or prepare for.

But at least I'll have a solid team behind me as we march into the unknown.

My dad pushes the doors open and the first chords of

the wedding march play. Traditional and historical and modern. A hundred paces ahead of me, Edam's standing just out of reach of the waves, in the black tuxedo that no one wears as well as he does. His sapphire eyes, the exact color of my dress, shine so brightly I can see them from here. He smiles, his white teeth biting his lower lip when he sees me.

I can't suppress my answering smile. As I walk toward him, my dad at my elbow, my sisters all gathered in a row as I pass, my heart is full. At the sound of a giggle in front of me, I look down to where Melina and Noah trip along with baskets of flower petals chucking enormous handfuls so hard they pelt the legs and feet of the people on either side of the aisle.

Dad chuckles next to me.

"This is everything I ever wanted," I say.

"It's exactly what you deserve."

I'm only a few feet from Edam when an enormous crane flies from the Garden across our path, and then out toward the sea. Cranes symbolize good luck, blessings, and peace. I look up and offer up a silent prayer of thanks, for the peace and health of this new world, my many blessings, and most of all, for my family.

Balthasar lifts my elbow up and I step up onto the raised platform next to Edam. His eyes meet mine, and they never waver.

Job stands between us, but back a step so that he can look out on the audience. "I was delighted when Chancery asked me to officiate today. She told me she wanted me because I have pursued healing for many years—and that's what this union is about. The world suffered a great deal for a very long time, and she has healed us, at great personal cost."

He looks at me for a moment before turning his attention to Edam. "In fact she and Edam have both suffered.

But with great sorrow comes wonderful perspective and insight into the depths that exist within both joy and gratitude. I've never seen a couple more grateful for their time together and for the bond that they share. I had the opportunity to watch both of them grow up, right here in Ni'ihau. They grew and changed and suffered, and ultimately they decided to turn toward one another through all the trials."

"I think that's what will keep them going, and will help their love to endure. So this is my admonition to you both today—no matter what comes, keep turning toward one another, today, tomorrow, next century and the many that come after. If you can do that, this is a love that will endure anything." He sighs. "I understand you don't have vows. You would prefer that something so personal not be broadcast worldwide?"

Edam's face flushes. "I wanted to say something. It's short."

"By all means," Job says.

"You already know how I feel about you," Edam says, his eyes intent. "You already know what I would give for you, what I would sacrifice. Anything, everything, utterly all that I have or will have or will be." He licks his lips. "But I know marriage isn't about grand gestures, so this is my pledge. I will do the small things, day in and day out. I won't fault you for your well-intentioned errors, and I'll always give you the benefit of the doubt. Because the small things add up to very big things, and I want every single good thing in this wide world for you."

I reach out for him, and he takes my hand. "I'll promise you something too," I say. "My life is full of people I love and that means there are a lot of demands on my time. My children, my sisters, my brother." I glance at Moses with a smile. "Pets, friends, and a demanding job. You already know how much the people of this world mean to me, and you understand the importance of my responsibility to them." I bring his hands to my lips and kiss them. "But I'll put you above them all. I love you *more*, so if you ever tell me that you need me—you *need me*, I will drop whatever is pressing on me, and I will run to you. Now. Tomorrow. Next week. Forever. You're my first, my everything, and my always."

"I would never ask you to drop anything and run to me," Edam whispers. "Because I'll already be there, right by your side."

Job murmurs the words of the marriage ceremony, and I do hear him, sort of. But something starts then, a pull that grows into a tug. It's been developing for years now, a yearning that reels my heart toward Edam's. Its pull strengthens as I say, "I do," and he says the same, and then I lean and lean and lean toward him, until our mouths finally meet.

The people gathered cheer and shout, but I don't care. The only person who really matters to me in this second is happier than I've ever seen him. "Mrs. Edam ex'Alamecha," he says. "You look exhausted." He sweeps me up in his arms. He whispers the next words against my ear, so soft that I can barely hear them myself. "I've never been happier about your brilliance—in holding a sunset cere-mony, and in having the reception tomorrow so that tonight is *ours*."

Our friends and family go wild as he carries me through the water and around the other side of the palace to go in through the back door of my old bedroom. It's fine though —I have nothing to hide. Not anymore.

Edam kicks the door between the rooms so hard it nearly flies off its hinges.

"Careful," I say. "You bust that, and we'll have to bring people in here all day tomorrow to work on fixing it."

He kisses me quiet. "Can't have that." He barely moves

his mouth away from mine, his words tangling against my lips.

"Can Mom not walk?"

Noah's voice from behind us is a bucket of ice water over my head.

"Are her legs working?" Melina asks. "Because if they aren't, we can run get Job."

Edam sets me down on the foot of the bed. "They work just fine," he says.

"They do?" Melina tilts her head, focused on my legs.

"I'm sorry," Kali says, a little out of breath behind me. "They just took off."

I laugh. "It's fine." I walk a step toward them and crouch down. "Come here, babies."

"Grandmother says we can't sleep with you tonight." Noah frowns.

Edam musses his hair. "Why would she say that?" He crouches down too. "You're always welcome with your mom and me."

"Really?" Noah smiles.

"Always." Edam swings him around in a circle and tosses him on the bed.

And something impossible happens. My love for Edam expands again. And if we end up snuggling with two toddlers until they fall asleep, and then carefully transferring them to their room on our wedding night, well. Things are always better when you have to wait for them.

Love is no different.

In fact, it might have been the inspiration for the rule. Because when Edam tosses me up on the bed in *almost* the same way he tossed Noah a few hours before, my heart nearly bursts in my chest. "We're finally alone," he says, his voice rough and low, just like I like it.

"Yes," I say. "We really are, and I find that I'm not exhausted at all."

He smiles, his eyes sparkling. "Me either."

For the rest of the night, it turns out we agree on nearly every single thing. And Edam's right. It really is the little things that bring the most joy.

⚜

I hope you enjoyed the Birthright Series! It was such a labor of love on my part. If you aren't ready to stop thinking or talking about it, join me and some other super fans on my FB Reader group! https://www.facebook.com/groups/750807222376182

And if you enjoyed the Birthright Series, and I really hope you did, you might be looking for your next read! I'd love it if you took a look at either my YA post apocalyptic series (starting with Marked), or my romantic women's fiction series, starting with Finding Faith. I've included a sample of Finding Faith next, if you want to scroll on and give it a try.

I think you'll find it's not like most "romances" you've read before. (And the series gets better and better, I swear. Books 4, 5, & 6 are my absolute favorites. They are all standalone stories, but they do go in chronological order and have overlapping characters.) Grab the boxset with the first three books here. They'll be available on all platforms in January.

Of course, if you're looking for another speculative ya storyline, you'll probably enjoy Marked better.

Finally, if you'd like a FREE full length novel, you can grab my standalone ya romantic suspense, Already Gone, if you join my newsletter at www.BridgetEBakerWrites.com.

If you don't want another single email, I totally understand. You can follow me for updates on social media and simply buy Already Gone. It's a twisty ya romantic suspense available everywhere books are sold.

31

SAMPLE CHAPTER FINDING
FAITH

By the time my friends turned seven, not a single one of them actually believed in Santa.

Ironically, that's the year my faith in the big guy began.

I was skeptical from the start. A fat, bearded man shoots down chimneys or climbs through windows to deliver presents to lots of kids he doesn't even know? He travels via a sleigh that's powered by flying deer?

Yeah, right.

I always gravitated toward science and math, because their clear-cut answers helped make sense of the world. I learned about Occam's Razor while preparing my science fair project in second grade. It dictates that all other things being equal, the simplest explanation is probably the correct one. That's why, the Christmas after I turned seven, when all my friends were catching up to what I'd known all along, that Santa's a big, fat, phony, I began to believe.

After all, that year I woke up to a decorated tree with blinking lights, and a whole truckload of fancy, beautifully wrapped presents. My options to explain this baffling event were: 1) a red-suited man who lives in the North Pole brought me toys in a magical sack; or 2) my dad actually saved some of the money he would otherwise spend on beer to buy the presents for me as a surprise. I could count on one hand the number of times Dad left the house, if I excluded walking around the corner to the auto-repair place where he worked, or walking to the convenience store for more alcohol.

In fact, if I hadn't learned to steal tiny amounts of cash from my dad's paycheck stash, my little sister Gertrude and I wouldn't have even had hotdogs and ramen to eat. Trudy and I still twitch every time we pass a hotdog stand.

It was clear, given what I knew, that Santa must exist.

I stand up, and clear my throat. Almost a hundred sets of eyes turn toward me, and the thrill I feel every year when Sub-for-Santa season commences fills my chest. Large nutcrackers stand guard by the door, and faux holly garland drapes along every surface. A sparkly, rainbow lit tree covered in ornaments we've been given by grateful parents as thank yous over the years decorates the conference room. It looks cheerier than usual, but it's still essentially one big table with a podium up front, and a hundred folding metal chairs in rows toward the back.

"Welcome to the organizational meeting for this year's Sub-for-Santa program, sponsored locally by the United Way. I'm delighted you're all here. We can't wait to work with you to bring a little wonder to a lot of children who haven't had enough of that in their lives. My name is Mary Wiggin, and I'm the President of the Sub-for-Santa program here in Atlanta."

Smiles sprout on the faces of volunteers all around me, which is more impressive given the fact that they're all sitting on hard, metal chairs.

I continue. "We are here to uplift the lives of as many kids as we possibly can. I'm proud to say that this program has grown consistently each of the eight years that I've been in charge, and I hope to be able to say the same next year."

Everyone claps and I wait for them to finish.

"Many of you are familiar, and I'm so pleased to see you returning year after year. Do any of you repeat sponsors recall the number one rule?"

Three hands shoot up. I point at a lady in a bright pink sweater sporting a reindeer wearing magenta lipstick.

"Only nominate families who are super poor?" she asks.

I nod my head. "We do want to ensure the families placed on our list are in need, mostly because our resources are limited and we want to help as many people as we can, but it's not our number one rule. Anyone else remember that?"

Now that one of them was wrong, they're all nervous about answering. Only one hand stays raised, the green polished fingers waving wildly, like a kid waving down an ice cream truck. "Yes, Paisley?"

My perky secretary from work is helping me run the program for the third year in a row. She's paid for some of her time, but at minimum wage. Ironically, she doesn't seem to care about anything at our real job where she's paid far, far more, but she's my most enthusiastic volunteer with Sub-for-Santa. Paisley's just made for Christmas, I guess.

She beams. "Don't ruin the magic."

"Exactly, yes, that's rule number one. We do not want any of these children, not a single one, to know where these presents really originate. The reason this program works is that these kids believe in the cultural fiction that a jolly fat man with a loving, hardworking wife supervises a host of tiny elves. The kids need to believe that someone has noticed the kind things, the good things, and the right things they've done this year. They need to believe that someone cares about them. If they think these presents stem from pity, how will they feel instead?"

Paisley's hand shoots up again, and she bounces up and down in her chair. I suppress my grin and call on the heavy-set man sporting a full beard with his arm raised behind her.

"But isn't that kind of a lie?" he asks. "I mean, eventually they'll figure it out, and they'll either be mad or feel like idiots."

I frown. I should never have trusted a man with howling wolves printed on his t-shirt.

"Were you ever a recipient of Christmas gifts, something like the Sub-for-Santa program?" I ask.

He shakes his head. "Nah, my parents didn't need handouts."

I grit my teeth. "As someone who was a recipient, trust me. They won't be angry when they find out people cared enough to keep their donation a secret."

"You're only one person. You don't know how everyone will feel."

Note to self: install ejection seats before next year's opening meeting.

"I can't speak for everyone," I say, "but neither can you. Respectfully, speaking from ten years of experience with this program, I think you're wrong. I've seen a lot of reactions and heard from a lot of children. I've heard from kids who were participants year after year on both sides. Many of them are involved to this day, just like me. We aren't lying to these children, and anyone who believes that Sub-for-Santa is perpetuating a lie should leave."

I pause and glance meaningfully toward the back door. No one stands up. "If you're all staying, I'd love to share something with you that might help you understand how this will work. When I was younger, my mom left our family. My sister was not quite four years old. After Mom left, our dad started drinking heavily. Now I have a label for what he was: a poorly functioning alcoholic. Those were difficult times in the Wiggin household."

Paisley gives me two thumbs up and I want to stop this presentation to hug her.

"That Christmas I was old enough to know that Santa wasn't real. He was a lie, and I knew we'd wake up Christmas morning the same as every other morning. I'd make ramen for my sister, and we'd pretend it wasn't the crappiest day of the year."

I make eye contact with a dozen people, making sure they're all listening.

"Except that's not what happened. For the first time in a very long time, something great happened to us. Santa Claus was real, and he brought us a beautiful tree with multitudes of presents underneath it. Once a year, I knew that even if my parents thought I was worthless, someone somewhere cared. When I did finally discover that it wasn't Santa, but in fact a group of extraordinary people who wanted me to have a fantastic day, that meant more to me than the fiction of Santa."

A tear springs to my eye, as it always does this time of year when I think back to that first Christmas. I wipe it away.

"Sub-for-Santa," I say, "is a program that allows good people to give to those who need love, for no benefit to themselves. We should be doing things like this all year, but that's too tall an order, so we settle for one day a year of selfless service and love to children who will truly appreciate the gesture. The real reason we never, ever, let the children know where the presents come from is that—"

Paisley's waving so frantically I'm worried she's going to poke the guy next to her in the eye. A lawsuit would eat up all our funds and the program would collapse. I sigh, but the corners of my mouth turn up a little anyway.

"Yes, Pais?"

"If the kids figure out it's coming from a charity, they'll feel patronized. We want them to feel like someone values them, like they're worthwhile, not like they're getting presents out of pity or guilt. Eventually, they'll be old enough to realize that there may be a real Santa somewhere, but he can't really reach everyone, so other people help out and do some of his work for him."

There may be a real Santa somewhere? I can't help but smile, because other than her small delusion, she's spot on. If she exhibited half this much zeal in the tax office where we both work, she wouldn't still be my secretary. She'd have been promoted to office manager.

"Well said Paisley, thank you. If these children believe in Santa, they also believe that they matter to someone. If these children know rich people are donating things to poor kids who aren't loved, they'll feel lesser. That's obviously the opposite of our goal."

As I work my way through the rest of the rules, my heart lifts and it finally starts to feel like the holiday season is upon us. Eventually, it's time to pass out nomination forms and sponsor requirements.

"I have a list of volunteers that we've collected from several church groups and businesses, as well as employees, friends and neighbors. You're all here because you offered to sponsor a family, or be part of my core team to help administer the entire operation, or both. I appreciate that greatly. We still have one more week to collect volunteers and then I'll finalize the nominations for participants. Please write down the information on anyone you have now, and bring it to me. The sooner we have nominations, the sooner we can contact them for permission, and request the documentation we need to ensure our efforts go to the right place. Last year, we helped five hundred and thirty-two families, with more than eleven hundred children. My goal for this year is to reach six hundred families and fifteen hundred children. If you'll all help, I think we can get there."

Paisley passes out nomination forms, and cards with the website URL where they can submit nominations once they've left tonight. "Thank you all, and please feel free to call me with any questions. My phone number and email address are both on that card, below the website listing. I try to reply as promptly as possible during the holiday season. I don't want details to impede our desire to bless these children."

Pais and I each take a door and people hand us nomination forms on their way out. Once the last person waves and walks out the door, I lock it behind her and blow out all but one of the Christmas Cookie candles. Paisley and I buckle down to work immediately, compiling a list of people to contact. A few people added names to the volunteer column as well, and my heart swells. Several others indicated they'd be willing to sponsor more than one family.

"We're almost done with the nominations," I tell her. "Why don't you take the volunteer names and update that spreadsheet for me. I'd love to send out the introductory email tomorrow. We always get a flurry of new sponsors when that goes out, plus maybe you can post our numbers and our mission statement to the Facebook group and hopefully get some shares that way."

Paisley is a whiz with lists of any kind. Sometimes I think she manages lists better than the computer. Whenever I comment on it, she says her parents had her working on lists of things before she could even talk. I've never asked her about her parents, and she's never volunteered much more than that.

"Sure boss, right away."

"I'm not your boss here, Pais. You're a volunteer same as me."

She rolls her eyes. "Except you're the Chair, and I'm still getting paid. But whatever you say, boss." She salutes me.

Paisley hops on the computer with a saucy grin on her face, and the clacking of her fingers on the keys soothes me. After a long and exhausting tax season, it's a relief to be focusing on the one thing I love more than taxes for a few weeks before we start all over again.

"Umm," Paisley says, "I found something a little odd on this list."

I tilt my head sideways. "Odd? What does that mean?"

"Well, I need to compare something first." She walks across the room and peers over my shoulder at the list I'm finishing up of nominated families. "There." She points. "That says Lucas Manning, right?"

I squint at the screen of my laptop and nod. "Yes, Lucas Manning, at 236 Sunset Cove."

"Can the same person be both a nominee and a volunteer?" she asks.

I scrunch up my nose. "No. If they're a legitimate participant in the program, they shouldn't be able to afford to sponsor a family."

Paisley walks back over to the desktop, and I follow. About a third of the way down her list, there's his name again. Lucas Manning, 236 Sunset Cove."

"Gah," I say, "what a mess. We must've included his name by accident. We'll have to go over the initial forms and figure out which one he really is."

We search and search, but sure enough, we didn't make a mistake. His name and address are listed here on the nominee form, and someone filled his name and address out as a sponsoring family as well.

"Now what?" I wonder out loud.

"Has this ever happened before?" she asks.

I shake my head. "Not that I know of."

"What do we do?"

Take the bull by the horns, I suppose. "I'll call him and set up an appointment to discuss the program. I don't think it's a subject I should broach over the phone, because if he's a sponsor, he'll be offended someone nominated him, and if he's a nominee, he'll wonder if other people disapprove of him taking things as evidenced by his name being listed as a sponsor. What a snarl. Hopefully the answer will be glaringly obvious once I reach his house, and I can play it off as a standard preliminary meeting either way."

"Good idea," Paisley says.

I dial the number listed, and the phone rings and rings. Finally it goes to voicemail. Lucas Manning has a deep voice with a faint accent I can't place, at least, not from hearing only ten words. I leave a message asking him to call me at the United Way office.

Not five seconds after I end the call, my phone rings and the words UNKNOWN CALLER pop up on the screen. Probably Lucas returning my call.

"Wow, that was fast," I say.

"Mary?" My boss Shauna's voice, even just saying my name on the phone, is unmistakable. "What was fast?"

I cringe, not that she can see it. "Your phone number came up as unknown, and I thought you were someone with Sub-for-Santa returning my call." Which was stupid, because I only gave him my office number.

"Ah, okay. Are you busy tonight? I was hoping you could meet me for dinner. I need to talk to you, and it's important."

"That sounds ominous," I say.

She laughs. "Well, we do have a lot of data to review. I got our analyst's reports on numbers and performance for the year."

My stomach turns. "You're not firing me, right?"

"I'd hardly do that over dinner. I'd have to wait until the

end of the meal to tell you, which would be beyond awkward when I finally got around to firing you."

She also wouldn't be making a joke about it if it were happening. I relax a little bit. "Where did you want to meet?"

"Bentleys, eight sharp. Dress nice." Shauna hangs up the phone.

"Was everything okay?" Paisley asks.

"I'm wearing black pants and a red sweater. Does this count as 'nice enough for Bentleys' do you think?" It's one of the premiere steakhouses in Atlanta, and I've only been once.

Paisley scrunches up her nose. "Well, I've never been there, but…"

"That bad?" I sigh. "Shauna wants to see me, and she said to meet her there. She reminded me to dress nice, like I need someone to tell me how to pull my pants on the right legs."

"Bizarre. Although you are her rising star. Probably just another client that asked for you specifically. If she's giving you more work, I know it goes against every part of your character, but you need to demand a raise. You already work harder than everyone else in that stupid office."

I wish. "No way is she calling me over to give me a raise. In any case, I have forty-five minutes until I'm supposed to arrive, and it's fifteen minutes to get to my house for a change of clothes. Bentleys is a solid twenty minutes away from home. I'm sorry to ditch you, but I better run."

"I have a cocktail dress in my trunk. If you ask nicely, I might be persuaded to share."

I raise one eyebrow. "Do I even want to know why you have a dress in the back of your car?"

She grins. "I'm single, and I like to be prepared. You never know where the night may lead."

I always know where mine will go. My nights beeline

toward a TV dinner in front of an episode of Gilmore Girls. But that's kind of pathetic. I should have a cocktail dress in my trunk. I should be spontaneous and fun.

"I'm single too," I say, "and the only thing in my trunk is dust bunnies, hiding amidst old tax files."

"You want the dress, or not?" she asks.

"I might. Lemme see it." I follow her out to her car.

She lifts the trunk and slides a black bag out. She pulls the zipper down to reveal a blood red sheath dress with black piping. I gasp. "Yes, I'd love to wear that, but I doubt it'll fit me."

Paisley eats like a bird and it shows, but one quick try on won't hurt. If by some miracle it fits, I'll spare myself a lot of anxiety about traffic and changing in time to reach Bentleys.

Paisley snorts. "It'll look better on you than on me I imagine, especially with your coloring. I mean come on, this vibrant red with your blonde hair and hazel eyes? Not to mention your golden tan. Remind me why we're friends again?"

I don't bother correcting her, but my skin isn't actually tanned. My dad's half Italian, so my skin's darker than your average white person.

I roll my eyes. "Obviously I've been using you this whole time for the day I would need a cocktail dress with no notice."

I leave the conference room and walk around the corner to try on the dress in my office. Paisley stands guard by my door just in case. It's late enough that everyone who normally works here is gone, but I'm not taking any chances on janitorial staff. The dress is red satin, with panels that alternate between shiny and matte in vertical stripes. It's a little snug, which means it shoves my chest up near my collarbones.

"I don't think I can go out in public looking like this."

"You have to at least show me," Paisley whines. "Come on, lemme see it. I have no exciting news, so I need to live vicariously."

I step out of my office.

Paisley whistles and claps. "If you were going on a date instead of to meet our boss, I'd totally force you to wear that. Since it's just a work thing, it's your call. You're welcome to borrow it as long as you dry-clean it afterward."

I bite my lip while I think about it. "It will be way easier than trying to drive home first, so I'll borrow it if you're sure it's okay."

She nods. "Totally fine."

"Thanks." I slide into my boring black pumps and grab my purse. "Actually, I should probably use the time I'm saving to help you finalize the nominee list."

Paisley shrugs. "I can finish the last few up here, no problem. Order the most expensive thing on the menu. Frank & Meacham owes you a nice meal for coming in on no notice, and late at night. Not during tax season." She scowls. "Those guys abuse your work ethic."

"I'll order the lobster and the steak."

"Oh man, then bring me leftovers. And to pay me back for the loan, text me and let me know what's going on. I love firm gossip."

"Will do." I pull my light brown leather jacket on over the stunning red dress, and walk out the door.

I run through a list of things Shauna might need to tell me. It can't be a promotion, because I'm a senior associate, which means she's got the only position above mine. I can't imagine she'd fire me. My hands shake. Could she be transferring me? There's a rumor going around that the London office is struggling. I can't leave my baby sister Trudy here in Atlanta alone, and she'd never follow me to London. If that's it, I'll have to tell her no. Can I tell her no?

I'm deep in thought, and only a few steps away from the comfort of my Honda Accord when I bump into someone.

My heart accelerates and I stumble backward, blinking my eyes in the cold air to help focus them. Strong hands wrap around my upper arms, steadying me. "Mary?"

I look up into the face of my ex-fiancé, Foster Bradshaw. He looks every bit as aristocratic and perfect as ever. I shouldn't be surprised to see him here, since he runs United Way's Atlanta office, but he's not usually here after hours. His dark hair falls softly over his forehead and ears. His deep blue sweater exactly matches his eyes. He knows it, too. With Foster, nothing is ever a coincidence.

"I'm so sorry, Foster. I didn't see you."

"Obviously." The humor in his tone rubs me the wrong way, or maybe it's my body's reaction to his cologne that makes me cranky. "Do you have a few minutes to spare? I need to talk to you about something."

Get in line, buddy. "Sorry, I don't actually. I just got a call from my other boss, the one who pays my bills. I've gotta run."

"Always working, even after tax season has ended. Typical Mary. Well, don't let me stop you, but I'd love to touch base sometime in the next few days before things get crazy." He releases me and steps back. "Be careful. It's icy out there."

I practically sprint to my car. Whatever my boss has to say, it can't be worse than spending another second with Foster.

Grab Finding Faith here.

Or Grab the first three books here.

32

APPENDIX

1. ALAMECHA: United States of America, England, Ireland, Scotland, Canada, Cuba, Puerto Rico
Eve
Mahalesh 3226 BC
Alamecha 2312 BC
Meridalina 1446 BC
Corlamecha 553 BC
Cainina 273 AD
Enora 1120 AD
Chancery 2002 AD
H. Judica 2002 AD

2. MALESSA: Germany, France, Netherlands, Switzerland, Norway, Sweden, Finland, Australia, New Zealand, Papau New Guinea, Iceland
Eve
Mahalesh 3226 BC
Malessa 2353 BC
Adorna 1451 BC
Selah 618 BC

Lenamecha 211 AD
Senah 1022 AD (Denah dead twin)
Analessa 1820 AD
H. DeLannia 1942

3. LENORA: All of South America (including Chile, Argentina, Brazil), Mexico, Spain, Portugal
Eve
Mahalesh 3226 BC
Lenora 2365 BC
Ablinina 1453 BC
Leddite 652 BC
Selamecha 379 BC
Priena 460 AD
Leamarta 1198 AD
Melisania 1897 AD
H. Marde 1987

4. ADORA: India, Japan, Korea, Indonesia, Thailand
Eve
Mahalesh 3226 BC
Adora 2368 BC
Manocha 1461 BC
Alela 590 BC
Radosha 192 BC
Esheth 638 AD
Lainina 1444 AD
H. Ranana 1967

5. SHAMECHA: Russia, Mongolia, Kazakhstan, Pakistan, Uzbekistan, Philippines
Eve

Mahalesh 3226 BC
Shamecha 2472 BC
Madalena 1639 BC
Shenoa 968 BC
Abalorna 299 BC
Venoah 333 AD
Reshaka 936 AD
Melamecha 1509 AD
H. Venagra 2000

6. SHENOAH: Continent of Africa, Saudi Arabia, Iran, Iraq, Turkey, Greece, Italy, Jordan, Afghanistan
Eve
Shenoah 3227 BC
Adelornamecha 2385 BC
Kankera 1544 BC
Avina 670 BC
Sela 467 BC
Jericha 135 AD
Sethora 399 AD
Malimba 708 AD
Adika 1507 AD
H. Vela 1990

ACKNOWLEDGMENTS

My editors, Carrie and Carla, are AMAZING. I love you guys.

My husband does EVERYTHING so that I can work. No one can compare to him, and I could not do what I do without him.

My kids are little champs.

Do I just thank the same people with every book? Probably.

And my readers. I love you guys, so much. I don't think you know how much your reviews, your comments, and your messages mean. <3 I am SO GLAD that you love Chancery's world and her family and friends in the same way that I do.

Bridget loves her husband (every day) and all five of her kids (most days). She's a lawyer, but does as little legal work as possible. She has three goofy horses, two scrappy cats, two adorable rabbits, one bouncy dog and backyard chickens. She hates Oxford commas, but she uses them to keep fans from complaining. She makes cookies waaaaay too often and believes they should be their own food group. In a possibly misguided attempt to keep from blowing up like a puffer fish, she kick boxes every day. So if you don't like her books, her kids, her pets, or her cookies, maybe don't tell her in person.

ALSO BY BRIDGET E. BAKER

The Finding Home Series:

Finding Faith (1)

Finding Cupid (2)

Finding Spring (3)

Finding Liberty (4)

Finding Holly (5)

Finding Home (6)

Finding Balance (7)

Finding Peace (8)

The Birthright Series:

Displaced (1)

unForgiven (2)

Disillusioned (3)

misUnderstood (4)

Disavowed (5)

unRepentant (6)

Destroyed (7)

The Sins of Our Ancestors Series:

Marked (1)

Suppressed (2)

Redeemed (3)

Renounced (4)

A stand alone YA romantic suspense:

Already Gone

My Children's Picture Book

Yuck! What's for Dinner?